Softly he said, "Put the stool in the middle of the floor, Charlotte."

"Why are you doing this?" she asked.

"Because you want me to."

He knew. Somehow, he knew everything. A stranger, someone she'd met mere minutes ago, had just locked her into a torture chamber. The situation should fill her with foreboding. There was a certain measure of that, to be sure, but mostly what she felt, God help her, was an intoxicating thrill of arousal underscored by a sense of rightness, a sense that she deserved whatever this enigmatic stranger would do to her, and more.

She lifted the stool, which was remarkably heavy, and set it down in the middle of the floor.

"Take your clothes off," he said.

She turned to stare at him.

"It has long been customary," he explained, "when punishing females to make them undress. It tends to have a . . . humbling effect."

Charlotte met his eyes for a moment, then looked down, her gaze lighting on the front flap of his breeches, stretched tight over a bulging erection. She felt suddenly starved for air; her heart thudded in her ears.

Darius noticed the direction of her gaze, but seemed unperturbed, perhaps even slightly amused. "Strip," he said.

Charlotte took a deep, tremulous breath, and set about unlacing her bodice.

House of Dark Delights

Louisa Burton

BANTAM BOOKS

HOUSE OF DARK DELIGHTS
A Bantam Book / February 2007

Published by Bantam Dell
A Division of Random House, Inc.
New York, New York

This is a work of fiction. Names, characters, places, and incidents either are the product of the author's imagination or are used fictitiously. Any resemblance to actual persons, living or dead, events, or locales is entirely coincidental.

Cover art: *Lesbia* by Weguelin, John Reinhard (1849–1927)
© Private Collection / © Christie's Images / The Bridgeman Art Library
Cover design by Jorge Martinez

Book design by Lynn Newmark

ISBN 978-0-553-38412-3
Printed in the United States of America
Published simultaneously in Canada

www.bantamdell.com

BVG 10 9 8 7 6 5 4 3 2 1

For Rich

I owe a tremendous debt to my agent, Nancy Yost, who lit a spark that set fire to my imagination. The result is Château de la Grotte Cachée and its extraordinary residents, whom I would never have met but for Nancy.

Many thanks also to Pamela Burford, Susan Uttal, and Rigel Klingman, who read pieces of this book as it was taking shape, and kept assuring me that I was on the right track. Their encouragement and support was invaluable.

Sexual Demons

There were personages connected with the worship of Priapus who appear to have been common to the Romans under and before the empire, and to the foreign races who settled upon its ruins...

Woe to the modesty of maiden or woman who ventured incautiously into their haunts. As Incubi, they visited the house by night, and violated the persons of the females, and some of the most celebrated heroes of early mediæval romances, such as Merlin, were thus the children of Incubi. They were known at an early period in Gaul by the name of Dusii, from which, as the church taught that all these mythic personages were devils, we derive our modern word *Deuce,* used in such phrases as "the Deuce take you!"

From *The Worship of the Generative Powers*
by Thomas Wright, 1865

&

When house or harth doth sluttish lye,
I pinch the maidens black and blue;
The bed-clothes from the bedd pull I,
and lay them naked all to view.
'Twixt sleep and wake,
I do them take,
And on the key-cold floor them throw.
If out they cry
Then forth I fly,
And loudly laugh out, ho, ho, ho!

From the seventeenth-century ballad,
"The Mad, Merry Pranks of Robin Goodfellow"

House of Dark Delights

'Twixt Sleep and Wake

Almost midnight,
July 30 of this year

SHE WAS out there somewhere, watching him. Halfway up the north postern tower of the castle, Elic paused, one hand gripping a chink in the soot-black stone, both bare feet poised on a narrow corbel. He looked over his shoulder, peering off into the darksome woods, nostrils flaring as he tasted the night: juniper and wild roses, honeysuckle, musty earth, ancient oaks . . . and Ilutu-Lili. The jasmine oil with which she anointed her throat and breasts, her salty-sweet skin, her heat, her desire drifted around him on a waft of sultry air.

"Why him?" she'd asked earlier this evening, in the extinct Akkadian tongue she'd taught him so that their conversations, some of them, could be theirs and theirs alone. "Why Larsson?"

"He's a *gabru,* Lili." *A strong, mighty young man.* It was what they called certain guests of the chateau, those in whom Elic took a particular interest. Inigo, in that merrily smirky way of his, had dubbed them "Elic's Alphas."

"That's not the only reason," she said.

Elic had turned without answering her.

"Urkhish," she'd said as he stalked away. *Go, then.*

He could have invited her to join him tonight, could have shared this *gabru* with her, as he sometimes did, but not this time. Not this one.

The oriel window of the bedchamber assigned to Viktor Larsson loomed just overhead, its stained glass casements thrown wide open on this unusually warm night. In a whispered growl, Elic cursed those, like Larsson, who insisted upon locking their chamber doors here, as if Château de la Grotte Cachée were some *hôtel public* instead of what it was: the most private of private homes.

The moon was full tonight, illuminating the topography of the tower wall as if it were midafternoon—though Elic could have scaled it on the blackest night, having done so countless times over the six centuries in which it had stood. Straining upward, he got a good grip on a notch meant to secure battle scaffolding, though it had never been used for that purpose. This castle was built not to repel outsiders, but to conceal and safeguard its permanent residents. Elic hauled himself up one-armed, quivering with the effort, until he could just reach the stone bracket supporting the window. Sweat trickled from beneath his black woolen cap, stinging his eyes, as he clambered over the projecting bay and stole into the room through one of the narrow openings.

He found his footing on the velvet-upholstered window seat, curled into a crouch, and rubbed his eyes with the hem of his black T-shirt. The moonlit Chambre de Mille Fleurs was large and opulent, its walls draped with fifteenth-century tapestries for which the Louvre or the Met would offer a fortune, if their existence were known. He breathed in a blend of musk, spices, and orange peel—Larsson's cologne—along with whispers of linseed oil, old wool, fabric softener, and lemon verbena.

The bedcurtains were tied back to reveal a tall, strapping young blond man lying faceup on a mound of pillows, naked under the sheet rucked around his hips. On one nightstand sat a ripped-open box of twelve protein bars, a strip of condoms, and the June issue of *Sports Illustrated* with a photograph on the cover of Larsson holding the Wimbledon cup aloft. On the floor next to the bed was the electric fan he'd demanded when he discovered, to his outrage, that the chateau was without air-conditioning except for a few window units in Inigo's suite. It was an old fan, though, and made quite a racket, which was probably why it wasn't running.

A pink leather makeup case sat on the other nightstand, along with a cell phone, a copy of American *Vogue,* and a book called *Medical Instrumentation: Application and Design.* These belonged to a statuesque American blonde whom Larsson had introduced during dinner yesterday, with obvious pride and affection, as "my beloved Heather." Heather's left ring finger sported a square-cut diamond the size of her thumbnail. When Inigo had suggested she might want to put it somewhere safe before taking the waters, for fear of losing it, Larsson said he'd forbidden her to remove it, even to have it cleaned. "If she loses it, I'll buy her another. I want every man who sees her to know she's mine." This devotion was quite a departure for the Swedish tennis star, whose appetite for models and actresses was legendary.

At this moment, Heather was partaking of a solitary, late-night soak in the bathhouse built onto a rocky mountainside about a hundred yards east of the chateau. It was an expediency engineered by Elic, who'd slid the idea into her mind, along with a certain something else, while "accidentally" brushing up against her earlier today.

"Excuse me," he'd said in English as he stepped down into the square, mosaic-floored marble pool in which Heather, Larsson, and several others, including Lili, were bathing in the therapeutic waters trickling from the adjoining cave—the *grotte cachée,* or hidden grotto, for which this valley had been named. English, in which the group were chatting, had become, over the past couple of hundred years, the lingua franca of Grotte Cachée due to the preponderance of visitors who spoke that language and none other.

Elic sighed as he settled chest deep in the water, which ran agreeably tepid on hot days like this. In the winter, it emerged warm and steaming, a peculiarity of the stream that fed it, which had its origins deep in the extinct, lushly vegetated volcano that loomed over their secret little *vallée*; it was not, however, the only anomaly of nature at Grotte Cachée, not by a long shot.

Reaching behind him, Elic scooped up a handful of blueberries from the afternoon repast laid out on a low iron table next to the pool: summer fruits, farm-cured ham, smoked duck, wheels of Saint-Nectaire and Bleu d'Auvergne, and a big round of crusty, wood-fired bread surrounded by pots of honey, butter, and traditional Auvergnat fruit pastes.

The pool, housed in a white marble edifice dating back to Grotte Cachée's Roman occupation, had submerged steps all around, the top one serving as a bench on which the bathers reclined. All, that is, except for Inigo, who sat on the edge of the pool in a pair of baggy plaid shorts with just his calves and feet in the water, a joint in one hand, cigarette in the other, half-empty bottle of tequila tucked between his legs.

The roof of the bathhouse, the center of which was an open "moon roof," as Inigo called it, was buttressed by pillars at the four corners of the pool, each supporting a life-size statue of a nymph being ravished in a novel position by a satyr. It was the same satyr in each tableau, a handsome young fellow with a tail like that of an ox, slightly pointed ears, and a pair of bony protuberances poking through his cap of close-cropped, corkscrew curls. His most extraordinary feature, though, would be a cockstand of heroic proportions. A thick, sinewy shaft jutting a good twelve inches from its wiry nest, it put one more in mind of a rutting stallion than of a man.

There'd been a visitor to the chateau a while back, sometime in the 1880s, as Elic recalled, who'd taught mythological studies at Harvard. Professor Wheeler couldn't fathom why satyrs sculpted by Romans around the time of the birth of Christ—in fact, it was the autumn of A.D. 14, hard for Elic to forget because the news of Augustus's death came while the statues were being erected—should look so decidedly un-Roman. As the professor had explained it, the Romans had usually depicted satyrs as being hairy and goatlike from the waist down, with prominent, often ramlike, horns. The statues in the bathhouse looked far more like the satyrs' original incarnation from ancient Greece.

In fact, the bathhouse satyrs bore a striking resemblance to Inigo in every particular save for the cabochon ruby in Inigo's left earlobe, the faded tattoo over his heart—*In Vino Veritas*—and the hair, which he cultivated in a boisterous black mop in order to conceal the horns and ears. He'd had the tail surgically removed soon after the advent of chloroform in 1847 because, as he'd told Elic at the time, it spoiled the cut of his trousers. He'd have done it centuries earlier were he not a self-admitted "sniveling crybaby" when it came to pain. He'd drunk himself insensible before getting that tattoo.

Inigo's entertainment this afternoon was in the form of two voluptuous Australian girls lounging in the water to either side of him. A redhead and a dark-rooted blonde named Kat and Chloe, respectively, they lolled against his legs with lazy smiles as they sucked on his weed and gulped his tequila. Both wore thong bikini bottoms sans tops, navel rings, and too much makeup; they reeked of the same overly sweet, one-note lily of the valley scent. Chloe had a silver barbell in her tongue and a bosom comprised of two staunchly perfect spheres. Kat's breasts were colossal, and jiggled like Christmas pudding every time she let loose with one of her frequent belly laughs.

Gesturing toward Chloe's chest with his cigarette, Inigo asked her, in the American accent he'd absorbed from watching too much satellite TV, "Are those real?"

"They're a damn sight realer than what I had before, mate."

"What about yours?" he asked Kat.

The redhead grinned and arched her back, putting her endowments on proud display. "What do *you* think?"

As casually as if he were testing a melon at a fruit stand, Inigo reached down and took hold of her left breast, kneading it with the relish of a true connoisseur of female flesh. Heather blinked; Larsson grinned; Lili looked on with a yawn.

"Sweet," he praised as he squeezed and stroked. "That's one nice, jolly set you've got there."

"Jolly?" Chloe said. "I think you're confusing Kat's yabbos with her."

"No, no," he said. "Breasts are like people. They all have their own personalities, their own needs and wants."

"Oh, yeah, and what do mine want?" Kat asked.

"What we all want—to get greased up and ridden like a pony."

Kat threw back her head and guffawed.

"Have you been in the cave?" he asked the girls, nodding toward the mossy gap in the black volcanic rock face that formed the back wall of the bathhouse. "There's this ancient stone figure in there that's got some seriously fucked-up anatomy. Come on," he said as he grabbed the tequila and rose unsteadily to his feet. "You gotta check this out."

As the girls clambered out of the pool, dripping and giggling, a blue rock thrush swooped down from its perch on the edge of the skylight, forcing Inigo to dodge it as it shot past his head. The bird circled one of the columns before lighting on the right shoulder of the marble satyr who stood leaning against it with legs spread and hips outthrust, both hands fisted in the hair of the nymph who knelt before him, licking his monumental organ like a cat.

"Dude," Inigo chuckled when the bird let loose with a series of harsh, scolding cheeps quite uncharacteristic of its species. "Chill, bro. We're not going in that far, just to the *Cella.* I want to show them Titty Man, that's all. Your space is your space."

Darius, evidently mollified, fluttered up through the moon roof in a bluish blur.

"After you, ladies," said Inigo, gesturing them into the cave as he surreptitiously pocketed the little butter pot off the table. He gave Elic a wink as he ducked into the mossy opening, for of course it was *his* fucked-up anatomy—or, as he liked to refer to it, his "heroic dimensions"—which Kat and Chloe were about to discover, no doubt with a fair measure of girlish enthusiasm once the initial shock wore off.

Jolie, one of the pretty young bath attendants, wheeled in a double-decker cart laden on top with drinks, and underneath with stacks of towels and robes. "Your papaya juice, *monsieur,*" she said as she offered a frosty glass to Larsson.

He accepted it mechanically while staring at the cave into which Inigo and the girls had just disappeared. "Was he . . . He wasn't talking to the *bird,* was he?" Larsson asked Lili in his melodic Swedish accent.

"Was that what it looked like to you?" Lili asked with a little hint of a smile. Her own accent was very subtle and very obscure. People meeting her for the first time were always curious as to her origins, about which she was always vague. "I'm from the Near East," she might say, or, if she were feeling droll, she might tell them she was from "the Fertile Crescent," or "the cradle of civilization," and let her interrogators make from that what they would. What she never said was "I'm from Iraq," which was what her homeland was called today. "The dreary questions," she said, "the tedious conversations. No, thank you."

"It *did* seem like he was talking to that bird," Heather said. "He was looking right at it and—"

"*Nä,* you're right," Larsson told Lili. "It's absurd. I've been a little . . . *snurrig i huvudet.* 'Light-headed,' I think is the word. Just for the past day or so, since I got here. The heat, maybe, *ja*?"

"That's probably it." Lili caught Elic's eye and cast him an eloquent smile.

Even after having known Lili for two and a half centuries,

Elic still got a little clutch in his chest when she gave him one of those intimate looks reserved just for him. Nonchalantly naked except for her ever-present gold anklet, her inky hair swaying on the surface of the water, her eyes dark and slumberous, she looked every bit the Babylonian goddess she'd once been . . . to some. To others, she'd been, and still was, a succubus who paralyzed sleeping men in order to rob them of their vital seed.

Lili, alone among her companions, was entirely unclothed; Larsson and Elic wore swim trunks, Heather one of those unlined racing suits, a red one, the kind that clung like skin when it was wet. She was leggy and lovely, with sun-gilded cheeks and the sleek musculature of an athlete. Her stomach was utterly flat, her breasts high and taut, with stiff little nipples that made Elic's teeth itch to bite them. She wore no perfume, but Elic did detect a hint of lemon verbena soap.

He grew hard, imagining Heather thrashing beneath him as he pumped a torrent of seed deep inside her. Lili had his heart, but he could never possess her, not with his body.

"Do you know him, this Inigo?" Larsson asked Lili. "*Did* you, I mean, before you came to this place?" As far as the chateau's houseguests were concerned, Elic, Lili, Inigo, and the reclusive Darius were just invited visitors, like them.

Lili shook her head as she accepted a glass of red wine from Jolie.

"You?" he asked Elic.

"No." It was the truth. Elic had known no other follets, as their host called them, before coming to Grotte Cachée.

"Does our host know him?" Larsson asked.

"Seigneur des Ombres has known Inigo his whole life," Elic told Larsson.

"His whole life?" Larsson said. "I was thinking *le seigneur* was elderly. No?"

"He's thirty-six," Elic said, "but an old soul." A very lonely old soul, his isolation being not so much by choice as by duty. The sense of responsibility that kept him here at his ancestral home, providing for Elic and his kind, made it difficult to establish relationships.

Stretching his arms out on the edge of the pool, Larsson said, with a measure of authority, "He's gay, this Inigo."

"What makes you say that?" Elic asked.

"You know. Always the girly chatter," Larsson said, miming a flapping mouth with one hand. "And the earring on the left, it means he likes to take it in the ass, no?"

"I don't know," Heather said, murmuring her thanks as she took a bottle of Vichy from Jolie. "He seems quite taken with those Australian girls."

Larsson dismissed that observation with a flick of his hand. Without so much as a glance in his fiancée's direction—for he appeared to have forgotten his "beloved Heather" the moment Lili entered the dining room last night—he said, "The gays, they love girls like that. It's what they all want to be, a silly little *fladermuss* with big balloon tits." He cupped his hands in illustration.

Heather said, "Viktor, how would Lars feel if he heard you—"

"Why would you bring him up?" Larsson snapped.

"Because you love him, you told me so, and you said you were going to try to learn to accept—"

"*You* need to learn when to shut your big mouth."

An uneasy silence fell over the group. The blood rose in Heather's cheeks. Jolie emptied Inigo's ashtray and left.

Larsson took a swig of his papaya juice and said, to the group as a whole, "My brother, he's a little confused right now. He'll come around."

Heather sighed.

"Real men," Larsson continued, "normal men, they like a woman who is . . . how do you say it? Elegant. Serene. Smooth skin—golden, not too pale—with shapely legs and a very tiny waist. A good handful on top, soft but firm, like crème brûlée. And long hair, very long, like a sheet of satin." That this was a spot-on description of Lili did not escape the notice of Heather, who looked away, her jaw set.

Lili met Larsson's gaze over the rim of her wineglass before casting her eyes down in a coy gesture as old as humankind. It shouldn't have infuriated Elic, but it did.

"Me, I have no quarrel with the gays," Larsson said. "They stay in their place, I stay in mine, *ja*? Everybody gets along fine."

"How tolerant of you," Elic deadpanned.

Larsson didn't seem to register the sarcasm, but Heather captured Elic's gaze and held it for a good long moment. Finally, she said, with an engaging little smile, "You have the loveliest accent, Elic—mostly French, but with hints of something vaguely Germanic."

"I was born elsewhere." Elic knew what she was doing: giving Larsson a taste of his own medicine. Good for her. "You must work out, Heather. You look exceptionally fit."

"Thank you." The smile intensified. "I'm on the women's crew team at Johns Hopkins."

Larsson got a flinty look in his eye, a thrust to his jaw. He didn't like his fiancée paying attention to another guy. Never mind how he'd just snapped at her, or the way he and Lili had been sniffing around each other for the past twenty-four hours. For some reason, this particular *gabru* incited more than the usual ache of desire in her. Perhaps it was his cornsilk hair; she'd always been partial to men who were as fair as she was dark. Or perhaps it was something more obscure. Fleshly passion was complicated; Elic knew that better than most. He didn't like it, but he couldn't blame her for her primal drives any more than he could blame himself for his own.

Lili was adept at revealing only as much as she cared to—but Elic, who knew her better than anyone, saw it all, felt it all, loathed it all . . . the spots of color staining those majestic cheekbones, the dilation of her pupils, turning her eyes to onyx, and most tellingly, a quiver of desire that sizzled through the water like an electric current.

om the grotto's spring was exception-
conductor of moods and sensations,
al nature. Even humans could detect
coursing through the pool. The more
ould even sense the erotic hum that
g after its occupants had left. Simply
water when it was laden with such a
thtaking surge of lust, although hu-
are of its true source.

e Lili. Nor should he really blame
the way he'd turned his back on
en she set her gaze upon a man, was
Nevertheless, every time Larsson
l y time his lust crackled through the
w , Elic wanted to drive his fist into the bastard's face. Instead, he smiled and chatted and bided his time.

Having walked this earth for nearly three thousand years, Elic had learned to disregard the urge to teach lessons and settle scores . . . until exactly the right time.

It's time, Elic thought as he stood in the Chambre de Mille Fleurs, contemplating the rise and fall of Viktor Larsson's chest in the moonlight. The shape of the sleeping man's penis, draped softly over his right thigh, was just visible through the rumpled white sheet.

You can't have this one, Lili.

This one is mine.

Is she still watching? Elic wondered as he set his silent feet upon the floor and uncoiled to his full height. *Can she see me through the window?* Lili's vision was preternaturally keen, as keen as a hawk's, and then some. He whipped off the cap and shook out his hair, which fell halfway down his back. "*Narru dishpu,*" she called it. *A river of honey.* His skin she likened to sweet cream, his eyes to seawater.

Normally he would close the window and draw the curtain even on a sweltering night like this, for there was inevitably a certain amount of noise once things were underway. But tonight he felt the need to disturb—to disturb Lili in particular, to let her hear this *gabru* with whom she was so captivated groan and beg and perhaps even, if Elic was skillful enough, scream. Viktor Larsson wouldn't seem so strong and mighty then. He'd have been vanquished, possessed, used. What was that Americanism Inigo was so taken with? Ah, yes.

He'll be my bitch.

And Lili will know it.

Elic shucked off his T-shirt and jeans, drew a deep, cleansing breath, and cleared his thoughts to prepare himself. So as to avoid injury during the transmutation, he lowered himself to the floor, carpeted in a centuries-old Oriental rug, and knelt on his haunches, naked and ready. Closing his eyes, he whispered the words he'd learned as a boy, the rhythmic, age-old incantation that brought about The Change.

It began as always, with a slow roiling from within, then the trembling and nausea and terrible sense of wrongness. And the pain. There was always pain, but somehow that was easier to deal with than The Change Sickness, as he thought of it.

Elic hunched forward, his fingers digging into his knees, eyes squeezed tight, lungs pumping, as the worst of it peaked and then faded. The only lingering discomfort was the sense of being starved for air as his bones compressed and his muscles softened. The narrowing of his ribs always incited a sense of panicked asphyxiation, but within a minute or so his breathing steadied; his pulse slowed.

Then came the part that he always found both unnerving and thrilling, even after all these years: the tightening and pulling inward of his loins, as of a dark, secret furrow being ploughed into damp earth. His cock, throbbing from the excitement of The Change, contracted into a tight, pulsing little knot;

his nipples itched as the flesh there swelled into buds, then breasts, heavy and soft.

Where there had been Elic, there was now a new incarnation, identical to the former in certain respects—same hair, same eyes—yet with a body whose form and chemistry were fundamentally different. He was *She* now, the female Elic might have been but for a fluke of nature at the moment of conception. Elic was not so much replaced during these occasional metamorphoses, as subsumed, incorporated into a being whose feelings and desires were purely female, but whose thoughts and memories—whose *self*—were still very much Elic.

Sitting back on her heels, she stretched her back and rotated her shoulders to the accompaniment of muted pops and cracks. She massaged her hands, flexed the delicate little fingers, and brought them to her breasts, which she lifted and squeezed. The part of her that was still Elic, still *He,* marveled, as always, at the softness of them, their weight and resilience. She pinched the rubbery little nipples, feeling a sting of arousal all the way down to her clit.

And then she turned her attention to the man in the bed across the room.

Viktor Larsson hadn't moved this whole time. The big Swede still lay sprawled on his back, arms and legs outstretched, like a Viking washed up on the shore. Shafts of moonlight illumined the hard musculature of his chest, the broad shoulders and striking face. He was magnificent—powerful, yet with an innate athletic grace even in sleep. Elic's female persona, the succubus, understood Lili's captivation with Larsson in a way that Elic himself could never hope to, especially given that Lili's high-test hormones made her that much more susceptible to the allure of a man who was, despite his flaws, utterly breathtaking.

Rising carefully to her feet, she shook out her legs and arms. She was tall for a woman, almost six feet, but that was still half a foot shorter than Elic. The difference in height conspired with the smaller, peculiarly balanced body to produce a slight disorientation for the first few minutes after The Change. When she felt as if she could walk without falling over, she took two guarded steps toward the bed, only to recoil with a gasp of pain as something sharp stabbed the sole of her right foot. Larsson turned his head, let out a grunty little breath, and stilled. Bending down, she lifted the offending object: Heather's engagement ring.

Mega-carat diamonds didn't end up on the floor unless they were thrown. It would appear that Heather was rethinking her future as Mrs. "Real Man" Larsson.

She slipped the ring onto her right hand and held it up; it flashed like lightning in the moonlight. Crawling up onto the bed with catlike stealth, she knelt next to Larsson and stroked her fingertips ever so lightly over the bulge between his splayed legs. Even through the sheet, and even in its flaccid state, his cock felt so warm, so vital. She stroked it again, and again, very slowly, a featherlight caress, until it began to thicken and stir.

Twisting the ring so that the diamond faced inward, she let the big stone graze him up and down along his member until it shifted like a live thing, rising hard and long against his belly. He made a little growly sound as she lowered the sheet and trailed her fingertips along the shiny-smooth organ. It radiated heat, twitching as she caressed it.

She took her time, stroking him lightly so as not to rouse him too soon from his slumber. The more sexually excited he was when he awoke, the more malleable he would be. And, too, it was critical that he be right at the edge when she took him; the more violent his orgasm, the more profuse the ejaculate—and that, after all, was her ultimate purpose in being here.

But not her only purpose, she thought as she slid her middle finger into the slick, hot cleft of her sex; there was her pleasure, too. The outer lips had already swelled and parted, exposing the little bud between them, which she circled with a gentle, fluttery touch until she was breathless and wet and ready. Larsson was ready, too, judging from the way his hips tensed and released with every brush of her fingertips.

She straddled his chest, leaned over, and said, "Viktor. Wake up, *chéri.*" Her English bore vague northern European inflections, like Elic's, and her voice had the same husky quality as his, though of course it wasn't as deep. When necessary for purposes of discretion, she could keep a *gabru* asleep, or half-asleep, while she tapped his seed, but the quantity nearly always suffered. More often, she would rouse him, but with just a touch on the forehead, convince him it was all a dream. Rarely did she take the risk, as she was doing now, of letting him remember it all the next day.

"*Vem är det?*" Larsson mumbled groggily as he rubbed his eyes. "Heather?"

"Not tonight." Reaching behind her, she closed her hand around his cock and stroked it firmly from root to tip. "Tonight you're mine."

He moaned, thrusting twice into her fist before he gathered his wits enough to say, "Wait . . . what . . . who the hell . . . ?"

"I don't look familiar?" she asked.

He studied her with a bewildered scowl, his eyes luminous in the shaft of moonlight drifting over his face. God, he was beautiful.

She told him what she always told them, because the resemblance was too profound to disregard. "I'm Elic's twin. Elle." *Elle,* that was how she always thought of herself during the transformation. *She.*

"Have we . . . ?" He groaned helplessly as she squeezed his cock in a way she knew—or rather, Elic knew—would excite him beyond reason. "*Jösses . . . Herre Gud,*" he moaned, gripping her waist as he writhed beneath her.

"We haven't met, but I've been watching you. And thinking about you." She dipped her fingers into her pussy, daubed the slickness onto a nipple, and teased it while she pumped him harder, faster. "I've got to have you, Viktor. Just for tonight."

"But . . . Heather . . . ," he managed.

"No one will know. You'll never see me again. Please, Viktor. Please . . ."

"*Helsike,*" he muttered, rubbing his eyes. "*Ja.* Fuck it. Okay. Yes." Eyeing the strip of condoms on the nightstand, he said, "Just let me—"

"Patience." Shifting forward, she knelt over his face and spread her labia to expose her aching clit. "Suck it."

He gripped her hips to bring her into better contact with his mouth. Shoving her fingers through his hair, she tilted his head up slightly, shivering at the gust of hot breath on her wide-open slit.

"No, Viktor, not with the tongue," she told him. "With the lips, like you're drinking from a straw. Right here. Yes," she sighed as he suckled her. "Like that. Oh, God, yes." Having your cock sucked was wonderful, as she knew very well, but having your cock shrink into a tiny little organ jammed with thousands of nerve endings, and having *that* sucked . . . there were no words to describe the sensation. The pleasure escalated swiftly, too swiftly.

He protested when she rose off of him. "But you haven't—"

"I want you inside me when I come. Wouldn't that be nice? If we came together?"

"*Ja,*" he agreed, sitting up. "Okay. Sure."

Leaning over him, she grabbed Heather's pink makeup case. "Lie back down, Viktor."

"*Nä,* I like to be on top."

"I know you do." All the *gabrus* did. She'd been looking for some kind of night cream or lotion, but found a little plastic bottle of personal warming lubricant instead. Just the thing. "Viktor, are you going to lie down, or do I have to tie you up?"

His surliness gave way to a sly grin. "Maybe I should tie *you* up."

"Does it frighten you to think of losing control to a woman?" Elle untied one of the gold cords securing the bedcurtains and snapped it to test its strength.

With a snort of laughter, he said, "I am not so easily frightened."

"Prove it," she said as she took his right hand and looped the cord around it twice. Softly, seductively, she said, "Lie down, *chéri.*"

He did, watching her closely while she knotted the cord securely to the bedpost. His erection, which had waned a bit during their verbal sparring, filled and rose as she lashed his hands and feet to the four corners of the bed. The gauzy curtains fell closed, enveloping them in a dreamlike little bower.

Taking him in—the golden god spread-eagled—she said, "You remind me of *Vitruvian Man.* That's a drawing by Leonardo da—"

"*Ja, ja,* inspired by a treatise on proportions by the Roman architect Vitruvius. What do you think, I'm just some dumb jock? You'll have to put a rubber on me."

"Shh." She flipped open the bottle of lube and drizzled a bead up the length of his penis.

He groaned in pleasure as she coated his cock and balls with the slippery balm, which heated up deliciously as she worked it in. Ah, the delights of twenty-first-century technology.

"*Sjysta prylar,*" he breathed as he writhed to her touch. "Put a rubber on me. Now."

"I'm disease-free," she said, "I promise."

He shook his head. "Once, back home, I got slapped with a . . . a *faderskaps* . . . You know, with the court and lawyers."

"A paternity suit?"

"*Ja.* Put a rubber on me. Just do it."

Elle got off the bed, retrieved the strip of condoms from his nightstand, and tossed them out the window.

"What the hell!" He yanked at his tethers as she returned to the bed. "*Slyna!* You crazy bitch, why would you do that? You *want* to get pregnant. That's it, isn't it? This is a setup."

"Relax, Viktor." She grabbed a pillow and shoved it under his butt to give her better access for her next assault. "I can't even get pregnant."

"*Skitsnack!* Bullshit! You're a lying bitch."

"Viktor, really—relax," she said as she dripped a little of the lube onto the tip of her right middle finger. "This next part will go easier for you if you do."

"*Äsch!*" he cried as she pressed her fingertip to his anus, circling the tiny opening to slacken it. "*Vad gör du?* What are you—?"

"Relax," she repeated, pushing through the sphincter. Crooking her finger toward his belly, she located a nutlike bulge, which she rubbed toward her in a slow, steady rhythm as the lube warmed up. "You'll like this, I promise you. You'll come better than you've ever come in your life." And far more copiously, which was really the point.

Larsson struggled against his bonds, spewing invective in English and Swedish, until the stimulation just got too much to ignore. He dropped his head onto the pillow with a sigh and some muttered Swedish curses; his eyes rolled up.

Elle pleasured herself as she milked Larsson. He turned his head to watch her with evident fascination, his breath coming faster now, hips straining in tempo with the prostate massage. His balls began to swell, the skin of his scrotum growing taut as the sac drew upward. His cock looked as if it were carved out of polished pink marble—rock-hard and glossy, with a network of delicate blue veins, the glans inflamed a deep, purplish red. Preejaculate oozed like syrup from its tiny slit, puddling onto his belly, an exquisite sight. He was ready now, bursting with come and about to explode.

"Suck me," he rasped, his head rocking on the pillow in sensual delirium.

"Sorry, no," she said as evenly as she could, given her own white-hot arousal. "But I'll fuck you if you ask me nicely."

"*Nej då!* Don't you dare."

"But we were going to come at the same time, remember?"

"Suck me!" he yelled, his voice raw and unsteady. "Do it. Just do it, you fucking bitch!"

"Viktor, trust me—the only way I'm going to let you come is if I fuck you. But you have to ask me first."

"Sug min kuk!" he screamed, straining at the cords, red-faced and wild-eyed. "Suck it!"

Soothingly Elle said, "I know you need to come, *chéri.* Just ask me and I'll—"

"Din satkäring! Sur-fjas!" he roared, the bed quaking and creaking as he thrashed. "Bitch! Whore!"

Sliding her finger out of his body and backing off the bed, she said, "I *could* just leave you here, tied up and helpless, with those poor balls of yours turning bluer by the—"

"*Nä,* don't! Don't! *Varsågod!* Please!" He was heaving and quivering, every muscle in his body bulging with veins, a tethered beast straining for release.

"Please what?" she asked from the foot of the bed, still fingering herself. "Please fuck you?"

"Vad som helst," he groaned. "Okay. Okay, goddamn it, just do it. Do it."

"Do what?" she asked, plucking absently at a nipple.

He let out a snarl of frustration that degenerated into a hoarse little sob. "*Jösses.* Fuck me."

"You didn't say please."

"Please!" he screamed. "Please, you fucking cunt, will you please just fuck me!"

"You're sure, now?" she asked as she crawled over him.

"Slyna! Hora!" he yelled as he thrashed against his bindings. *"Do it! Fuck me! Just fuck—"* A quavering moan issued from him as she took hold of his cock, which was almost too stiff to tilt up, and seated the head inside her. With a grunt of effort, Larsson snapped his hips, filling her; she groaned in agonized pleasure. He bucked beneath her, sweat-sheened and moaning. It didn't take long, of course. Quite soon he stilled and shuddered, a low, grinding sound, almost like a death rattle, rising from his chest.

Elle ground hard against him, igniting her own climax. Larsson roared, his cock jerking as it shot out a jet of hot come. It went on and on, burst after burst striking the mouth of her womb. He shouted with every spasm, his entire body flexing like a bow. It went on so long that he was hoarse and quaking by the time the final tremors coursed through him.

Larsson went limp, his eyes half-open as he sucked in lungfuls of air. Elle's hands shook as she pulled the pillow from beneath him and fumbled with the cords knotted around his wrists and ankles. He didn't seem to notice when he was finally freed; she had to push his left arm and leg aside to flop down next to him.

"*Ofattbar,*" he muttered. "Fucking *satans helvete.* That was... *häftigt.* Amazing. What did you say your name was?"

Reaching over to stroke his damp forehead, she whispered, "Take a little nap, *chéri.* Just for a few minutes."

He closed his eyes and went slack, his mouth slightly open, breathing deep and regular.

Dragging her hair off her face, Elle closed her own eyes and whispered the words that would change her back into Elic. The "return ticket," that was how she thought of it. From female to male... succubus to incubus.

It was much the same on the inbound trip as on the outbound: the queasiness, the pain... This time, though, her bones were expanding, her muscles solidifying, her skin stretching. The widening of her ribcage always made her want to vomit, but the feeling never lasted more than a few seconds.

The discomfort was all but gone when she felt a biting tightness on her right hand. "*Merde!*" The diamond ring, which she'd forgotten about, was digging into that finger as it grew. She sat up and tugged at the narrow band, growling in pain as she struggled to get it off before the finger finished enlarging. It wasn't easy; although the finger was coated with lube, so was the hand that was trying to remove it. She closed her teeth over the ring, took a deep breath, and yanked. It slid into her mouth, thank God. She tasted gold and blood; the finger was abraded up to the middle knuckle, but at least she—or rather, Elic—wouldn't have to end up getting Heather's engagement ring cut off. The questions would have been awkward.

She spat the ring onto the floor and slumped back down, swearing under her breath as the transformation ran its course. Her breast tissue shrank back into the pectorals; her genitals felt as if they were turning themselves inside out. It was only when he felt a penis and scrotum lying heavy between his legs that he truly felt like Elic again. He ran his hands over his face, his chest and arms, reassured by the firmness of the flesh, the unabashedly masculine contours. Diverting as it was to be Elle from time to time, it was always comforting to come back home into the body he'd been born with.

During The Change, Larsson's semen had become imbued with an incorporeal essence unique to Elic. It was a precious elixir, this *zeru,* as Lili called it, a merging of superb human genetic material with certain more ethereal qualities of the dusii race. The pressure of it, the lust it generated, made Elic's cock grow heavy, rising just a bit in anticipation of his next stop: the bathhouse.

Feeling a grating emptiness in his stomach—he was always famished after tapping seed—Elic sat up and grabbed one of Larsson's protein bars, a never-tasted novelty. He lounged back against the headboard to unwrap it, smiling when he found it to be coated in chocolate, a weakness that had rubbed off on him from Lili. He bit off a mouthful and chewed, only to gag in disgust at the shocking, nostril-flaring foulness of it. Spitting the grainy mush into his hand, he squinted in the semidarkness at the wrapper: *A heavenly combination of chocolate fudge and soy crisps guaranteed to delight your taste buds.*

Lying goddamn humans.

He hurled the bar, pre- and post-masticated, into the wastebasket. Larsson stirred at the noise, blinking his eyes open as he looked around. "Heather?"

"Not exactly."

The big Swede focused on Elic, his obvious bafflement giving way to recognition as he took in the hair. "Oh, you," he said, clearly thinking he was looking at the woman he'd just bedded, only to gape in stupefaction when Elic turned to face him fully and he realized there was a man in his bed. "*Jösses!*" he exclaimed, sitting bolt upright. "*Vem*... Who the hell... *Elic*?"

"Let me ask you, do you actually *like* those things?" Elic asked, nodding toward the protein bars, "or do you just eat them for the—"

"What the fuck...?" Scrabbling back toward the edge of the bed, Larsson said, "What the hell are you doing here?"

Elic allowed himself a puzzled little smile. "You don't remember?"

Larsson stared at Elic, his eyes glowing like silver coins as he thought about what he'd just done with the woman who bore such an uncanny resemblance to the man now lounging in his bed—the buck-naked, half-erect man. He looked down at himself, at the oily sheen on his cock and balls, the little plastic bottle of warming lube; he'd feel it in his ass, too. "*Nej*," he said, shaking his head in revulsion and disbelief as the possibilities crystallized.

"Sorry to have awakened you," Elic said. "You really conked out there. I'm not surprised, given—"

"Get out!" Larsson yelled. "Get the fuck out of here!"

"Hey, what's gotten into—"

"*Get out!*" He lunged across the bed, taking a wild swing that Elic easily ducked.

Elic drew back and landed a swift punch to Larsson's head, dropping him in a heap on the bed. Grimacing, he examined his injured finger, now throbbing from the blow. What would Larsson think, he wondered, when he came to? Would he rationalize it in his mind, convince himself he'd dreamed the whole thing, or perhaps hallucinated it? The chateau's guests tended to experience all kinds of unexplainable phenomena.

There was the lube, but wishful thinking being what it was, he could conceivably decide he'd done that to himself while sleep-fucking or whatever.

Rising from the bed, Elic pulled on his jeans and black T-shirt. Larsson had razzed Elic about the shirt earlier that day, both because it bore the Adidas logo—he'd just signed an endorsement contract with Nike—and because it had faded in the wash. "Look at Elic's shirt, how worn and shabby it is," he'd told Lili with an amused little shake of his head. "Even ball boys don't wear shirts like that."

Elic whipped off the shirt and tossed it on the floor for Larsson to find in the morning.

She's still watching.

Elic smelled it in the night air as he crossed from the chateau to the bathhouse, that heady fusion of jasmine and pheromones that told him Ilutu-Lili was still somewhere at the edge of the woods, keeping an eye on him—and an ear, as well. She would have heard Larsson pleading with Elle to fuck him, heard him roaring in relief when she finally did. She'd be disillusioned with her mighty *gabru,* and perhaps a bit miffed with Elic for putting Larsson through all that when he could have been tapped with a good deal less drama. She wouldn't stay cross at him long, though, she never did; nor he with her.

Lili... my beloved, mins ástgurdís. *Would that it was you I was coming to now,* Elic thought as he approached the bathhouse. *Would that I could possess you as I possess all these others for whom I care nothing. Would that I could lie with you and love you and make you truly mine.*

Elic's cock stretched the fly of his jeans as he stood in the arched doorway of the temple-like structure, watching Heather take her midnight soak. She reclined on the steps in a far corner of the pool, head back, eyes closed, the red swimsuit a little puddle on the marble floor behind her.

He entered the bathhouse and circled the pool, taking no care to be silent. The other spell he'd cast upon Heather this afternoon, when he'd put it in her mind to take this late-night bath, had ensured that she would be deaf to any sound produced by humanfolk or follets from the moment she lowered herself into the pool. So Larsson's groans and pleas and screams of lust, audible, Elic was quite sure, to the entire Grotte Cachée valley, had not been heard by his fiancée.

Moonlight streamed in through the skylight, infusing Heather's sleek, damp body with a silvery radiance. Her hair, even wet as it was, looked like spun gold, her nipples like little copper coins balanced just so on her petite breasts.

Arkhutus, that was what Lili called the female guests in whom Elic, the incubus incarnate, chose to plant the seed he took such care to harvest. That Heather was engaged to Larsson was purely a fluke. The *arkhutu* needn't be involved with the *gabru* who'd produced the seed, nor even know him. All they need have in common was excellent genetic potential, as demonstrated by such factors as physical vitality, accomplishments, and intellect. Archer referred to them, in that aridly British way of his, as "prime breeding stock."

Standing at the edge of the pool not far from Heather, Elic realized she wasn't dozing, as he'd thought. Her submerged right hand, which rested in her lap, was moving in a slow, sensual rhythm. Elic stripped off his jeans and stepped down into the pool—cautiously, so as not to betray his presence by disturbing the water. Lust quivered up his legs, settling hot and insistent in his loins; the water would have contained a lingering sensual charge from this afternoon even before Heather stepped into it, thus kindling her own sexual heat.

He grew fully erect within a matter of seconds, his cache of *zeru* only fueling his lust. Standing in the water about two yards from Heather, Elic stroked himself in time with her own caress, very lightly, just the fingertips playing up and down the shaft as he gritted his teeth to keep himself in check. It wouldn't do to go off in his hand, thus squandering all that precious seed, but he'd learned that it paid to be as primed as possible. The greater the discharge of seed, the more likely the *arkhutu* was to get pregnant. The position in which he took her was important, too, conception being likeliest if she was on her back, although he sometimes made them lie on their sides, or kneel facedown. And, too, it was imperative that he coax her into the most powerful orgasm possible, the contractions of which would force her cervix into contact with the ejaculate.

If Lili were with him now, she might milk Elic's seed, as he had milked Larsson's, while he pumped away with measured strokes inside this *arkhutu*, trying to make it last, to make the pleasure mount and mount until he was wild with it. Lili sometimes did that for him, amid soft kisses and intimate whispers, often with a little curved steel rod she'd had forged for that purpose by the royal swordsmith to Louis XVI.

Tonight, however, Lili was just a distant, if not quite disinterested, observer.

Elic grasped the head of his cock to squeeze out a few thick drops of pre-come, which he rubbed over the aching instrument to facilitate penetration. *Now.*

He crossed to Heather in two strides; by the time she opened her eyes, he was upon her. She drew in a breath to scream. He clamped a hand over her mouth and willed her hearing to return.

"It's me—Elic," he said, but she was already kicking and struggling. She rammed a fist into his nose, sparking a bolt of pain that had Elic swearing harshly even as he thought, *Good girl.*

He tried to pin her into the corner of the pool, but she thrashed and fought like a wild thing, and she was surprisingly strong. She bit his hand to get it off her mouth, but as she was filling her lungs, he clamped a hand to her forehead and said, "*Láta... liggja...* Shh, Heather. Easy. Easy."

She quieted, her breath coming rapidly as she stared at him.

He felt the tension ease from her muscles as her mind and body surrendered to his desire, his aching need—always a heady moment, filled with the promise of exquisite pleasures to come. Her eyes glittered darkly as she held his gaze; her legs fell open. Elic knelt on the floor of the pool and slid his cock up and down the cleft of her sex, feeling the heat and dampness of her arousal even underwater.

Closing his hands over her breasts, he whispered against her lips, "You're about to have the most extraordinary dream."

Lick of the Flame

One

May 1749

DARIUS, CURLED up in his little box of straw in the gatehouse, awoke to Frederic, the guard on duty, barking out, "*Halte! Qui va là?*"

"It's Mrs. Hayes with the virgins," responded a woman in English. "Sir Francis is expecting us."

Darius rose, quivering as he stretched the kinks out of his back, and leapt from his box. A lady stood silhouetted against the setting sun on the other side of the portcullis barring the arched entryway. She was plump and matronly, her steely hair mostly hidden beneath the hood of a long red cloak.

"What is the watchword?" demanded Frederic, whose English, like his French, bore a pronounced Swiss-German accent. He was, like the two dozen other guards charged with maintaining the peace and privacy of Grotte Cachée, a Swiss mercenary, members of a breed prized throughout Europe for their discipline, skill, and prudence. So discreetly did Frederic and his brethren fulfill their responsibilities that the chateau's guests rarely noticed them, despite their rather garish red and blue striped uniforms.

"Do what thou wilt," she said with a sigh of annoyance. "Now, will you kindly raise this bloody thing and let us pass? We're late as it is, and Sir Francis doesn't like to be kept waiting."

"The cart, it must go 'round back to the stable," said Frederic as he cranked the windlass that operated the portcullis's pulley system. There came a battery of creaks and groans, underscored by a high-pitched metallic grating that Darius could only hear in his present feline incarnation.

Slinking beneath the big iron grate as it rose, he crossed the drawbridge that spanned the dry moat. On the path out front stood a cart full of prettily attired young women, gazing up at Château de la Grotte Cachée as if awestruck.

"Leave your shawls and mantles in the cart, lasses, but don't forget those fans," Mrs. Hayes ordered. "Necks high, shoulders down, arms curved lightly outward. Pinch your cheeks and plump up those bubbies."

The cartman repeated the instructions in French as he handed the girls down from his vehicle. They were young and creamy skinned, fresh little peaches in dainty lace caps and frocks of dimity and flower-sprigged lawn. They giggled and whispered as Mrs. Hayes ushered them through the gatehouse and into the chateau's enclosed courtyard, their gaits naively rustic, their skirts swishing against Darius as he followed along. They all wore exactly the same scent, an all-too-common *eau de parfum* redolent of rosemary, bergamot, and orange blossom, no doubt supplied by Mrs. Hayes.

"They await you in the withdrawing room next to the chapel." Frederic pointed toward an arched doorway in the castle's west range.

"What ho," said Mrs. Hayes when she noticed Darius. "Seems a little gray ghost has thrown in with us." She squatted down to pet him, but he dodged her before she could. He could mingle with the chateau's guests on those rare occasions when curiosity got the better of him, such as this evening, so long as he was careful to steer clear of actual physical contact. "Skittish, are you? Aye, but you'll fit right in with the rest of these coy little pusses."

The girls fell silent as they neared the fountain in the center of the courtyard, a stone pool surmounted by a statue of a man and a woman joined in carnal union as water sluiced over them from a jug held aloft by a handmaid. It wasn't the sculpture, indelicate though it was, that had stunned the girls into silence, Darius knew. It was the gentleman kneeling over the edge of the pool with his gold-shot silk coat thrown up and his breeches around his knees, grunting in pain as a lady in an ornate silver half-mask whipped his buttocks with a length of rattan.

"God's balls!" he cried. "Have mercy, my lady."

"Is that you, Your Grace?" asked the whoremistress. "Came all the way to France for a good caning, eh?"

The prostrate gentleman, a duke judging from the term of address, raised his head and grinned like a basket of chips. "Mrs. Hayes! I see you've brought the cherries for the banquet."

"Did I say you could speak?" demanded the masked lady. "You shall take a dozen more strokes for that," she said as she brought the cane down with whistling speed.

The duke emitted an ecstatic little moan even as he reached between his legs to frig himself.

"Fie!" His tormenter smacked the offending hand with her cane, saying, "You may spend when I say you may spend, and not a moment sooner."

"As you please, my lady," muttered the duke as he lowered his head and raised his rosy ass.

"Come, poppets," said Mrs. Hayes as she led them, along with Darius, through the arched doorway and into a little vestibule.

A burly guard, one of the expansive retinue who'd accompanied the chateau's current guests from England, said, " 'Tis high time, Mrs. Hayes. I was thinkin' you'd been set upon by bandits."

"Sorry, Tommy. Two of the wenches tried to hold out for more money, so it took a bit of dickering to get them to come."

"Aye, but they'll all come before the night's through," Tommy snickered.

Extending her hand, Mrs. Hayes said, "Fifty quid apiece, as usual, plus my traveling expenses."

Tommy made a quick count of the girls, then pulled a sack of coins from inside his coat and handed it to the procuress. "Come along, then."

Unlocking the door behind him, he gestured the group into the chapel withdrawing room, a candlelit chamber furnished with silk settees and low marble tables. The centuries-old tapestries that normally graced these walls had been taken down and replaced with paintings depicting men in white monks' robes disporting themselves with nubile, half-naked nuns. Over the central dining table, where a crystal chandelier normally hung, dangled a lamp shaped like a batlike monster with an erection almost as big as itself. A carved wooden sign hanging over the doorway to the chapel read *Fay ce que voudras:* "Do what thou wilt," the motto of England's Order of the Friars of St. Francis of Wycombe, better known as the Hellfire Club.

About two dozen gentlemen and half as many ladies occupied the room, some standing and some reclining, all exquisitely attired. The ladies, he saw, all wore silver brooches inscribed *Love and Friendship* on the bosoms of their deeply décolleté gowns. Two of them had their gowns half-unlaced, exhibiting embroidered satin stays so low cut as to display their breasts in their entirety. One lady's gown had been fashioned with a skirt that opened to the waist in back; her petticoats and panniers had likewise been split to reveal tantalizing glimpses of flesh every time she moved.

The perfumes and scented accoutrements of the assembled company—handkerchiefs, sachets, and powders—merged in a flowery-sweet miasma. There were two maidservants, as well, serving wine and such aphrodisiacal delicacies as oysters, caviar, almonds, pine nuts, and figs. They all turned to watch as Mrs. Hayes ushered in the young women, but the only man who was mannerly enough to rise was Darius's fellow follet, Inigo.

"*Bonsoir, mesdemoiselles,*" Inigo said with a bow. The charming young satyr was attired for the evening in a gold-embroidered satin coat of some dark hue which Darius's feline eyes couldn't quite place—something reddish or brownish, most likely. His unruly curls were caught in a ribbon at his nape, leaving just enough on the sides to cover those telltale ears. He captured Darius's gaze and winked.

Darius winked back.

The rest of the gentlemen appraised the procession with a frankness that would have seemed grossly rude under ordinary circumstances. Two ladies lounging side by side, one wearing a mask trimmed in peacock feathers, conferred behind their fans as they pointed to this girl and that. Darius swiveled his ears to home in on their whispered comments. ". . . in the yellow stripes, with those big blue eyes? Wouldn't you just love to bend her over your knee?"

Darius wove his way between the ladies' rustling silk skirts and the men's white-stockinged legs to the doorway that led to the chapel, where he was less likely to be noticed and pestered. If he'd thought about it, he would have made himself invisible before coming in here; it was the safest course of action in a room this crowded.

"Mrs. Hayes! You are late," said a gentleman seated at a dining table in the center of the room as he snapped an enameled snuffbox shut. He was a gangly fellow of perhaps forty, with a long nose and a pale, oddly soft-featured visage. Like some of the other men, he wore a wig, but his was by far the most ornate and heavily powdered.

"My apologies, Lord Sandwich, and my compliments," said Mrs. Hayes with a little curtsey. "Pray, where might Sir Francis be? I was to deliver these charming lambs to him personally."

"The chief friar grew weary of waiting and retired to the chapel to make ready for the mass. These are the virgins, then?"

"Yes, and please you, m'lord." Herding the girls into a semicircle, the better for viewing, Mrs. Hayes announced, "For your delight and diversion, gentlemen, eight unpolluted and intact maidenheads, fresh from the local villages. In the roseate bloom of youth, each and every one, virgin rosebuds as yet uncropped. I have tutored these innocents myself in the many and varied arts of love, the better to enhance their defloration during your rites of Venus."

The whoremistress clapped her hands twice, a signal to the girls to execute awkward curtseys, glancing at one another as if to make sure they were doing it right. From the way they jostled each other, it was clear they were unused to the wide, hooped skirts in which they'd been outfitted for their presentation.

Scanning them with a critical expression, Sandwich said, "Intact, you say?"

"Pure and unsullied, one and all."

"We shall see." Lord Sandwich snapped his fingers at the girl closest to him, a buxom beauty with coppery hair, and signaled for her to approach. "Come, come," he said, pushing his chair away from the table so that there was room for her to stand before him.

"Step lively, Nadine," urged Mrs. Hayes as she prodded the girl.

He gestured her closer until she stood between his outstretched, cat-stick legs. "I shan't hurt you."

"He'd rather she hurt *him*—eh, Sandwich?" some wag remarked.

"Lift your skirts, then," Sandwich said.

Nadine greeted that command with a blink of bewilderment.

Mrs. Hayes said, "They only speak the parleyvoo, your lordship."

"Soulevez votre robe." Indicating the girl's skirts, Sandwich flicked his hand, cloaked to the fingertips in frilly lace cuffs.

Nadine looked around at the raptly attentive audience, cheeks blossoming with color.

"I'll have that one," someone remarked. "I do so love it when they squirm and blush."

"I daresay they've been well trained to do so," someone else observed. "Is that not right, Mrs. H?"

Ignoring the taunt, Mrs. Hayes stepped forward and started lifting the young woman's dress, but Sandwich slapped her hand away. "What's the chit being paid for, if not to do our bidding? *Soulevez-le, mademoiselle.*"

Closing her eyes, Nadine gathered her skirts and raised them to her knees.

"Oh, for pity's sake," Sandwich growled. "*Plus haut.* Like this." Leaning forward, he grabbed her hands and forced her to raise the mass of dimity, stiffened petticoats and panniers chest-high, leaving her naked from the waist down.

"By Jove, her cunny's as red as her face," someone chuckled.

"A ripe little split apricot, just begging to be licked."

"Be a sport, Sandwich," said an Italian-accented fellow who was craning his neck to see. "Turn her 'round so the rest of us can have a peek."

"Unlace her! Let's have a taste of those apple dumplings."

"All in good time, gentlemen." Nudging the girl's slippered feet apart with a high-heeled shoe, Sandwich parted her red-tufted slit and pushed his middle finger in. She sucked in a breath, her eyes shut tight, as he probed that which had ostensibly never felt the touch of a male hand.

"Right. She'll do." Pointing to a row of nuns' habits hanging by hooks in the robing alcove behind him, Sandwich told her, in French, to change into one of them, leaving herself completely unclothed beneath. He instructed one of the ladies, a Mademoiselle de Beaumont, to assist the virgins in their disrobing, which for reasons beyond Darius's ken prompted much appreciative laughter.

"So soon?" asked Mrs. Hayes. "It took me all day to get them properly flashed up, and now you want them to take it all off?"

" 'Tis your fault for being late. They need to be ready for the banquet as soon as the mass has ended." Sandwich beckoned to the next girl in line, who lifted her skirts without being asked and barely flinched during the examination. "You may take your leave, Mrs. Hayes. I'd say we have the matter well in hand here."

He inspected the girls one by one, pronouncing them either intact or "close enough," before sending them off to the alcove to disrobe in full view of the guests. The gentlemen—some of the ladies, too—opined liberally on their various charms as they unlaced their dresses and peeled off their underpinnings, assisted by the fair-haired, French-accented Mademoiselle de Beaumont. A few of the maidens struck Darius as remarkably blasé about the lewd exhibition, one or two genuinely embarrassed. Others appeared so overwrought despite their cooperation that he suspected they were acting the part they'd been taught to act.

In any event, their spectators seemed appreciative enough. Several of the men stroked themselves as they took in the little performance. Darius noticed Inigo ushering a pretty little thing from the room, his front trouser panel already half undone, one hand fisted around a wine bottle.

A strikingly handsome man lowered his raven-haired lady companion from his lap to the floor between his legs and unbuttoned his knee-breeches to free his erection. Those sitting nearby watched with undisguised interest as the lady licked and fondled the rigid organ. "Brava," they praised when she swallowed it to the very root, causing the recipient of her ministrations to clutch her head, moaning, "Ah, Lili, but you are a talented wench."

On a red silken couch in the corner, two men positioned the lady with the split skirt on her hands and knees so that one of them could roger her from behind as she took the other in her mouth. A bewigged gentleman whom Darius recognized from newspaper illustrations as Frederick, Prince of Wales, bent a masked lady over the back of that same couch and canted up her petticoats. He lubricated his weapon with spittle and slammed it into her so hard she shrieked.

"Good show, Your Highness," praised a bacon-faced fellow in a too-tight, fancily embroidered coat who'd come over to watch the bawdy tableau while working himself off. "Give her a taste of the royal cutlass," he grunted as he thrust into a lace handkerchief. "Stab it in and twist it! Split the wench! Spank her arse! That's it, good and hard. Aye, that's it..."

"What have we here?" The voice was male, softly deep, German accented—and far too close.

Darius's whiskers thrummed a warning just in time for him to leap away from the hand that was about to scoop him up.

There came a chuckle as his would-be captor straightened up, tugging a scented handkerchief from his voluminous, fancily embroidered coat sleeve. He was Prussian-pale, with gray eyes, full lips, and a hard, outthrust jaw. Although his hair was concealed beneath a fashionably small powdered wig, Darius could tell from his eyebrows that he was blond. Like many of the other gentlemen, he had a ceremonial sword hanging in a sheath at his side.

"Bashful, are you, *mein kleiner freund*?" he asked. "Methinks thou hast wandered into the wrong place."

"Chatting to yourself, Lord Turek?" inquired a lady who sauntered toward them, fluttering her fan. " 'Tis the sign of a degenerated mind. I knew there was something about you I fancied."

It was the woman in the silver mask who'd been caning the duke out by the fountain. Although English, judging from her voice, she wore, like all ladies of fashion, a luxuriant *robe à la française,* its overskirt of quilted silver brocade extending a good three feet to either side. The weapon she'd wielded earlier, a slim rattan crook, like that of a British schoolmaster, hung from a silken ribbon around her waist. Her face was artfully painted, right down to the little black silk patch near a corner of her mouth; her flaxen hair was styled in a complicated arrangement studded with diamonds, and more diamonds adorned the velvet ribbon around her throat.

"Oh, a cat!" she exclaimed. "I loathe the wretched things. Go! Shoo!"

She lifted her skirts and made kicking motions at Darius, who turned to dart away, only to find Turek directly in his path. "I've got him." He crouched down, arms outstretched and grinning in a predatory way that provoked a searing hiss from Darius.

"There you are!" A pair of female hands snatched him off the floor before Turek could grab him. Darius shot his claws, ready to spring, as she clutched him to her bosom, whispering, "Easy, Darius. 'Tis I, Elle."

He looked up at her, calming when he recognized the blue-eyed honey-blonde who'd captured, or rather, rescued him: Elic in his female persona, dressed for the evening in a lavish gown of pale blue painted silk. Other follets posed no risk to Darius, only humans, whose slightest touch assaulted him with a barrage of desires that he was helpless to ignore—all manner of desires, from a hankering for iced creams to the most bizarre sexual fetish. Darius relaxed into Elle's embrace, reassured by her familiar scent, barely discernible beneath a saccharine haze of rose oil.

"The beast is yours?" asked the masked lady, eyeing Darius warily over her fan. "You would do well to remove it before it bites someone."

"He really is quite harmless," said Elle, cradling Darius protectively, "but he cannot abide the touch of strangers."

"That is the only kind she *can* abide," said Turek, indicating the lady who'd just joined them. His grin revealed a mouthful of teeth a bit too white and even to be real, a suspicion that was confirmed when Darius noticed a narrow ribbon of gold around his gumline. Bowing to Elle with a luxuriant sweep of the hand that held the handkerchief, he said, "Anton Turek, at your service, mademoiselle. And this lovely but rather imperious peasant is Charlotte Somerhurst."

Darius's nose twitched, not at the perfume wafting from Turek's handkerchief, but from an almost indiscernible whiff of something raw and dark that excited the hunter in him.

"Really, Turek," said Charlotte. "You must learn to introduce people by their titles, as we British do, else one never really knows to whom one is being presented. I am the Countess of Somerhurst," she told Elle, "and this barbarous Hun is, in fact, a baron from one of those murky little countries no one ever visits."

"Bohemia," Turek said. "But I make my home in Vienna, for the most part."

"And in London, and Paris, and Venice, and who knows where else," Charlotte said. "Upon my word, Lord Turek has so many homes, I should think he has forgotten where most of them are."

Elle introduced herself with a little curtsey.

"Just 'Elle'?" Charlotte asked. "No family name?"

"Nor title, I confess."

Charlotte smiled in a coldly remote way that wasn't hard to decipher. Having been judged and found lacking in all that was meaningful, namely social standing, Elle could now be crossed off Charlotte's list of people who mattered.

"I say, but you are the very image of a local fellow who was inducted into the Hellfires yesterday," Charlotte told Elle. "An acquaintance of our hostess. Evidently he'd been intrigued by the order for some time, and was eager to participate. I believe his name is Eric."

"Elic," Elle corrected. "He is my twin brother."

"Indeed." Charlotte glanced slyly in the direction of Turek, whose gaze had frosted over at the mention of Elic. "Well, I suppose there can be no mistaking the resemblance. There's a handsome family if ever I've seen one."

A maid came by with a tray laden with wineglasses and two cut-glass carafes filled with wine. "Regular or enhanced?" she asked.

"Oh, enhanced, definitely," Charlotte replied.

"I would advise you to avoid that kind unless you've a tolerance for cantharides," Turek advised Elle. "Spanish fly," he explained in response to her quizzical look.

Elle waved away the tray altogether. Turek chose the unadulterated wine, saying he found the notion of consuming ground-up blister beetles both repulsive and dangerous, and that cantharides, in any event, merely excited the flesh as opposed to the passions.

"I take my excitement in whatever manner I can acquire it," replied Charlotte as she raised her glass. "To sin in all its varied and wondrous forms."

"How came you to join our little romp this evening, Elle?" Turek asked as he raised his wineglass to inhale the bouquet.

"Like my brother, I am a friend of la Dame des Ombres. She thought I might find it diverting."

"Pray, where *is* Madame?" he asked as he scanned the room. "I've yet to make her acquaintance."

"She tends to keep to herself." Elle stroked and nuzzled Darius, coaxing a deep purr of contentment from him. "Her *administrateur*, Lord Henry Archer, sees to the needs of her guests."

"Ah, yes, Archer," Turek said. "Capital fellow."

Lord Henry, second son of the Marquis of Heddonshaw, was an affable young dilettante and the first Englishman ever recruited to oversee the affairs of Grotte Cachée. It was he who'd suggested to the chateau's *gardienne*, Camille Morel, Dame des Ombres, that she invite the Hellfire Club to spend a fortnight at the chateau. They'd been meeting at a London pub called the George and Vulture, but it had burned down recently, leaving the Hellfires betwixt and between. Madame, mindful of the carnal needs of the three follets in her care—Darius, Elic, and Inigo—had written a letter of invitation to the club's founder and chief "friar," Sir Francis Dashwood. Having read references to Grotte Cachée in the erotic memoirs of Domenico Vitturi, a sixteenth-century Venetian nobleman, and eager to experience the rumored haven of licentiousness for himself, Dashwood had gratefully accepted the offer. He, his colleagues, and their female followers had disported themselves for two weeks at the chateau, and were to depart on the morrow—but not before a final orgiastic celebration tonight.

"Are you a frequent visitor to the chateau?" Turek asked Elle.

"I've been a guest here for some time."

"Can you enlighten me at all about that rather curious stone figure in the cave next to the bathhouse? The one they call Dusivæsus?"

"Been snooping, have you?" Charlotte asked him.

"Exploring," he corrected. " 'Tis a more worthy pastime, I daresay, than spending the better part of every day as you do, being bathed and groomed and dressed."

"That sculpture is the oldest thing at Grotte Cachée," Elle told him. "It predates the birth of Christ." She did not volunteer the information that it was, in fact, a representation of herself—or, more accurately, herself and himself.

A chorus of cheers drew their attention to a pair of bewigged and liveried footmen entering the room with something that looked like a hobbyhorse in the form of a black swan; its head curved backward so that its gilded beak, carved into a remarkably realistic phallus, jutted upward from the seat.

"My word," Elle said.

"Just something to get the nuns in the proper frame of mind for the banquet. An *idolum tentiginis,* Sir Francis calls it, one of several little playthings the friars brought with them from London." Charlotte's eyes, just visible through the holes in her mask, slid toward Elle as if to gauge her reaction for its amusement value.

Mademoiselle de Beaumont took the hand of one of the local maidens, now garbed in the tunic and wimple of a nun, led her to the device, and instructed her in French as to how to mount it. The girl was balky at first, but, emboldened by the mademoiselle's gentle encouragement, she finally lifted her habit and sat astride the creature, impaling herself on its beak.

"That was far too easy," Charlotte sneered. "She's no more 'intact' than I am."

The girl proceeded to rock back and forth on the swan, prompting applause from the onlookers and praise from Mademoiselle de Beaumont.

"Why did everyone laugh when Mademoiselle went to help them undress?" Elle asked.

Charlotte and Turek shared a knowing chuckle. "Take a good look at her," Charlotte said.

Elle did. "She is very beautiful."

"She is the Chevalier d'Eon," Turek said.

"Chevalier?" Elle said. "She's a *man*?"

"No one knows for certain," Turek said. "There are countless wagers riding on her true sex. One can speculate on the matter through the London Stock Exchange. I've done so myself."

From behind her fan, Charlotte said, "She is an intimate friend of King Louis's mistress, Madame de Pompadour. They say she spies for the king. I know for a fact that she's a lethal hand with the sword. She has won a number of duels, sometimes dressed as a man, and sometimes as a woman."

The girl on the swan began rocking in earnest, her breath coming faster, color rising in her face. The spectators cheered her on as they pleasured themselves and each other.

"This is a most curious gathering," Elle remarked.

With a dismissive wave of her fan, Charlotte said, "These are just preliminaries, my dear, a little *ouverture* to put us all in the mood for the banquet that's to follow the mass. That is when the true festivities will begin. We shall be in nuns' habits ourselves, then, most of us—until they start ripping it all off us, of course." The wicked spark in Charlotte's eyes betrayed her desire to see Elle swoon with shock. "I do hope you've a fit constitution, my dear, because the entertainments can be a bit acrobatic. There is always a physician on hand, though, to revive those who faint, as well as to prepare the various . . . invigorating tonics on which some of our members have come to rely."

"I'm afraid I shan't be able to attend the banquet," Elle said.

"A pity," Charlotte said. " 'Tis a most singular experience."

"About this mass . . . ," Elle began. "You cannot mean there's to be an actual religious service." Of course, she knew all about the mass, having been well briefed on it following her—or rather, her male alter ego's—initiation into the order yesterday. Perhaps, Darius thought, she was trying to determine just how seriously the Hellfires actually regarded the pseudo-religious aspects of their order.

" 'Tis a sort of backward mass meant to invoke the Prince of Darkness," Charlotte said matter-of-factly. "A *missa niger,* we call it." Narrowing her eyes at Darius, she said, "Did that cat just *snicker*?"

"He made a noise," Elle said. "I don't know that I would call it a snicker."

Darius gave Charlotte his most guileless feline smile.

"The *missa niger* is a very special event for us, and rather infrequent," Turek said. "Our detractors seem to think we conduct one every night, but it's really no more often than once a month. Its purpose is more to ridicule religious pomposity than to summon the Devil—although it does celebrate our own, rather unorthodox philosophies and values. Usually only the superior members are permitted in the chapel during the rites, what Sir Francis calls the twelve apostles. Oh, and a couple of footmen, to serve as acolytes. And, of course, the lady who has been chosen to be our Bona Dea for that particular mass."

"Bona Dea?" Elle said. "She was a Roman goddess of fertility, yes?"

"Quite right," Turek said. "The Bona Dea serves, in essence, as our altar. She lies naked upon the altar table, and the mass is said over her body. To be chosen as Bona Dea is the highest honor we can bestow upon one of our female companions. Sir Francis will announce her name shortly before the mass. Our fair Lady Somerhurst expects to be chosen for the first time tonight."

With a self-satisfied little smile, Charlotte said, "I will admit to having heard rumors to that effect. I must say, it's about time. I've frequented these gatherings for about two years."

"What, exactly, happens to the Bona Dea during the mass?" Elle asked. "Why must she be naked?"

"I regret that I cannot reveal the particulars," Turek said.

Charlotte said, "Everyone who participates in the masses is sworn to secrecy. Before one begins, the lady who's been chosen to be the Bona Dea, if it is her first time serving in that capacity, is taken aside by the lady who served most recently, for instruction as to what is expected of her. Tonight's tutoress will be Emily Lawrence. She would be the one in the backless skirt over there on the couch, taking it fore and aft."

"Suffice it to say," Turek said, "certain acts are performed upon the Bona Dea that would strike the uninitiated as highly obscene, but they are all part of a ritual that we superior friars take very seriously."

"If you do serve as the Bona Dea tonight," Elle asked Charlotte, "will you keep the mask on, or—"

"*Nein,*" Turek said quickly. "The Bona Dea could not possibly be masked. 'Twould be absurd. 'Tis absurd even here, if you ask me." To Charlotte, he said, "You really ought to take that blasted thing off. Everyone who is coming has already arrived."

Elle said, "I've been wondering why you wear it."

"If the wrong person were to encounter me here, it could be quite awkward. I leave the mask on till I'm quite certain it's safe." Charlotte surveyed the room over the rim of her wineglass, stilling when she noticed the darkly beautiful Lili, she of the clever mouth, walking toward them. Snagging Turek's gaze as she untied her mask, she said, sotto voce, "Your little infidel is headed this way."

"Ah. Yes, well, I shall be taking my leave, then. Ladies. *Auf wiedersehen.*" Turek executed a deep continental bow, turned, and strode away, stone-faced, passing Lili without so much as a nod.

"He doesn't care for her?" Elle asked.

"On the contrary." Tucking the mask into a hidden pocket of her skirt, Charlotte whispered, "He's mad for her, desperate to have his turn with her, but she can't bear him for some reason, utterly avoids him. God knows why—she's nobody." She tapped her lips with the fan as Lili joined them, bringing with her a whisper of jasmine.

"What a darling little cat," Lili said in a throaty, mildly accented voice. "I say, do either of you ladies have a pot of lip rouge? I seem to have misplaced mine."

"Left it all on Lord Bute's sugarstick, did you?" Charlotte produced a tiny, diamond-encrusted case from her pocket and handed it over. "Elle, Lili. Lili, Elle. Well, that was easy."

"You must learn to close your ears to her, Elle." Lili graced Elle with a disarmingly warm smile. " 'Tis the only way the rest of us can bear her company." She was an exquisite creature with almond eyes and high cheekbones, her ivory gown providing a sharp but pleasing contrast to her olive skin and sleek black hair.

"We were just talking about Lord Turek," Charlotte said with a sly little smile.

Lili gave a theatrical little shudder as she thumbed open the rouge pot.

"Turek was to get a leg over Lili tonight, whether she wanted him or not," Charlotte told Elle, "but that's been foiled. You see, 'twas his turn to be Abbot of the Day, which means being a sort of co-celebrant in the mass, along with Sir Francis, who is our chief friar. Once the mass is over and the banquet has begun, the Abbot of the Day has first pick of the nuns, and they do not have the option of refusal."

"Ah," Elle said.

Lili patted her generous lips with the rouge, rubbed them

together, and handed the pot back to Charlotte. "Thank God Sir Francis replaced him."

Elle said, "Yes, Elic told me he's been given the honor."

Lord Henry had taken Sir Francis aside yesterday evening and asked him, on behalf of la Dame des Ombres, to name the newly inducted Elic Abbot of the Day. A presumptuous request, perhaps, but Sir Francis granted it as a gesture of thanks to Madame for her hospitality.

"Have you met Elic?" Charlotte asked Lili.

"I'm not sure."

"He's hard to miss," Charlotte said. "Tall, fair, devastatingly handsome, with a look in his eye that suggests he could give a lady quite a ride. There is little chance you could have met him and forgotten."

"They haven't met," Elle said, whereupon the other two women glanced curiously at her, wondering, no doubt, how she could be so certain of this. "That is, I think Elic would have told me if he'd met a lady as lovely as yourself, Lili. He's my brother, you see, and we're very close."

"I'm just relieved that he managed to get himself appointed Abbot of the Day," Lili said. "I cannot imagine what I would have done if Turek had been given the power to choose any one of us, like it or not."

"And he *would* have chosen you, darling," Charlotte said. "You've seen how he looks at you."

"Like a snake eyeing its prey," Lili said.

Casting her gaze at the ceiling, Charlotte said, "Are you not perhaps being a bit hasty in your judgment, my dear? Turek is well built, unbelievably strong . . . and you must admit he's a handsome devil, 'specially with the wig off. You've said yourself, you have a weakness for blond men."

"I've heard all about him," Lili said. "I know how he treats his bedpartners. Pours gin down their throats till they're reeling, sometimes completely unconscious, then ravishes them like a beast. I've seen the bites and bruises on the women he drags off. I've seen them on *you*."

"One mustn't discount the allure of the beast, my dear," said Charlotte with a wicked little smile. "When it comes to lovers, I'll take a devil over an angel any day."

"It's not just that," Lili said. "There's his smell. He smells... wrong somehow."

"Bah!" Charlotte scoffed. "There's nothing foul about his smell. Now, Bubb Doddington, there's a ripe one. Would you rather have that great, rancid bladder of lard huffing and puffing on top of you?"

"I wouldn't say *foul,* exactly," Lili said. " 'Tis subtle, to be sure, but Lord Turek smells almost... metallic, but in a slightly dank way. Like a handful of copper pennies."

"I know what you mean," Elle said. "I've smelled it, too."

So had Darius, now that he thought about it. It *was* subtle, but his feline nose was sensitive, especially to certain smells.

It wasn't copper pennies. It was blood.

"Well, Lili," Charlotte said, "it would appear you're to be spared your lovelorn swain's attentions, at least for tonight. Frankly, I cannot imagine why Elic even wanted to take his place, given the reams of Latin he's had to memorize between then and now."

"My brother relishes new experiences," Elle said—a disingenuous statement, for what Elic truly relished, with compulsive zeal, was the transference of seed from an exemplary male to an equally superior female. As Abbot of the Day, he would have his pick, following tonight's mass, of the beautiful, well-bred adventuresses who kept company with the Hellfires.

Charlotte said, "Turek was quite the rusty-guts when he found out that he would not be serving as Abbot of the Day. He took it like a gentleman, of course—in front of Sir Francis—but he gave me an earful in private last night. He was snarling, sputtering, raving like a bedlamite. Went on and on about how irregular it was, how Elic's only just become a member of the order, and a rank-and-file member, at that, how he shouldn't even be permitted to observe the mass, much less officiate. Of course, it's not really the lack of propriety that got to him. It's knowing he won't get to bang our dear Lili until the next *missa niger*, which will have to wait till Sir Francis can find a proper venue for it."

"With any luck," Lili said, "that will take a good long while."

"What an unusual accent, Lili," said Elle. "If you don't mind my asking, where are you from?"

"The Ottoman Empire."

"You are Persian, then?" Elle asked.

"Good heavens, no," Lili said. "At one time, my homeland was under Persian rule, but I've no Persian blood in me."

"Lili likes to cultivate an air of mystery," Charlotte said, gazing about the room as if in search of more diverting company, "the better to ingratiate herself with Sir Francis. Ah. Speak of the devil."

The gentleman who'd just entered from the anteroom to the chapel was built like a shoulder of mutton, with genial good looks and an appealing smile. His dark hair—his own, not a wig—was unbound, his attire surprisingly plain and dignified. He sat at the table to confer with Lord Sandwich. Training his ears on the conversation, Darius heard him say, "Mrs. Hayes finally brought the vestals, I see."

"Yes, indeed," replied Sandwich as he offered his snuffbox to Dashwood. "And a fetching lot they are."

"What sort of gentleman is Sir Francis?" Elle asked, although Darius happened to know that she—or rather, Elic—had taken the waters with Dashwood that very afternoon, along with Inigo, Archer, Charlotte, and Lord Sandwich.

Lili said, "He is quite charming, really—witty, engaging, admired by everyone who knows him. And very accomplished—a patron of the arts and one of King George's inner circle. An unabashed libertine, of course, and he swears like a cutter, but that didn't prevent him from being appointed Chancellor of the Exchequer. A brilliant man in many respects."

"Brilliant and debauched," Charlotte said. "The perfect combination. They say he seduced Empress Anne of Russia during his Grand Tour, whilst disguised as King Charles of Sweden—all the more remarkable when one considers that King Charles was dead at the time."

"My word," Elle said as she gazed across the room at the subject of their conversation. Curled up against her chest, Darius felt her heartbeat quicken and her skin grow warm.

Sir Francis Dashwood was the man on whom she'd set her sights tonight, Darius realized. He was the chosen one, the man whose seed she intended to acquire. She'd best be quick about it, given the evening's program; there would be a fairly narrow block of time in which to do the deed and transform herself back into Elic in time for the mass and ensuing orgy.

Charlotte said, " 'Tis a testament to Sir Francis's personal magnetism that he has lured men of such rank and accomplishments to the Hellfire Club. The Prince of Wales himself is a member. He's the one who just finished rousting Lady Cavendish. He doesn't know it, but he's being cuckolded by that dashing fellow Lili just larked, the Earl of Bute."

"Cuckolded?" Elle said. "My English..."

Lili said, "Prince Fitz's wife, Princess Augusta, is Lord Bute's mistress."

Pointing discreetly with her fan, Charlotte said, "We've got the Duke of Queensbury, the Duke of Kingston... The fellow with the sketchbook is William Hogarth, the painter. Those two young bloods playing in-and-in with Emily are the Marquis of Granby and George Walpole, heir apparent to the Earldom of Orford. That gundiguts over there combing his wig is George Bubb Doddington—rich as Job, and a bosom friend of the prince. And, of course, the gentleman sitting with Sir Francis is John Montagu, Earl of Sandwich and First Lord of the Admiralty. A rake of the first order, of course, wagers hundreds of thousands of pounds at the gaming tables. Loves to have his arse whipped, can't raise the old quimstake any other way, but he's hardly alone in that."

"*Le vice anglais,*" Lili said. "I was astounded the first time I saw them bring out all their whips and birches and canes."

Rising from his seat, Lord Sandwich waved his handkerchief and called for the attention of the assembled company. "Ladies and gentlemen, *mesdames et messieurs.* The chief friar informs me that our *missa niger* will commence in approximately an hour. It is taking a bit more time than we had anticipated to get the chapel properly outfitted. In the meantime, Sir Francis would like to announce the identity of the lady who is to serve as our Bona Dea this evening, so that she may learn what is required of her and prepare herself to receive our worship."

The room fell into silence as Francis Dashwood pushed back his chair and stood. Charlotte arranged her gown's flowing train, her rouged lips pinching into a bright crimson sphincter of a smile.

"The lady I'm about to name," said Dashwood, "has never before served as our altar, though there have been many who've wished it so. 'Tis an honor that's bloody well overdue, I think we can all agree. She is a flower of rare scent and beauty whose presence in our little secret garden has been a source of immeasurable delight since she first graced us with her company some two months past."

Charlotte, who had been glancing about the room in self-satisfied anticipation, grew deathly still, her smile fading—for of course, she'd been keeping company with the Hellfires much longer than two months.

Dashwood said, " 'Tis my pleasure to inform you that our goddess for this evening is to be our lovely and enchanting Lili."

Two

A ROAR of approval filled the room. Lili blinked. Charlotte's mouth fell open. She gaped at Lili, who seemed at a loss for words.

"You bitch," Charlotte rasped.

"Lady Somerhurst, I—"

"You conniving little gutter-slut. You've been scheming against me from the first, campaigning behind my back."

"I've done no such thing. I never even wanted—"

"Liar!" Charlotte flung the contents of her wineglass at Lili.

A hush enveloped the room as all eyes turned toward Lili, who stood perfectly still in her ivory gown with its bloodlike stain, regarding Charlotte with remarkable calm. With a sad little shake of her head, she said, "I'd have stepped aside if you'd only asked."

The silence was punctuated by a snicker from across the room, and the observation that "Charlotte Somerhurst doesn't ask—she decrees."

"She's cooked her goose now," someone muttered.

"By my word, I shall lie upon that altar before *she* ever does," remarked the pudding-gutted Bubb Doddington, to gales of laughter.

"Charlotte—" Dashwood began, but the mortified Lady Somerhurst was already stalking out of the room, her train billowing behind her.

"Oh, Charlotte," murmured Lili, shaking her head at the retreating woman. "Why must you do these things to yourself?"

"You almost sound sorry for her," Elle said.

"There is a real person underneath all that paint and hauteur," Lili said, "and a fairly interesting one, at that."

It was a testament to Lili's character, Darius thought, that she was praising the woman who'd just called her a scheming bitch and doused her with wine in front of a roomful of people. She struck him as warmhearted and insightful. What on earth, he wondered, was a woman of such sterling qualities doing with a bunch of randy reprobates like the Hellfires?

Lili said, "Charlotte was educated at one of the finest seminary schools in London—brought up there, actually, from about the age of seven, after her mother died. She's the only female in this circle who's got more than a smattering of Greek and Latin. Well, apart from myself, but don't tell any of these horny goats. They wouldn't look twice at me if they knew I had a functioning brain. Most of them don't know B from a bull's foot, and they prefer their women as muddleheaded as they are."

With a conspiratorial little smile, Elle said, "I daresay my stockings are as blue as yours, so your secret is safe with me."

The awkward interval that followed Charlotte's departure was lightened when Dashwood turned to one of his companions at the table and said, "Whitehead, you scurvy old bastard. Why don't you haul that withered arse of yours off that chair and lead us in that new song of yours."

The song in question turned out to be a stately English hymn called "Lo! He Comes," its lyrics replaced with an outrageously bawdy tale of a man on a quest to cure his impotence through ever more inventive sexual escapades. Those who knew the words sang them with gusto, while those who didn't howled with laughter.

Dashwood, sitting at the table with a glass full of some sort of clear swizzle that was probably gin, had entered into a deep tête-á-tête with Lord Sandwich. With all the raucous singing, Darius could barely make out their conversation, which had to do with Charlotte Somerhurst.

"She's always off the hook about something or other," grumbled the earl. "Bloody shrew."

Dashwood shook his head. "This time it's my fault. I should've warned her it was to be Lili. I'd meant to, but then came all that bothersome shit with the chapel, and it slipped my mind. I'll talk to her tomorrow, bring her to her bearings."

Sandwich gave a skeptical grunt. "So you think she can be coaxed off the high ropes, do you? I wish you luck, my friend."

Gazing off at the silken couch in the corner, Lili said, "It looks as if Granby and Walpole have finished up with Emily Lawrence. I'd best go find out what's expected of me during the mass."

Her pensive expression was not lost on Elle, who asked, "Are you nervous?"

Lili looked as if she was going to deny it, but presently she smiled a little sheepishly and said, "A bit. I've no idea what's to be done to me with all these lechers looking on, only that no one ever speaks of it. I'm no blushing maiden, God knows, but to make such a spectacle of it, and in such an irreverent way..."

"Are you Catholic?" Elle asked.

"No, but I am not without spiritual inclinations, and I do harbor some deference for places of worship. A *débauchée* I may be, but there are some things even one such as I am loath to do in God's house."

"Grotte Cachée's chapel has never even been consecrated, you know," Elle said. "No mass has ever been celebrated there. It may look like a chapel, but I doubt very much that God takes any special interest in it."

"Thank you for telling me." Clasping Elle's hand, Lili said, "How refreshing to meet someone like you in the midst of all this loose baggage. Will I see you at the banquet later?"

"I regret that you will not." A half-truth, more or less, since Elic would be there.

Leaning close, Lili said with a smile, "You shan't regret it on the morrow, when you're the only lady in this place who can walk without wincing. I hope we can spend some time together tomorrow, then, before my departure."

"As do I."

After Lili left, Elle, still cradling Darius, negotiated her way through the revelers toward Dashwood. He noticed her and turned to look, giving her a thorough but admirably discreet appraisal. She held his gaze, something no lady of refinement would ordinarily do—but then the protocol of polite society hardly seemed to apply to this particular gathering.

Sandwich looked from Dashwood to Elle. With a knowing smile, he patted his friend on the shoulder, got up from the table, and left.

Dashwood rose from his seat and bowed when she came up to him. "You must be Elic's sister. Elle, is it?"

"It is indeed, sir." She curtseyed, her gaze still locked with his. "I've been looking forward to meeting you."

Dashwood reached out to pet Darius, prompting her to clutch him to her chest. "He's shy."

"Aye, but you're not." The smile turned intimate, knowing.

"If I were, I would hardly be here," she said.

Gesturing her into the adjacent chair, he retook his seat, set a glass in front of her, and reached for a carafe of wine. "No, thank you," she said, covering the glass with her hand.

Too close now to Dashwood for comfort, Darius leapt from Elle's lap and sat at her feet.

"Are you enjoying our gay little saturnalia?" Dashwood asked.

"To be sure. But in truth, all this noise and activity is beginning to wear a bit. I thought I might seek out some quieter, more private place. I don't suppose you would care to join me."

He chuckled as he sipped his gin. "Most ladies would flirt and tease for a bit, make it seem like the chap's idea—even at such a gathering as this. Not one for the chase, are you?"

"The chase is so much pretense and posturing," Elle said. "I much prefer the thrill of capture."

"With capture comes possession," he said softly, his dark gaze trained on hers.

"One would certainly hope so." Lowering her voice, she said, "Come with me, Sir Francis. I know a place where we can be alone."

Dashwood leaned toward her to trail his fingertips down her throat and over the soft swell of her bosom. "You're assuming we must be alone for this . . . possession to occur."

"I do not perform for the amusement of an audience, *monsieur.*"

"The presence of others can be most stimulating to the passions," he said. "Have you never enjoyed the sport of Venus in a room full of people?"

"Never with such people as these. The notion of all these Lotharios watching and fondling themselves . . ." She shook her head. "I can't imagine I would take pleasure in it."

"They needn't know what we're doing, if we're discreet about it."

She cast him a dubious look.

Smiling, he scooted his chair back and patted his lap. "Come."

She looked around the room, as if to buy time while she thought it over. Presently, she rose and smoothed down her dress. Glancing about to make sure they weren't being watched,

Dashwood gathered up her skirts in back as she lowered herself onto his lap. He turned her so that she was facing away from him.

"Rest your elbows on the table," he said quietly.

Leaning forward, she did as he asked.

"Relax," he murmured, lightly stroking her back. "Listen to the singing. A damned sorry effort, that!" he called out as the song ended. "Like pigs farting in mud. Let's have another one, and do try to carry the tune this time."

Dashwood slid his right hand beneath the great silken blossom of Elle's skirts, whispering, "Rise up a bit so I can get to these buttons." He shifted slightly, smiled. "You're wet."

Smiling at him over her shoulder, she said, "You're inspiring, *monsieur.*"

Dashwood gripped her waist and pressed her back down with a little grunt of effort. She drew in a breath. "*Mon Dieu.*"

Dashwood sat back in his chair with a sigh, his right hand still buried beneath her skirts. "You're wonderfully tight, *mademoiselle.*"

Darius moved aside to avoid Dashwood's foot as he hooked it around a chair leg beneath the table. Elle's silk skirts rustled languidly as he caressed her.

"Oh...," she breathed. "Yes..."

For some time, they sat joined but unmoving, or nearly so. Dashwood's foot flexed slightly against the chair leg and released, and again, and again, in a leisurely, steady rhythm. Elle widened her legs, bracing her feet on the carpeted floor.

Darius could hear them breathing as the tension mounted. Elle stretched out her legs, her feet trembling. The chair leg creaked in an ever-quickening cadence.

Dashwood's gaze grew unfocused. He sat forward, grimacing. Elle closed her eyes, one hand clutching the edge of the table, the other fisted around her empty wineglass.

He shuddered, a guttural little sound rising from his throat. The stem of the wineglass snapped in Elle's hand. Prince Fitz glanced idly in their direction, then looked away. For a long moment, they sat rigid and flushed, sharing a crisis of pleasure while their oblivious companions sang and caroused.

Dashwood slumped against her, his lungs emptying in a lingering sigh. Elle chuckled breathlessly.

He planted a tender little kiss on the back of her neck. *"Merci, mademoiselle."*

"De rien, monsieur."

The song concluded to rousing applause, whereupon Whitehead launched into yet another. Having had quite enough of that, Darius got up, stretched, and strolled from the room. Seeking his favorite refuge within the chateau, he padded down the hall to the southwest tower, and pawed open the door. He sprinted down the winding stairwell and through a torchlit passage to the slightly ajar door at the very end, which he slipped through.

It was blessedly quiet in the long disused *chambre de punition,* and dark, but with his sharp feline vision, Darius had no trouble locating his little pile of straw in the corner beneath the whipping stool. With his forepaws, he scooped out a nice, comfortable hollow and settled in. Twitching his nose at the smell of rose oil on his fur, he gave himself a thorough licking, finishing with his face, which he cleaned by rubbing it with his dampened paws.

Curling up in the straw, his head pillowed on his paws, he closed his eyes and surrendered to the darkness.

Don't you dare cry, Charlotte Somerhurst commanded herself as she roamed the halls of the chateau, trying vainly to shake off the rage and humiliation seething inside her. *Don't give those worthless curs the pleasure.*

They had no real breeding, no taste, no refinement. She'd given herself to them for two years, let them use her like a Drury Lane vestal, and what did she have to show for it? Jeers and laughter. And Dashwood, that scurvy Captain Grand, had just stood there and let it happen. Like a fool, she'd believed that she would finally, after all this time, have the privilege of lying upon the altar as an object of veneration and desire.

The exquisite little gift she'd brought Dashwood as a gesture of thanks for the honor only underscored her mortification. Thank God she hadn't yet given it to him. The moment she got back to her guest chamber, she'd have Bridget build a fire and burn the bloody thing to ashes.

No, first things first. She must arrange with Lord Henry to hire a private coach and driver for tomorrow. The notion of sharing accommodations with the Hellfires, in light of what had just occurred, was unthinkable. She would return to London alone and be quit once and for all of those insolent beau-nasties with their fine silk coats and beer-garden manners.

No, not London; it would be impossible to avoid the Hellfires there. She'd go to her country house in Cambridgeshire. She'd take a handsome young lover, several of them. She'd host her own outré little house parties, weeklong bacchanals of sensual indulgence that would have all of London society abuzz. She would render the Hellfire Club passé, ridiculous. People who mattered would laugh at their childish rituals just as the Hellfires had laughed at her.

Charlotte drew up short when she heard muffled singing and realized she must have wandered back in the vicinity of the chapel withdrawing room, where the Hellfires were gathered—but how? She could have sworn she'd been headed in a clockwise direction around the castle, but if so, she couldn't possibly have come back to where she'd started without encountering the gatehouse. Had she turned around and retraced her steps without realizing it? It was possible, she supposed. She'd felt a bit queer ever since her arrival here, almost as if she'd been breathing in a haze of opium smoke the entire time.

A surge of wooziness overtook her as she gazed around at the near-black stone walls, identical to all the rest of the walls in this place. She closed her eyes, but that only made everything whirl drunkenly, so she opened them and drew in a deep breath. *Get yourself in hand, Charlotte.*

No more wandering these halls feeling sorry for herself, Charlotte decided. She must find her chamber on the second floor of the northwest tower, but she couldn't begin to guess which direction she was facing at this point. There was a corner tower directly ahead of her, at the end of the hall; unfortunately, they all looked alike. If this wasn't the right one, she thought as she entered it and climbed the winding stairwell, she would simply try the next one, and the next.

It was, in fact, the wrong tower, as she discovered when she opened the door on the second-floor landing to a sitting room decked out *à la Chinois* with sumptuous, Oriental-inspired furnishings and objets d'art—the latest rage in London and Paris. In the center of the room stood an exotic lacquer-and-gilt table on which pretty little Millicent Holmes lay naked and panting, her legs draped over the shoulders of a curly-haired fellow who knelt on the floor, licking her notch as he thrust something in and out of it.

The young man, clad in nothing but his long, ruffled shirt, looked up and smiled at Charlotte while continuing to frig Millie with what appeared to be an ivory statuette. "What a delightful surprise! Come to join our little private party, have you?" He spoke like an English aristocrat, but Charlotte knew he hadn't come there with the Hellfires.

"I . . . no, actually, I'm just looking for my own chamber," Charlotte said as she backed up onto the landing.

"Oh, do stay, Charlotte," Millie breathlessly implored. "He's got more than enough pikestaff for both of us, believe me."

"Perhaps later." Charlotte shut the door and headed back downstairs, thinking as she did so that perhaps she'd been too hasty in rejecting the invitation. That "enhanced" wine she'd drunk earlier had begun to take effect, provoking a tingling warmth between her legs that would only grow hotter and more insistent as the evening wore on. Of course, she could simply retire to her room and bring herself off by hand, but experience had taught her that she could come a dozen times under the influence of cantharides and still be aching for more.

Charlotte thought about that handsome young buck upstairs, with his wild black ringlets and boyish smile. That shirt hid most of his body, but she could see that he had well-muscled legs and...

She paused on the stairs, frowning at the memory of something peeking out from the hem of his shirt in back, something curiously... tail-like. Not a tail, of course—it couldn't have been—but then, what...?

She shook her head, wondering if her wine had been spiked with more than just an aphrodisiac. Or perhaps there was something in the water here, or in the air, that made people's minds play tricks on them.

At the bottom of the stairwell, Charlotte paused and looked around, baffled to find herself in a narrow, unfamiliar hallway lit by a single torch. The walls and floor were of the same near-black stone as the rest of the castle, but more rough-hewn. In the floor of beaten earth was a stone-lined well, on the lip of which sat a bucket tied to a rope. Preoccupied with her thoughts, she'd evidently bypassed the first-floor landing and ended up in the cellar.

She was about to turn around and head back upstairs when she noticed, at the end of the passage, a slightly open door comprised of a thick, iron-banded slab of oak with a small, barred window carved out of it; it was the type of door one might encounter in a prison or lunatic asylum. Charlotte approached it curiously and stood on tiptoe to squint through the little window, but it was too dark on the other side to see much. Using both hands, she hauled the door open and stepped inside.

Yellow torchlight spilled through the doorway, illuminating a groin-vaulted stone undercroft with a floor of beaten earth, its six arched bays supported by a pair of massive, drumlike columns. Embedded in the columns at various heights—and in the ceiling and floor, as well—were a number of iron rings, some of them dangling chains, manacles, and foot irons. The bay in which she stood housed a long, sturdy table with a frame around the edge, fitted out with three rollers to which ropes were attached—a torture rack, Charlotte realized with a little shiver of fascination.

She circled the device, trailing her fingers over it as she recalled an etching she'd seen once of a naked young woman being stretched on the rack by a group of masked inquisitors. One of them was squeezing her nipples with pincers while another manipulated some unidentifiable device in the hairless slit between her legs. The woman had her head thrown back and her mouth open, but it was unclear whether she was crying out in pain or ecstasy—or both.

Charlotte's arousal intensified as she imagined what it must feel like to be tied up and pulled taut while nameless men did as they wished to her naked and exposed body. She would be completely at their mercy. They could use her in unspeakable ways, make her feel whatever sensation they wanted her to feel, and she would be helpless to resist. That notion should have repelled someone like Charlotte, who was accustomed to power and relished the wielding of it, yet for some reason she found it darkly exciting.

In an adjacent bay stood an old bed covered with a wool blanket, a fat coil of hemp cord looped around one of the bottom posts and a covered chamber pot tucked underneath, next to a little cluster of empty oil lamps. A collection of sinister devices sat on wooden shelves next to the bed. Charlotte recognized the thumbscrews and the spiked "cat's paw" designed to tear the flesh from bones. There was a Spanish boot, a tongue tearer, iron collars and belts, and a number of helmetlike devices meant to do unspeakable things to the wearer's head.

Most of the other implements were unfamiliar to Charlotte, although in most cases she could guess which body part they were intended to crush, pierce, or restrain. An unlabeled brown glass vial sat on the bottom shelf, the contents of which she could only begin to imagine. Poison? Flesh-eating acid? The images that came to mind sickened her.

Charlotte strolled through the rest of the cellar, whose furnishings included a hanging cage, a pillory with head and wrist holes, and an iron chair with built-in shackles. Tucked away in a far, dark corner amid a pile of straw was a low wooden stool equipped with leather restraints, a device not unfamiliar to her. There was a whipping stool in most village squares, right next to the stocks. She'd never actually seen one used, but the notion of a miscreant being bound to such a stool for a humiliating public flogging had intrigued her since adolescence. In her fantasies, the offender was always some aloof, powerful nobleman, someone like that bastard who'd sired her, then shunted her off to London the very afternoon of her mother's funeral; and she, Countess of Somerhurst, would, of course, have the honor of wielding the whip.

But now, contemplating the deceptively simple bench with its straps and buckles, Charlotte couldn't help but visualize herself being shoved to her knees by some burly peasant whose job it was to mete out justice to the black-hearted and bloodstained. She could almost feel the bite of leather around her arms and waist as he lashed them to the stool, the cool air on her naked hindquarters as he flung her skirts up so that they hung down over her head. He would yank her thighs apart to strap them to the back legs of the stool, leaving her kneeling over it with her arse lifted indecently high, like a bitch in heat.

There would come a pause. She would feel his breath on her most intimate, cruelly exposed flesh . . . and then would come his bemused, almost pitying chuckle. He would see how her sex lips had flushed and parted, revealing her erect little clit and dripping quim, and he would know the shameful truth—that the high and mighty Lady Somerhurst found degradation so arousing that she was on the verge of release even before the first lick of the whip.

Charlotte crossed to the whipping stool in its shadowy corner, nipples prickling against her tight-laced stays, her sex wet and inflamed. The walls in that bay were festooned with an astonishing assortment of floggers, paddles, horse crops, canes, birches—and most ominous of all, a wooden handle sprouting three lengths of heavy steel links. Chain whips were true implements of torture, devilishly efficient at tearing the flesh from the back.

What must it feel like, she wondered, to be overpowered, bound, disciplined... *used*? To be a slave to the will of another, a *thing* with no will of her own? No expectations, no decisions, no responsibility except to meekly accept the punishment that was meted out to her, knowing it was just and right; for there was blood on her hands, the blood of a life cut short through her doing. Invisible though it might be to others, it was a stain that would haunt her until the end of her days.

She ran her hand over the top of the stool, a hefty chunk of satin-smooth walnut carved with rounded edges and a downward slant meant to keep the buttocks elevated, a perfect target for the whip. The leather straps were age-worn, but thick and wide. Charlotte ached to feel their buckles digging into her as she embraced the whipping stool in a posture of abject submission.

She *could* feel it, if she really wanted to, Charlotte realized. She could bind herself to the stool, leaving just one hand free with which to ease her raging lust. There would be no sting of the whip, of course, but she could close her eyes and imagine it as she caressed herself. The cantharides would keep her in an agony of arousal for hours; the pleasure could be extraordinary.

The only problem was the position of the stool itself, which was tucked too tightly into the corner to be usable. Crouching down, the straw crackling beneath her feet, she gripped it from underneath. As she started to lift it, something furry brushed her hand.

Charlotte screamed and dropped the stool, tumbling onto the floor as a flash of gray—*a rat?*—darted out of the straw. She kicked out instinctively, bunting the creature into the wall. It yowled, which was when she realized it wasn't a rat at all, but that gray cat of Elle's—which was almost as bad.

Charlotte scrabbled backward across the floor, squealing in alarm. Yanking the rattan crook off its ribbon around her waist, she whipped it back and forth to ward off the offending beast. "Begone! Get out of here!"

The cat made a dash for the door. Charlotte chuckled at the idiocy of her reaction as she rose to her feet and shook out her skirts. Thank God there'd been no one about to witness it.

Her relief was short-lived, for a shadow drew her attention to the doorway through which the cat had just disappeared. There, silhouetted against the torchlight in the hallway, stood the figure of a man.

"You don't loathe cats at all, do you?" he asked in a deep, slightly accented voice as he rubbed his shoulder. "You're afraid of them."

"Who is that?" Charlotte asked. He was somewhat taller than average, well muscled and coatless—which meant he was most likely some menial servant or day laborer, for no gentleman, or even a footman, would dream of appearing before a lady half-dressed. "Answer me," she demanded, brandishing the crook, "or I shall report your insolence to your mistress."

"I have no mistress." He retreated to the hallway, returning a moment later with the torch, which he jammed into a sconce near the door. "I am here, like yourself, at the sufferance of our Dame des Ombres."

In the enhanced light, she could see that he was younger than his voice would suggest, with dark, wavy hair pulled into a leather-wrapped queue. Vestless as well as coatless, he wore an unadorned shirt tucked into fawn breeches, and the plainest of white silk cravats.

He crossed his arms and leaned against the wall. "I am Darius."

It occurred to Charlotte to fling out some quip about the curious new fashion for introducing oneself by first name only, but her wits seemed to have fled the moment this Darius fixed his gaze upon her. To say he was striking would suggest that he was merely handsome. In fact, by the standards of London fashion, he was anything but; with his humble attire and half-grown beard, he put her in mind of a Cossack, perhaps even a pirate. But those eyes . . . Charlotte had never seen eyes quite so huge and dark, a gaze so shockingly direct, so *intent.* Yet there was a quietness to him, a stillness that was mesmerizing.

"I am the Countess of Somerhurst," Charlotte said when she found her voice.

Darius nodded thoughtfully. "Are you a countess in your own right? I can't imagine any self-respecting English earl tolerating a wife who plays camp follower to the infamous Francis Dashwood and his cronies."

She hesitated, uneasy as always when someone raised the subject of the late Nathaniel Wickham, Earl of Somerhurst. "Not that it is any of your affair, but my lord husband went to his maker several years ago."

"Before or after you took up with the Hellfires?"

"You are an ill-mannered boor, sir."

Darius smiled. "And you, madame, are a foul-tempered bitch."

"H-how dare you . . . ," she sputtered.

"Ladies who make a habit of kicking cats should expect to be called bitches—and worse."

"I took it for a rat," she said, while wondering how he could have seen her do that; she would have noticed if he'd been watching.

"You'd have done it anyway. You're terrified of cats." Before she could summon a response to that, he said, "Whatever possessed you to get involved with the Hellfires, Charlotte?"

"How do you know my Christian name? And what makes you think you're entitled to call me—"

"Were you so very bored... *Lady Somerhurst*?"

She turned away and hooked her rattan crook back onto its ribbon, thinking she really ought not to linger here, encouraging this audacious lout with his prying questions. She should lift her chin, stalk past him, and be gone from this place.

She cast Darius a sideways glance. He still stood leaning against the wall with his arms crossed, regarding her with that unnervingly serene absorption. She didn't quite know what to make of him. He didn't behave like a gentleman, didn't look like one or talk like one; yet he was no peasant. He was unlike anyone she'd ever met.

Charlotte realized she was staring, and wrenched her gaze from his. "Of course I was bored," she said, as if that were the real reason she'd embraced the Hellfires' extreme brand of libertinage, or rather, the only one. "There are only so many tablecloths one can embroider, so many cups of tea one can pour..." She sighed disgustedly. "So many beef-brained stablemen one can seduce, before one starts to look elsewhere for diversion."

"Why the Hellfires?" he asked.

" 'Twas Sir Francis." Buzzing with nervous energy, Charlotte lifted a handsome black riding crop from the wall. It aroused her anew, just stroking the braided leather handle with its wrist loop, feeling its weight and balance in her hand. "He was the first man I ever met—the only man—who regarded me as a person of learning and intellect, not just some light-heeled young widow. He knew I was a bit loose in the rump, of course, but he also knew I had a brain. I cannot tell you how refreshing that was. When he told me about the Hellfires, I begged to be a part of it. It all seemed so enlightened, so exotic and exciting."

"And now?"

"Well, those mock masses are absurd, of course. It always escaped me why Sir Francis felt the need to cloak a bit of harmless sport in all that ritualistic drivel."

"You didn't seem to feel that way before Lili was chosen to lie upon the altar in your stead."

"How could you know that?" she asked. "You weren't there."

"I can blend in when I choose to." Pushing off the wall, Darius came toward her. He moved with an unhurried, feral grace, like a predator closing in on its prey in such a way as to keep that prey blissfully off guard. "Disenchanted with the Hellfires, are you?"

Stroking her hand along the length of the riding crop, she said, "It's all one great, smutty joke, isn't it? Hogs in armor, the lot of them. Schoolboys sharing bawdy jests, passing 'round dirty pictures. Half of them can't even raise the old rogering iron unless their mates are watching and cheering them on. The other half need a good flogging before they can rouse their passions."

"It rouses your passions, too, does it not?" Darius was standing directly in front of her now, his gaze on the crop she was fondling with all too evident fascination. "The flogging?"

She shrugged with feigned nonchalance. "I shan't pretend I don't relish the opportunity to redden the occasional bum."

"But not half as much as you might relish having your own bum reddened." He took the crop from her, inspecting it in a leisurely way. "I think you wish there was someone who could take you in hand and deal out the punishments you so ardently desire . . . and richly deserve."

Charlotte swiftly weighed and rejected the option of feigning outrage; this Darius was, for whatever reason, far too perceptive for such a disingenuous display. Instead, she merely said, with studied calm, "Deserve?"

"For kicking the cat," he said.

"I told you, I thought it was a rat. It darted out at me, and I was startled, so I—"

"Why did it dart out?" he asked. "Because you disturbed it, perchance?"

"Well…"

"You were moving that." He nodded toward the whipping stool as he ran his hand along the crop's slender stock. "To what end?"

Charlotte stared at him, heat scalding her face; she couldn't remember the last time she'd blushed.

He held her gaze. "You were curious. Yes?"

She groped for words, but what could she say?

Gesturing toward the stool with the crop, he said, "Carry on, then. You've got *me* curious now, too."

She didn't move.

He took a step toward her, stroked her face lightly with the little leather paddle on the tip of the crop. The smell of the leather made her quim throb. She closed her eyes, swallowed hard.

Softly he said, "Put the stool in the middle of the floor, Charlotte."

"Why are you doing this?" she asked.

"Because you want me to."

He knew. Somehow, he knew everything.

She looked toward the door, still half-open; anyone could come down here and walk in on them. Before she could voice that concern, Darius crossed to the door, pulled it shut, and tugged a rusty steel plate down over the little window. He took a key from a hook on the wall, twisted it in the keyhole, and stowed it in a pocket of his breeches.

Charlotte felt both more secure now and more vulnerable. A stranger, someone she'd met mere minutes ago, had just locked her into a torture chamber. The situation should fill her with foreboding. There was a certain measure of that, to be sure, but mostly what she felt, God help her, was an intoxicating thrill of arousal underscored by a sense of rightness, a sense that she deserved whatever this enigmatic stranger would do to her, and more.

Rejoining her, Darius nodded toward the whipping stool as if to say, *Go ahead.*

She lifted the stool, which was remarkably heavy, and set it down in the middle of the floor.

"Take your clothes off," he said.

She turned to stare at him.

"It has long been customary," he explained, "when punishing females, or attempting to coax confessions from them, to make them undress. It tends to have a . . . humbling effect."

Charlotte met his eyes for a moment, then looked down, her gaze lighting on the front flap of his breeches, stretched tight over a bulging erection. She felt suddenly starved for air; her heart thudded in her ears.

Darius noticed the direction of her gaze, but seemed unperturbed, perhaps even slightly amused. "Strip," he said.

Charlotte took a deep, tremulous breath, and set about unlacing her bodice.

Three

"I MET YOUR sister." This was Sir Francis Dashwood's greeting to Elic in the chapel's shadowy little narthex, where Elic was waiting, along with the two footmen serving as acolytes, for the mass to begin. "Lovely girl."

The Hellfires' chief friar had a speculative glint in his eye as he smiled at Elic. He was wondering, no doubt, whether Elic was privy to his covert little assignation with Elle in the withdrawing room.

"She told me it was a most rousing encounter," Elic said.

"Did she," Dashwood said with a little quirk of the eyebrows. "You two must be close."

"We share everything." Including the seed that Elle had tapped from Dashwood, and which Elic would transfer, before the night was over, to some estimable woman—which was his sole reason for participating as Abbot of the Day in this absurd mock mass, in order to have first pick of the Hellfires' female followers afterward. The seed formed an insistent presence in his lower belly, causing his bollocks to tighten in anticipation, his shaft to grow thick and heavy.

The monkish robe he'd been given to wear—white silk with a scarlet-lined hood, like that of the twelve "superior" Hellfires now murmuring quietly in the chapel—served to conceal his state of arousal. Beneath it, he wore nothing, as instructed—a blessed relief from the constriction of Elle's rigid, cone-shaped corset. The robe closed down the front with a mere four little hooks, for ease in opening when required during the dark rites and the banquet to follow.

The two brawny young men serving as acolytes had been outfitted for the occasion in white satin breeches and jackets. The darker of the two held a pair of lit black tapers in mammoth iron candelabras, the other a brass censer full of hot coals dangling from the end of a chain, and a matching incense boat. From their expressions of amusement as they whispered together, Elic gathered their attitude toward the impending ritual fell short of reverential.

As ridiculous as Elic felt enveloped in white silk, at least it was a fairly simple, straightforward garment. Dashwood, as chief friar and primary celebrant in the mass, sported gold buttons on his hoodless robe, a stole embroidered with phalli and demonic symbols, and a tall red cardinal's hat trimmed in rabbit fur. The hat was particularly remarkable, so much so that Elic had to chew on the inside of his mouth to keep from smirking. Oblivious of the figure he cut, Dashwood carried himself with regal bearing, clearly confident that he looked entirely as solemn and dignified as he felt.

How on earth, Elic wondered, could his distaff counterpart have found this man sexually alluring? For Elle had not simply appreciated Dashwood's amiable disposition and many accomplishments, as Elic did; she had *desired* him, intensely. Elic could not have re-created that desire in himself even if he wanted to, his bodily humors, which governed his sexual appetites, having reverted to the masculine. He recalled all too clearly, though, how much Elle had wanted Dashwood, how exciting it had been to feel him thrusting inside her, unhurriedly at first, then with quivering urgency as their pleasure crested together—all the while surrounded by revelers who had no idea what was transpiring beneath the great silken mass of her skirts.

Dashwood asked whether Elic was fully acquainted with his role in the upcoming ceremony.

"I am," said Elic, withdrawing from a pocket of his robe the little red leather missal stamped *Order of the Friars of St. Francis,* which he'd been given during his induction into the Hellfires yesterday. It had been little trouble to memorize the verses and responses, given his familiarity with Latin from the half-millennium during which Grotte Cachée had been under Roman rule. What amused Elic about the order of service for the Hellfires' *missa niger* was that it was patterned after that of a standard Roman Catholic mass. If Dashwood was as contemptuous of religion as he purported, he would simply turn his back on its rituals, put them altogether out of his mind. Instead, he chose to celebrate his decadent ideology by conducting his own solemn, albeit obscene, versions of those rituals, thus betraying their true importance in his mind.

"Archie." Dashwood caught the eye of the acolyte with the candles and motioned him into the chapel.

The young man straightened his back and strode between the two fat columns that separated the narthex from the chapel proper.

"Slowly," Dashwood whispered.

Archie duly adjusted his pace. When he was halfway up the center aisle, the white-robed congregants noticed him and rose to their feet, flipping up the seats in their small double bank of ornately carved misericord chairs.

Grotte Cachée's unconsecrated chapel, constructed when the castle was rebuilt in the early 1400s, was quite small, its walls and low, vaulted ceiling crafted from the same dark volcanic rock with which the castle had been built. Red glass lanterns, installed by the Hellfires along with various other trappings, cast a sinister, ruddy luminescence. The effect was reinforced by the smoke rising from braziers in which a mixture of herbs crackled over hot coals. The mousy stink of hemlock was predominant, but Elic's keen nose detected a bittersweet note that had to be belladonna, and a whiff of something else that smelled almost, but not quite, like tobacco: henbane.

The sanctuary at the far end of the chapel was a raised, semicircular niche, its curved rear wall draped in black velvet to cover a large stained-glass window. Against this funereal backdrop hung an oil portrait of a demonically handsome young man with wings and horns floating on a plume of smoke—a laughably romanticized rendering of Lucifer perfectly in keeping with the overwrought tone of the proceedings. Built onto a platform in the center of the sanctuary was an altar table of volcanic stone some eight feet long and half as wide, its top inlaid with a geometric mosaic of darkly shimmering black lava glass. Archie placed the candelabras to either side of a tiny black pillow on the left edge of the table, then struck a Chinese gong once with a hammer padded in black leather.

"Harry," Dashwood whispered.

The other acolyte carried his censer and boat up the aisle, followed at stately intervals by Elic and Dashwood, who entered the sanctuary with heads bowed and hands clasped before them. On the altar table, arranged around the candelabras, were such accoutrements as a silver chalice topped with a black cloth-covered plate, a tiny silver ladle, a dish of fragrant olive oil warming over a little brazier, a small silver cauldron half-filled with water, and a jewelry casket of ebony inlaid with mother-of-pearl in the shape of a six-pointed star within a circle. Most curious was a brass aspergillum such as those used for sprinkling holy water, which was shaped like a dildo with a bulbous, perforated glans. To these paraphernalia Elic added the missal, which he laid with feigned veneration on the black satin pillow.

Harry took his place next to an iron censer stand forged to look like a rearing serpent, while Archie struck the gong three times. The congregants turned en masse toward the narthex in anticipation of the Bona Dea's entrance—all save one, who stood motionless, staring straight ahead. Like the other congregants, including Elic, he wore his hood low over his face, casting his eyes into deep shadow. From his powder-paleness and the grim set of his jaw, Elic recognized him as Anton Turek.

Between the two columns flanking the entrance to the narthex there appeared a dark form that seemed to hesitate for a moment before advancing slowly up the aisle. Elic had assumed that Lili would make her entrance naked, but in fact she wore a mantle of fur-lined black satin that trailed heavily behind her. Over it she was swathed head to toe in a sheer black veil that floated and fluttered as she walked, making her look like a specter materializing from the smoky pall.

As she came closer, Elic saw that the mantle was secured at the throat with a pair of cloakpins connected by a chain, causing it to fall open and reveal, through the gauzy veil, the tantalizing promise of bare, golden flesh and a glimpse of the shadowy arbor between her thighs. She smelled like jasmine and desire.

Elic's cock filled and rose as he watched Lili walk toward him. As Elle, he had thought this woman lovely, but in an abstract, purely esthetic sense; more than her beauty, he had admired her character and intellect. As a man, he was struck by her in a far more corporeal way. She was a magnificent creature, exquisite in mind and body, serenely sensual, and, it would appear, in thrall to the appetites of the flesh—as, for better and for worse, was he.

Lili ascended the altar steps and turned to face the congregants, who executed a deep bow in unison. She turned back toward the sanctuary, whereupon Elic, Dashwood, and the two acolytes reverenced her in the same manner.

Reaching beneath her veil, the acolytes removed the luxuriant mantle and laid it on the table like an altar cloth, fur side up; it was mink, Elic saw, dyed jet-black. Escorting Lili onto the platform, they handed her up onto the table's right-hand edge. She sat with the veil stretched out behind her over the lustrous black fur but still cloaking her in front to her feet, around one of which she wore an anklet of hammered gold.

Elic glanced up to find her regarding him with interest through the shroudlike veil. He'd seen that look many times before, when someone who'd already made the acquaintance of one of his alter egos met the other and found the resemblance astonishing. He gave her a slight smile, which she acknowledged with a little nod.

Dashwood executed another profoundly deep bow toward Lili and made a left-handed, backward sign of the cross. "*In nomine magni Dei nostri Satanas introibo ad altare Domini Inferi,*" he intoned. "In the name of our great God Satan, I shall enter the altar of the Infernal Lord." He opened his robe and produced his half-hard member.

"*Ad Eum qui laetificat meum,*" Elic responded. *To Him who gives joy unto me.*

The acolyte Harry lifted the little dish from its brazier and offered it to Dashwood, who dipped his fingertips in the warm oil and smoothed it over his member. "*Adjutorium nostrum in nomine Domini Inferi.*" *Our sustenance is the Name of the Infernal Lord.*

Who reigns on earth. "*Qui regit terram,*" responded Elic as he dipped his own fingers into the dish, coating them with oil.

Elic turned toward Lili, who, in keeping with her instructions, leaned back with her weight on her hands behind her and her legs spread wide. The position caused the veil to cling to the contours of her flat belly and high, full breasts. Her nipples were wine-red through the whispery muslin.

Elic slipped his oiled hand up under the hem of Lili's veil until he reached the thatch shielding her sex, as soft and black as the fur on which she sat. She closed her eyes as he parted the tufts of hair, then the soft, damp purse within, sucking in a breath when he pushed two fingers deep inside. The flesh there was hot, snug, and already slippery, but he oiled it anyway, per his own instructions. He took his time about it, using slow, rhythmic strokes, gratified when he noticed her nipples stiffen and push against the veil.

"Domine Satanas, Tua est terra." Dashwood stroked himself to full erection, his gaze on the portrait of Lucifer as he delivered an encomium of praise to his dark lord and the world of luxury and gratification that was his creation and his domain.

As Dashwood concluded his statement, Elic reluctantly slid his fingers from Lili's sweet little *chatte,* stepping aside so that the chief friar could take his place between her widespread legs.

Entreating Satan for strength, Dashwood lifted the bottom part of Lili's veil, bunching it around her hips, and brought her closer by tugging the mantle on which she was poised.

"Et plebs Tua laetabitur in te," Elic responded. *And Thy people shall rejoice in Thee.* Elic moved behind Dashwood, gripping Lili's ankles as she stretched her legs out so that he could keep them positioned, during the *Introit,* "as high and wide as possible to either side of the chief friar," in keeping with his duties as set forth in the little red missal.

Thanks to his being a good head taller than Dashwood, Elic had an unobstructed view as the chief friar seated the oil-sheened head of his cock just inside the *belle-chose* that had been prepared for him, while pleading with Satan to demonstrate his power. *"Ostende nobis, Domine Satanas, potentiam Tuam."*

Elic delivered his line, something about soliciting Lucifer's beneficence, as he grappled with the sudden, baffling urge to seize Dashwood and tear him away from the *altare* he was about to *introi.*

Steadying Lili by clutching her hips, Dashwood entreated his Infernal Lord to hear him clearly—*"Domine Satanas exaudi orationem meam"*—as he rammed himself into her.

Lili, still leaning back on her arms, gasped at the abrupt impalement, her body arching as she threw her head back. Elic fretted for one missed heartbeat that she might have been hurt, until he looked at her veiled face and saw, in her eyes, an expression of utter bliss.

This was what she lived for, he realized—sexual possession, the thrill and succor of fleshly delights.

Elic managed, despite his maelstrom of conflicting emotions, to recall and recite his responsum. *"Et clamor meus ad Te veniat,"* he said. *And let my cry come unto Thee.*

Lili opened her eyes and looked beyond Dashwood to Elic, curious, no doubt, as to the stress in his voice, or perhaps to the tension in his grip as he held her legs open for another man. Elic could not, for the life of him, wrest his gaze from hers as Dashwood slowly withdrew and resheathed his cock while offering a demonic version of the familiar salutation, "The Lord be with you." *"Dominus Inferus vobiscum."*

"Et cum tuo," Elic replied, along with the entire congregation—the first time they had participated in the response, although they would do so throughout the remainder of the *missa niger.* A glance revealed that several of them were fondling themselves through their robes as they took in the lascivious ritual.

"Gloria Deo Domino Inferi," chanted the chief friar, his thrusts echoing the slow, measured cadence of the incantation as he glorified, praised, and thanked Lord Satan, his Infernal King and Almighty Emperor.

Dashwood uncoupled from Lili without spending and rebuttoned his robe. He strode solemnly to the opposite end of the table, bowing to Lili as he crossed in front of her, and removed the black cloth from the silver paten that sat atop the chalice. The little plate held a reddish, triangular biscuit made from angelica root, which the Hellfires waggishly referred to as "Holy Ghost Pye." Lifting it in both hands toward the portrait of Lucifer, he beseeched his lord to accept the offering of their "host."

Elic, in keeping with his role in the profane pageant, helped Lili to lie down on the mink-draped altar table so that she was stretched out faceup along its length. He peeled back the sheer muslin only as far as her throat, leaving her face veiled and the rest of her utterly, breathtakingly nude. Bathed in the sanguine haze that filled the little chapel, she could have been Aphrodite herself, rendered in Titian's supple, luminous brushstrokes. She was, indeed, the very embodiment of beauty and erotic desire.

Setting the wafer back on the paten, Dashwood lifted it from the chalice. Uncovered, the silver goblet's contents released the sweetly noxious aroma of brandy infused with what could only be sulphur. He raised it to the image of Satan while reciting a prayer of offering of the "chalice of fleshly lust."

Setting the chalice on the altar, Dashwood held his arms out, palms down, and implored his "dark Lord and Sovereign" to arise, that his servants might kneel before him in adoration. Harry handed him the incense boat, opening the censer to be filled. Spooning up a few of the tarry little nuggets from the boat, Dashwood sprinkled them onto the hot coals, producing a thick, resinous smoke unlike anything Elic had ever smelled before. Not so Lili, whose eyes, even through the veil, widened with surprised recognition.

Holding the censer by its chain in his left hand, Dashwood encircled the chalice and wafer three times counterclockwise. He bowed, swung the censer thrice in the direction of the Satanic portrait, and bowed again.

Archie offered the dish of warm oil to Elic, who dampened the fingers of both hands and rubbed his palms together to slicken them. Lifting Lili's left arm, he oiled it with long, sleek strokes up to the wrist, then did the same to the right. Re-oiling his hands, he smoothed them down over Lili's shoulders and chest. He paused at the upper slopes of her breasts. They were round and ripe, in contrast to her slender limbs and exquisitely tiny waist.

Dashwood, meanwhile, set about censing the altar itself by walking slowly around it with the censer spewing smoke as it rocked back and forth. Passing behind Elic as he anointed the Bona Dea, the chief friar said, "*Dominus Inferus vobiscum.*"

"*Et cum tuo.*" Elic kneaded the lush mounds until they glistened. His fingers were so long that most breasts felt small when he cupped them, but these were a perfect handful—warm, full, and wonderfully soft.

Lili's eyes drifted shut on a sigh as he squeezed and stroked. Her tight little nipples grazed his palms, making his cock stir.

Oiling his hands yet again, Elic glided them over Lili's stomach and mons veneris, burrowing his fingers through her silken muff. Although it was not part of the protocol for this segment of the *missa niger,* he couldn't resist the urge to glide a finger lightly along the gaping slit. Her hips twitched; her breathing quickened.

Reluctantly, Elic moved on to Lili's legs, feeling the muscles beneath the supple flesh; she was strong for a woman. The gold anklet was an archaic, even primitive-looking piece of jewelry, burnished with age. Hanging from it was a deep blue, gold-rimmed disc that looked like lapis lazuli.

"*Sursum corda,*" Dashwood said as he completed the first of three slow circumambulations of the altar. *Lift up your hearts, brothers.*

"*Habemus ad Dominum Inferum,*" responded Elic, along with the rest of the congregation. *We lift them up to the Infernal Lord.*

Harry brought the ebony jewelry chest to Elic and raised its lid. Tucked into its velvet-lined interior were two pairs of gleaming gold circlets in the shape of snakes, one pair bracelet-sized, the other somewhat larger, each circlet dangling a short length of chain. Elic chose one of the smaller bands and slid it onto Lili's upper arm close to the elbow. Making sure the little chain was in front, he snugged the armlet in place by squeezing the soft gold until the snake's head was almost touching its tail. The chain terminated in a little clasp made to look like the talons of a bird of prey. Taking hold of Lili's right nipple, Elic affixed the clasp to it.

After adorning her left arm and nipple in the same manner, he raised both arms over her head, wrapping her hands around the shafts of the two iron candelabras just above their heavy bases. This position arched her back and pulled the chains taut, thrusting her breasts up high and tugging her nipples in a manner that Elic surmised, from her expression, to be more productive of pleasure than of pain.

Still circling the altar, Dashwood said, "*Gratias agamus Domino Inferno Deo Nostro*" as he swung his censer, adding to the cloud of darkly aromatic smoke hovering overhead. *Let us give thanks to the Infernal Lord our God.*

"*Dignum et justum est*"—*It is right and just to do so*—replied Elic as he withdrew one of the larger gold circlets from the casket. He slid it up Lili's right leg to the very top of her thigh and squeezed it in place with the chain once again positioned in front. At the end of the chain was another talon clasp. This he attached, very carefully, to her right outer labium.

A sort of drunken wooziness overtook Elic as he repeated this process on the left side, although he'd taken not a drop all evening. He saw himself as if from above, adorning this naked, faceless stranger with these obscene ornaments, and experienced a peculiar detachment, as if he were watching the actions of another man through the eyes of Satan in that ridiculous painting. Noticing Dashwood's glassy eyes as he handed the censer back to Harry, it occurred to Elic that the incense, or whatever it was, must have some sort of narcotic power.

Having completed his censing, Dashwood extended his arms and recited a paean to "Lord Satan, God of Power," concluding it with "*Hosanna in profundis.*"

A dozen voices echoed, "*Hosanna!*"

Dashwood stood before the altar with his back to the congregation and unbuttoned his robe, prompting the congregants to do the same. Gazing reverentially at the portrait of Lucifer, his cock in one hand and his balls in the other, as if in offering, he exhorted his God Satan to gather his power and arise. The rest of the Hellfires followed suit, save for Elic, to whom Archie handed the aspergillum. The brass shaft felt heavy, hard, and cold; he chafed it with his hands to warm it.

"Credo in Satanas, qui laetificat juventutem mea." Dashwood stroked himself erect, as did those congregants who were not yet fully tumescent. "I believe in Satan, who enriches my youth. I worship Thee." Bowing, he kissed the dark nest between Lili's thighs.

Elic, standing across the altar table from Dashwood, widened Lili's legs until her heels were at the very edges of the altar. This had the effect, because of the chains attached to the leg bands, of pulling her sex lips wide open, exposing the entrance of her damp little nick, against which Elic positioned the aspergillum. The instrument being more sizeable than that of the average man, and a good deal more rigid, he nudged it in slowly to allow her flesh to yield to the harsh intrusion. He heard a ragged little sigh issue from her throat, though perhaps it had come from him. In his befuddled state of mind, he couldn't be sure of anything—except his own white-hot arousal.

"In spiritu humilitatis suscipiamur a Te, Domine Satanas," chanted Dashwood as he rubbed himself faster, Archie beating the gong in time with his strokes. *"Et sic fiat sacrificium nostrum in conspectu tuo hodie, ut placeat tibi." In a humble spirit may we be received by Thee, Lord Satan, and may the sacrifice we offer be pleasing in Thy sight.*

Elic pressed the aspergillum deeper into Lili's weeping quim. Her hips rose and fell languorously, her breath fluttering the veil over her face. She let out a little growl of gratification as he buried the instrument fully inside her. He thrust it in rhythm with the gong while caressing the slippery folds of her sex, very lightly for now, and avoiding the clitoris lest she come off too soon. The Bona Dea was not to spend until the chief friar's initial discharge; Elic's instructions had been quite exacting on that point.

Harry fetched the cauldron of water, standing at the ready as Dashwood masturbated in earnest.

"Come, Lord of the Temple," chorused the congregants, still displaying their privates, though most had ceased diddling themselves, no doubt in order to save their pent-up lust for the banquet. "Come, Lord of the World. Come from the Gates of Hell."

"Behold Satan's bride," Elic said as Lili writhed to his teasing touch, her expression rapturous through the veil. "The Infernal Lord is within her."

The candelabras quivered in Lili's grasp, casting an odd, stuttering luminescence over her shuddering body. In Elic's intoxicated state, it seemed as if time itself were advancing in jerky little snippets instead of smoothly and seamlessly, as it ought to.

Archie beat the gong faster and faster in time with Dashwood's strokes as the chief friar beseeched Satan, in a voice grown hoarse, to accept his offering. "*Hanc igitur oblationem servitutis nostrae sed et cunctae familiae tuae, quaesumus, Domine Satanus, ut placatus occipias.*"

Dashwood, his face blood-flushed, nodded to Harry, who positioned the cauldron to receive the impending oblation. Thus forewarned, Elic grazed the edge of Lili's clit with a slick fingertip, drawing a gasp of startled pleasure from her. She thrust her hips up in a wordless plea for release. *Not quite yet.* Elic gentled his touch, withholding that release as she writhed in an agony of need.

Gripping the edge of the altar table, his hand fisted in the fur, Dashwood gave himself a few firm strokes, then stilled. A low groan rose from his throat as he ejaculated into the chalice held by Harry.

Now. Elic thrust the aspergillum faster as he massaged Lili's most sensitive flesh in a way that he knew, from long experience in pleasuring women, would bring her off instantly. She cried out, her back bowed, as she climaxed. What an exquisite sight she was, thrashing in sensual abandon. Elic's cock rose against his belly, hot and hard and aching; his balls felt as if they were stuffed to the bursting point with gunpowder. Were he to climb atop this table and take this woman right now, he'd go off like a howitzer the moment he entered her.

Panting, Dashwood squeezed out the final spurts into the chalice, straightened up, and rebuttoned his robe. Taking the chalice from Harry, he raised it to the portrait of Lucifer. "*Domine Satanas corda nostra mundet infusion, et sui roris intima aspersione foecundet.* May our hearts be cleansed by the inpouring of our Lord Satan, and may He make them fruitful by sprinkling them with the dew of His grace."

"*Ave Satanas,*" Elic said as he drew the aspergillum out of the breathless, sated Lili, stroking her trembling hip as he did so.

"Hail Satan!" cried the Hellfires.

Elic handed the aspergillum to Dashwood, who dipped it into the chalice of water mixed with his spendings. Crossing to the back wall of the sanctuary, directly beneath the Satanic portrait, he shook the brass phallus twice onto the floor while blessing it, in the name of Satan, with the "seed of life." He repeated this benediction at all four corners of the sanctuary and returned the aspergillum to the altar table.

Turning to the congregation, Dashwood said, "Let us pray."

Together with the Hellfires, Elic recited, "*Pater Noster. Qui es in Inferis...*" *Our Father, who art in Hell...*

At the conclusion of the heretical Lord's Prayer, Archie handed the chalice with the ladle in it to Dashwood, who bowed over it, saying, "*Hic est calyx carnis stimulous.*"

Taking the chalice from Dashwood, Elic held it over his head. "Behold the chalice of voluptuous flesh which gives joy to our life."

Archie then offered the paten to Dashwood, who lifted the little wafer. "*Hoc est corpus Inferno Deo Nostro.*" He touched the red-tinged wafer to each of Lili's nipples, then pushed it into her damp slit, saying, "Blessed is the womb that bore Thee, and the breasts that gave Thee suck." Withdrawing the wafer, he held it aloft, saying, "Behold the body of our Lord Satan. Accept the body of Satan and the chalice of voluptuous flesh in the name of the Infernal Lord."

The congregants, their hoods still low over their eyes, filed out of their bank of misericord chairs and approached the sanctuary in a single file procession. The first man, whom Elic recognized from his stature as Lord Bute, withdrew his cock as he ascended the altar steps. He bowed to Dashwood, who said, "*Corpus Satanus,*" as he touched the wafer to the tip of the semi-erect organ.

"Amen," responded Bute, who came to stand opposite Elic at the altar table as the second man approached Dashwood. Lowering his hood, Bute bent to confer a ritual kiss upon Lili's quim, gliding his tongue along the pink flesh in a way that made her sigh with pleasure.

"*Sanguis Satanas,*" said Elic as he ladled a bit of brandy from the chalice into the little hollow of Lili's navel. Bute lapped it up with evident relish, straightened, and said, "Amen." Raising his hood, he stepped aside for the next communicant.

One by one, the Hellfires took their turns. Bringing up the rear was Lord Turek, who walked up to Dashwood holding a rigidly erect penis that was bowed, narrowing toward the tip rather like a Turkish dagger. After receiving the host, he lowered his hood and approached the altar table, eyeing Lili with icy rapaciousness.

Elic caught Turek's eye and gave him a warning glare, to which he responded with a mildly amused nod of acknowledgment. Indeed, the kiss he bestowed upon Lili's sex was surprisingly brief and chaste. It was only when he went to lick the brandy from her navel that he employed his tongue, which was unusually long and pointed, recalling Lili's characterization of him as a snake.

"Amen." With a frosty smile at Elic, Turek returned to his seat.

Extending his arms, palms down, toward the Hellfires,

Dashwood intoned, "Lord Satan saith, in chaos and drunkenness, I rise again. You shall revel in the lusts of the flesh, which are fornication, ribaldry, luxury, sorcery, drunkenness, and revelry. My flesh is meat indeed."

"*Caro mea vere est cibus*," repeated the Hellfires in Latin.

"Brothers," Dashwood continued, "we are slaves of the flesh, meant to revel in fleshly things. May the almighty King of Hell grant you the fullness of life and the attainment of all you desire. May He shower His blessings upon you and fill your fiery lance with never-ending streams of the milk of life. *Ego vos benedictio in Nomine Magni Dei Nostri Satanus.* I bless you in the name of our Great God Satan."

"*Ave, Satanas!*" the congregants roared. "Hail Satan!"

"*Ite, missa est*," Dashwood said. "*Fornicemur ad gloria Domine Satanas.*"

And so ended the dark mass, with the chief friar's final exhortation to go forth and fornicate to the glory of their dark Lord.

Four

KEEP THOSE on," said Darius as Charlotte, having undressed down to her shoes and stockings, bent over to untie an above-the-knee garter. The stockings were the plain white ones ladies had taken to wearing of late, but the shoes were fashioned of brocaded silk with sharply pointed toes, an ornate silver buckle, and very high, curved heels. He liked how the height of the shoes shaped her slender body, forcing her back into an arc that accentuated her dainty breasts and firm, shapely derriere. "And leave the ribbon 'round your neck, as well."

"I prefer to take them off," she said as she continued untying the garter. He knew why. There was something reassuringly natural about complete nakedness, a kind of purity. The shoes and stockings imparted an aura of salaciousness that unsettled her, despite her dark longings.

Darius stepped behind her and swung the riding crop at that tempting little ass; leather struck flesh with a satisfying snap. Charlotte shrieked as she fell to the floor of packed earth. "You *cur*!" she cried, rubbing her bottom as she knelt on her haunches. "You . . . you . . ."

Crouching so that they were at eye level, Darius seized a handful of her hair, still in its diamond-studded coiffure, and tugged her head up, forcing her to look at him. Softly, calmly, he said, " 'Tis best that we understand each other from the outset, my lady. You may remain here, in which case you will abandon yourself to my will and comply without hesitation to my demands, no matter what they be. 'Twill be a compact between the two of us, a binding covenant."

He stroked the riding crop lightly down her throat and over a trembling bosom, giving the nipple a sharp little flick. "Or you may put those back on." He nodded over his shoulder at the heap of finery and underpinnings on the iron chair, which she'd laboriously divested as he'd watched, making no move to assist her. "I'll even help you with the laces and hooks," he continued. "And then you may leave here, and we shall be quit of each other. Which shall it be?"

She stared at him for a long moment, then lowered her gaze, licking her rouged lips. "The first."

"Say it."

"I . . . I suppose I shall stay."

"And enslave yourself to my will? Say it."

"And enslave myself to your will."

"Look at me." Darius tilted her chin up. He was no mind reader—he sensed desires only, not other thoughts or feelings—but a human's eyes revealed much, if one searched thoroughly enough. Charlotte's revealed a frisson of apprehension at this rough handling . . . as well as a breathless surge of excitement.

She craved this rough treatment, she thrilled to it. Did she not, he would hardly be doing it. It was she who had set this particular caprice in motion, not he. He was just a peaceable, reclusive djinni who'd had the poor fortune to brush up against this rather complicated human when all he'd wanted was a bit of slumber in a dark, quiet place. Now, having sensed that human's hunger to be mastered and punished, he had no choice but to appease it, to play the role in which he'd been involuntarily cast.

Ah, but if only it were a mere performance, a simple matter of acting the brute in order to satisfy the lady's predilection. It was the curse of Darius's kind to absorb a human's desires to the point where one was not just willing, but eager to act upon them—to become, if only temporarily, a different man, the kind of man who would, for instance, relish the opportunity to abuse and degrade a woman such as this.

Darius could feel it already, as he knelt staring into Charlotte's eyes, sensing a riot of wants and needs—*cold chains, tight ropes, the crack of his palm, her tears of shame and relief at being whipped, bound, caged, penetrated, used.* She didn't just want this brutal treatment; she wanted him to want to inflict it, and so, God help him, he did. He wanted to make her writhe and groan and suffer, he wanted to spank that pert little ass of hers raw, he wanted to force his cock into every part of her that could take it, but most of all, he wanted to make her submit. She needed to bend to his will, utterly and completely, to be thoroughly chastened and taken to task. He wasn't quite sure why she craved this as she did, but the need for punishment consumed her—as, now, did Darius's need to be the instrument of that punishment.

Pointing with the riding crop to the whipping stool, he said, "Mount it."

She made as if to rise. He planted a booted foot on her shoulder and shoved her back down. "Did I tell you to stand?"

"I . . . No, I just thought—"

"Don't think," he said. "Just do as I say. No more, no less."

After a moment's thought, she turned and crawled on all fours toward the stool.

"Good girl," Darius said as she slid herself onto it, its sloping top canting her buttocks upward—quite the tempting target. She gripped the front legs of the squat bench as Darius circled her, tapping her with the crop as he issued instructions. "Head up. Keep your gaze on that bullwhip up near the ceiling. Spread those legs," he said, slapping her inner thighs with the crop. "Your knees should be as wide apart as the back legs of the stool. That's it."

He stood behind her, admiring the pose, which displayed in frank offering her hotly blushing, completely hairless vulva. She burned with lust, quite literally, since cantharides excited lust by inflaming the body's most sensitive flesh. The red-hot tingling and itching stimulated the genitals to a fever pitch, leaving one desperate for sexual release.

"You shave?" he asked, stroking the tip of the crop over the slick, rosy petals of her labia.

"Y-yes," she said with a little shiver. "Bridget—my ladies' maid—she does it during my bath."

"Why?"

"My... my husband was an art collector, and he wanted me to look like the women in his paintings—the nudes. You know."

"Hairless."

She nodded.

"And you obeyed, like a compliant little wife? I can't quite fathom it."

"I was fifteen when we were wed, and I'd lived a sheltered life."

"In the seminary, yes?"

"How... how could you know that?"

She yelped as he smacked her ass with the crop. " 'Tis I who ask the questions, Charlotte, you who answer them. You are not to speak except to respond to me, and then with the most sincere and humble demeanor. Do you understand?"

She nodded. "In... in the seminary, yes. I knew nothing of men or marriage, or... anything, until Somerhurst and I were wed."

"Your father arranged the union?"

"He did."

"Your husband, he was older?"

"Much. And . . ." She looked over her shoulder at him, as if asking permission to continue.

He nodded.

"And a very commanding sort of man. Very particular, very set in his ways. He would brook no disobedience."

"Did he hit you?"

"No. Well, once, but . . . not as a general thing. He didn't have to," she said with a sort of bitter weariness. "I was completely cowed by him. Everyone was. Even other men."

"Was he faithful to you?"

She shook her head. "He had his mistresses. And his whores."

"All very young," Darius said.

"Yes. How . . ." She glanced warily at him, as if worried she'd overstepped herself by starting to ask a question.

"It strikes me that a man's fondness for hairless quims might reflect a penchant for those too young to have sprouted any hair there." And yet Darius, who had never, in his long existence, been attracted to a female of tender years, found Charlotte's naked gash deeply arousing—because, of course, she wanted him to. The smoothness of it made him want to stroke and lick her, bite her, fuck her. Without hair to obscure his view, he could see, between the pouting lips, every detail of her female anatomy, blood-flushed and sheened with moisture.

"Your husband has been dead for—how long?" Darius asked.

"Five years."

"During which time you've become adept at giving orders rather than taking them. And yet you continue to shave."

"It takes weeks to grow out, and the itching maddens me. And, too, I've found that men, most of them, rather like me bare there, especially when they . . . well . . ."

"Gam you."

"Yes."

"This Bridget, is she pretty?"

"Y-yes."

"Yes, of course," he said as he grazed the crop up and down her bare vulva. "A pretty little Irish girl with milky skin and freckles. You like spreading your legs for her, making her lather you up and take a razor to your most private, secret parts. You relish your power over her, and the way the razor feels as it scrapes you clean. It excites you, doesn't it? And she can tell. She can see your cunt swelling, your clit stiffening, just as I can now."

He tucked the crop's little paddle into her gaping slit and turned it on its side, spreading her sex lips wide open. A little whimper rose from her as he stood there, scrutinizing her most secret flesh, his cock pulsing at the sight. "Do you make her lick you, this Bridget?" he asked. "Do you make her shove the handle of the razor in you as she rubs your—"

"N-nay," said Charlotte, squirming in evident shame, and perhaps arousal, at being so exposed.

"But you do it to yourself after she leaves, don't you? You send her away and finger yourself and imagine it's Bridget being forced to attend to your basest needs. Either that or she gets the cane. Isn't that right?"

Charlotte hesitated.

Darius dealt her ass another taste of the crop, harder this time. "Isn't it?"

"Yes . . . sometimes."

He slapped the crop down on the small of her back. "Back arched, head up, ass high. You're getting sloppy."

"I . . . I'm sorry," she said as she corrected her pose.

"When I position you, Charlotte, I expect you to maintain that position until I give you leave to move. You expect discipline in others, but you lack it yourself. Discipline cannot exist without humility and a willingness to obey. You must be punished when you falter in your obedience, else you'll never learn. You're like some wild, wicked little mare that bucks and kicks whenever someone tries to saddle her. You must learn to be ridden, Charlotte. You must be broken to the whip. Like so."

Stepping back, Darius set about thrashing her with the crop, a rapid battery of smacks alternating in direction so that each backhand struck the left cheek of her ass, each forehand the right, as if he were whipping a horse into a gallop. She greeted every blow with a little high-pitched cry that excited Darius on a primal level, the level of the beast. Each slap of the paddle left a rosy little stain in its wake. He found himself aiming his blows so as to form two hot blooms of color, one on each alabaster globe.

"Hold the position," Darius ordered as she squirmed, instinctively trying to avoid the blows.

"I... I'm trying."

"Did I ask you a question? Did I say you could speak?" He shifted the direction of the crop, giving her quim a slap that was sharp enough to shock her but light enough to do her no harm.

"Oh, God." She squeezed her legs together, stammering, "Please, I... I..."

"You're hopeless." Hurling the crop aside, he knelt behind her and wrested her legs apart. "Spoiled, headstrong... There's only one thing for it."

She drew in a breath, trembling in anticipation, as she envisioned him ramming his cock into her and fucking her, fast and furious, slapping her ass as he did so. The image was so real, so clear, that it took Darius a moment to realize that it was coming from her rather than him. Not that he didn't want to fuck her. He did, desperately. His erection pushed against the front flap of his breeches, nearly popping the buttons from their holes; if he didn't take her soon, he'd end up spurting in his drawers.

It would be so easy to give her what she hungered for, and so gratifying, too; because she wanted it so badly, so did he. Yet her deepest, most compelling desire right now was for him to punish her for some unspoken sin by mastering her, bending her to his will. Were he to give her the good, hard spank-fucking she secretly craved, at least in this moment, he would be doing her bidding, instead of forcing her to do his.

"You've asked for this." Lifting the leather strap attached to the left-hand leg of the whipping stool, he buckled it around her thigh, good and tight, then bound her other thigh in the same manner. He leaned over to secure her upper arms to the stool's front legs, his loins pressed to hers as if he were about to take her from behind. The suggestive nature of the pose, and Darius's erection, weren't lost on Charlotte, who rubbed against him in a way that urged him perilously close to orgasm.

"Feeling a bit ruttish, are we?" he murmured in her ear as he reached around her to squeeze her breasts.

"Please..."

"Yes?" He grasped a hard little nipple in each hand and pulled, coaxing a breathy little moan from her.

"Please... oh, God, please..."

"Please fuck you?"

"Yes. Oh yes, do it," she begged, thrusting against him again. "Do it now."

"Charlotte, Charlotte..." Backing off her, he buckled the waist strap around her, which had the effect, in concert with the leg straps, of forcing her rear end up and keeping it there. "You speak when you ought to hold your tongue and move when you ought to be still, forcing me to restrain you. And now you expect to be rewarded for your defiance in dictating when and how I shall take my pleasure? I think not."

Rising, he came to stand before her, unbuttoning his trouser panel from the waistband. "You must earn the right to slake your lust, Charlotte. In the meantime, I shall slake mine, but not in that greedy little twat of yours." He knelt and pulled his rampant cock through the slit in his drawers as he gripped the back of her head. "Can you swallow a lob whole, like Lili?"

"I... I can try."

"Do more than try, Charlotte," he said as he pushed himself into her mouth, "and I just might let you come."

She proved herself an accomplished fellatrix, employing a firm, rhythmic suction without once scraping him with her teeth. The way she looked, bound to the stool in a posture of submission as she sucked him in and out of her mouth, only heightened the sensation. On the verge of spending all too soon, he pulled himself out and told her to lick just the tip, then the shaft and balls, lightly, teasingly, as he fought the urge to shoot, letting the pleasure mount higher, higher…

"Take it in your mouth again," he ordered her, in as calm and authoritative a voice as he could muster, under the circumstances. "Deep this time, as far as it will go."

She struggled to obey him, eyes watering as he shoved deeper, deeper…

"You can do it," he said. "Open your throat. That's it…"

He withdrew when she began to gag, waited a moment for her to regain her breath, then said, "Again—deeper," and pushed himself in even farther before retreating. "Again. Take it all the way to the root. Good girl."

He fucked her mouth, thrusting faster and faster as the pleasure sizzled through his veins, surging in his loins like lava ready to spew. "I'm coming," he rasped. "Swallow it down. All of it."

He gritted his teeth to keep from crying out as he exploded in her mouth, pumping it full as he hunched over her, clutching her head. Breathless and sated, he slid out from between her lips and tucked himself back into his drawers with unsteady fingers.

Charlotte dropped her head, her back heaving as if she were struggling for air.

"Charlotte?" he said gently as he crouched down.

There came a sound like a cough as she spat her mouthful of come onto the floor.

He stood and rebuttoned his trouser flap.

She looked up at him, her eyes wide and contrite. "I…I couldn't," she said. "I never could. I just can't bear the thought of—"

"*Silence,*" he roared. "You refuse to follow commands, refuse to keep your mouth shut. You claim you want to be here, that you're ready to bend to my will, yet—"

"I do," she exclaimed. "I am. I . . . I just . . ."

"You just need a little assistance in overcoming your natural willfulness, is that it?"

"I . . . suppose . . ."

"I had hoped you wouldn't start out quite so obdurate," he said as he crossed to the shelves next to the bed. "I must say, I'm disappointed in you, Charlotte. It seems you're going to require much in the way of external restraint before you can be trusted to exercise that restraint of your own accord."

Darius stood for some time, examining the various implements of punishment on the shelf. From the corner of his eye he saw her watching him fretfully.

He paused to contemplate the brank, a hinged, skull-shaped framework of iron welded to a heavy band meant to encircle the lower part of the face. Dangling from the front was a chain with which to control the movements of the wearer. There was a triangular opening for the nose and mouth, the bottom of which was fashioned to accommodate one of two iron appendages designed to serve as gags; these Darius examined one by one. The most benign was a flat tab. More sinister by far was a fat little shaft studded with spikes.

"No," Charlotte begged as Darius scrutinized the latter, even going so far as to fit it speculatively into the mouthpiece. "Please don't, not that. I won't speak out of turn, I promise."

"And yet you're doing so right now." Removing the spiked bit, Darius inserted the iron tab. "Calm yourself, Charlotte. My intent is not to maim you to the point where you can never speak again, but rather to teach you to master that insolent tongue of yours on your own."

Kneeling before her, Darius pried the brank open and fitted it around Charlotte's head, shoving the knob over her tongue as he snapped the device shut. He secured it with the attached padlock and slipped the key into his trouser pocket.

Standing back, he admired his captive, now not just naked and bound to the whipping stool, but gagged with an instrument designed as much to humiliate as to silence. Emitting muffled little mews of distress, Charlotte twisted her head about like a puppy trying to divest itself of its collar, her little breasts bobbing and swaying with her efforts.

Darius felt a heaviness unfurl between his legs as his arousal reasserted itself. She was entirely within his power, this iron-masked strumpet, and of her own volition, no less. He could do with her what he wished, his excitement, and hers, escalating in direct proportion to her suffering.

It was a heady, even thrilling sensation, yet at the same time unsettling. This wasn't the first time Darius had been compelled through casual contact with a human to change into something he was not, to feel things he wouldn't ordinarily feel, to do things that, when recalled later, would appall him. Experience had taught him that the longer such an episode lasted—and it would not end until the human was ready for it to end—the deeper his immersion in the sensations and desires he'd been forced to embrace. Right now, there was still a part of him that was Darius, the *real* Darius, with his familiar ideology, principles, likes and dislikes, *self*. Before Charlotte was done with him, however, he might be so consumed by this new, casually brutal persona that his old self was barely a memory.

She had ceased struggling, and was regarding him warily through the iron bars of the brank, wondering, no doubt, what further indignities he had in store for her. Her eyes were a golden green, and quite fetching, really, or would have been but for all that ridiculous paint.

"So much for your training," he told her. "Now for your punishment."

Five

ROOTING AMONG the heap of clothing she'd deposited on the iron chair, as Charlotte craned her caged head to watch him, Darius came up with her crook.

"Methinks you deserve a taste of that which you so liberally dole out to your gentlemen associates," he said. "What's sauce for the gander may be sauce for the goose, eh?"

Taking up position beside her and facing her upraised ass, he bent the slender cane this way and that, testing the whiplike suppleness of the rattan. "Have you ever been caned, Charlotte?" he asked.

She shook her head.

"But you've wondered what it feels like."

After a moment's hesitation, she nodded grudgingly.

He said, "There are—as you must know, this being your weapon of choice—any number of techniques one may employ with the cane, depending on whether one's aim is to inflict excruciating pain and permanent scars, or merely a few temporary welts. I would imagine that you wield it with a relatively judicious touch."

She nodded vigorously.

"Of course," he continued, "your purpose in administering canings is erotic stimulation. Mine is chastisement."

He whipped the rattan switch through the air with a malevolent whistle.

She cringed.

"How many strokes do you generally deliver?" he asked. "Five?"

She shook her head.

"Four?"

She shook it again, her gaze on the crook.

"Fewer?"

She nodded.

He cocked a skeptical eyebrow. "You shall receive six." Taking careful aim at the plumpest part of Charlotte's bottom, still flushed from the riding crop, Darius said, "One."

He delivered a stroke of the cane, just a short one, with a little twist of the wrist to give it some sting. It connected with a snap that drew a muffled gasp from its recipient, who strained vainly against her bindings.

Across the rosy mounds of her bottom there arose a thin, pale welt, which reddened as Darius watched. From the way she squirmed and groaned, it was apparent that the pain was actually intensifying, rather than easing, as blood rushed to the point of impact. It took her close to a minute to settle down, at which point Darius took aim again.

"Two," he said, and dealt her a new welt just below the first.

He waited, as before, for the pain to blossom fully, the welt to redden prettily, before counting off and delivering strokes three, four, and five, each time connecting just a little farther down.

"Six." With his final blow, he aimed for the crook of her thighs, a location that seemed, from her reaction, particularly sensitive. When he was done, she bore a neat ladder of welts down her hindquarters that struck Darius as cruelly beautiful.

Charlotte's little snatch looked, if anything, more inflamed than before. Moisture glistened between the distended lips. "You found pleasure in that," he said. "The pain, the humiliation, it rouses your passions, does it not?"

When she hesitated, he flicked the cane again, leaving a fresh mark just below the last one. "Does it not?"

She nodded.

He stroked the crook upward over her quim to the little puckered aperture above it, pressing into it just deeply enough to force a natural ridge near its tip into the tight sphincter. Charlotte drew in a sharp intake of breath. He popped the ridge out, then in again, and again, and again, provoking a satisfying gasp every time.

"Have you ever been ass-fucked, Charlotte?"

She hesitated, then nodded.

"Did you fancy it?"

She shook her head violently.

"Why not? Because it's degrading?"

She shook her head.

"Because it's painful?"

She nodded.

"It needn't be," he said, "if one is properly conditioned."

Tossing the cane back onto the chair, he unbuckled her restraints, took hold of the chain attached to the brank, and tugged. "On your feet."

She stood, bending over to swipe at her stockings, grimy from her having crawled across the earthen floor.

He yanked her up by the chain. "Are you *utterly* incorrigible? I said, 'On your feet,' not 'Get up and dust yourself off.' Stand up straight, damn it. Shoulders back, tits out, hands clasped behind your waist."

She did as she was told.

"When you are standing or sitting," he said, "you shall maintain this posture unless I instruct you otherwise. When I say, 'Down,' you are to turn away from me and kneel while keeping your hands behind your back, and lower your head until your forehead touches the floor as close as possible to your knees. At all times, you are to keep your back arched, your movements graceful, and your bearing humble. Do you understand?"

She nodded.

"Yes, of course you understand," he said, "but knowing you, you will need a little help in learning to comply."

He strode back to the bay housing the bed, Charlotte stumbling along behind him as he pulled her leash. One of the shelves held several straight belts—hinged bands of iron made to fit around the waist and pinion the arms by means of attached rings, some on the sides, others on the back. As luck would have it, the smallest belt had its rings on the back. This Darius fitted around Charlotte's waist, instructing her to interlock her fingers behind her as he clamped the rings around her wrists.

"This will serve as a reminder of proper demeanor," he said, "till you've learned to exercise it on your own."

Turning to the bed, Darius pulled off the mattress and blanket and tossed them onto the floor, exposing an interlaced network of ropes—hemp cord, like that coiled around the bedposts. Tugging Charlotte forward, he ordered her to lie facedown.

She hesitated, blinking at the bare rope bed. Darius unceremoniously lifted her and laid her down with her vulva and each breast positioned over one of the six-inch-square gaps formed by the intersections of the ropes; then he reached for the coil of hemp. Pulling her stockinged legs wide open, he secured them to the rope bed by wrapping them tightly from ankles to upper thighs, tying off the bindings just short of the bottommost welts from her caning. Bound and gagged with iron restraints, her legs utterly immobilized, she was as helpless as a fly in a spiderweb.

Charlotte observed Darius fixedly through the brank as he returned his attention to the items on the shelves. Most were ugly, monstrous even, but a few struck him as malevolently beautiful, like the collection of pear-shaped shafts forged of embossed steel with ornate knobs at the stem ends. He chose the smallest one; six or seven inches in length, its bulbous tip—the blossom end of the "pear"—was about as thick around as the head of a prick.

Sitting on the edge of the bed, Darius glided the little instrument over Charlotte's red-striped ass and between the lips of her sex, still inflamed by cantharides and damp with lust. She emitted little pleading moans through her gag, lifting her hips reflexively. He obligingly pressed the pear against the mouth of her quim.

"Are you so very eager to be fucked?" he asked as he worked it around and around, teasingly, in the dewy little opening. "Even by cold, hard steel?"

She nodded.

He slid it into her, sheathing it to its full length. She thrust her hips, wordlessly begging him to frig her.

" 'Tis a rather cunning machine you've just invited into your cony," he said as he shifted it this way and that inside her. "Lovely to behold, but with a nasty little secret. *La poire d'angoisse,* they call it."

He waited for her to translate it in her mind from French to English: *the pear of anguish.* Her movements ceased. She turned her caged head to look at him.

"Would you like me to demonstrate how it got its name?" he asked.

She stared at him for a moment, shook her head.

He said, "Come now, surely you're a little curious. You see, this knob is actually connected to a screw. If one turns it, like so"—he gave it a short twist, making her gasp—"it causes the steel petals that form the pear to spread outward, rather like a flower opening up. The more one turns it, the wider it opens, eventually producing a fair degree of pain and mutilation—and, in many cases, death. In times past, *la poire* was employed both for punishment and to extract confessions. The sin of the accused would determine into which body cavity it would be inserted, sometimes coated with some noxious or caustic substance. Heretics would take it in the mouth, sodomites in the ass. Of course, for strums such as yourself, the orifice of choice was Cock Alley."

He turned the knob again. Charlotte began to writhe and twist, struggling against her bonds, more from fear, he knew, than from discomfort; he'd barely begun to expand it.

"Don't like the feel of it in that pampered little snatch of yours, eh? As it would happen, I've other plans for it." He screwed the pear closed and slid it out.

Lifting the brown bottle from the bottom shelf, Darius pulled out the stopper and dribbled a yellowish, syrupy fluid over the tip of the pear, turning it this way and that until it was well coated.

Charlotte shook her head wildly, emitting muffled protestations.

"It's olive oil," he said dryly as he restoppered the bottle and put it back. "For the lamps."

Charlotte closed her eyes and turned away from him, clearly as embarrassed as she was relieved.

"You see, the aperture for which this device is destined," he said as he spread the cheeks of her ass, "is somewhat less accommodating than—"

She bucked and thrashed as she realized where he was about to insert the pear.

"Be still," he demanded, forcing compliance by pressing down hard on the small of her back. "My intent is not to injure you, merely to stretch you a bit. The pear will remain inside you, gradually expanding, until you've learned not to merely tolerate it, but to find it arousing. You'll thank me for it when that which you once found painful elicits instead a rare degree of pleasure."

She looked dubious, but she stopped squirming.

This time, when he spread her cheeks, she lay still and rigid, her eyes squeezed shut. She flinched as he pressed the pear's slick, rounded base into her, penetrating only half an inch or so before her body tightened around the intrusion.

"Ease up," he told her as he twisted and pushed, making little headway. "If you're tense, 'twill only make it hurt. You're taking it either way—you've no choice in the matter—so you may as well open up and accept it."

She nodded, drew in a breath, and let it out.

This time, when he pushed, the pear slid in a good inch, thanks in large part to its slippery coating of oil. "That's it," he murmured as he worked it in deeper, deeper. "That's it." Reaching between her legs with his free hand, he cupped her smooth, warm sex. "You may come now for being such a good girl."

She bore down, rubbing her wet slit and stiff little clit against his fingers, and again and again, hips thrusting in a carnal rhythm. With every upthrust, Darius shoved the pear a little deeper, wriggling it a bit to enhance the internal stimulation. The more she associated such stimulation with pleasure, the more satisfying it would be for both of them when his cock was inserted where the pear was now.

By the time he'd buried its entire length inside her, Charlotte was in a paroxysm of lust. The bed creaked with every thrust against his now-slippery hand.

Charlotte screamed through her gag as she spent her passion, grinding wildly against his hand. Darius frigged her with shallow thrusts of the pear, caressing her gently as her pleasure ebbed, then more purposefully as it renewed itself. She spent thrice more, and would doubtless have continued to do so had Darius indulged her wordless pleas for release, but for now, his own need for release had become far too distracting to ignore.

He untied her legs from the rope bed, then helped her to rise off it and stand up. "If I take off your restraints," he asked, "can you be trusted to comport yourself as if you were still wearing them?"

Charlotte nodded, whereupon he unlocked and removed

first the brank, then the straight belt. Without being prompted, she clasped her hands behind her waist, standing with her shoulders back, breasts outthrust.

He circled her, appraising her posture and nodding in approval. "Take down your hair," he said.

She did so. It fell to her waist in a thick, gleaming braid. "Shall I unplait it?" she asked.

"Nay, leave it as it is. But give me those," he said, indicating her handful of little diamond-studded hairpins. "Are they real or paste?" he asked, holding one up to admire in the torchlight.

"Real, of course."

He shoved them into his pocket. She looked as if she was about to object, but she stilled her tongue.

He pointed to the mattress on the floor. "Down."

She stepped onto the mattress and began lowering herself to her knees, forcing him to remind her to turn away from him first. This she did, then knelt and bent forward with her hands still clasped behind her, head down.

He flicked open the buttons of his trouser flap, savoring as he did the sight of the pear's beautifully crafted knob emerging from between the cheeks of her ass, with its neatly spaced embroidery of welts. Her pussy was wet, red, and wide open. Kneeling behind her, he grabbed her hips and filled her with a single, slick lunge that forced a startled cry of pleasure from her.

He wrapped her braid around his fist like a horse's rein and fucked her with sharp, deep strokes, relishing her posture of submission, her meekness, her complete surrender to his will. On the verge of coming, he paused and twisted the knob of the pear, just enough so that he could feel it widening inside her, making her as snug as a fist. She moaned at the added pressure, but voiced no objection.

He twisted the knob again.

"Stop, I beg you," she implored.

Darius yanked on the braid, jerking her head up and forcing

her back into a nice, ass-hiking curve. "We have a covenant, you and I. 'Tis my place to decide what you can bear, and yours to take it. Is that not what you agreed to?" He dealt her bum a stinging smack, the red-wealed flesh hot beneath his palm; she cried out in a way that he found intensely arousing. "Is it not?"

"I... Y-yes, but—"

"*But?*" Still pulling on the braid, he slapped her again, harder. "Mouthy little scab." And again. "Bitch." And again, and again... "Jade. Trollop. Whore."

He knelt unmoving with his cock deep inside her, every slap reverberating through her sex and into his, the rhythmic vibrations making him achingly, impossibly hard, driving him closer, closer...

She'd wanted to be spank-fucked; now she had her wish, but on his terms, not hers. Not that she didn't enjoy it. Either because of the pain, or in spite of it, she was wet and swollen, her initial trepidation replaced by guttural moans as she pushed back against him in an effort to take him even deeper, harder.

"Be still." Withdrawing halfway, Darius pried her hands apart and shoved them between her legs, ordering her to stroke his cock and balls but not to dare touch herself. "You have to earn the right to come."

He kept still while she did as he'd ordered, but her soft, cool caress soon had his entire body shaking, his breath shuddering. He climaxed explosively, and with a shout that echoed like thunder throughout the cellar.

Once he'd regained his breath, he withdrew from her, inciting a little whimper of frustration on her part. Rising to his feet, he refastened his trousers with palsied hands. "You may spend when you've been good and obedient," he said, "not when you've whined and complained and questioned my..."

Looking down at her, he saw that the right cheek of her ass, the one he'd spanked, was alarmingly red, the welts so inflamed he was surprised none had started bleeding.

"*Mon Dieu,*" he muttered, appalled at how close he had come to really hurting her—to *wanting* to hurt her. His control was slipping, a sign that he was losing his grip on Darius, the real Darius, and becoming, in his heart and soul, the pitiless rakehell she wanted him to be.

Charlotte turned her head slightly to look at him, as if wondering what was wrong. He should have chastised her for moving out of position, but he didn't. Taking the door key from his pocket, he went out to the hallway to draw a bucket of water from the well. This he set next to the mattress, along with the chamber pot from beneath the bed.

"I'm going upstairs to get something to eat." To get away from her, actually, away from her maddening influence on him, but it wouldn't do to let her know the effect she was having on him, the unwitting power she wielded over him. "Wash yourself while I'm gone." He pulled out his handkerchief and tossed it in front of her. "Be quick about it, then resume your position. I'll expect to find you just as you are when I come back."

Indeed, when he returned about half an hour later, Charlotte was precisely as he'd left her, crouched facedown on the mattress with her hands clasped at the small of her back. The chamber pot and bucket were tucked into a corner, with the damp handkerchief neatly draped over a crossbar of the hanging cage, like laundry hanging out to dry—a domestic touch he wouldn't have anticipated. Charlotte followed him with her eyes as he approached, a dinner tray in one hand, lantern in the other.

Hanging the lantern on a ceiling hook, Darius lifted her head by the braid and set down the tray, which held three stone china bowls and a folded napkin. "Eat," he said, indicating the largest bowl, which contained *soupe au chou* left over from the servants' supper, the broth drained off so all that remained was a mound of cabbage, bacon, and potatoes amid flecks of aromatic herbs and vegetables. The two smaller bowls were filled with wine.

Clearly dismayed that he expected her to dine without the use of her hands, crouched over her food like a dog, Charlotte said, "I . . . I'm not really—"

"I won't have you swooning from hunger while I've still some use for you." Darius leaned against a column, arms crossed, and watched her. "Eat."

Charlotte regarded the soup for a long, bleak moment, and then she took a tentative nibble of potato.

"Good girl," he said.

She used her teeth to pick up the rest of the chunk of potato and ate that, and then some bacon, some cabbage, some more potato . . .

"Don't neglect your wine," he said. "The bowl on the left contains Spanish fly. That on the right is unadulterated. You may have whichever you prefer."

Charlotte lowered her head and dipped her tongue into the cantharide-spiked wine with the delicacy of a kitten. It took her a few licks to develop an effective technique, but before long, she'd learned to curl her tongue so as to lap it up more efficiently. There was something crudely titillating about the sight of this golden-haired countess hunkering over her meal with her face in the bowl, hands dutifully clasped behind her, a steel knob emerging from her whip-scarred ass.

"Pick up the napkin," he said when she'd eaten enough to suit him.

She started to unclasp her hands.

"Uh-uh-uh," he said.

She paused, then lifted the napkin with her teeth.

"Stand and come to me."

She rose with admirable grace and came to stand before him, back arched, hands behind her, the napkin still clutched in her teeth.

He took it and used it to dab her mouth, wiping off that absurd lip rouge in the process, then tossed it onto the tray.

"Step back," he said, "under the lantern. Let me get a good look at you."

She did as she was told.

"Turn 'round," he told her. "Slowly."

Charlotte had the fragile beauty of a porcelain figurine, exquisitely pale but for her nipples and vulva, which were blood-flushed from the cantharides. Her body was elegantly proportioned, her skin smooth and flawless—save for a few barely visible little silvery streaks on her lower belly, which Darius would never have noticed but for the bright overhead light.

"You have children?" he asked.

"I'm barren."

Pointing to the evidence that her belly had once been greatly stretched, he said, "These marks testify otherwise. You've given birth."

She frowned at the marks as she composed her response. "Just . . . just once," she said. "I became barren afterward."

"When?" he asked. "When did you give birth, I mean."

Charlotte took her time answering, and when she did, it was with obvious reluctance. "Nine years ago." She evidently didn't care for this line of conversation, didn't like being reminded that she was the mother of a young child by the man who'd been fucking her and whipping her and shoving things up her ass.

"A son or a daughter?"

"A son," she said stiffly, looking straight ahead, but not at him.

"A son and heir—that must have made the late Lord Somerhurst happy. And how does a wanton widow dispose of an inconvenient nine-year-old earl while she's off lifting her skirts for the Hellfires? Pack him off to some suitable boarding school where he can learn to be a proper peer of the realm, I should think."

She didn't answer, merely continued staring beyond him.

"You lied to me," he said. "When I first asked if you had children, you said you were barren."

"But it's true, I *am*—"

"You deliberately misled me. I see no substantive difference between that and an outright lie."

She sighed.

" 'Tis of little import *why* you lied," he said. "I won't have it. You must be taught a lesson, one that will sting."

She met his gaze then.

"Come." He gestured for her to follow him to the bay that housed the rack. The massive table was bordered with a framework of iron and fitted out with three wooden rollers about eight or ten inches in diameter, one at either end and one in the middle, connected by a pair of ropes that wound around all three rollers. Darius ordered Charlotte to climb onto the device and lie down. This she managed rather awkwardly on her own; he was in no humor to offer any help.

Seeing that she'd situated herself with the small of her back curved over the middle roller, he repositioned her so that the roller lay beneath her hips with the knob of the pear just accessible in case he should choose to employ it. He lifted her arms up and out so as to lash her wrists to the top roller by means of noose-like loops at the ends of the two ropes; yanking her feet apart, he secured them in like manner to the bottom.

As he touched her, a tableau materialized in his mind's eye of a woman being tortured on the rack by men in masks and robes. To many women, such an image would summon feelings of repulsion and terror—but not to Charlotte Somerhurst. He felt her fascination with the notion of being tied up and stretched, tormented, penetrated, and her excitement that she was about to experience such treatment firsthand.

It vexed him that Charlotte's penalty for that insolent lie should be something she secretly craved. Never mind that everything that had transpired between them this evening was rooted in her baffling desire for punishment. The things he'd done to her, the things he'd made her do—they were all, essentially, at the behest of her dark, unspoken longings. Nevertheless, the more immersed Darius became in the role she'd prescribed for him, the more he felt like—the more he *became* like—the disdainful, vicious, easily roused persecutor she wanted him to be.

On each end of the middle roller was an iron winch with holes all around in lieu of handles; a long, iron-tipped pole meant to operate the winch leaned against the wall nearby. Darius jammed the tip of the pole into the winch and hauled it toward him, using both hands and putting his weight into it, for the machinery was very old and very heavy. The middle roller rotated with a grinding creak, drawing the ropes, and Charlotte's arms and legs, somewhat tighter. He cranked the winch several more times, until she was stretched out with her hips raised high by the middle roller, drawing Darius's gaze to her upthrust sex. It was, if anything, even pinker than before, the slit glistening with moisture.

"You're enjoying this a bit too much." He shoved the pole back into the winch. With each successive crank, the ropes grew more taut, exerting that much more pressure on Charlotte's limbs.

"No more," she gasped. "Please."

Darius whipped the cravat from around his neck and balled it up. "One would think you'd have learned to keep your mouth shut by now." Prying open her mouth, he stuffed the wad of silk into it.

Thus gagged, the only sounds she could produce were muffled whimpers. She tried to capture his gaze as he reached once again for the pole, her expression one of silent pleading. Ignoring her, he gave the winch one final turn, just to remind her that it was he who wielded the power here, he who had the right to dispense pleasure or pain at his sole discretion.

Crossing to the shelves near the bed, Darius chose a pair of petite thumbscrews and brought them back. Maliciously ingenious little devices, they were comprised of two strips of iron joined by screws, the interior surfaces, which were meant to crush thumbs or other small body parts, studded to enhance their effectiveness. Charlotte lifted her head—the only part of her that she could move even slightly—to watch him pinch and pull her right nipple to full stiffness and fit the little instrument over it. He tightened the screws to squeeze the plates together, stopping when she winced. He did the same to the left, then twisted and tugged both thumbscrews until she moaned through her gag.

Was it pleasure that had produced that moan, or pain? So confounded was Darius by his role in this strange drama that he didn't know which he most hoped to elicit anymore.

Parting her sex lips, he slid a finger into her tight little puss, hot juices running like sap down his hand. She shuddered in obvious pleasure. Whatever discomfort Charlotte might be enduring, she was clearly in a state of excruciating arousal—only heightened, no doubt, by the suffering to which he was subjecting her.

"Shall I attach one of those thumbscrews to your clit?" He rolled the slick little bud between his thumb and forefinger, noting with satisfaction how it engorged and reddened in response to his ministrations. "Nay," he said, "I've a better idea."

Bending over her, he took the little pearl between his teeth, biting just hard enough to make her tremble with uncertainty, wondering how far he would go. He kept her in suspense for a bit, working his teeth back and forth so that she could feel their sharp edges. Presently he moved on to the delicate little folds of her inner labia, then the outer, which he nibbled and nipped and finally—enticed by the silkiness of her denuded mons—lightly tongued. She was warm, soft, luscious. Little wonder her lovers preferred her hairless when it came to gamahuching.

Darius thrust his middle finger, then two more, into Charlotte's dripping quim as he twisted the knob of the pear, all the while gamming her with featherlight strokes of his tongue. She was quivering, lungs pumping like a bellows, head thrown back.

A vivid fancy of the imagination—Charlotte's, of course—bombarded him like cannon fire: two handsome lovers writhing against her, filling her, pummeling her from within, groaning as their arousal peaked along with hers. It was a pleasure she'd never experienced, given the discomfort she associated with Greek lovemaking, but it was one she'd often dreamt of—a pleasure that Darius, like it or not, was now obligated to provide for her. Would it satisfy her at last? Would it end this maddening travesty?

It mattered not. She wanted it; Darius, her master and her slave, must make it happen.

She was close now, so close, hovering on the breathless verge of climax.

"No." He pushed away from her, shaking his head. Was he mad? Was this how he would pay her back for lying to him? By giving her pleasure, by letting her come? Fucking bitch, she always managed to get to him, to get him turned around from what he'd intended. So lost was he in her thoughts and feelings that he couldn't keep his own straight anymore. He couldn't command himself, much less her.

Charlotte, her eyes wild with frustration and outrage, strained against her bindings as she watched him rummage in his pocket for the key to the door.

"I told you the lesson would sting," he said.

She shook her head frantically, desperately, until the makeshift gag loosened and she could spit it out. "Don't leave! Oh, God, Darius, *please.* You can't leave me like—"

He slapped her face so hard her head whipped to the side. "Don't tell me what I can't do!"

She stared at him, her cheek reddening.

A distant, diminishing part of him, the part that was still the Darius of old, was appalled that he'd struck a woman in anger—

but the new Darius, Charlotte's pet monster, reveled in her shock and her pain. God, how he loathed what he'd become, what she'd made him, but most of all he loathed her for doing this to him.

"Darius," she said. "Don't go. Darius, please . . ."

He turned and left.

Six

"TO THE powers of darkness," Francis Dashwood toasted as he raised his horn-shaped glass of brandy.

"To the powers of darkness," echoed Lili, along with the others who'd gathered in the great hall for the traditional post-mass banquet: the superior Hellfires in their white silk monks' robes, the rank-and-file members in their ordinary garb, and the women, all now identically attired, local virgins and imported adventuresses alike, in black nuns' habits.

All save Lili, who stood next to Dashwood with her hair still loose, and wearing the voluminous veil she'd worn during the mass, sans cape and body ornaments. The Bona Dea always retained the veil during the banquet, but rather than draping it over her entire body head to foot, as was customary, Lili had chosen to wrap it about herself, knotting it on one shoulder like the *lubushu* of her homeland. This way, although her body was still visible through the gossamer folds to those who stared hard enough—which seemed to be every man in the room, and some of the women—there would be something left to the imagination. And imagination, in Lili's view, fueled the passions ever so much more effectively than crude displays of flesh.

"Archer, old chap!" Dashwood called out. "You've joined us after all."

All eyes turned toward the main doorway, which framed the earnest young Lord Henry, their mysterious hostess's majordomo.

"I, er, shan't be lingering," Archer said. "Just dropped by to, you know, make certain you've got what you need, see that the hall has been readied per your instructions." He surveyed the majestic hall with its lofty, oak-trussed ceiling, polished wainscoting, and tall windows, blinking as he took in the various playthings set up among the settees and fainting couches: a spanking horse, a whipping frame in the shape of a St. Andrew's cross, a set of stocks, a pyramidal ladder fitted out with restraints, a rack of assorted shackles and ropes, and of course the rampant black swan that served more or less as the Hellfires' mascot. He stared at Lili's translucent attire for a fleeting moment, met her eyes, and quickly looked away.

Lili followed his gaze to an easel near a window open to the night sky, where Mr. Hogarth sat painting a canvas based upon one of his earlier sketches, his oils, brushes, and solvents arranged on a table beside him. Hanging on the wall nearby was the slate on which the Hellfires' steward, Paul Whitehead, would keep score of the members' amorous accomplishments during the festivities to come.

On the dais at the far end of the hall, servants put the finishing touches on a row of candlelit, damask-draped banquet tables laden with a quintessential Hellfire Club feast. Most of the victuals had been chosen for their stimulating qualities and flavored with such aphrodisiacal spices as gingerroot, saffron, aniseed, and chili peppers. Platters of silver and cut glass were heaped with exotic game, roast beef carved to resemble female buttocks, breastlike pairs of squabs adorned with cherries, deer penises *Suédois,* snails, sardines, hard-boiled eggs, avocado pears, pomegranates, asparagus, artichokes, leeks, truffles, chestnuts, orchid bulbs, a dozen varieties of oysters, gallons of wine, gin, and treacherously potent "Hellfire Punch," and most seductive of all, from Lili's viewpoint, a cluster of little copper pots on braziers filled with luscious, fragrant chocolate.

Dashwood was assuring Lord Henry that they had everything they needed and telling him how reluctant they would be to leave on the morrow. "Most sporting of Madame des Ombres to have invited us, sight unseen," he said. "Must be a damned fine lady—*damned* fine."

"Er, yes, I daresay she is," Archer said as he backed out through the door, stealing another furtive glance at Lili as he did so. "Good. Jolly good. Well, then. I shan't detain you any longer."

Once Archer had closed the door behind him, Dashwood announced that, in keeping with Hellfire tradition, the Abbot of the Day would have first choice of the ladies, after which the others could pair up as they saw fit. He waved a hand, whereupon the "nuns" formed a line to either side of Lili.

"Right, then." Dashwood made a come-forward gesture to Elic, who looked remarkably like his charming sister. They had the same radiant gaze beneath those dark, slashing eyebrows, the same fine bones and burnished gold hair, which Elic wore in a ribbon-tied queue that trailed halfway down his back. He was lean and rangy, with squared-off shoulders and the kind of controlled grace that Lili found irresistible in a man. Something else she found irresistible was compassion, a quality sadly lacking in many of his sex. But the heartening little smile Elic had graced her with at the beginning of the mass, the way he'd flinched when Dashwood had entered her so roughly, the way he'd looked at her, touched her...

His touch had both thrilled and comforted her, a heady combination, and a novel one. The life Lili led, the life she was forced to lead, afforded her ample opportunity to ease her relentless lust, but none to ease her sense of isolation. The Hellfires and their ilk—for they weren't the only such voluptuaries with whom Lili had thrown in her lot over the years—seemed fixated on sexual gratification to the virtual exclusion of other forms of personal communion. When they conversed, it was about sex; when they touched, it was to fuck or suck, or to ready themselves for such sport. And it was always sport with them, never, ever lovemaking.

For the most part, Lili was content enough with this state of affairs. After all, it would only complicate matters to have to cultivate an actual relationship every time she felt the need for sexual release, which was almost constantly. Yet there were times, even when she was surrounded by others, as now, that she felt utterly, crushingly alone.

"Well, Elic?" Dashwood said. "Which of these delectable creatures will favor you with her company this evening?"

Elic looked directly at Lili, didn't even pretend to consider the others.

She might have looked away coyly, but instead she held his gaze, wordlessly acknowledging the invisible ribbon binding the two of them together.

He walked up to her and bowed. "*Mademoiselle.*"

She smiled up at him. "Your servant, *monsieur.*"

No sooner had Lili put her hand in Elic's than the rest of their company launched into the debaucheries that were the highlight of most Hellfire gatherings. In groups of two, three, and four, they laid claim to the various furnishings and devices scattered throughout the hall, stripped off their clothes, and had at it.

"Let me take you to my chamber." Elic had a deep, raspy, Gallic-seasoned voice that sent a giddy little tickle up and down Lili's spine.

She shook her head. "We must remain here, among the others—at least in the beginning, while those who matter among the Hellfires are still sober enough to notice our presence."

"Those who matter?" Elic looked around, shaking his head. "They're bad actors in silly costumes. None of them matter."

Lowering her voice as she glanced about, Lili said, "Perhaps not, but they have their way of doing things, and if I don't comply, I shall find myself dismissed from their company in short order."

"If they don't matter," he asked, "why should that trouble you?"

She turned to watch Winnie Aldridge being gamahuched by George Walpole whilst the Duke of Kingston lashed her to the ladder. A few yards away, several bodies writhed in unison on two pushed-together couches, a fleshy tangle of torsos and limbs.

"There are few venues where a lady with certain appetites may satisfy them without restraint," she said. "The Hellfire Club may be absurd in many respects, but it is a godsend for one such as I."

Elic looked around, his gaze lighting on the minstrels' gallery over the screens passage. "I don't think anyone's up there. We'd still be in the hall, more or less."

Bemused but gratified by Elic's desire to be alone with her, or as alone as could be managed, Lili allowed him to guide her toward a narrow stairwell. Just before she ducked into it, she turned and saw Anton Turek standing still as death in the midst of all that carnal bedlam, watching her with an intensity that made her shiver. Had Archer not prevailed upon Dashwood, at Madame des Ombres' request, to name Elic Abbot of the Day, it would be Turek escorting her to a trysting place right now instead of Elic. Thank God for meddling hostesses.

The gallery was small, with a single curtainless window and no comfortable furnishings—just a semicircle of hard-backed chairs paired with music stands. Elic's hopeless expression as he looked around touched something in Lili's chest that made her smile.

"Come," she said, drawing him by the hand to a dark corner as far as possible from the railing overlooking the hall proper. With her back to the wall, she tugged him closer. *Mamitu,* but he was tall; the top of her head didn't even reach his shoulders. "Here," she said as she set about unhooking his robe. "Take me here."

Bracing his hands against the wall, Elic bent his head to touch his lips to Lili's, an unexpected gesture that drew a little huff of surprise from her. The Hellfires rarely kissed during their orgies; when they did, it was with much mashing of lips and thrashing of tongue. Elic's kiss was warm, lingering... filled with sensual promise, but with an underlying tenderness.

Perfect.

"I know you're not permitted to refuse the Abbot of the Day," he whispered as their mouths parted. "But if this isn't what you want—"

"If you hadn't chosen me, I'd have wept," she said, astounded that she meant it. Parting his robe, she stroked her hands downward over his sinewy chest and abdomen to the straining shaft between his legs.

Elic groaned as she caressed him. He yanked her *lubushu* up to her waist and lifted her against the wall. But as she guided him to the mouth of her sex, or tried to, the flesh that had felt like a rod of steel just moments ago grew limp in her hand.

He looked not just surprised, but astounded. Muttering something in a language that sounded vaguely Nordic, he rubbed against her, his fingers digging into her hips as he ground her against the wall.

"Elic," she said, but he just thrust harder, almost violently, though to little effect. "Stop," she said gently. "Elic, please. It's all right."

"No, it's not." He set her down, looking truly confounded. "I can't... I... It makes no sense."

"It happens," she said as she pulled her *lubushu* back down.

"Not to me."

Reaching up to stroke his face, she said, " 'Tis the *azulla,* I think."

"The what?"

"The incense they burn during the mass. My people called it—call it *azulla.* You probably know it by its Arabic name, hashish. It makes the mind spin. Be patient, *khababu.* Give the *azulla* time to wear off, and soon you will be—"

"No," he said as he refastened his robe. "You don't understand. This doesn't happen to me. It *can't* happen to me, *azulla* or no *azulla.*"

"Forsooth," she said with a gently mocking smile. "Are you so very different, then, from other men?"

"I'm not—" He bit off his words and looked away, his jaw rigid.

"You're not what?" she asked, scalp prickling.

With a flurry of laughter, the Marquis of Granby burst forth from the stairwell with one hand wrapped around a bottle of wine and the other around the naked waist of Emily Lawrence. "Bugger me, someone's beat us up here," Granby slurred. "Say, you don't mind if we join you?" he asked as he tripped over a music stand and tumbled to the floor, along with a merrily shrieking Emily.

Bowing to Lili, Elic said, "Forgive me, *mademoiselle,* for having taken so much of your time," and left.

Seven

LILI STOOD in the entrance of the bathhouse watching Elic float facedown in the pool. The skylight overhead framed a mere sliver of moon, not enough to alleviate the darkness—unless, like Lili, one had eyes that could capture any faint hint of illumination, however thin, and magnify it several times over.

Had she not been blessed with this gift, she wouldn't even have known Elic was here. After he left the musician's gallery, she'd looked through the window and seen him striding away from the chateau toward the bathhouse. Anyone else would have seen little more than the blackness of night.

She'd gone downstairs and sipped a cup of chocolate while contemplating what had just transpired, meanwhile fending off carnal invitations from any number of half-naked, whip-wielding men—but not from Turek. The gloomy Bohemian sat leaning on his elbows in a darkened corner, a pair of steel wrist cuffs dangling absently from one hand, legs irons from the other, both prettily embossed and of dainty proportions. Lili recognized them as one of half a dozen sets commissioned by Dashwood for the express purpose of restraining females.

Turek's hood was pushed down, and he'd removed his wig for the mass, as required, exposing an unruly thatch of straw-colored hair. He glanced up and, upon spying Lili looking his way, his hang-gallows look gave way to a glint of interest. He rose and started toward her.

She gulped down the rest of her chocolate and slipped away through the crowd. Twice, as she'd traced Elic's path to the bathhouse, she'd paused and turned, probing the night with her keen eyes to make sure Turek hadn't followed her; there'd been no sign of him.

Lili approached the bathhouse with guarded, silent steps, the only sound a faint gurgling from the cave stream that fed the pool. Mist rose like smoke from the surface of the water; viewed with her nighttime vision, it looked like a sheet of that black volcanic glass that covered the altar in the chapel. Elic's prone, naked body might have been carved from alabaster, with every muscle painstakingly sculpted and polished. His hair, now unbound, flowed like streams of honey over the surface of the water.

Lili watched Elic's inert form float slowly in her direction on a current from the stream, until his feet touched the edge nearest her. When they did, he lazily stretched out his arms and scooped the water, pushing himself forward until his head nearly touched the far end. It took several long minutes for him to drift back down to her end of the pool, which was about fifteen feet square. Again, as soon as his feet brushed marble, he propelled himself back to his starting position.

At no time did he lift his face from the water.

Slowly, warily—for Lili had bathed in this pool and knew of its conductive powers—she crouched down and dipped a hand into the balmy water. A terrible yearning swept over her—not just a sexual yearning, though that was part of it. She felt, in her very soul, a sudden, excruciating loneliness.

Elic bolted to his feet and whipped around to face her, water sluicing off him as he stood hip-deep in the pool; he was fully erect, every muscle tensed in readiness. "*Que se produit?*" he demanded, clawing strands of wet hair out of his eyes. "*Qui est là?*"

"*C'est moi—Lili.*"

Elic searched the mist until his gaze met Lili's. He lowered himself onto the benchlike top step with a weighty sigh.

"Shall I leave?" she asked.

"No, stay." He rubbed his hands over his face. "Please."

She untied her *lubushu,* dropped it on the marble floor, and stepped down into the water.

"My God, you're beautiful," he said in a low, earnest voice. "Perfect." She was about to thank him when he asked, "What are you?"

Lili ducked beneath the surface of the water and covered the distance between them with one fluid underwater glide. Standing before him, she twisted the water out of her hair. " 'What,' not 'who,' " she mused. "That means you already know."

"I've been thinking about it. 'Tis only with other follets that I am unable to act upon my desires."

"With *all* follets, or . . . ?"

"With most of them. No matter how aroused I am, how much I want her, I wilt the moment I try to enter her. There are reputed to be exceptions, but I've yet to encounter one. I've been sheltered here for years, so I've met very few of my kind—our kind."

"I must say, it always strikes me as odd to hear another follet refer to follets in general as 'our kind,' given our variety, all the different races." She took a seat next to him, submerging herself with a sigh of contentment. "There must be scores the world over, each with its own sub-races—and within those races, untold variations among individuals. When I happen across another follet, and am able to identify him as such, he's usually so different from me that I wouldn't begin to think of him as 'my kind.' "

"Yet, every race of follet is descended, in one way or another, from Frøya," he said. "That makes us all cousins, however distant or removed."

"They don't call her Frøya where I come from. They call her Ishtar."

"Darius calls her that, too," he said. "Inigo calls her Hecate. Where *are* you from?"

"Babylonia—or what *was* Babylonia. And you?"

"The coast of Norvegr, what you call Norway. But I've lived here, at Grotte Cachée, for centuries."

"How many?" Rarely did Lili pry into the lives of others, follet or human, but there was something about being here with Elic—the womblike warmth of the water, the mist and darkness, and their remarkable affinity—that emboldened her.

"How many centuries?" He looked away with an engagingly sheepish grin, skimming the hair off his face. "Eighteen."

"*Eighteen?*" She sat up, laughing incredulously. "You've been tucked away here, in this remote little valley, for eighteen hundred years?"

"I do venture out into the greater world from time to time," he said. "In fact, I enjoy traveling. But I couldn't hope for a better home than Grotte Cachée. This is a haven for our kind. Our needs are seen to without our having to keep our true identities a secret every minute of every day. We have—"

"We?"

"There are two others," Elic said. "Darius and Inigo. Darius was already here when I came, though it was some time before I met him, because he's something of a recluse. He lives in a chamber deep in that cave," Elic said, cocking his head toward the mossy entrance to the grotto behind him, from which emanated an almost imperceptible glow. "Has ever since I've known him."

"That must be why Lord Henry asked us to stay within a quarter mile of the entrance, where the torches are, if we decided to go exploring in there," she said.

"That, and humans tend to experience a certain . . . derangement of the senses if they venture much farther than that. So did you?" he asked. "Go exploring?"

"God, no, I've had my fill of caves," she said with a shiver. "I've had to live in them, or rather, hide in them, once too often. So cold and dank, even in the summer."

"Our Grotte Cachée is actually quite cozy, year-round, even with the stream running through it. Not that I'd care to make my own home there, and God knows Inigo wouldn't. He's far too enamored of his creature comforts—the quintessential sybarite, lives entirely for pleasure. He arrived with the Romans when they occupied this valley after the Gallic Wars."

"How came *you* to settle here?" she asked as she skimmed her hands across the glassy surface of the water to watch the trails and ripples.

"Desperation." Elic settled back with his head against the lip of the pool, gazing up through the skylight.

"If you'd rather not talk about it..."

" 'Tisn't a very pretty tale," he said.

Lili found Elic's hand underwater and threaded her fingers through his, a gesture that felt as natural as if she'd done it a thousand times. "Tell me."

Turning his head to look at her, he said, "I was forced to flee my native land when the farmers came. The hunters and fishermen who'd been there before, they had understood me and my ways. They called me an *álfr,* which means *elfe* in my present tongue. 'Tis much the same in English, I think."

"It is," said Lili, thinking, *Of course.* Elvenfolk—tall, stalwart, and fair-haired—were regarded as the most beautiful follets in existence.

"At that time," Elic continued, "before the rise of the *Æsir,* which is to say the principal gods and goddesses, *álfafólk* were considered deities, and treated as such. The humans offered me *blóts,* which were sacrifices of meat and mead—and beautiful young women. It was their way of ensuring that there would always be enough elk and seals and salmon to feed them."

"Did they...you don't mean to say they killed these women."

Chuckling, Elic said, "They would hardly have been much use to me dead. Nay, they were very much alive, and not at all reluctant. They always told me they considered it an honor to give themselves to me."

An honor, Lili thought, and a thrill. What young woman in her right mind wouldn't have leapt at the chance to perform her sacrificial duty with the likes of Elic?

" 'Twasn't a bad life for one such as I," Elic said. "But gradually, the wild places along the coast were plowed under by newcomers and turned into farms. One year, a terrible blight destroyed most of their crops. Having no one else to blame, they decided I must be a *dökkálfr* in disguise. They're pure evil, the *dökkálfr.* They bring nothing but disease and misery. The farmers thought if they destroyed me, it would protect them from future misfortune. I retreated into the forest, scrounging for food—and making occasional forays into the villages at night in the hope of finding a female."

"Wasn't that risky?"

"Insanely so, but I need carnal release the way humans need to breathe. 'Twouldn't be such a problem if I could achieve that release on my own, but I'm not made that way."

"Nor I, more's the pity," Lili said. "If I could pleasure myself, I wouldn't have taken up with the likes of the Hellfires, I can tell you that. Unrelenting lust, which roars back the moment we satisfy it—'tis the price some of us must pay for immortality."

"Or near immortality," he said. "Surely you're susceptible to fire, like the rest of us—well, most of the rest of us. Darius is a djinni. Fire doesn't harm him, but he can drown. And of course the various bloodsuckers each have their own particular Achilles' heel—decapitation, sunlight, staking..."

"No, I'm rather drearily typical in that regard. Fire will make short work of me. I rue the day humanfolk discovered how vulnerable we are to it."

Elic said, "I'm not sure how the farmers knew, but they did. They sent out search parties that winter, and one night they found me sleeping in a little stone hut deep in the woods. It was the home of an old hermit named Ingvarr, a human who'd been my friend for decades. He'd taken pity on me and insisted I share his roof until the spring. I should have refused his hospitality, but I was so cold and so exhausted, and . . ." Elic looked away, his expression grim. "They wrapped me in chains and beat my old friend to death while I watched—'twas his punishment for harboring me. They built a crude pyre in front of the hut and threw Ingvarr onto it, and then me next to him, still in chains. And then they lit it."

"*Mamitu*," Lili breathed, staring at him in shock and horror.

"My clothes and hair burned first. When my skin began to blister and char, the farmers decided there was no point in waiting 'round in the bitter cold, when they could return to their warm homes. As soon as they were gone, I gathered my strength and rolled myself off the pyre and into the snow."

Squeezing his hand, she said, "My God, Elic. It must have been agonizing."

"I've forgotten the pain, but I'll never forget the utter despair that gripped me. 'Twas the first, and only, time in my life when I've pined for the comfort of death."

"I'm surprised you lived through it," she said.

"Evidently, it takes a somewhat more thorough roasting to do in the likes of me. Once I realized I was going to live, I managed to creep, inch by inch, into the hut. I lay there for days, half-delirious in my chains, while the burns healed."

"It took *days* for them to heal?" So powerful were the recuperative abilities of most follets that wounds, even the most grievous, generally repaired themselves within hours—a day or two, at the most.

"The burns covered most of my body. I had to not only mend, but grow a great deal of new skin, all the while bound in chains. One morning, Ingvarr's granddaughter, Sigrún, came looking for him. I knew her well, but at first she didn't even recognize me, with all that fresh, pink skin and no hair or eyebrows. Sigrún's husband, Valdís, was a blacksmith, and he freed me from the chains. They offered to shelter me in their home, but that was unthinkable, after what had happened to Ingvarr. I decided to leave Norvegr and look for another place to make my home. Valdís gave me some clothes and a hunting knife, and Sigrún packed me some food. I spent the next few years journeying in a southwesterly path, through Germania and into Gaul."

"Posing as a human, I assume."

"Aye, but I've always found it difficult to hide my true nature over an extended period of time. The longer I go without a woman, the more irrepressible my mating drive becomes. It makes me wild, rash. I tried to keep my contact with the Gallic tribes to a minimum, but eventually I was always found out and exposed, usually by the local druid."

"The druids, they were the priests, yes?"

"The *high* priests—there were lesser ones. Each tribe had a different name for me, but they all regarded me as a demon of the worst order, a lust-crazed monster out to despoil their women. Several times, I was almost captured and burned, but I fought like the devil and always managed to escape. It didn't help that the Romans were invading Gaul at the time, which meant I had to avoid cohorts of soldiers, too. I began to wonder if there was any place on Earth where I could live in peace, or if I would spend my entire existence wandering from one location to the next, trying desperately to appease my hungers while pretending I was something I wasn't."

"That is how most of us live," Lili said.

"Is it how *you* live?" he asked quietly.

She sighed. "As I said, I am drearily typical. How did you end up in this particular area of Gaul?"

"I'd decided to go to Spain, and if Spain wasn't hospitable, into Africa. Ideally, I wanted to find a place where they knew nothing about my kind."

"There are follets all over the world," she told him, "even in Africa."

"I didn't know that then. In any event, while traveling south, I encountered the volcanic highlands occupied by the Arverni tribe, the region we call Auvergne now."

"This region."

He nodded. "I was tempted to circumvent it because of the difficulty of negotiating such rugged terrain. But then again, it was easier to keep myself hidden, with all the dense woods and gorges and narrow little valleys. By that point, I'd resolved to allow myself no contact with people at all until I reached Spain."

"None at all?" she asked. "But what of your mating drive?"

"Oh, I was half-mad with lust, but by that point, I knew enough about the Gauls to know that I couldn't risk any more exposure, however minimal. I'd no desire to relive the experience of being captured and set on fire. I traveled through the thickest forests, which slowed down my progress but kept me out of sight. I thought I was safe because I didn't seek out any humans. I didn't expect them to seek *me* out—how could they even know I was there?—but they did. There was a small clan called the Vernae, an offshoot of the Arverni, who lived in this valley. They trapped me and brought me back to their village, but not so they could burn me. They wanted to use me to sire offspring with special powers to perpetuate their druidic line."

"You can sire children by human women?" she asked. Most follets, including Lili, couldn't reproduce with humans; it was why she could disport herself as she wished with no risk of pregnancy. But given that Elic could only have relations with humans, perhaps he was one of the few who could father half-human offspring.

He said, "I actually have a very strong urge to reproduce, and I *can*—in a manner of speaking."

"Either you can or you can't," she said. " 'Tisn't very complicated."

"In my case, it is. You see, I make no seed of my own, so if I couple with a woman in the ordinary manner, which is generally the case, there is no possibility of conception."

" 'The ordinary manner'? And what, pray, would be the *extra*ordinary manner?" she asked.

A little hesitantly, he said, "I . . . have the ability to take a female form in order to mate with a male of superior quality. As I change back into a male myself, the seed I've secured from him is enriched by certain of my own—"

"You're a dusios," she said in a tone of wonderment. The term had been bandied about quite liberally in past times, becoming more or less synonymous with "demon," but a true dusios, with the ability to shift genders, was a great rarity. "I didn't know there were elfin dusii."

"Any race of follet can produce dusii," he said. " 'Tis a random aberration among nonhumans."

"Elle . . . ," she breathed, staring at his face—the sea-blue eyes and sensual mouth, the godlike beauty. "My God, you're *Elle.* No wonder she looks so much like you. She *is* you."

"I'm glad you know," he said. "I didn't like keeping that from you. My intent this evening was to capture Francis Dashwood's seed, but now that I've got it, I'm at somewhat of a loss as to what to do with it. By rights, it should only be bestowed upon the worthiest sort of female. That was why I got myself appointed Abbot of the Day and took part in that absurd mock mass, so that I could have first choice of the women afterward."

"I was hoping you'd choose me," said Lili as she touched his cheek, "even if it didn't quite work out as you'd planned."

Turning, he gathered her in his arms. He smoothed the damp hair off her forehead, stroked her face, her mouth. Ducking his head, he kissed her, very gently, his lips warm and soft and sweet against hers. It felt so pure to her, and yet so thrilling, as if she were fifteen again, and feeling a man's mouth on hers for the very first time.

"You taste like chocolate," he murmured.

" 'Tis my only vice."

He laughed at that, his chest shaking against hers; she laughed, too. They kissed again, with more passion this time, more purpose, as he caressed her throat, her breasts, the curve of her waist. He slid a hand between her thighs, grazing a finger very lightly along the seam of her sex. The flesh there felt so hot and sensitive; every brush of his fingertip provoked a little whimper of desire from her.

"I wish..." She sighed. "I just wish we could..."

"Shh..." Gripping her hips, he pulled her astride his lap and pressed her to him, his erection like a column of heat against her most intimate flesh.

She said, "But you can't..."

"You can."

Elic rubbed against her, rocking her hips slowly but firmly. Lowering his head, he drew a nipple into his mouth, sucking and tonguing it with a deeply rhythmic pressure that heightened her arousal to an almost excruciating degree. Only a dusios, she thought, who knew firsthand the sensitivities of female breasts, could do this so well.

"Yes," she breathed, her thrusts growing faster, more erratic as water sloshed in waves over the edge of the pool. From his low groans and the straining of his muscles, Lili could tell that he, too, was in a high fever of arousal—and doubtless a fair measure of frustration, given his inability to spend this way.

Elic held her tight as she came, whispering things she couldn't hear over the roar of blood in her head, and her own helpless cries of release. He tucked her head into the crook of his shoulder and stroked her back with a quivering hand. "Lili... you're so beautiful," he whispered into her hair.

Reaching between them, she closed her hand around his erection.

He bucked at her touch. "Oh, God," he groaned. "Lili . . ."

Gliding her fist up and down his length, she said, "Is it possible, if I were to use my hand, or perhaps my mouth . . . ?"

He shook his head. "I can't spend save between a woman's legs—a human woman. Never in my life have I so ardently wished it otherwise." Gently removing her hand, he said, "Were you to continue that, 'twould evoke only pain, not pleasure. After I've tapped a man's seed, I'm left in a state of fierce arousal until I can transfer it. Too much provocation when I've no outlet for my passions can leave me in agony."

"You'll be in this state until you find a suitable woman to give the seed to?" Lili asked.

"The problem is, there *are* no suitable women here, not right now."

"Surely you've found yourself in this fix before," she said, "having—how do you put it?—tapped a man's seed, but with no one appropriate to transfer it to. What do you do when this happens? Just pick the least objectionable female and hope she doesn't become pregnant?"

"Yes and no," he said. "I use a condom, much as I hate to."

"Because they diminish your pleasure?"

"That, and it's a terrible waste of seed that I've gone to some trouble to obtain, but better to waste it than for the wrong woman to conceive a gifted child."

"Is that what you'll do tonight?" she asked. "Use a condom?"

Elic slumped down, his forehead resting against hers. "I wish . . . I . . ."

"I know," she said, fighting a pinch of unaccustomed jealousy at the prospect of this man—whom she'd only just met—lying with another woman tonight. An absurd reaction, of course, especially in light of her own sexual appetites, which were all-consuming and utterly ungovernable. Elic was as much a slave of his carnal humors as was she; regardless of their feelings, that would never, could never, change. "So . . . which of

Francis Dashwood's 'nuns' do you think you will choose?" she asked as coolly as she could.

Elic lifted his big shoulders. "Does it matter? It isn't as if there's one who stands out above the rest."

"They fancy themselves so forward-thinking," Lili said, "so worldly-wise, but really they're just children playing dress-up."

"As are the Hellfires themselves," Elic said. "You've been keeping company with them for what—two months now? I can't imagine how you've tolerated them for that long."

" 'Tisn't easy," she conceded. "They can be a tiresome bunch, with their rituals and their whips. But by throwing in my lot with them, I've been able to satisfy my cravings without drawing too much attention to myself. 'Tis no easy matter for one such as I to pass for human. I tend to stand out, and that can be a dangerous thing. In almost every culture I've encountered for the thousands of years I've been alive, a female who lives for the pleasures of the flesh is reviled. I've been driven from my home countless times. I've been beaten, stoned, flogged, even hanged."

Elic wrapped his arms around her, whispering her name.

"In most communities," she said, "I've two options. I can do what desperate females have always done, sell myself to any man with enough coin to pay for me. In that case, although I'm still held in contempt, I'm understood and generally tolerated. But it is a miserable existence. It eases my lust, but depletes my soul. In my homeland, I was worshipped. A temple was built in the city of Akkad to honor me as the goddess of the new moon."

"That disc of lapis on your anklet..."

She nodded. "A symbol of the new moon. I've worn it for over four thousand years. But those times are long gone. New deities have replaced the old—'tis the same everywhere. From goddess to whore," she said bitterly.

"And your other choice?" he asked. "Besides selling yourself?"

Laying her head against his smooth, hard chest, she said, "I can choose the man I want, and wait until nightfall, and steal into his bed while he sleeps. There is a *mashmashu* I can say, some words in the old tongue, that will allow me to control him after he awakens. I can prevent him from moving altogether if need be—or rather, he can move, but just slightly—and that's usually what I do. He's aware of what is happening, what I'm doing to him, but powerless to stop me—not that he'd want to even if he could. The *mashmashu* ensures that his pleasure will be extraordinary, far more so than he could experience through normal human coupling."

She had *mashmashus* for other purposes, too, ancient spells that could make a person feel things, or experience things, that defied the boundaries of reality—or rather, the reality that most humans were capable of comprehending. Rarely did she have cause to use such spells, but they were at her disposal should she require them.

"I can do something like that with my own ancient words," Elic said, "except that the person I'm taking can move and speak. But if I like, I can make it all seem like a dream."

"In my case, unfortunately," she said, "he is left entirely aware of what has transpired—and entirely able to identify me afterward. For that reason, I sometimes take the form of a woman he knows, though I'd rather not, because of the concentration it takes. I can even determine, by searching his mind, what his notion of the ideal lover might be, in terms of appearance and comportment, and become her. In those cases, he might choose to interpret it as a dream, but usually it's such a strong memory that he knows it really happened. Eventually I'll find myself labeled a succubus. Things took an especially ugly turn when the Roman Church decreed that females of my breed were in league with Satan. Being labeled a whore was nothing to being labeled a witch. I can survive any form of torture or execution except burning, which is, of course, how witches are dispatched."

"Or were," Elic said. "The witch mania seems to have pretty much run its course, thank God."

"Not quite. Three years ago, while I was traveling through Germany, I found myself rounded up along with two other women—innocent midwives who'd aroused the suspicions of the local *bürgers* by being just a bit too skilled in the healing arts. We were imprisoned in a village called Mühlbach, and sentenced to burn. They did burn the other two, poor things, but I escaped as they were building my pyre, by seducing my jailer. I fled to England. A woman can still be burned there for murdering her husband, but not for consorting with the Devil—or making it appear that she is by being too light in the heels. Of course, I still tended to attract a fair amount of attention, which was why I took up with the Hellfires once I discovered them. With them, I'm just another wanton among..."

Lili trailed off, staring through the doorway of the bathhouse into the darkness beyond. "Someone is walking this way," she said.

"Qui va là?" Elic called out.

"C'est moi," replied a brusque male voice as footsteps approached. *"Je vous avais recherché."*

" 'Tis my friend Darius," Elic told Lili. "He says he's been looking for me."

"The one who lives in the cave, yes?"

Elic nodded, his gaze lowering to her bare, albeit mostly submerged body. "I'll ask him to leave," he whispered.

"Don't be silly," she replied, amused but touched by his solicitude. "I'm hardly shy, and this *is* the entrance to his home."

"He doesn't generally come in this way," Elic said. "Too much risk of bumping into humans. There's another entrance hidden in the woods, closer to his chamber. He likes to use that."

"Elic?" A darkly handsome fellow in shirtsleeves stood at the other end of the pool, squinting into the mist until his gaze lit on Lili. "Ah." He backed up, schooling his expression, but not before she detected a grimace of disappointment at her presence in his friend's arms. "Lili. I—I beg your pardon. I didn't realize—"

"You know me?" she asked.

When he hesitated, Elic said, "Darius was in a more . . . feline mood when last you met."

"Ah, yes, that watchful little gray cat," Lili said. Darius's ancient and mysterious race, the djinn, were blessed with the ability to assume animal forms. The most powerful among them could even, it was said, make themselves invisible at will.

Darius, clearly taken aback by Elic's having revealed his shape-shifting powers to a presumed human, glared at his friend. "Elic, what the devil are you—"

"She's one of us," Elic told him.

Darius stared at her for a moment, then scowled at his friend. "You might have told me."

"I just did. Is anything wrong?" Elic asked him. "You seem a bit . . . out of sorts."

"You've no idea," Darius muttered. Taking in the two of them, curled up together in the water, he said, "I had a favor to ask of you, but I can see that you're . . . occupied, so—"

"Wait," said Elic as his friend turned to leave, his hands fisted at his sides. Excusing himself to Lili, he waded to the opposite end of the pool and asked quietly, "*Quelle faveur?*"

Crouching down so that he was at eye level with Elic, Darius glanced at Lili and whispered for a minute in French, his voice so low that she could make out only the occasional word or phrase . . . *belle et insatiable . . . elle veut deux hommes . . .*

"*Où est-elle?*" Elic said. *Where is she?*

"*Dans le cachot.*" *The dungeon.*

"*Le cachot?*"

"*Elle veut être là,*" Darius said tensely. *She wants to be there.* With another glance at Lili, he said, "*Mais si—*"

"*Non.*" Elic looked down, shaking his head disconsolately.

"C'est impossible," he said with a frustrated sigh. *"Je ne peux pas—pas avec Lili." I can't—not with Lili.*

"Oui, naturellement," Darius said soberly. *"Je suis désolé."*

"J'aurai besoin d'un condom," Elic said.

Darius shook his head, something like a smile banishing his grim expression just for a moment. *"Elle est stérile."*

"Stérile? C'est bon." Raking his hair back with both hands, Elic said tightly, *"Je vous rencontrerai là." I'll meet you there.*

"Merci, mon ami." Rising, Darius said to Lili, "I apologize for my foul mood, *mademoiselle.* 'Twas an honor and a pleasure to have made your acquaintance. Dare I hope your stay with us will be a lengthy one?"

"Would that it were so," she replied, "but the Hellfires are to depart tomorrow, and I with them."

"I am sorry to hear it. Perhaps you can visit us again. Until then"—he bowed—"*au revoir.*"

"Au revoir."

Elic continued gazing through the doorway for some time after his friend had disappeared into the darkness. Finally he turned to face her, but he didn't meet her eyes as he said, "I must leave."

"I know," she said. "You must release your seed." To some woman Darius had found, a woman who was "beautiful and insatiable," and who wanted two men.

"Lili." He crossed to her swiftly, banding his arms around her in an almost painful embrace, his face buried in her hair, his erection pressing rigidly into her stomach.

"I know, *khababu.*" She pressed her lips to his chest, his throat. "You have your destiny, just as I have mine."

"Stay with me tonight," he rasped. "Let me hold you in my arms, just for tonight."

"Yes. Of course."

"I live in the northeast tower, at the very top." He kissed her head, stroked her face. "Go there and wait for me. I shall join you as soon as I can."

Don't think about it, Lili told herself as she watched him striding back toward the chateau, his monk's robe flickering like a white flame in the darkness. *Don't think about* her, *whoever she is.* She was nothing to him, a mere vessel in which to relieve his lust.

A beautiful and insatiable vessel.

Don't think. Turning, Lili stretched out onto her back, suspended like a leaf on the surface of the warm, soothing water. *Just be.*

The sliver of moon in the center of the skylight—the symbol of all she once was, and would never be again—taunted Lili until she closed her eyes, whispering, "Just be... just be..."

Her mind floated along with her body, which drifted on the subtle current until her head just touched the edge of the pool nearest the entrance. She lay there, weightless and dreamy...

Until a pair of hands gently cupped her head.

"Elic?" Lili opened her eyes to find herself staring into the upside-down face of Anton Turek, kneeling over her at the edge of the pool, his eyes glowing red in the swirling mist.

"Your Abbot of the Day seems to have abandoned you," Turek said in a low, oddly sibilant voice. "You won't mind if I step in and take his place."

"Get away from me." Lili seized his wrists, thrashing in the water as she struggled to free herself from his grip.

He tightened his hands like a vise, canting her head back so that all she could see was his lurid gaze against that chalk-white skin. Leaning closer, he whispered something under his breath in his own language while stroking his thumbs over her forehead.

Lili opened her mouth to scream, but it was as if her throat had grown suddenly thick and useless. Her lungs heaved, her heart hammered, but not the slightest sound could she force from her mouth.

Her hands, still clasped around his wrists, felt strangely rubbery. She tried to tighten them so as to free herself from his grip, but nothing happened, hard as she strained. Her legs, equally unresponsive, sank like dead weight into the water.

"Now you know how it feels, *mein liebes,*" he said softly, almost tenderly, "to be immobilized as you immobilize your own prey. Paralysis—'tis your weapon of choice also, is it not?"

Her eyes must have betrayed her alarm, because he said, "Oh yes, I know all about you. I know we are two of a kind, you and I. I know that we belong together."

His lips drew back, revealing, in lieu of the ivory dental bridge he normally wore, a mouthful of yellowish stumps—save for the pair of narrow little incisors flanking his two front teeth, which curved into needle-sharp points, like the fangs of a snake.

"And soon," he said, "we shall *be* together, for all eternity. *Jetzt schlaf.*" He touched his lips, cool and dry, to her forehead, inciting a strange, thrumming pressure in her skull. A white hiss filled her ears; her eyes drifted shut.

She fell, grasping and clawing, into oblivion.

Eight

THANK GOD, thought Charlotte as she heard the key turn in the door. Darius hadn't been gone all that long, really—fifteen or twenty minutes—but it had felt much longer, with her stretched out on this rack, her limbs pulled taut, nipples smarting with every breath. And, of course, there'd been the fear that he would never return—that she would languish here, bound to this infernal machine until she'd given up the ghost. They would find her months from now, or years—just her skeleton, two little thumbscrews, that damned pear, and a white silk cravat—and wonder how the devil she'd gotten herself in such a fix.

That slap had shocked her more than hurt her, unlike the other punishments he'd dealt out, which had been administered with a ruthless but cool dispassion. The slap had been furious, impulsive, the act of a man whose self-control was slipping.

Darius entered the chamber, locking the door behind him. He regarded her in weighty silence for a moment before approaching. She was disquieted by the look in his eyes—black and brooding, almost murderous, yet with a hint of uncertainty that made him seem, if anything, even more dangerous.

He removed the thumbscrews from her nipples and the loops of rope from her wrists and ankles and ordered her to follow him to the rear of the dungeon, and to bring the cravat with her. She hastily shook out arms and legs and rubbed her rope-burned wrists—her stockings had protected her ankles—then assumed his prescribed stance and did as she'd been told.

The bay to which he led her was that which housed the whipping bench. Charlotte wondered for a moment whether he intended to use it again, until he told her to move it back into its corner. "And fluff up the straw beneath it," he said, an order that Charlotte found baffling, but obeyed without comment.

When she turned back around, she found him maneuvering a pair of iron manacles hanging by chains from the ceiling; he was lowering them, she saw.

"Give me that," he said, indicating the cravat.

Using his teeth, he tore the scarf into two strips, which he wrapped around her abraded wrists, tying them off like bandages.

She thanked him automatically, only to silently curse herself for disregarding, yet again, his admonition against talking.

Darius closed his eyes and shook his head, jaw outthrust, hands curling into fists, as if it were all he could do to keep from throttling her. "Did I say you could speak?" he said in a quietly menacing tone.

"I . . . I just—"

"Goddamn it, Charlotte!" His fury was confoundingly real, if the livid streaks staining his cheekbones were any indication. "The rules haven't changed, yet you persist in flouting them, like the cosseted, willful little strum you are. And as for these"—he nodded toward her silk-swathed wrists—"I assure you your comfort is the least of my concern—quite the contrary. It's just that these manacles were forged for a man, and I don't want your hands slipping through."

Raising first her right arm, then her left, he closed the iron loops around her wrists, locked them, and pocketed the key.

This isn't so bad, she thought. To be sure, she could do without the stretching of her arms after all that time on the rack, but at least she could turn her body, move her legs.

As if he'd read her mind and was hellbent on subjecting her to the maximum possible suffering, Darius adjusted the height of the manacles so that only the pointy little toes of her brocade shoes touched the floor. He stalked away wordlessly, returning a minute later with a padlock in one hand and a device in the other that she took for a horse's bit until he came closer and she got a good look at it. It was a curved strip of iron with chains dangling from either end and a rather phallic knob in the middle.

"Open your mouth." He shoved in the knob, wrapped the chains around the nape of her neck, beneath her braid, and locked them together—a bit more snugly, she thought, than was strictly necessary. The knob, which was fatter at the tip than at the base, didn't just compress her tongue; it filled her mouth so completely that she couldn't even breathe through it, much less produce any noise.

"Since you've proven incapable of holding your tongue on your own," he said, "the iron gag shall do it for you. 'Tis a most effective apparatus, very popular among inquisitors for its ability to block out even the most anguished screams."

There came a rusty rattling from the other end of the dungeon as someone tried to open the door, followed by the pounding of a fist. Through the thick oak slab came a man's voice. "Darius?"

Panicked, Charlotte tried to meet Darius's gaze, but he was already striding toward the door. She craned her neck to watch him, but the mammoth columns blocked her view as he unlocked the door and, to her astonished dismay, said, "*Entrez.*"

"*Où est-elle?*" asked the intruder. *Where is she?*

Dear God, thought Charlotte as two pairs of footsteps

headed her way. *It can't be.* He'd invited someone else down here to witness her abuse and humiliation at his hands. Her "covenant" was with Darius and Darius alone. How could he? How *dare* he?

Her dismay was compounded when the two men came into view and she recognized their visitor as Elic, the friend of Madame des Ombres who'd finagled Sir Francis into naming him Abbot of the Day. Most of the "monks" looked a bit foolish in those white silk robes, but Elic, with his height, his bearing, and his extraordinary beauty, looked positively magnificent. He was one of those men who exuded masculine sensuality, a true devotee of women who, she suspected, could fuck like a stallion while whispering the kind of heartfelt endearments every female was born wanting to hear. Charlotte had entertained the hope, before her self-imposed exile from the Hellfires earlier this evening—the very fervent hope—that she could capture Elic's eye during the banquet and discover firsthand just how hot-blooded he was beneath that cool Nordic exterior. But now...

To have this man with whom she was more than a little besotted see her like this, naked, gagged, and trussed to the ceiling... oh, and that blasted pear!

Cheeks scalding, she turned her face away as the two men came to stand before her.

"Eyes forward," Darius snapped.

She hesitated.

He seized her chin in a painful grip and wrenched her head around to face them. "Take care, Charlotte," he warned. "I am in no mood to tolerate defiance. Be accommodating to our guest, or you shall suffer the consequences. You have made my friend's acquaintance already, yes?"

"All too briefly. Lady Somerhurst." Elic bowed, an act of common courtesy that struck her as incongruous, bizarre even, given the situation; yet she found a measure of comfort in the gesture. "My friend can be a bear, I know," he said with a conspiratorial little smile, "most especially when he is of a choleric disposition, as now. Perhaps my presence here can lighten the atmosphere a bit."

With a scornful little roll of the eyes, Darius said, "If you are done playing the gallant, perhaps you'd care to inspect my little gift, and tell me if it is to your liking."

Darius gestured for Elic to take a turn around Charlotte, which he did. He paused behind her. She felt a little tremor deep within her as he fiddled with the knob of the steel pear, the stimulus sending pulses of arousal into her quim. "You've been a busy fellow," he told his friend.

Darius sighed. "She's very demanding."

She was demanding? Was it not he who was lord and master in this unholy liaison? A stinging retort was on the tip of her tongue. Perhaps it was best, after all, that she was gagged.

"Did you shave her?" Elic asked.

"She came to me that way. Do you like it?"

"It suits her."

A pair of unfamiliar hands—long-fingered, warm, and ever so slightly rough—stroked her backside almost reverently. "*Parfait,*" Elic murmured. "Has she ever been shared?" he asked as he circled her, admiring and caressing.

Shared? Did he mean at the same time? wondered Charlotte, heart skittering. Two men at once?

"Never," replied Darius, who remained behind her, pinching and kneading her arse. "But she craves it more than anything else. Don't you, my pet?" He spanked her hard when she didn't respond quickly enough to suit him. "*Don't you?*"

She nodded, thinking, *How could he know that?* She'd never told him, never even hinted at it. From the beginning, it was as if he were privy to her most secret and shameful longings, most especially her need to be punished for Nat's death.

The pear shifted inside her again, this time sliding out a bit, then back in, easily because of its sheen of oil and how accustomed she'd grown to its unyielding presence within her. Darius pushed it in and out, in and out, slowly, turning and twisting, as if readying her for what was to come.

Two men at once. She'd had offers before, tempting offers, which she'd rejected from fear that the pain would outweigh the pleasure. Now, with that fear assuaged, she trembled in anticipation.

Standing in front of her now, Elic took her breasts in his hands and squeezed them gently. She started when he thumbed her nipples, which the thumbscrews had left distended and keenly sensitive.

He stepped closer, his erection nudging her through his robe as he tilted her face up and lightly kissed her cheek. "You want this?" he whispered in her ear, too softly for Darius to hear.

She nodded.

"All of it?" He glanced at the gag, the manacles.

She nodded again.

He smoothed a hand downward over her belly, sliding a finger into her sex as if to confirm the extent of her willingness. A soft little hum of pleasure rose from his throat upon finding her wet and ready. He stroked her with just the right touch—deep but soft, in a deliciously unhurried rhythm. So raw and hot was her flesh there, thanks to the cantharides, that every brush of his fingertips kindled a little firestorm of pleasure. She widened her legs as best she could, poised as she was on the tips of her toes, and rocked into the caress, feeling the pleasure rising, rising...

"Quite a sweet little notch she's got there," said Darius. "Surprisingly snug, considering how much company it must have entertained over the years. She's wonderfully fuckable, comes explosively. *Uses promptos facit,* eh?" Turning his head, he purred a translation into her ear, "Practice makes perfect."

Charlotte glanced at him, wanting to say, *My Latin's probably better than yours, you arrogant bloody bastard.* Good thing she was gagged; God knows how he would have reacted to that, in his present surly humor. He'd changed since they'd begun this dark adventure. In the beginning, he was commanding, but in a quiet, restrained way, a way that inspired trust and confidence—else she never would have put herself in his hands as she did. In the interim, though, for reasons Charlotte couldn't fathom, his attitude toward her had taken on an angry, bullying edge. He'd become high-strung, belligerent. With any luck, Elic's presence here would help to keep his friend on his bearings.

She felt Darius's arm brush against her as he unbuttoned his trousers. He pulled out the pear and tossed it aside, provoking a gasp from Charlotte and a sudden, aching emptiness. "Lift her up for me," he told Elic.

Elic did so, saying, "Wrap your legs 'round my waist, my lady. Aye, that's it."

She felt Darius's fingers in the cleft of her arse, and then a hard pressure as he positioned the head of his cock where the pear had been. Widening his stance as if to brace himself for the effort, he gripped her hips and drove in, filling her in one slick, groaning thrust.

She shuddered—not from pain, precisely, more from shock at such swift and absolute impalement where she was least accustomed to it. He felt thick and huge inside her, stretching her open, his balls pressed right up against her.

"Are you all right?" Elic asked her.

"She's fine." Darius reached between Charlotte and Elic with both hands, spreading her sex lips as he crooked a finger into her quim. It clenched reflexively, a telltale sign of the depth of her arousal. "Oh, yes, more than fine. It's what she's been dreaming of, a nice, hard cock buried deep in her ass, and another in this red-hot little cunny. Isn't that right, *my lady*?"

God help her, she nodded, her head rolling back against his shoulder. Raising his hands to her breasts, Darius rubbed her sex juices onto her inflamed nipples, plucking and teasing. Gripping Charlotte's legs, still banded around his waist, Elic rubbed against her, his silken robe as liquid smooth as a layer of oil between his sex and hers. She writhed deliriously, causing Darius's cock to slip in and out of her with a lubricious friction that felt like nothing else she'd ever experienced.

Elic's breath grew hectic as he ground against her, his gaze unfocused. "Hold her," he told his friend.

Darius curled his hands under her thighs, spreading her legs wide open. He flexed his hips, thrusting her own hips forward, her own naked, flushed sex, as if in offering to his friend.

Elic fumbled with the hooks of his robe, swore under his breath and yanked it open with both hands. He had the physique of a young god, lean and muscular, his cock rearing up sleek and hard and ready. He moaned as if in an agony of lust as he entered her, pausing halfway to close his eyes and hiss something in a language unfamiliar to Charlotte, not French; it sounded Scandinavian. His cock felt almost impossibly hard, as if there were a rod of steel beneath its taut, shiny-smooth skin. Just the sight of it, wedged half-buried in her slit, made her feel as if she might spend at any moment.

Elic pressed in another inch or so, arms quivering. "Are you all right?" he asked her, a little breathlessly. "It's not too—"

"God's bones," growled Darius.

Charlotte nodded reassuringly to Elic, whereupon he clasped her waist and sheathed himself fully. He stood unmoving for a moment, as did Darius, letting her savor the feeling of being penetrated by two men. She felt incredibly full, utterly stuffed; the sense of possession was absolute, even more so than she'd imagined.

"Mind you don't spend till we do," said Darius as he withdrew his cock and shoved it back in. "Else you get the whip."

Elic muttered some exasperated imprecation under his breath, but he let it go.

Both men started thrusting then, falling into the same measured rhythm, Elic clutching Charlotte's waist, Darius her hips as she dangled like meat from the ceiling. She closed her eyes and gave herself over to the bliss of two cocks stroking her tingling-hot flesh from within—and stroking each other, as well, for how could each man not feel the presence of the other inside her?

Their thrusts grew ever swifter and more erratic. It was utterly intoxicating—two hard male bodies, grinding and pumping, two men clutching, panting, groaning...

Don't spend, Charlotte told herself, even as she writhed in mindless pleasure, feeling the inevitable approach of a climax she couldn't hope to forestall. She bit her lip as it gathered, thinking perhaps, if she kept still and didn't cry out, he wouldn't know. But so jolting were the spasms, in her ass as well as her quim, that her whole body rocked with them.

Both men stilled for one long, rigid, trembling moment. Darius cursed; Elic roared. Then came the extraordinary sensation of not one, but two cocks jerking and sputtering inside her amid a chorus of hoarse masculine groans.

Elic, breathless and damp with sweat, held her with shaking arms as Darius slid his cock from her ass a bit too swiftly for comfort. "Fucking little bitch," he growled as he rebuttoned his trousers.

"Easy, Darius," cautioned Elic as he eased himself out of her and gently lowered her legs. "She enjoyed it, same as we did, and why not? Why on earth should you—"

"*Why are you standing up for her?*" Darius bellowed at his friend. "Greedy little cunt, I *told* her to wait for us. She claims she wants to obey, she wants to bow to my will, but I'm bloody hard-pressed to believe it."

"Look, friend," Elic said evenly. "You're not yourself tonight. You and I both know why. This thing has gotten its claws into you." Gripping Darius's shoulder, he said, "You need to step back and look at things from a—"

"Don't!" Darius flung Elic's arm away, his face darkening, veins bulging on his neck, his forehead. "Don't tell me what I need to do. I know what I need to do." Stalking past Charlotte to the wall of whips behind her, he said, "You can stay and watch, or you can leave. I suggest you watch. Then you'll see how things really are. You'll see her moaning with every stroke—and not because she wants me to stop—quite the opposite. Nothing excites her like a good, hard lashing. Isn't that right, Charlotte? Tell him."

Elic met her gaze. She hesitated, then looked away, nodding.

"You're sure?" he asked quietly.

Another nod.

Dragging a hand through his hair, Elic said, "Very well, then." He bowed, saying, "I thank you, my lady, for indulging me this evening. I wish you well."

He walked away, rehooking his robe. Charlotte heard the door creak open, but she didn't hear it close.

"This'll serve you right," said Darius as he came up behind her. She heard a metallic rattling, which puzzled her for a moment until she realized what he'd taken down from the wall: the chain whip.

Charlotte managed just one frenzied shake of the head when the first blow struck, followed swiftly by a second, a third, a fourth . . . Pain slashed at her as she twisted and flailed—real, searing, bone-deep pain, the shock of it so blinding that for a moment, she couldn't even scream, and when she tried to, the gag rendered her mute.

God, help me, she prayed as blood ran from her ravaged back. *I don't deserve it, but have mercy, please . . .*

"Stop! Jesus, stop!" shouted a man. Elic?

He hadn't left after all, Charlotte thought as her legs gave out and her head slumped forward. Uneasy, he'd paused in the doorway, just long enough.

There came the sounds of a scuffle, Elic screaming, "Look at her! For God's sake, look what you've done."

Then a different voice—Darius's voice, low, stunned—saying, "Christ. Oh, my God."

"Help me get her down from here."

"Oh, my God," said Darius as the blood drained from Charlotte's head and the world swam from gray to black to nothingness. "Charlotte. Oh, my God. Oh, my God."

Nine

*F*INALLY, THOUGHT Anton Turek as he stood back to admire the sight of Ilutu-Lili bound and at his disposal, a sacrificial offering at the mercy of his whims.

After rendering her insensible, he'd wrapped her in her veil and carried her through the cave to the so-called *Cella,* a recess off the main passage that had been utilized, in primitive times, as a place of worship. Little wonder it had been chosen for that purpose, given the natural grandeur of its appearance. The mouth of the spacious alcove was rimmed in mineral icicles that had grown down from above and up from below. Some had merged to form columns in shades of cobalt, crimson, and orange that shimmered in the light from a pair of torches flanking the imposing entryway. Not torches of the primitive variety, Turek was pleased to note, but iron stanchions topped with round, cagelike cressets stuffed with flaming fuel—most likely pitch-soaked pine. They would burn a good long while without needing to be tended, which reduced the risk of unwanted company before Turek had finished with Lili.

Just inside ran the stream that meandered through the lower levels of the cave on its way out to the bathhouse. In a fortuitous fluke of nature, it was spanned by a bridge of rock with a relatively flat, walkable surface, enabling one to enter the *Cella* without wading through knee-deep water. To the right, the floor dipped into a shallow depression lined with a two-handled, tarnished bronze bowl that had been hammered to fit it perfectly; firewood and kindling were piled up in tall stacks against the wall next to a crook-shaped iron poker hanging from a hook in the stone. Overhead, in the center of the alcove's high, domed roof, was a vertical shaft, one of several in the labyrinthine cave that served as natural chimneys. This one, Turek had been told, terminated in a wooded crevasse so deep in the craggy, heavily treed mountain overhead that any smoke issuing from it dissipated long before it was ever seen.

The focal point of the *Cella* was an ancient effigy that loomed against the back wall between a pair of flickering torches—cressets again, atop tall iron spikes jammed into cracks in the bedrock floor. Some ten feet tall, the statue had been carved, along with the wide platform on which it stood, of the same dark volcanic rock from which most everything in this valley, save the bathhouse, was constructed. Its craftsmanship was simplistic to the point of crudeness, with a stylized face that put Turek in mind of a mask, each upraised arm bearing a cup to signify fecundity. There were two breastlike mounds on the chest, as well as a phallic protuberance rising between the massive legs. The hermaphroditic anatomy, in concert with the name neatly inscribed on the front of the platform, DVSIVÆSVS, suggested to Turek that this supposed fertility god had, in fact, been a dusios. Curiously, there was a second inscription carved—or rather, scratched—atop the first, but it was written in an alphabet Turek had never seen before.

Dusivæsus wore five rust-encrusted iron torques, one around each ankle and wrist, with the largest encircling his neck. The latter at first glance looked to represent a snake swallowing its own tail. On closer inspection, the serpent's mouth more closely resembled a yawning vagina, its half-consumed tail the head of a penis. Dangling from the neck torque was the pair of steel cuffs Turek had brought with him, locked snugly around the wrists of Ilutu-Lili.

Turek had stripped off Lili's veil and tethered her naked to the statue with her arms stretched overhead and her feet resting between those of Dusivæsus, the height of the platform putting her and Turek at eye level—or so they would have been, but for the way her head hung down, ropes of damp black hair cloaking her like a mantle. Turek lifted her chin, pushing the hair aside to admire that striking face and lush body, gold-sheened in the flickering torchlight. He cupped a breast, squeezing the warm, resilient flesh until she flinched, a kittenish little growl of distress rising from her throat.

His stomach responded with a grind of hunger; it had been days since he'd fed.

"*Wecken sie.* Wake up."

She stirred groggily, her eyelids fluttering. "What . . . ?"

"Naptime is over, my dear. We've much to accomplish this evening."

Lili blinked at him, her eyes—those dark, dreamy, painfully beautiful eyes—widening as she took in his cool smile, the cavernous *Cella,* the stone figure to which she was trussed like a flayed lamb in a butcher's shop. She stood up straight, yanking at the cuffs with a clatter of steel against iron.

Turek chuckled as she filled her lungs with air. "Go ahead, my dear. We're far too deep in this cave for anyone to hear you, but I find the sound of a woman's screams quite stirring to the senses."

"Bastard," she said in a voice quavering with outrage. "*Monster.*"

"Correct on both counts," he said. "But what particular breed of monster, eh? Have you managed to sort that out?"

Her gaze lit on his mouth, no doubt recalling the fangs he'd given her a good look at earlier. "Strigoi?"

He shook his head. "They are close relations, the Strigoi, but I am, in fact, an Upír of Carpathian lineage—the most venerable of the vampyric lines, if I do say so."

She addressed him with a frank contempt he couldn't help but admire, given her predicament. "A bloodsucker, imagining himself venerable. It's almost laughable."

"Ah, but you are not laughing, are you? You know, I think, why I have brought you here, what I have in mind for you."

"I assume you mean to feed from me. Go to it, then." She turned her head and raised her chin to bare the left side of her neck in a bold invitation that stole Turek's breath. Never before had his prey willingly volunteered to be taken. The gesture excited him in a far more visceral way than did mere hunger. His spine bristled as the little hairs all along it stood on end; a spasm quivered through his cock.

He stepped closer to brush his fingertips ever so lightly along her throat, feeling the carotid pulsing seductively just beneath the surface. She closed her eyes, waiting.

"Unafraid, are you?" Leaning forward, he glided the sensitive tip of his tongue along the artery's path, reveling in the hot thrum of blood beneath the flesh. "A curious reaction," he said. "Or it would be, if you were human."

She grew very still.

He stepped up onto the platform, seized her head with both hands and raised it, forcing her to look him in the eye. "I could suck you dry and leave you for dead, and within hours your veins would be humming with fresh blood, the color would blossom once again upon your cheeks, and you would arise and walk away, laughing at me. Is that not true, my sweet, devious little succubus?"

She held his gaze unblinkingly.

"I must admit," he said, "I failed to see through you when

you first joined us. Just another dasher who can't keep her legs together, that's what I took you for. I'd intended to use you as I use your sisters in harlotry at the first convenient opportunity."

"By knocking me senseless with gin, then feeding on me as you vent your lust," she said. "I'd have awakened in the morning too battered and bitten to notice the puncture wounds on my throat—"

"Or they may very well have been here," he said, reaching up to stroke her inner wrist. "Or here." He licked the inside of her elbow, feeling her shiver from the sensation. "Or even here," he added, fondling the aureola around her left nipple. "It can actually take very little to satisfy me if my hunger has been recently slaked, and I do love to suckle at a ripe breast from time to time."

"And if your hunger hasn't been slaked?" she asked. "If you're ravenous?"

"Do I drain my prey to the point of death?" He shrugged negligently. "More often than not, if I'm feeling peckish, but never with those whose demise would attract untoward attention. The nuns of the Order of St. Francis are quite secure in that regard, I assure you."

"A murderer who only kills when he doesn't think he'll be caught is still a murderer," she said. "How many have you butchered? Hundreds? Thousands?"

"Just as humans feed on the lower beasts, so vampyres feed on humans. 'Tis the natural order, the way of the world. I must say, I'm surprised to find you so sentimental about the welfare of humanfolk. After all, you've a bit of the vampyre in you already, no? You're a creature of dark passions and terrible, ungovernable hungers, as am I. We are really much the same, the succubus and the Upír—both predators seeking our own particular sustenance, which we derive from humans—willing or unwilling. We both do our prowling at night, for the most part. We are both singleminded in the pursuit of our prey. And we are both susceptible to the same means of destruction—immolation—which makes me suspect that your race and mine are perhaps more closely related than one would think."

"How long have you known what I am?" she asked.

"It came to me gradually, from observing you. You're quite the debauchee, to be sure, but not like the others. Their carnal appetites are juvenile and easily gratified, whereas it became clear over time that yours . . ." Turek slid a hand down her belly to brush the very edge of her sex, smiling to himself as she cringed away from his touch. "Yours are as deep as the night, dark, complicated, inexorable. My suspicions about you, about what you might be, came to fruition when you took a fancy to that handsome young vicar who showed up without warning during our weekend at Bute's country house last month. His nephew, was it? Painfully earnest, went on at some length about the poor 'unfortunates' selling themselves on the streets of St. Giles and Whitechapel, and our obligation to rescue them from their lives of sin. Joseph, I think his name was."

"Josiah," Lili said quietly.

"I followed you that night when you slipped upstairs to his bedchamber and—"

"Impossible," she said. " 'Twas the middle of the night, and there was no one about. I was very careful not to be seen."

"I followed you from outside the house, crawling along the brick walls while tracking your movements from within. I watched through young Josiah's window as you crept into his bed and whispered the words that rendered him immobile while you fucked him senseless. Lucky fellow, I thought, falling victim to the likes of you. Gets to eat his cake and have his virtue. He couldn't move, but he did manage a few halting words now and then. He called you . . . Eliza, was it?"

With a sigh, Lili said, "She's his housekeeper's daughter. He's infatuated with her."

"An infatuation the upstanding reverend would never stoop to act upon, of course—but he might dream about her, yes? About her coming to his bed and doing things to him, dark, bestial things he'd never imagined in that unsullied mind of his. 'Twas a revelation, Lili, watching you entice him, over and over again, into a frenzy of lust. The way you used your hands, so slowly and softly at first, then your tongue and teeth, that juicy peach from the fruit bowl, the knotted scarf, the candle . . . Ah, and the things you whispered in his ear to rouse his passions . . . Bless me if it wasn't the most exquisite filth I'd ever heard. More than once, I thought the poor boy might die of apoplexy, the way he shook and panted while you kept him hovering on the edge, his face gone purple, fingers clawing at the sheets. How many times did he come off, do you recall? Five? Six? And each time just as violently as the first."

Lili made no response to that.

"That was when I grasped what you were and resolved to possess you," Turek said as he caressed her face, her throat. "Not just for one night of casual bloodfucking, but wholly, and forever."

"You're mad."

"I'm actually quite rational, as vampyres go." Turek rubbed his thumb firmly along her right carotid to stimulate and plump it, making it easier to locate and pierce. "We incline toward lunacy, sad to say. Not the Upír so much, but the others."

He tilted her face to expose the side of her neck, his fangs prickling as the little nerves there prepared to draw blood up through the conduits in his palate to his own depleted vessels. Bending his head, he chose a spot high on her neck where the artery was likely to be closest to the surface, and planted a soft, preliminary kiss there.

Lili hitched in a breath at the first light touch of his fangs against her skin. Not so blasé now at the prospect of being fed upon, she twisted and writhed, wresting her head from his grasp.

"Fight me all you want, my dear. I rather fancy it." Grabbing a fistful of her hair, Turek jerked her head aside and pierced her throat.

She wrestled and kicked, crying out hoarsely as he worked his fangs through the shallow muscle, deftly puncturing the carotid sheath and the artery itself while taking care not to nick the jugular. So violent were her struggles that he was forced to unhinge his jaw and latch on hard to her throat, using his entire mouth—not a technique he liked to employ on such a beauty, given the unsightly bruising and teeth marks that would result, but with prey this frantic, it was the only way to keep his fangs seated. He lifted her legs to either side of him, both to thwart those painful kicks and to raise her to a more convenient height so that he wouldn't have to feed hunched over.

Lili's blood ran very warm, with a distinctive essence redolent of rainwater and figs. Turek moaned deep in his throat as he siphoned it, his fangs tickling as it pumped through them, gums pulsing. Like a nursing babe, he worked his tongue in a firm, steady rhythm so as to encourage the flow. Bracing his legs, he strengthened his grip on Lili as she strained vainly but heroically against the steel cuffs and the weight of his body crushing her to the statue.

Yes. Oh, here it comes... Lili's blood percolated through Turek's brain in a rush of pinpricks that made him feel weightless, exhilarated, his vision stained red, heart thudding in his ears. His hunger faded, replaced by the intoxicating bliss of fulfillment as the crimson nectar flooded his tissues and organs, infusing them with blessed nourishment. His cock and nipples grew erect, tingling at the surge of fresh blood.

As Lili's veins emptied, rendering her weaker and weaker, her struggles gradually devolved into a feeble, desperate writhing. Though she was, by now, too delirious to realize it, her languid movements as Turek stood pressed into the cradle of her thighs, feasting on her, only served to stoke his carnal excitement, his cock rising like a curved spike against his belly.

How tempting it would be to hammer himself into her now, as he fed on her, he feverish with lust and fresh blood, she too frail to resist him but knowing what was happening, knowing he could fuck her at will and that she, the proud goddess who'd spurned him for weeks, was powerless to stop him. Perhaps, given her succubitic nature, he could even make her share in his pleasure, despite herself. How he longed to feel the cool and indifferent Ilutu-Lili moaning and bucking in his arms, like any hot-cunted wench getting a good grind.

But how much better it would be, how utterly rapturous, to wait until he'd drunk his fill, then take her as she drank from *him.* To be inside a female undergoing vampyric conversion was always marvelous, sexual passion imparting a sharp, breathless intensity to the transformational process.

Of course, with female follets—those rare ones who were not only willing but able to be converted, for some were immune—the results were unpredictable and often unsatisfying. Some members of the faerie races, especially the sheltered and naive forest types, found the experience so overwhelming that, like infants, they would close their eyes and sleep through the entire thing. Skoggra and their first cousins, wood-wives—delicate and lovely despite their razorlike claws—tended to lose control, leaving Turek slashed to ribbons. Even worse were the rusalki of Turek's homeland. While splendid fucks, they were so unrelentingly vicious—toward him as well as toward their prey—that he'd all but given up trying to turn them.

Ah, but succubi... No claws, no killer instinct, no tiresome naiveté, just an all-consuming, inexhaustible hunger for the joys of the flesh. To screw a succubus while she underwent the change was sheer ecstasy, in large measure because her pleasure fed his, and vice versa. He felt it all as if it were happening to him—the thrill of penetration, the tang of hot blood, the synchronous pounding of their hearts with every sex-thrust, the woozy euphoria as their life forces mingled, recasting her bodily humors in a new mold, that of the noblest of predators... the Upír.

The succubus occupied, in Turek's estimation, a unique and lofty position in the distaff pantheon of follets—and Ilutu-Lili, with her moonlit beauty, her lush sensuality and keen mind, was the de facto queen of her race. They belonged together, she and

Turek. She didn't realize it yet, of course, but she would, once she'd shared his lifeblood and become as he was.

Through the blood-haze that held Turek in its thrall, he became dimly aware that Lili had grown heavy and limp in his arms. *Scheisse.* Lost in his reverie, he'd overfed. Were she human, she would be on the verge of death, if not lifeless already. He carefully extracted his fangs, unlatched his teeth from her flesh, and snapped his jaw back into place.

Her neck bore the imprint of his bite, so badly contused that his fang marks were all but invisible amid the purpling wound—or so they would have been but for the blood trickling from the pair of pinhead-size punctures, which Turek instinctively licked.

He lowered Lili's legs and stepped down from the platform. She hung slackly in her wrist cuffs, head slumped down. Pushing her hair off her face, he leaned her head against Dusivæsus's right breast. "*Wecken sie.*" He underscored the command with two sharp slaps on the cheek. "Come, my dear. You must feed now."

She muttered something incoherent.

"You'll feel better once you've got some fresh blood in you. Just a sip," he said in response to her drowsy look of disgust. "A drop, even. One drop of my blood is all it will take, one warm, sweet, miraculous little drop—and then you shall become as I am. But you must drink it of your own free will, knowing the outcome and accepting it, for the conversion to take effect."

Lili stared at him through heavy-lidded eyes, shook her head blearily. "Never."

It was remarkable that she could communicate at all, considering how much blood he'd drained. She was recovering with astonishing speed even for an immortal—just that much more evidence that Ilutu-Lili was an extraordinary being, worthy to take her place at his side until the end of time.

"Why do you suppose I went to the trouble of bringing you

here?" he asked. "Were it a simple matter of hunger, I'd have chosen one of the others." Taking her face in his hands, he said, with genuine feeling, "I don't just want your blood, Lili. I want *you.* I need you. I've been alone far too long, for my entire existence as an Upír."

"H-how long?" she managed.

She was probably stalling for time, hoping to figure out a way to free herself from his clutches. Still, why shouldn't she know something of his past, if they were truly destined to share eternity together?

He said, "I was born—as a human—in Prague in 1329, and I became an Upír in June of 1348, while studying to be a physician at the University of Bologna. So next month will mark the four hundred first anniversary of my vampyric conversion."

"A *physician*? You?"

"'Twas that or the priesthood. I wanted to help people," he said with a sardonic smile. "I settled on medicine because it didn't require a vow of celibacy. Even in my altruistic youth, I knew my limits."

"How... Why...?"

"Why did I trade in medicine for vampyrism? 'Twas the Black Death—it ravaged Italy that year. I tried to treat the poor bastards who'd been struck down, thinking surely God would keep me well so that I could continue His work. He had other ideas, though. One morning I awoke seething with fever, my hands and feet gone black, blood dripping from my mouth. I realized I'd be dead by nightfall. I knew a woman, Galiana Solsa—somewhat older than I, but dazzling, brilliant, reckless. She exuded danger like an aphrodisiac."

"She was a vampyre?"

"So she'd told me."

"She *told* you? Wasn't that risky?"

"We'd had a liaison some months before, very brief, but very impassioned. She'd wanted to turn me. She told me I could live forever if I were only willing to, in her words, harvest humans rather than healing them. I thought she was mad—literally. I thought, 'Dear God, I'm in love with a gibbering lunatic.' "

"You loved her?"

Turek looked away with a studiously blasé shrug, wishing he'd had the presence of mind not to blurt that out. "I was nineteen, and she was magnificent—or so I'd thought until she started in about the harvesting and so forth. I ended the affair, much to her sputtering rage, and threw myself into my schooling—until the morning I woke up dying. I knew no surgeon could help me, so in desperation, I sent for Galiana. She scoffed at me as I lay there vomiting and shaking and oozing blood, all the while pleading for her to turn me. She told me I'd made my bed, that I ought to have taken her up on her offer when I had the chance, that sort of thing. 'Twasn't till I was on the verge of death that she finally turned me. She'd intended to all along, of course—just having a bit of fun at my expense, which I suppose she was entitled to."

"Did you go back to being lovers?" Lili asked.

"God, no. She was much too vexed at me for having cast her aside. There's been no one since her, no one I've thought of as a lover, certainly, nor even a mistress."

"What about friends?" she asked.

"Vampyres don't form friendships easily, and humans are for feeding and fucking. No, as I say, I've been alone for four centuries."

A hint of something that might have been pity shadowed Lili's eyes for a fleeting moment, or perhaps it was just a fancy of Turek's imagination.

"And you," he said, "you've been alone, too, no? Roaming the earth like a gypsy, trying desperately to conceal your true self, to pass for human. But you aren't human. You're different, Lili. You're better than them, a higher being, an immortal—a goddess."

"Not anymore," she said.

"A succubus, then."

"A succubus," she agreed. "But not a bloodsucker. Not a murderer. I'd rather die than become what you are."

"Such pedestrian platitudes are beneath you, my dear," said Turek as he rolled up the right sleeve of his robe. "I changed my tune, and I wager you will, too. And I think you'll be surprised at how readily you take to the vampyric way of life. Before this night is through, you'll be reveling in it. You will prey on humans to appease not just your lust, but your hunger as well. Yes, you will kill them, time and time again, and you will feel not a moment's remorse. We will prey on them together, you and I, sharing our quarry as we share all else. We will savor their blood as if it were the sweetest wine. But first you must savor mine."

Turek raised his right wrist to his mouth and pierced one of the fat blue veins just beneath the surface of the skin, using the very tips of his fangs. Withdrawing them, he watched two slender red ribbons emerge from the minuscule punctures to crawl around his wrist like twin bracelets.

"One drop." Turek offered his blood-banded wrist to Lili, who turned her head, her lips pressed tightly together. He grabbed her jaw and forced her to face him. "One tiny lick—that is all it will take to initiate the change."

Eyeing him with revulsion, she said, "You *are* mad if you imagine that I would ever choose to become like you. You fancy yourself godlike, but to me, you're just some vile little bloodsucking insect—a mosquito with delusions of magnificence."

"You are testing my patience," he said between clenched teeth, his grip tightening on her jaw.

"No, not a mosquito," she said, her voice frosting over with contempt. "They at least have wings. You're more of a louse, I'd say, or perhaps a bedbug, scuttling about in the dark, antennae twitching at the scent of blood..."

He cuffed her, whipping his palm hard across her face, which struck the statue with a dull crack of skull against stone. "*Blöde Fotze,*" he spat out. "*Dumpfbacke.* You asked for that."

"Ah, yes," she said as she looked up at him, ugly abrasions

marring her forehead and cheek. "That's what bullies always tell themselves, especially bullies who like to hit women. If this is the kind of treatment I can expect from you, why on earth would I want to spend the rest of eternity at your side?"

"Things will be different after you've gone through the change," he said, "very different. You'll be like me. We'll understand each other. We'll be *part* of each other, sharing everything—our bodies, our prey, our very souls."

"I'll get to share my soul with the likes of you?" she asked with a little smirk that made Turek's hackles quiver. "That can't honestly be your best argument."

Yet, to Turek's dismay, it was. The enticement he usually employed to woo converts—immortality—was only effective with humans and non-immortal follets. "I'd expected some resistance on your part," he said. "You can't see any benefit to going through the change, but that's only because you don't understand our way of life, the lust for blood, the exultation of the hunt, the thrill of sinking your fangs into warm human flesh. And, of course, you care nothing for me—yet. But you will. Once you're a vampyre yourself, you'll come to understand me—dare I say, even hold me in the same esteem in which I hold you—and you'll thank me for turning you."

"You can't turn me against my will," she said. "And I assure you, there is no argument powerful enough to convince me to become what you are. I will never, ever taste a drop of your blood, Turek, and there is no way you can force me to do so. You can drain every ounce of my blood—I'll make more. You can beat me to a pulp—I'll recover."

Turek smiled as he reached into the right-hand pocket of his robe and pulled out the squarish brown bottle he'd pinched from Will Hogarth's painting supplies before following Lili to the bathhouse.

"What is that?" she asked warily.

He uncorked the bottle and held it under her nose; she flinched.

"Spirits of turpentine," he said, inhaling from the bottle as if it were perfume. "I'm actually rather fond of the aroma—though I can appreciate your distaste for it. As one also susceptible to fire, I understand your aversion to combustible substances."

"An ugly threat," she said in a thin, wavering voice, "and a curious one, coming from someone who claims to hold me in esteem. You say we're two of a kind, that we belong together, that you want to spend the rest of eternity with me."

"And so I do," he said. "Vampyres are creatures of passion—but also of ferocious pride. If, as you insist, I can't have you, then I shall see to it no one else ever will."

Setting the bottle down, Turek withdrew from his left-hand pocket the petite, ornamental leg irons crafted to match Lili's wrist cuffs. She kicked and thrashed, but she was no match for his strength; in short order, he had her feet tethered to the statue's ankle torques. He lifted the hammered brass bowl from the fire pit and set it on the platform, to the side of where Lili stood, then built a fire so high that it would burn like the devil when he lit it.

If he lit it, for of course he was hopeful that the threat of a fiery demise would prompt Lili to agree to undergo conversion. Should she persist in refusing, however, he would burn her to ashes.

Not that he was particularly eager to do so—she was, after all, an exceptional example of her race, and exquisitely beautiful—but far better that she should be destroyed than to spend the rest of her long, perhaps even infinite, existence laughing at the "bloodsucking insect" who'd had her in his clutches only to weaken and let her go.

Lili had observed these sinister preparations with commendable stoicism. It was all feigned, of course—the color had leached from her face—but that only made her display of composure more remarkable.

Retrieving her veil from the altar where he'd tossed it earlier,

Turek held it wadded up over the firewood-filled brazier, doused it with turpentine, shook it out, and wrapped it around Lili's legs and torso. Enveloped by the volatile solvent and its ominous reek, she began trembling.

Her trembles turned to shudders, racking her head to toe, when he wrested one of the torches from its hole in the bedrock and brought it close.

"Having second thoughts, *liebling*?" he asked softly. "There is no shame in entertaining a change of heart, especially when one's life is at stake. No one knows that better than I."

Lili shrank back from the torch, its flames sputtering in her huge, dark eyes.

Turek lowered the torch to the fire he'd prepared, which ignited with a *whump,* thanks to its spattering of turpentine. In no time, roaring flames leapt from the brazier, which stood less than a foot from Lili in her turpentine-soaked veil. The fire emanated a hellish heat, raising a sheen of sweat on her pallid face.

Replacing the torch, Turek retrieved the poker, hooking it around the handle of the brazier that was on the far side of Lili so as to pull it away from her a bit. "Wouldn't do to have a spark landing on you just as you're reconsidering," he said. "You'd go up like a torch yourself."

He stepped up onto the platform and pricked a fresh vein, this one in his left wrist. Holding it up for Lili to see the blood seeping from the tiny punctures, he said, "One drop, and you will live forever as one of my kind. Refuse this offer, and I shall move that brazier right in front of you and watch you burn to death, shrieking in agony. When the flames ebb, I shall replenish the wood. There is plenty, as you can see, to keep this fire raging all night, and that's long enough to reduce you to cinders. Surely any fate is preferable to that."

"Nay, there's a worse one by far, and that would be to spend eternity as a murderous little maggot like you."

With a surly thrust to his jaw, he said, "There is a limit to my patience, Lili, and you have reached it. Consider this my final invitation—and your final opportunity to spare yourself from the flames." Bringing his wrist very close to her mouth, he said, "One drop. One flick of the tongue..."

She raised her gaze to his and, still shaking like a rabbit, said, "Go to Hell."

"Lili, Lili..." Turek sighed in exasperation, anger, and genuine sorrow. Hooking the poker around the brazier's other handle, the one closest to Lili, he said, "I daresay you shall be there long before I am."

Ten

"GO TO my chamber in the cave," Darius told Elic as he laid Charlotte on the mattress—facedown, because her back was, if not flayed, damn close to it. The wounds were open, bloody, horrific. "I've got some hartshorn drops on the shelf with my medicines. Bring that and a jar of salve."

"Which salve? You've got—"

"The green one," Darius said, picking one at random as he pulled the blanket up to Charlotte's waist. It didn't matter which he brought; the point was to get Elic out of here while he healed these bloody awful wounds. "*Go.*"

"Should... should I bring back some sort of bandaging, or—"

"Bring back whatever the hell you want, just *go*!"

As soon as Darius heard the door slam shut, he drew in a calming breath to clear his mind, and contemplated the gashes on Charlotte's back. He'd done this to her, brutalized her in a bewildering black rage that had vanished the moment he'd realized the damage he'd wreaked. She'd fainted from shock and pain, and was still unconscious, which was all for the good. Healing those who were awake and aware provoked too many awkward questions.

Darius held his hands over the lower part of Charlotte's back, about an inch from her lacerated flesh, closed his eyes, and focused all his mental faculties. He began to tremble as his own energy, his own curative life force, funneled into Charlotte, knitting the torn flesh, closing the ghastly wounds. His hands grew warm, then hot, shaking as he strove to undo the terrible wrong he'd done to this complicated, confused woman who'd had the poor fortune to stumble upon the likes of him in this cellar full of instruments of torment. Slowly he moved his hands upward over her back, feeling the damage repair itself, the skin grow together strong and smooth.

He opened his eyes, drained and shivering but gratified to see that the lacerations he'd inflicted had all but disappeared, leaving only a network of faint pink streaks, like mild burns. Those would fade over the course of the next few days, leaving her whole and perfect once more.

Elic, despite their long acquaintance, knew nothing of Darius's ability to heal. Nor did Inigo, nor Madame des Ombres, nor any of her predecessors. If they'd given it any real thought, they might have suspected, given his compulsion to turn the wishes and desires of humans into reality. What more profound desire could there be, when one was sick or injured, than to be made well again? There wasn't a human alive who wouldn't take advantage of such a talent, for their loved ones if not for themselves, as Darius had learned all too well a long time ago. Every healing tapped into his own vital humors, leaving him exhausted, sometimes cripplingly so. He'd even been known to lapse into a coma, if the injury or illness was exceptionally severe. Incessant, indiscriminate healing, such as had once been forced upon him, left him a depleted husk in short order. Worse, it interfered with the natural balance of life and death, spawning myriad treacherous repercussions.

Having journeyed halfway around the world to escape those who would exploit his healing powers, Darius was loath to reveal them to anyone, even those closest to him. Although he tended to avoid attachments to humans in the interest of self-preservation, Elic and Inigo did not. They befriended people quite liberally, both here at Grotte Cachée and in the course of their occasional travels—always without Darius, who didn't dare risk the possibility of physical contact with humans. If Darius's fellow follets knew that he could erase the suffering of those they cared about, they would inevitably pressure him to do so. "Just this one exception," they would implore. And then would come another exception, and another, and yet another. Those he healed, even if they were sworn to secrecy, would eventually send their own friends and family to Grotte Cachée to be healed by him . . . and so it would all begin again.

Darius drew the blanket up to Charlotte's shoulders and stroked her hair off her face with a tremulous hand, saying her name. She stirred, murmuring something he couldn't make out.

He reclined on his side next to her, too fatigued to sit up anymore. "How are you feeling?"

She squinted her eyes open. "Darius? Wh-what . . . ?" Her expression shifted from bafflement to fear as she remembered what had happened, what he'd done to her. She shrank away from him, flinching when he closed a hand over her shoulder.

"I'm sorry," he said earnestly. "I'm so sorry, Charlotte. I don't know what . . ." He shook his head, grimacing, for of course he did know what had come over him. It was the same thing that came over him every time he suffered passing contact with a human, the gradual displacement of his own identity with a new, unfamiliar, and entirely unpredictable Darius—not that it always ended with such savagery, thank God.

She was staring at him, as if wondering how to react to an apology from a man who'd just torn up her back with a chain whip.

"Forgive me," he said. "Or don't forgive me, but please know that I didn't mean to hurt you, not like that. I promise nothing like that will happen again."

She reached around beneath the blanket to touch her back, frowning in confusion. "I thought... It felt..."

"You'll be fine," he said.

"Wh-where is Elic?"

"I sent him back to the cave for some tonic and salve."

"The cave?"

"It's where I live, as a sort of permanent houseguest of Madame des Ombres."

"You live in the *cave*?"

It felt good to smile. "A suitable abode for a bear such as I, wouldn't you say?"

"Madame won't give you a room in the castle?"

"I prefer the cave for its privacy," he said. "I like being alone, just dusty old me and my dusty old books."

"Books?"

"They're a weakness of mine. I've been gathering them for cen—for years."

"What kind of books?"

He shrugged as he stroked her arm over the blanket. "There are a number of medical treatises, some very old. The healing arts are a special interest of mine. Quite a bit of history, philosophy, religion, some fiction—whatever appeals to my various interests." With a devilish grin, he said, "I've got quite a few volumes of erotica, dating back to the ancient Greeks and Romans."

"Indeed." She rolled onto her side, gathering the blanket around herself. "My favorite of that era would be the verses of Catullus. So witty and vigorous. I never tire of reading them."

"Which translation?"

"The original Latin, actually." Charlotte caught his eye with a slyly sweet smile.

Darius ducked his head and rubbed the back of his neck. "I'm a blockhead."

Charlotte laughed, happily and carelessly. Darius stared at her, astonished not only by this display of good spirits, after all they'd been through, but by how girlishly pretty it made her.

She said, "I don't suppose it will surprise you that I, myself, have amassed a rather shamefully vast collection of bawdy literature. Have you gotten yourself a copy of *Fanny Hill* yet?"

He shook his head with a quizzical frown, not having heard of it.

"Oh, but you must!" Pushing herself up onto an elbow, she said, "It's an entire novel of the most *delicious* smut, written by some poor bloke in debtor's prison who's trying to earn enough money to free himself. Do snag yourself a copy before the English Church manages to get it banned. I hear they're trying."

"I shall write to my dealer in London on the morrow. I've learned one mustn't hesitate about these things. I did manage to acquire the complete works of Sappho before the Church burned her writings."

"You must be older than you look, then," observed Charlotte with a chuckle. "Weren't those burned in the Middle Ages?"

Forcing a little laugh, Darius said, "I meant they were *published* before the burnings." *Little lies,* he thought. Even his most innocuous encounters with humans were buttressed with a framework of little lies, insignificant individually, but onerous when taken together. "I was lucky to get the Sappho. Some books that were censored are virtually lost."

"Aretino's *Postures,*" she said.

"Precisely. The most famous—or infamous—erotic work in European history, and yet I've never been able to get my hands on a copy. What I wouldn't give for a first edition."

Charlotte studied his eyes for a moment, looked down, picked at the blanket. She seemed about to say something, but hesitated, as if rethinking it. Finally she said, "You . . . you're not at all the man I'd thought you were when . . . I first came down here."

"I wasn't myself," he said quietly, stroking a stray tendril of hair off her forehead. "You seem different, as well."

"Because you realize I'm not some illiterate little hoyden?" she asked with a smile. "That I am, in fact, a rather erudite little hoyden?"

"I confess, it didn't occur to me that there was much of anything beneath your highly polished, if somewhat brittle surface—not even a past. I, er, I apologize for making you talk about your son. That was callous of me. I knew you didn't want to drag motherhood and all that down into this den of sin—why would you? I'm sure you're an excellent mother, very loving. What I said about him being inconvenient, and your packing him off to boarding school—"

"Nat isn't in boarding school," she said in a soft, strained voice, her gaze on the mattress.

"Ah. Well, it was never any of my—"

"He died five years ago."

"Oh." Darius moved closer, gathering her in his arms and tucking her head against his chest. "I'm sorry, Charlotte. God, *so* sorry," he added, sick at the memory of how he'd taunted her about her son.

"I killed him," she said, "the same as if I'd thrown him under those carriage wheels myself."

"I . . . I'm sure you didn't—"

"I did," she said into his chest. "I don't why I'm telling you. I've never told anybody. You might think I'm immune to shame, someone like me, but *this* . . . It's hard enough to live with, much less talk about."

And yet, Darius realized, because she was curled in his embrace and couldn't hide her raw need, she felt compelled to talk about it now. To him. This, then—the part she'd played in her son's death—was the sin for which Charlotte had sought punishment at his hands, however dimly she recognized it. A doomed endeavor, of course, but perhaps not completely futile if it impelled her, for the first time in five years, to want to unburden herself.

"Tell me," he said.

She was silent for so long that he thought perhaps she'd had second thoughts, but then she said, very softly, "Somerhurst—my husband—he . . . he didn't want me after Nat came. Didn't want me in his bed, I mean. He said now that I was a mother, he didn't see me the same way. For the longest time, I tried to change his mind. I tried to be pretty, alluring. I stole in to his bed one night. He bloodied my nose, called me a hussy."

Darius let out a little huff of disgust.

"After that"—she lifted her shoulders—"he spent most of his time in London and left me to the estate in Cambridgeshire. He had no interest in his son, except as an heir—avoided him when he could, and ignored him when he was forced into his presence. He had his whores and his mistresses, and I had Nat. I had the better end of the bargain, to my way of thinking. I adored Nat, he was the world to me. He was a real boy, daring, adventurous, but a cuddler, too. He—" Her voice cracked.

"It's all right," murmured Darius as he held her closer. "It's all right."

"For four years, I had Nat and nothing else—no one else."

"Were you lonely?" Darius asked. "For adult companionship, I mean."

"I had a few friends, not many—but of course, I hadn't been touched by a man since I'd told my husband I was in the family way. My sister Livy used to write to me, urging me to take a lover, but that seemed so unsavory, and anyway, I had Nat, and he needed me. But then . . ."

She lapsed into silence again.

"Who was he?" Darius asked.

"Hugh Stapleton, heir to the Viscount of Granthorpe, and a horse grenadier. Very dashing, very charming, but not like so many of the rest of them, those privileged youngbloods who only care about whoring and drinking. He was a real gentleman in the very best sense—warm, kind. I met him at Livy's home in the Cotswolds. Hugh was her husband's brother's army chum. He was... God, he swept me off my feet. Nothing happened between us during that visit—well, one brief, stolen kiss—because I had Nat with me, and I still didn't think it would do to let things go too far. But then, after I came home, I was lonelier than ever, having had what little I'd had with Hugh. I hadn't realized how terribly I'd missed just being... cared about."

"Of course you did. It is what all humans most desire."

"Hugh wrote me the most moving letter, tender but so impassioned. I actually wept when I read it. Livy was due to come spend a fortnight with me, and he asked if he might come along. He said he'd pose as a coachman so as not to arouse suspicions. Livy urged me to let him come, said he'd been pining for me horribly—so I agreed. I wanted to be free to spend time with him, and I'd already resolved to share my bed with him, so of course I had to make other arrangements for Nat, who slept in the nursery right next door. I asked my husband to take him on a two-week visit to London."

"And he agreed to that?"

"He was appalled by the idea. For that matter, so was Nat. He'd been to London and hated it, said it smelled like smoke and dung. But I pressed the matter like a bulldog, and off they went. Of course, Nat needed someone to look after him, so I sent along his nursemaid, Carrie, not thinking about the consequences in my zeal to be alone with Hugh. Carrie, you see, was very young, very comely, and not at all conversant in the ways of the world—just the way Somerhurst liked them."

"Ah," said Darius.

"While she was being deflowered in the garden of our London town house—she gave me quite the tearful account of it afterward—Nat left the house and went wandering out into the street."

"Oh, Charlotte." Darius held her tight as her shoulders began to shake. "Charlotte, Charlotte..."

She sobbed until she was too exhausted to continue, soaking his shirt with her tears. "The messenger came while I was in bed with Hugh," she said through the stuttering little gasps of her breath. "Livy knocked on the door and gave me the news. I think I would have killed myself if he hadn't been there to comfort me and talk sense to me. I know I would have."

"I'm glad you didn't."

"Two months later, Somerhurst contracted smallpox during an outbreak in London and died. I didn't mourn him for a second."

"One can hardly blame you," said Darius as he dried her face with the hem of his shirt.

"Hugh wanted to marry me," she said, calmer now, although her breath still came in little hitches. "I told him someone like him deserved better. He persisted. I slept with his best friend, Livy's brother-in-law. That did the trick. But then, about a year later, he wrote to me saying he knew I was in anguish, otherwise I wouldn't be 'scourging myself' the way I was. He said I should never forget that I could always find comfort in his arms. Every few months I get another letter from him. I've never answered any of them, but that doesn't keep him from writing."

All Darius could do was shake his head.

"There were other men after that," she said. "About two and a half years ago, I realized I was with child. The father was married. I, of course, was not. Nevertheless, I was thrilled. I thought, surely God wouldn't let me bring another child into this world if I weren't a good person deep inside, a good mother. For the first time since Nat's death, I was able to feel something other than guilt and torment. I had hope. I felt so light, so happy. It was as if I suddenly had a purpose again, a reason for being."

"Were you not at all concerned about your reputation?" Darius asked.

"I planned to spend my confinement on the Continent, so

that no one would be the wiser, then raise the child as my ward. But before my stomach had even started to grow, I lost the baby. The physician who treated me said I had growths in my womb that weren't life-threatening, but that would make it difficult for me to conceive, and impossible to carry a baby to term. I'd become barren." Bitterly she said, "God had known best after all."

"Well..."

"Soon after that, I learned about the Hellfire Club. At last, I thought. Hell on Earth. 'Twas as if Sir Francis had invented it just for me."

"I very much doubt that," Darius said.

"I feel like Lady Macbeth sometimes," she said. " 'Tis as if my hands are covered with blood, and they'll never come clean."

Darius raised her palm to his mouth and kissed it. "There's no blood here, not one speck."

Shaking her head, she said, "You can't see it, but—"

" 'Twas an accident, Charlotte."

"Nay. If only I hadn't—"

Bracketing her face with his hands, Darius said, "Did you mean for Nat to die? Was that why you sent him away? Was that why—?"

"Jesus, no. Of course not."

"Then why *are* you scourging yourself?" he asked gently.

She stared at him, groping for an answer.

Darius rolled Charlotte on her back, slipping a hand beneath the blanket to rest it on her lower abdomen. "If you could have carried that child to term, would it have changed the past two and a half years?"

" 'Twould have changed the rest of my life."

Darius moved his hand over her belly, feeling, exploring...

"Darius?"

"Shh. Relax."

He felt the growths in her womb, clusters of fibrous knots massed within and without. Closing his eyes, he drew a channel of healing warmth through his hand and into the pearlike organ. The tumors withered and shrank, disappearing altogether within a minute or so.

Smiling, he lowered his head and kissed her on the lips, the first time all evening he'd done so.

"What were you doing?" she asked.

"I suspect you shall find out soon enough."

Eleven

"OH, GOD," Lili breathed as Turek tugged the brazier closer, its flames so near now that she could feel the little hairs on her arms crackling with heat.

"It's a bit late to be calling on Him now," said the vampyre. "As one makes one's bed, so must one lie in it."

From beyond the *Cella* came the soft scruff of bare feet on stone as someone sprinted toward them through the cave.

Turek heard it, too. He turned toward the sound as Lili screamed, "Help me! Please!"

"*Halt's maul!*" Whirling on her, Turek whipped his fist across her face, igniting an eye-watering burst of pain in her nose.

"Lili?" Elic appeared on the bridge in the entryway, taking in the scene with an expression of horror. "Christ, what—?"

"He's a vampyre," Lili choked out through the metallic taste of blood in her mouth. "He can be k-killed—"

"*Gusch!*" Turek struck her again as Elic bolted across the room, roaring in rage. Seizing a handful of Turek's robe, he slammed his fist into the vampyre's head, sending him stumbling back with a shout of pain.

"Let her go," demanded Elic as he stalked toward Turek, "or I swear to God I'll—"

"You'll what?" Turek yanked one of the tall torches out of the floor by its iron spike and swung it while striding toward Elic, who backed up onto the bridge to avoid the flames. "What do you suppose you can do to me while you're burning to death, eh?"

"He can burn, too." Lili cocked her head toward Turek. "He told me."

Elic grabbed one of the shorter torches that flanked the entrance, prompting a malicious little chuckle from Turek. "Perhaps you haven't heard, but 'tis more often than not the gentleman with the longer weapon who has the advantage." Smirking at Lili over his shoulder, he asked, "Is that not right, *mein liebes*?"

Taking advantage of Turek's having turned away, Elic leapt at him, aiming his torch's flaming cresset at the vampyre's robe. Turek raised his own torch like a battering ram, using it to push Elic away.

"Elic!" Lili screamed.

Flames sputtered on the chest of his robe, the silk burning with a smell like singed hair. He slapped at them with his hands, wincing.

"Elic, watch out!" she yelled as Turek stabbed at him with his torch, aiming the ball of fire at his long, loose hair.

Elic ducked and lunged, swinging his torch, but Turek blocked it easily.

"We could perform this tedious dance all night," said the vampyre as he backed up toward Lili, "but I've a more entertaining idea. Do you recognize the new scent our lovely Lili is wearing this evening? She'll be a column of screaming flame in about two seconds—and then I shall let the brazier finish the job. How delightful that you could be here to watch," he said as he dipped his torch toward the hem of Lili's veil.

Elic sprang forward and slammed his own torch down, pinning Turek's at the front edge of the platform with a spray of sparks and cinders. Straining with the effort, Turek heaved his torch up, flipping Elic's smaller, lighter one across the chamber and leaving him empty-handed. He looked toward the other tall torch, but it was across the chamber, behind Turek.

This is it, thought Lili, shaking uncontrollably as Turek returned his attention to her. *Don't scream. Don't give him the satisfaction.*

Turek aimed his torch at Lili. Elic reached for it, jumping back as the vampyre wheeled on him, stabbing at him with the fiery end.

Elic made another grab; Turek jabbed again, laughing.

"Poor, doomed Lili," Turek taunted, keeping Elic at bay by prodding at him with the flame-filled cresset. "Your champion has failed you. Bested by a bloodsucking insect."

"Aren't you getting ahead of yourself?" Visibly steeling himself, Elic reached into the fireball, locked his fingers around the searing-hot iron cage, and yanked the torch out of Turek's grip.

Lili screamed Elic's name. Turek gaped.

Elic, grimacing in pain as his flesh sizzled, took one long stride toward the dumbstruck Turek, hauled back with the torch, and rammed its pointed end into the vampyre's chest.

Turek let out an ungodly howl as he fell to the ground, stabbed through the heart—not a fatal injury to his variety of bloodsucker, perhaps, but one that would certainly slow him down for a bit. He twitched and shuddered, grabbing at the iron spike as if trying to pull it out.

Elic shoved the spike in deeper, groaning in pain and exertion, until Turek quivered and went slack; then he let go of the cresset and stumbled back. His hands were charred and blistered; flames leapt from his sleeves.

"Elic!" Lili cried, but he was already crossing to the stream. Falling to his knees, he plunged his arms into the icy water with a hiss.

Within seconds, he was hauling himself, somewhat unsteadily, to his feet. "The key," he said, gesturing toward her restraints with a ravaged hand.

"In his pocket."

Elic retrieved the key and stepped up onto the platform to unlock Lili's wrist cuffs, wincing.

As soon as her hands were freed, she lowered Elic's head to hers and kissed him. "Thank you," she said, shaking in relief. "Thank you. Thank you. God, I don't know what else to say."

"Say you love me. You don't even have to mean it. I just long to hear those words from your—"

"I love you," she said. "It's mad—we've only just met."

"Then I'm mad, too," Elic said, and kissed her again.

Twelve

"A VAMPYRE, eh? Is he still here?" Shielding his eyes against the bright morning sun, Inigo scanned the procession of carriages lined up along the flagstone drive that curved around the castle to the stable at the edge of the surrounding woods. The Hellfires and their followers were chatting and fanning themselves in little clusters as they waited for the journey north to Calais and the Channel. Meanwhile, an army of servants—theirs and their hostess's—loaded their luggage into the waiting vehicles.

Chuckling to himself—Inigo was like a little boy, eager for a glimpse of the monster—Darius said, "No, Turek's already on his way to Paris, bound in chains and with an escort of Madame's Swiss Guards. She's going to use a *lettre de cachet* to have him—"

"*Lettre de cachet?*"

"King Louis gives them to his favored few, left blank so they can fill in the name of any miscreant they'd like to condemn to indefinite confinement in the Bastille, for whatever reason suits them."

"Indefinite?" asked Inigo. "This vampyre, he needs blood to survive, yes?"

"Perhaps he'll feed off his fellow prisoners. Perhaps they'll put him in a cell all by himself and he'll . . . well, I'm not sure he can actually die without being burned to death. In any event, I don't think Madame is too troubled over his fate. After what he did to Lili, I can't say I'm very concerned, either."

Darius heard Charlotte Somerhurst greeting someone. It was Henry Archer, crossing the drawbridge from the gatehouse. They shared a brief conversation, Charlotte smiling and laughing amid a cluster of other ladies, and then Archer noticed Darius and Inigo and excused himself to join them.

"Morning, gentlemen." Turning to Darius, he said, "Must say, old man, I wouldn't have expected to see you here, milling about among the pesky humanfolk."

"I'm waiting to say good-bye to Charlotte Somerhurst." He would have done so already but for the risk of getting too close to the women she was talking to.

"I've just come from Madame," said the young *administrateur,* looking up at the top floor of the gatehouse, which housed the study that was her private refuge. She stood at the window, a shadowy form holding Yseult, her St. Charles spaniel. "She tells me that Lady Somerhurst has a silvery radiance emanating from her."

"Is that so." Darius's gaze shifted to Charlotte's belly, hidden behind a paper-wrapped package she held clutched in her arms.

"He's smiling," Inigo muttered to Archer while staring at Darius. "He never smiles. What does it mean, a silvery radiance?"

"It means there will be a blessed event in the lady's future," Archer replied. "A very blessed event. The child is gifted."

"Chalk up another druid for Elic," Inigo said. "Good show!"

"A druidess," Archer corrected. "It's a girl. She also tells me that her ladyship's aura has until present been muddy-colored, with ominous streaks of black, which would indicate maladies both of the body and the spirit, but that there's no trace remaining of any morbid energy at all."

"Interesting," Darius said, wishing he could stop smiling.

Archer glanced around and lowered his voice. "I do hope Elic knew what he was doing with this one."

"Meaning...?" Darius prompted.

"Meaning is she really worthy of—"

"She is," Darius said in a tone that would brook no argument.

Archer addressed him with a penetrating look as Inigo elbowed him in the ribs to communicate the fact that the lady under discussion was strolling toward them.

Charlotte looked exceptionally fresh and young this morning in a gown of green-striped lawn, her face shadowed by a wide-brimmed straw bonnet bedecked with silk daisies. Darius and his companions all bowed as she approached. "Gentlemen," she said, then she looked directly at him and smiled. "Darius."

Archer and Inigo made their excuses and took their leave.

Darius dug in his pocket for the handful of diamond-tipped hairpins he'd taken from her last night, and handed them to her. "These are yours, I believe."

"Thank you." In a tone of quiet wonderment as she stowed the pins in her reticule, she said, "I awoke this morning with the most extraordinary feeling of... lightness. 'Twas as if I'd gone to sleep weighed down by a pile of stones I'd been carrying 'round for years, and when I woke up, they were just... gone."

"A good night's sleep can be most rejuvenating," he said.

"It was this place," she said, then added softly, "It was you. I'm not sure exactly how it happened, but I do know I owe you a debt, one which I can never repay—though I couldn't live with myself if I didn't offer some gesture of thanks, however inadequate."

"You owe me nothing," he said, "but if you are so moved, there is something you can do that would please me greatly."

"Anything," she said.

"This Hugh Stapleton," he said, "the one who keeps sending you letters . . . I'd like you to write to him."

She looked a bit taken aback, as if it were the last thing she'd expected him to say. "What . . . what shall I write?"

"Whatever you'd like. Whatever you're moved, in your heart, to say to him."

Charlotte looked down for a long moment, the brim of her hat concealing her face. When she met his gaze again, her eyes were shimmering. She cleared her throat and said, "I shall. There is, however, something else, something I'd like to give you, both as a token of thanks and as a memento of my visit."

She handed him the package, a rectangular parcel folded in brown paper and tied with string, a note in an elegantly feminine hand inked on the front. *My Dearest Sir Francis*, it began.

"Ignore the inscription," she said. "I'd intended to give this to Dashwood, but I've washed my hands of him—of all of them."

Darius unwrapped the paper to reveal a book bound in weathered oxblood leather, the title worn off with age. He turned to the frontispiece, an accomplished but remarkably lewd engraving of a couple locked together in carnal bliss. Facing this illustration was a title page in Italian:

Il Verse d*i* Pietro A R E T I N O
con acquaforte da Guilo R O M A N O

"Aretino's *Postures,*" Darius exclaimed, thumbing through the slim volume of poems and the etchings that had inspired them.

"I cannot guarantee it's from the first sixteenth-century printing," she said, "but it's got all of Romano's original etchings, so I think it's likely. He was a student of Raphael, you know."

"I know. I . . . Where on earth did you . . ."

"I found it in a Venice junk shop, if you can believe it."

"What I have a hard time believing is you setting foot in a junk shop," he said.

"I tend to like books other people are inclined to cast aside."

"Your generosity leaves me speechless." Ducking his head beneath the brim of her bonnet, Darius kissed her lightly, sensing as he did so the desires that were even now taking root in her heart. They were the same desires that most humans held dear: a comforting home, someone to hold at night, and somehow, despite the odds, a family.

As they drew apart, Charlotte's gaze lit on something over his shoulder. Darius turned to find Elic and Lili strolling across the drawbridge, Lili in a gauzy morning dress, a fluttery little lace cap in lieu of a bonnet. They were walking hand in hand, which meant that Elic's burns from last night were healed, or mostly so.

Charlotte said, "Lili's staying behind, have you heard? She and your friend Elic have apparently hit it off quite well."

"Yes, he told me earlier this morning."

How long will she be staying? Darius had asked.

A few months. Elic had shrugged, smiling. *A few centuries. As long as she can stand me.*

In that case, she'll be gone by the end of the week.

"I must speak to her before I leave," Charlotte said. "I... ruined one of her gowns, and... well, there are things I must say to her."

"Go ahead," said Darius. "I shall take my leave now."

They shared another kiss and said their good-byes.

Elic greeted Charlotte with a bow, then left the two women to their conversation and walked over to Darius. "Is she a follet?" Elic asked.

"Charlotte? Of course not."

"She appears to have recovered from last night's injuries with remarkable speed," said Elic, gazing across the driveway at the subject of their conversation.

"She wasn't as badly hurt as we'd initially feared." *Another little lie,* Darius thought. Even with his fellow follets, he could not escape them.

Elic turned to look pointedly at Darius, his expression doubtful. It wasn't the first time Darius had seen that look in his eyes.

Cocking his head toward Lili as she took Charlotte's hand and kissed her cheek, Darius said, "They seem to have put their differences behind them."

With a little smirk at Darius's clumsy redirection of the subject, Elic said, "One of these days, friend, there's something you and I need to discuss."

Quietly, soberly, Darius said, "No, we don't."

Elic studied Darius gravely for a moment, then patted his shoulder and rejoined the ladies. Darius lingered a moment to watch the three of them talk.

Charlotte met Darius's gaze and smiled.

He returned the smile, and then he turned and walked back to his cave and his books.

[illegible]

[illegible]

[illegible]

[illegible]

[illegible]

Body of Knowledge

One

August 1884

"NOTICE, IF you will, the heroic dimensions of the generative organs," said Professor Elijah Wheeler, gesturing toward one of the satyr statues as he reclined in the pool, sipping a glass of wine.

Inigo smiled to himself as he contemplated the statue, which depicted the penetration from the rear of a buxom beauty bent over at the waist with her arms gripping a column of the bathhouse. *Heroic dimensions.* Not horselike, or grotesque, or even freakish, as they'd ofttimes been described, but *heroic.* He liked that.

"In concert with the normal legs and the diminutive horns," Wheeler said, "such a representation would appear to suggest the original concept of a young satyr as envisioned by the early Greeks. This bathhouse, on the other hand, is clearly Roman, and of much more recent construction—around the time of Christ, give or take. Romans in that era generally depicted satyrs as half man, half goat, with hooves, thick, shaggy haunches, larger ears, and less prominent, or certainly less tumescent, genitalia. Wouldn't you agree, Lee?"

The dark-haired, bespectacled young man soaking in the far end of the pool with his nose in a history book—Thomas Lee, Wheeler's assistant in his mythological studies courses at Harvard University—looked up, blinking. "Sorry, Dr. Wheeler. What were you . . . ?"

"The satyrs. More evocative of ancient Greece than of Rome, given the outsized penis and so forth, wouldn't you agree?"

Lee's ears flushed crimson as he glanced at the third member of their party, who had arrived at the chateau just the evening before for a weekend visit while touring the landmarks of Europe.

Catherine Wheeler, the professor's petite, auburn-haired daughter, was one of those independent-minded young females who, despite a fair degree of natural comeliness, inherited in this case from her father, did her best to cultivate an aura of seriousness. A self-proclaimed "disciple of the natural sciences," she wore, despite the oppressive heat, a high-buttoned shirtwaist, tweed vest, and sensible, ankle-length riding skirt. A drearily utilitarian leather pouch hung from her belt, next to the chain of a man's pocket watch that she had checked twice during the half hour she'd been sitting there, for reasons that eluded Inigo. Equally baffling was her habit of calling her father by his Christian name. When Inigo had asked her why, she'd replied, *Because that's his name.* She appeared to be corsetless, given the natural contours of her waist and bosom, a fact that might have imparted some sexual allure but for her calculated dowdiness.

Of the four people lounging by the pool that afternoon, Catherine alone had declined to immerse herself, explaining that, unlike her traveling companions, she'd neglected to pack a bathing costume. At breakfast, Lili had offered to lend her one, but the young woman had declined. She wasn't much for taking the waters, she'd explained, and in any event, she didn't plan to linger very long at the pool, having planned to spend the greater part of the afternoon exploring the geological formations in the cave.

"Rest easy, Lee," chuckled Wheeler, having noticed his assistant's discomfiture. "Catherine's sensibilities are not so fragile that she would swoon at the proper anatomical terms. She's a scientist, don't forget. And really, these statues aren't much worse than what she saw at Pompeii, and she was only twelve then."

"Elijah's right. Don't be such a square-toes, Thomas." Catherine, sitting with her legs curled under her at the edge of the pool, a walking stick across her lap, pulled a cigarette case from a pocket of her skirt and flipped it open.

"Are those American?" asked Inigo, sitting up eagerly.

"Lucky Strikes. Help yourself." She leaned over to offer the smokes to Inigo, lounging in the water several feet from her.

"Much obliged," he responded, employing an expression he'd picked up from an American dime novel called *The Adventures of Buffalo Bill from Boyhood to Manhood.* He slid a cigarette from the case, sniffing it appreciatively.

Thomas Lee scowled as he watched Catherine light Inigo's cigarette, a reversal of traditional roles that amused Inigo far more than it seemed to amuse their young visitor. A subtle, covetous undercurrent coursed through the water from Lee's direction.

Jealousy! thought Inigo as he drew in a lungful of fragrant Virginia tobacco. *Excellent.* Perhaps he would pretend to woo her, just for the melodrama. Not that he had any serious designs on her. Her avowals of sophistication aside, it was abundantly clear to him from her dress and demeanor, not to mention the way she avoided looking directly at the statues, that she wasn't at all comfortable with Grotte Cachée's atmosphere of casual licentiousness. She might call Lee a square-toes, but he'd bet anything she was just as much of a prig, if not worse. The seduction of such a woman was, in Inigo's experience, a tedious venture that, even if successful, yielded lackluster results. He preferred his conquests experienced and enthusiastic. One peek at the old heroic dimensions was all it generally took for that type to lie down and throw up her skirts.

"Julia did insist on keeping Catherine out of the Pompeian brothels so she wouldn't see those frescoes," Wheeler continued, Julia being his beloved wife, whom he'd lost to cancer five years earlier; he'd mentioned her several times during supper last night, and again at breakfast this morning. "She'd wanted to keep her away from Pompeii altogether. She was concerned for her daughter's innocence, as any mother would be, but she relented when I explained the historical significance of the ruins, and the benefit to Catherine's intellectual advancement. Julia and I felt strongly that females, especially those as thirsty for knowledge as Catherine, deserved the same academic opportunities as males. So, what do you make of them, Lee?"

"Sir?"

"The satyrs. More Greek than Roman, yes?"

"I . . ." The young man peered over his reading spectacles to survey the statues, his brows quirking in interest. "Yes. Yes, I suppose they are."

"Why on earth would first-century Romans have sculpted satyrs in the style of Greeks from centuries before?" Wheeler asked rhetorically. "It's a conundrum, and a maddening one. I shan't get a good night's sleep till I figure it out."

Catherine sighed through a plume of smoke. With an indulgent smile, she said, "As always, Elijah, I shall never understand how you and Thomas can devote so much time and energy to all this mythological twaddle. I'm sure there are interesting facets to it—I loved fairy tales myself when I was a girl—but is it really worth the devotion of minds such as yours? Who cares which variety of satyr some long-dead sculptor chose to carve? They're *satyrs,* for heaven's sake. They aren't even real."

"They were real to whoever carved these statues," Thomas countered.

"He was a sculptor," she said. "He was told to carve satyrs, so he carved satyrs. He probably just made them up out of his imagination, using statues he'd seen in the past for reference."

"Not at all," said Inigo.

All heads turned toward him.

"I, er, would assume someone posed for him—just some ordinary fellow," he lied. "I mean, look at them, they're so true to life."

"What they're true to," Catherine said, "is a male fantasy of sexual freedom and prowess."

"Precisely," Wheeler said, "except that I wouldn't say it's a fantasy so much as an ideal. A satyr like those represented here, being both macrophallic and ithyphallic, which is to say both well-endowed and erect, personifies the supreme in masculine sexual vigor, which has been a highly underestimated force in the development of civilization. You should have read my second book, *Mythological Carnality and Its Impact on Western Europe.* I went into great detail on the subject."

The supreme in masculine sexual vigor, Inigo mused as he lounged against the side of the pool, puffing on his cigarette. He liked that, too. In fact, though he normally had little patience for scholarly types and their long-winded discourses, he found himself liking Elijah Wheeler more and more as the conversation progressed.

"The satyr was a type of incubus," Wheeler explained, "as was the dusios, which is what the statue in the cave would appear to represent, given the inscription, Dusivæsus. I'm not sure what *væsus* meant in Gaulish—I shall try to look it up—but the root word *dusi,* in conjunction with the anatomy, couldn't really mean anything else." Wheeler and Lee had spent most of that morning in the *Cella,* taking notes and making drawings.

"I wish I knew what the second inscription meant," Thomas said. "The one that's scratched over the first."

"As do I." To his daughter, Wheeler said, "It's crude and irregular, but I can just make out the letters, and I swear they look like runes. That can't be right, though, because runes were native to Germany and the Scandinavian countries, not France."

"I copied that inscription down, the runic one," Thomas said. "The library here appears to be exceptionally well stocked in books of ancient lore. Perhaps we can find the answer there."

"I'll ask Kit Archer if we can have access to it." Wheeler and Christopher Archer, second-in-command to Émile Morel, Grotte Cachée's current Seigneur des Ombres, had been friends for some twenty-five years. They'd met at Oxford, where they both did their postgraduate work, Wheeler in classics and his American roommate in the history of Europe and the Mediterranean. Inigo knew this because the two old friends had reminisced at length during last night's long, wine-fueled supper.

Wheeler said, "Dusivæsus, if I may call him that—"

"Or her," Thomas pointed out.

"Point taken," Wheeler said.

"Or her?" Catherine said. "The statue is either male or female, no?"

"The dusios, in his classic incarnation, had hermaphroditic qualities," her father responded. "He was, in fact, sequentially hermaphroditic, in that he could change from male to female, and back again."

She said, "From the way you speak, one would think you really believed in these creatures."

Creatures? Inigo dismissed the notion of even pretending to woo Catherine Wheeler. Lucky Strikes aside, she just wasn't worth the effort.

With a shrug, Wheeler said, "There are some invertebrates and fish that have been documented as being sequentially hermaphroditic. Who's to say it's not within the realm of possibility?"

Catherine raised her hand, her expression droll.

"As I was saying," her father continued with a sigh, "that statue predates these satyrs—by how much, it's impossible to say, but it's clearly Gaulish in origin." With a glance at his daughter, he added, "The Gauls, of course, being the branch of Celts who lived in France, Belgium, and Switzerland."

Eyeing her father balefully, Catherine said, "I am well aware of who the Gauls were, Elijah. I studied other things at Cornell besides physics and geology, you know."

"Forgive me if I find that difficult to remember," Wheeler replied, "given your conviction that the answers to all of life's mysteries can be found within the realm of bloodless science."

"I beg you, both of you," Lee groaned, "spare me another of these tiresome debates till after dinner, when I've got a brandy or two under my belt to muffle the histrionics."

"Histrionics?" Catherine did not look amused.

"There's nothing wrong with a good, lively debate between friends—or family," Wheeler said. "Keeps the cerebral juices flowing."

"Histrionics?"

Not to be dissuaded from his impromptu lecture, Wheeler said, "St. Augustine wrote in *The City of God* of '*Dæmones quos "dusios" Galli nuncupant,*' or 'Demons the Gauls call dusii.' He characterized them as incubi, inasmuch as they 'often made wicked assaults upon women, and satisfied their lust upon them.' "

"I don't understand," Catherine said. "Aren't ancient statues usually of gods and goddesses? Why erect a statue to a demon?"

"To the ancients," Wheeler said, "the world was full of supernatural beings, and it wasn't always easy, sorting the good from the bad—or even differentiating one type from the other. For example, in the seventh century, Isidore of Seville included satyrs as real, living beings in his encyclopedia of all known things, which he called *Etymologiae.* He wrote that the Latin term for such creatures was incubi, and that the Greeks knew them as pans, the Gauls as dusii, and the Romans as fauns."

"He said dusii and satyrs were the same thing?" asked Inigo, outraged.

Wheeler shrugged. "It was complicated, sorting out—"

"But they're nothing alike." Inigo sat up straight, shaking his head at the mental laziness of some humans. "True, they're both incubi, but satyrs are . . . well, you know. Supremely masculine. Heroic. They've got the horns, the ears, the . . ." He held his hands about a foot apart, grinning meaningfully.

"The tail?" Thomas said dryly.

Inigo, pondering the faint surgical scar on his tailbone, said, "Right. Sometimes. But dusii, with that back-and-forth business, male to female . . . Not that I'm casting aspersions, God knows, because I'm very fond of . . ." *Careful.* ". . . .the *idea* of such a being, but they're a whole different *race,* for crying out loud."

"Who's a whole different race?"

Inigo turned to see Kit Archer lumbering into the bathhouse. Someone meeting the *administrateur* and Elijah Wheeler for the first time would never guess they were exactly the same age. Lean and handsome, with just the faintest dusting of gray at the temples, Wheeler wore his forty-six years with effortless grace. Archer, on the other hand, was one of those men who started losing hair and gaining pounds in his twenties, swiftly transforming into a shiny-pated, rotund version of his former self.

"We were just talking about certain . . . mythological creatures," said Inigo, ever mindful of Archer's constant exhortations to watch what he said in front of the guests.

"Ah, yes," Archer said with his omnipresent jovial smile. "Well, that would be Elijah's area of expertise, would it not?" Squeezing his bulk into one of the little iron chairs at the perimeter of the bathhouse, he leaned over with a grunt to untie a shoe. "Just thought I'd soak my feet and calves for a bit. Blasted gout, don't you know. Bane of my existence. The Gauls who once lived here ascribed healing powers to these waters. May as well give it a go. The doctors certainly aren't helping."

"Speaking of the Gauls," Wheeler said, "Lee and I were wondering if we might have a look around your library this afternoon, do a little research into the history of this place."

"Be my guest, old man, be my guest. I'm rather proud of that library, I confess. Built it up from a few paltry shelves to what it is now, which is one of the finest collections of ancient and classical history in Europe, if I say so myself."

Rising to her feet with the help of her walking stick, Catherine said, "I'm off to investigate the cave."

"Capital idea," Archer said. "Er, I must humbly request that you don't disturb any artifacts and leave everything as you find—"

"Yes, my father has already explained the rules to me."

"And that you stay on the lamplit path," Archer persisted, "and venture no farther than the *Cella*—that would be the chamber with the statue in it."

"What happens if I go farther?" she asked with a sardonic little smile. "Do I turn into a pumpkin?"

Archer looked up, the smile stiffened into place. "You will find yourself in inhospitable terrain."

Two

"CATHERINE!"

Catherine paused some fifty yards into the cave, next to one of the wall-mounted oil lanterns, waiting for Thomas to catch up with her.

"Mind if I tag along?" he asked a little breathlessly as he took off his spectacles and hooked them over the neckline of his damp white bathing suit.

"You'll get chilly, dressed like that," she said, thinking how silly men looked in their swimming clothes when they weren't in the water, as if they were just walking about in their underwear. "Caves tend to be—"

"I don't mind."

She knew why he wanted to be alone with her. As gently as she could, she said, "I'm not going to change my mind, Tom."

He held her gaze for a bleak moment, looked away, started to say something, sighed. "All I'm asking is for you to think about it. You answered so quickly, without even—"

"I thought about it before you asked. I've been thinking

about it since I was a child, about the impact on my career, my life, if I were to marry."

"For God's sake, Catherine, it's not as if I'm some Neanderthal who's going to tie you to the cookstove and beat you when you get out of line. It's *me,* Thomas," he said, his eyes dark and intense. "I'm the one who took you to that suffragist meeting, remember?"

"Actually, I took you."

"The point is, you can't seriously think I'm the kind of man who'd try to remake you into some mindless little baby mill. You've known me for how many years now? Three? Four?"

"Men change once they're married," she said. "They get covetous, domineering."

"Is your father like that?" he demanded. "He and your mother had an ideal marriage, a marriage based on equality, respect... Your mother was free to follow any pursuit she desired."

"You never even knew my mother, Thomas. Elijah romanticizes their marriage because he loved her so much." Which was why the poor man couldn't stop grieving for her, why he'd cocooned himself in the womb of academia after her death, and why he wouldn't even think about courting other women, even though he was the type of man who was never meant to be alone.

"Are you saying she was unhappy in her marriage?" he asked.

"I'm saying she made the best of her lot. She loved my father. She loved me, she loved being a mother. But I think—*I know*—she would have had a much richer, more fulfilling life if she'd followed her dream and become a physician."

"A *physician*?"

"She'd been accepted into the Female Medical College of Pennsylvania when she married Elijah and became pregnant with me. I think she'd intended to return to her medical studies eventually, but as the years passed, she found herself playing helpmate to my father in his career, accompanying him on his travels..." Catherine shrugged. "She used to tell me that a woman has a choice in this life, marriage and motherhood or a career. I want a career, Thomas. I want to go back to Cornell someday and teach. I can't do that if I'm shackled in wedlock to... to *anyone.* It's not you. This... this isn't about you."

He looked away with a dubious little grunt. He was right to be skeptical, of course, for it *was* partly about him, perhaps even mostly about him. Yes, the institution of marriage, with its ingrained subjection of women, made Catherine uneasy, but if any man could make it work, it would be Thomas. More troubling, though she was loath to mention it because it was about *him* and not about abstract principles, was his attachment to such an inane pursuit as mythology. To spend one's life classifying satyrs and demons and faeries struck her as an appalling waste of brainpower. Likewise, Elijah's devotion to the subject, much as she loved him, both baffled and shamed her. Thomas's distressed her even more, because she could see him making her happy if only she could respect his life's work.

"It *feels* as if it's about me," he said.

"I care for you," she told him truthfully. "You're one of the finest men I know."

"Then why won't you give me a chance? Give *us* a chance. I love you, Catherine. I want to marry you. Does that count for nothing?"

She looked away, groping for words, as she did every time he made that declaration, which she'd never returned.

Gentling his voice, he said, "You're afraid. Don't be. Let me prove I can give you a loving marriage *and* your freedom."

"And if it turns out to be a disaster—for both of us?"

"Neither of us can predict the future," he said, "but we can try our best to make it work and leave the rest in God's hands."

She said, "The very fact you put it that way, knowing how I feel about religion..."

"We'll leave it to fate, then. Is that better?"

"*No,* it's not better," she said heatedly. "I'm a scientist,

Thomas. I don't just launch into foolhardy endeavors willy-nilly and leave the outcome to fate—whatever that is."

"Foolhardy endeavors?" He reached out to grip her arms, startling her; they never touched. "I'm asking you to *marry* me, Catherine. You dismiss my proposal out of hand because the outcome is uncertain and you can't bear that. You can't bear not being in complete control every step of the way, you never could. But that's how life is. Life is full of uncertainty and risk, but there are some chances we take out of passion and love and faith just because we're human."

She backed away, wrenching herself from his grip. "Not me. I'm not made that way. I'm sorry."

"But—"

"Leave me alone, Thomas," she pleaded, surprised to find her throat closing up, as if she were on the verge of tears. "Please, just—" She swallowed to steady her voice. "I just want to be alone right now. Can I just be alone for a little while?"

Thomas regarded her in dreadful silence for a long moment. As he turned to leave, he said, "I'll be keeping that ring in my pocket for a year, in case you change your mind."

Catherine stood studying the statue in the lamplit *Cella* for a long time, as if, in understanding it, she would better understand Thomas and Elijah. On the front of the slab of stone that formed the base of the statue had been painstakingly incised the word DVSIVÆSVS. Scrawled over it in much larger letters, as if gouged by a knife, was the runic inscription the two men were so eager to translate: ᚲᛟᚾ•ᛈᚱᚨᛖᛚ

Her arms still felt the imprint of Thomas's hands. They never touched, she and Tom. His courtship of her, if one could call it that, had been so reserved and decorous—for he was both a gentleman and a creature of the mind—that it had taken her over a year to realize that he was paying her his addresses.

Not once had he tried to kiss her. If he had, Catherine

couldn't imagine how she would have responded. On the one hand, she'd striven to discourage him ever since she'd sorted out his intentions. On the other, she couldn't help but be a little curious. At twenty-two, she alone among her girlhood friends had never been kissed.

The statue was huge and crude, with its tree-trunk limbs and lascivious bulges—especially that between the legs. Dusivæsus's masculine organ was a monument unto itself, so erect that it had been carved with no space whatsoever between it and the statue's belly.

Did real men get that hard? she wondered. Did they rise that high? She might never find out, given her disinclination to marry. Not that she had any moral objection to the concept of free love, but she didn't quite see the point. For men, the appeal was obvious, inasmuch as they derived pleasure through ejaculation. But for women, who by all accounts merely tolerated the act in the interest of procreation or wifely duty, such relations were not only baffling, but fraught with peril. It was she, not he, whose reputation could end up in tatters, she alone who ran the risk of an unwed pregnancy. Why the women who got involved in such relationships didn't think the matter through to its logical conclusion was beyond Catherine's scope of comprehension.

Catherine left the *Cella* and stood in the outer passageway, looking back toward the way she had come, then in the other direction, leading farther into the cave. It was very dark that way, a tunnel of blackness.

You will find yourself in inhospitable terrain. Little did Mr. Archer know that Catherine had traversed such terrain before. She'd been exploring caves since she was an adolescent, squeezing herself through crawlways too tight for her male colleagues, climbing shafts they dared not, navigating ledges too narrow for their feet. And caving wasn't the extent of it. She'd stood on the banks of Kilauea's lakes of boiling lava, trekked across the Bering

Glacier, scaled Mont Blanc armed only with an ice pick, a rope, and her trusty compass.

She could handle Grotte Cachée.

Retrieving her notebook and pencil from her gear pouch, she flipped to the first blank page, checked her pocket watch, and wrote:

> 23 Aug. 1884, 3:25 pm
> Grotte Cachée, Auvergne, France—
> Lava cave (efflux) in extinct volcano: Extent unknown.

After consulting her compass, Catherine began a rough map of the cave, lifted a lantern from its hook outside the *Cella*, and set about tracking the waterway through its disappearances into sinks and its reappearances downstream. It turned out to be a maze cave comprised of a vast network of corridors, tunnels, chasms, and rooms, everything from nooklike alcoves to sprawling galleries festooned with jewel-toned stalactites and stalagmites, rippled shawls of dripstone, and thistly frostwork.

Catherine was finishing up a sketch of the most breathtaking crystal pool she'd ever seen when she realized she hadn't noticed the stream in a while. She went back the way she'd come, using her map as a guide, only to find herself at an unfamiliar crossroads where the corridors went off in three different directions. Could she have taken a wrong turn? She did feel a little light-headed, probably from thirst. She took out her watch, which gave the time as 10:04. She hadn't been down here *that* long. Lovely; now her watch was broken.

She consulted her compass, but its needle jittered crazily. Only once had she experienced this type of magnetic declination, when as a child she and her cousins had gone exploring in an abandoned iron mine near her grandparents' home in eastern Pennsylvania. The needle had fluctuated then, due to the presence of all that iron, but not nearly as wildly as now. The explanation, of course, was that she was standing in the heart of a volcano, albeit one that had gasped its last breath long ago. The lava, as it cooled, must have produced a flow of swirling electrical energy. Most likely this magnetic vortex was also responsible for her malfunctioning watch.

Catherine picked a corridor and took it, hoping that it would lead her back to where she'd started from, or to some other exit from this labyrinthine cave, but it only led to more corridors. At length, she began to realize that the floor beneath her was pitched upward, like a ramp. She paused, noting that the relative humidity was lower than it had been before, which made sense, given that she appeared to be heading to an upper level of the cave system.

Tucking her walking staff under her arm, she withdrew her compass, but the needle still spun and whirled. Just looking at it made her feel so dizzy that she wavered on her feet, the walking stick slipping out from beneath her arm. But instead of falling onto the stone floor, it stood straight up.

Catherine stared at it, thinking, *This can't be happening. I can't be seeing this.* The staff stood poised on its tip, quivering ever so slightly, as if animated by an electrical current. Absurd, of course; wood couldn't conduct electricity. She reached out and tentatively touched her fingertips to the stick, which popped into her hand with a sound like a gasp. It felt the same as always, just an age-burnished length of hickory, completely inert, utterly normal.

Nothing in this place is normal. Catherine glanced down at her watch, which now read 8:57. "Oh, blast." Now something was wrong with her watch. She experienced one of those little mental anomalies where one feels as if what's happening had happened before. But no; as dependent as she was on her watch, she would remember if it wasn't working properly.

A few hundred yards up the meandering, inclined corridor—or it could have been a few hundred feet; Catherine's queerness of mind was affecting her sense of space—she felt a fresh draft and brightened. *Please, please, please be a way out of here.* But it turned out to be a shaft in the roof, impossible to negotiate without the proper equipment. It was comforting, though, to see a patch of light, even if it was edging into dusk already, and to hear the tweets and trills of birds in the forest overhead.

No sooner had she entertained that thought about birds than one flew straight at her from the corridor up ahead, narrowly missing her as it sped past. Catherine laughed breathlessly even as she braced a hand on the wall to keep her balance. That bird was a good sign. Given the unlikelihood that one would enter a cave through a vertical shaft, and given from whence it had flown, chances were good that she'd find a navigable opening up ahead.

Catherine ventured onward, only to be attacked—for that was what it felt like—by the same little bird, a bluebird, she thought, given its coloring. Were there bluebirds in France? She should know that, after all those happy childhood hours she'd spent poring over Audubon's *Birds of America* and other bird guides, but her mind felt as if it were wrapped in cotton wool.

The bird fluttered past her from behind, turned, and flew at her with such fierce determination that she was forced to duck. She straightened, fighting a wave of vertigo, only to have to sidestep it as it streaked by her yet again, disappearing around a bend in the corridor up ahead. It was almost as if it were harrying her, like a hawk being harried by a smaller bird. She wondered if it had a nestful of chicks somewhere up ahead, to which it viewed her as a threat. It certainly seemed to be trying to keep her away from *something.*

She continued on, looking out for a nest in one of the nooks and crannies in the stone wall, only to stop short, gaping in stupefaction, when she rounded the bend. The corridor opened up into a cavernous gallery, the walls of which were lined, floor to ceiling and wall to wall, with books.

She stepped into the gallery and held her lantern aloft, turning around to take it all in—thousands, possibly tens of thousands, of volumes lined up on wooden shelves looming a good fifteen feet high against the cave walls. An armchair upholstered in age-crackled leather stood in a corner with a frayed needlepoint footstool tucked up against it, a reading lamp on a little marble table off to the side. The only other furniture was a rolling ladder of the type they had in the Cornell library, so that one could reach the volumes stored on the top shelves. The gallery was devoid of decoration save for a large tapestry on the opposite wall, very old—it looked as if it might date from the Renaissance—which hung all the way to the floor.

Catherine heard an irate little chirrup and looked up to see her avian tormentor sitting on a bank of unlit pendant lamps hanging from a chain strung between two stalactites. Brandishing her walking stick with mock ferocity, she said, "You'll keep your distance if you know what's good for you."

As if it had understood her, it responded with a battery of screeches and a furious batting of its wings.

"I'm bigger than you," she told it petulantly as she strolled around the strange library, scanning the titles stamped on the spines of the books. "*You* leave."

One wall held various sacred texts, Bibles, and works of comparative religion, philosophy, and theology. There were herbals and pharmacopeias, and innumerable history books going back hundreds of years—including quite a few medieval tomes inked on parchment and bound between leather- and silk-covered boards.

Another type of book that was represented in significant numbers, Catherine was intrigued to discover, had to do with matters of an amatory nature. These were arranged not by author, as was the rest of the collection, but by date of publication. The earliest were some very old anthologies in Latin of the verses of Sappho and Catullus, as well as a number of volumes that appeared to be of Oriental and Indian origin. The rest had dates on the title pages that fell within the past two hundred years.

Catherine looked for books written in the languages she was most conversant in, French and English, and thumbed through a few of them: Jean Barrin's *Venus dans la Cloître,* John Cleland's *Fanny Hill, or Memoirs of a Woman of Pleasure,* Giovanni Giacomo Casanova's *Mémoires de J. Casanova de Seingalt.* She was surprised to recognize one of the books, an academic treatise by Richard Payne Knight titled *A Discourse on the Worship of Priapus,* from her father's library at home. Toward the end of the last shelf was a set of English magazines, about a dozen and a half, called *The Pearl.* The last and most recent volume in this group, Sir Richard Burton's translation of *The Kama Sutra of Vatsyayana,* had been published a year ago.

As Catherine returned the *Kama Sutra* to its slot, she was overtaken by a wave of vertigo that left her clutching at the shelf for support. She looked about the gallery, only to see the rows of books swaying slowly, like waves rising and falling in the ocean, the tapestry fluttering and flapping. She rubbed her eyes with a trembling hand, whispering, "Hold on, Catherine, hold on. You've never been the swooning type—don't start now."

The bird made a cackling sound, almost as if it were taunting her.

"Bugger off," she said, then laughed in astonishment that such a rude phrase had passed her lips. What would her mother have thought?

The wooziness faded; the bookshelves stilled.

The tapestry, however, still fluttered just a bit, at the bottom. It continued to do so as Catherine slowly approached it, hoping it meant what she thought it did. "Please," she whispered as she pulled it aside, revealing another, much smaller chamber.

The bird flew past her into the little room, where it lit on a windowlike gap in the cave wall above a narrow iron bed.

"Yes! Oh yes!" Charlotte cried as she stepped into the little bedchamber. The irregular opening really did resemble a window, flanked as it was by a pair of green-painted wooden shutters standing wide open. Through it, she saw, in the purplish twilight, the branches of trees, their leaves trembling in the cool evening breeze. She wouldn't even have to squeeze through the window, she realized when she noticed the door next to it—an actual wooden door, also painted green and fashioned to fit the irregular opening. She turned the doorknob. It was locked, but a key hung by a leather cord from a nail next to it. The shutters were likewise fitted out with a latch hook lock.

Content in the knowledge that she could leave any time she wanted to, Catherine took a moment to look around. The chamber felt remarkably cozy and homelike, with a threadbare Persian rug underfoot and a quilt draping the bed. Against one wall were a pair of shelves attached to two magnificent, tangled formations that she realized were petrified tree roots. The top shelf supported yet more books between a pair of iron candlesticks, the bottom a collection of items—jars, vials, a small scale, a mortar and pestle—that looked as if they belonged in an apothecary.

Lighting the two candles with her lantern, Catherine turned her attention to the books. She slid out the first one, almost dropping it when the little bluebird on the windowsill let out a fiercely strident scream.

"Do go away," she muttered as she opened the cover of worn brown leather stamped SHAKESPEARE in gold on the spine. The rumpled, discolored title page featured a large etching of the likeness of the Bard below the title:

Mr. WILLIAM
SHAKESPEARS
COMEDIES,
HISTORIES &
TRAGEDIES
Published According to the True Originall Copies

At the bottom of the page were the words:

LONDON

Printed by Isaac Iaggard, and Ed. Blount, 1623.

Catherine's eyes widened. 1623? This was one of the few copies in the world of the coveted first edition of Shakespeare's collected works. She'd seen this very same book at the British Library just last week, except that it had been a third folio, published in 1664; they kept the priceless first folio under lock and key.

Slipping the book back into its space, she lifted the second, which was an exquisitely illuminated *Book of Hours* on silky vellum. Written on the flyleaf in an archaic hand, the ink rusty with age, was the inscription *Pour Darius, l'hermite qui aime des livres. Guillaume, Décembre 1505.*

Catherine worked her way down the row of books, growing ever more impressed, as the little bird continued to hector her. They were all first editions, some quite rare and valuable, the type of book one normally saw only in museums. Pierre Choderlos de Laclos's *Les Liaisons Dangereuses* had also been inscribed to "Darius" in October of 1782. A different Darius, perhaps? A many-times great-grandson of the Darius who had been gifted with the *Book of Hours* in the sixteenth century? What other logical explanation could there be?

She slid out a slim volume bound in oxblood leather, checked the date of publication—1524—and thumbed through its pages, finding it to be an illustrated book of verse in Italian. Her mouth dropped open as she realized that the engravings were all of naked men and women copulating. Their bodies—the females' as well as the males'—were meaty and lush, their positions... inventive. The only similar depictions of the sex act she'd ever seen were the statues of satyrs and nymphs in the bathhouse, and even they didn't seem as boldly lewd as these etchings, possibly because the white marble imparted an aura of cool classicism.

Catherine had seen cats and dogs mating, the male mounting the female from behind, and until recently, she'd assumed that was the standard position for human coition. But then she'd been assured by her cousin Abbie, who liked to natter on about such things in a salacious whisper, that people conducted the act face-to-face with the woman lying supine beneath the man. Other positions, Abbie had assured her, were a crime against God and nature.

"Nature doesn't judge," Catherine had archly replied. And if there were such a thing as God, she'd thought at the time, she couldn't imagine Him judging such things, either, but she'd kept that blasphemous observation to herself.

"Well, the state judges," Abbie had said. "People can get arrested for doing it the wrong way. And once they're dead, they'll go straight to heck. Even thinking about that sort of thing is a sin."

If that was true, Catherine thought, then she would roast in heck for eternity, because to her, the pictures in this book were among the most fascinating she'd ever seen. They pointed up all too vividly the gaps in her knowledge of those matters one couldn't learn about in college courses and science books. Ten minutes ago, she'd had no notion of the extent of her ignorance about what men and women did together in bed. Now, that ignorance appalled her. She, a scientist who prided herself on being informed and making logical decisions, had resigned herself to lifelong virginity without the slightest knowledge of what she'd be giving up. It took a book three and a half centuries old to make her curious.

Very curious.

The little bird, as if fed up with being ignored, lifted off from the windowsill and flew around the room, screeching.

"Stop it!" Catherine yelled as it circled her, forcing her to swerve this way and that. The room shifted jerkily, as did the bird. She'd think it was in front of her, then realize it was behind her. She whirled and spun, raising her walking stick to fend it off as it flew perilously close to her head.

"Go away!" She swung the stick, hoping to scare it off, but she hadn't counted on the bird's erratic movements and her own current lack of spatial judgment. The stick struck the bird with a sickening thump.

It dropped like a brick.

"Oh!" Catherine pressed a hand to her mouth as she stood over the little creature, lying utterly still on the Persian rug next to the book she'd been looking at. "Oh, no. Oh, you poor little thing. I didn't mean to . . . *Damn.*"

She grabbed her lantern and crouched down for a closer look, hoping to see a flutter of movement, to hear a weak little peep, *anything.* But it just lay there, immobile and probably lifeless, its eyes fixed and glazed.

She touched its little chest very softly with her fingertips, but there wasn't the slightest hint of movement. "I'm sorry, little fellow."

This close to the bird, and with the light from the candles and lantern, she could see that it wasn't a bluebird at all, but a blue rock thrush—a male, judging from the beautiful grayish-blue plumage.

Catherine rose to her feet, wondering what to do with it. Leaving a dead bird on the carpet of someone's home seemed like the height of rudeness. She should put it outside. In fact, sentimental though the notion was, she thought perhaps she should bury it. It had gotten pretty dark, she saw as she glanced out the window, but she did have her lantern, and perhaps she could find something to use as a shovel.

When she looked back down at the bird, it was gone.

Catherine stared at the empty expanse of carpet, as if waiting for it to magically reappear. Had it just been stunned? Perhaps, but she would have noticed, wouldn't she, if it had gotten up and flown off? How could she have missed it? Dead or living, birds didn't just vanish.

Then again, this wasn't the first strange experience she'd had since entering this cave. It was as if she'd become lost in a dream world where the physical rules didn't apply anymore. Not that that was possible. There was a logical explanation, there always was; there had to be. As her physics professor used to say, "There is a reason for everything. Just because you don't know the answer doesn't mean it's not there."

A soft noise drew her attention to the bookshelf, where she watched the volumes she'd replaced shifting one by one in order to line up more neatly in the row. The candles extinguished themselves with a little puff of smoke, first one, then the other.

There is a reason for everything, she told herself. She was tired. She was thirsty—hungry, too. She'd spent a stressful afternoon. Little wonder she was seeing things.

Catherine picked up the book from the carpet, and was about to replace it on the shelf when she had second thoughts. She'd barely glanced at it; when again would she have access to these kinds of revelatory images? Why not take a closer look while there was no one around to rip this font of information out of her hands and condemn her as a filthy-minded wanton on account of her very natural curiosity?

There being no chair in the room, Catherine set her lantern on the nightstand and reclined on the bed, propped on an elbow with the book open next to her. She perused it from beginning to end, studying each engraving as if it were an illustration in a biology textbook. One picture showed the couple in a luxuriously canopied bed, the woman astride the man as he inserted his erect penis into her vaginal opening. In another, the woman was again on top, but facing away from her lover, one hand gripping his erection so as to aim it between her legs. In two, the man stood while the woman reclined on a bed; in one, they coupled as animals did, he taking her from behind.

Several of the positions involved a good deal of lifting and twisting, with limbs entwined and heads thrown back in presumed ecstasy—the women included. Although Catherine had never taken Italian, it was close enough to Latin for her to make out parts of the verses, in one of which the woman was rhapsodizing about the "extraordinary pleasure" it gave her to feel the thrusting of her bedmate's penis inside her. In almost every illustration, the reproductive anatomy was depicted in frank and astounding detail—vulvas, labia, bulging scrota, rigid penises with their helmetlike tips...

In the picture to which she kept returning, a bearded man knelt with his lover's legs thrown over his shoulders, pressing his erection into her. Catherine had known, of course, that sexual intercourse involved the insertion of the male member into the female, but knowing about it and actually seeing it were two very different things. The sight of a distended penis half-buried in a woman's body was oddly exciting in a way that Catherine wouldn't have predicted. Her face and throat grew warm as she imagined the pushing and straining that must accompany the act; her breathing quickened.

How must it feel, she wondered, to be penetrated like that by a man, to be *taken* in an act of animal passion? She'd always assumed it must be rather distasteful, but the more she looked at the picture, the more she doubted that assumption.

Catherine closed her eyes and lay on her back, envisioning the couple in the picture, not as a black-and-white engraving, but as real, flesh-and-blood lovers sharing their bodies in the ultimate act of intimacy. The image was startlingly real, as if she were watching a stage play, albeit an extremely bawdy one, from the front row. She imagined how it would feel to open herself up like that, physically, to a man, to be made love to, to experience that kind of pleasure.

Extraordinary pleasure.

Catherine felt the most curious sensation of heat and swelling between her legs, and dampness, too, although she wasn't perspiring elsewhere. She hesitated, then pressed a hand to the juncture of her thighs, through her skirt and underpinnings. She rubbed her fingers back and forth slightly, which both relieved and exacerbated the feeling, as when one scratched an itch, only to find that the scratching itself heightened the irritation. She'd never touched herself like this, though she suspected men did occasionally, or at least some men. Abbie had once whispered of walking in on her brother when he was fondling himself "there."

A hand stroked her breast.

She jolted upright, every nerve on end. For a split second, she thought she saw a shadowy form looming over her in the semidarkness, but the illusion evaporated as she looked around, heart drumming.

No one was there. Of course no one was there. She was alone here. What she'd felt, or thought she'd felt, was a delusion, like the others she'd been experiencing these past few hours.

She lay back down again, an arm thrown over her face. *It isn't real,* she told herself. *It's a figment of my imagination.* From her reading, she knew that hallucinations could be brought on by many factors other than those, such as intoxication or lunacy, which she could discount out of hand in her particular case. Fatigue, dehydration, and stress, all of which she'd been suffering from this afternoon, could make one experience things that weren't really happening.

And then there was the magnetic vortex that had, at the very least, disabled her compass and watch. If it could affect inanimate objects that way, perhaps it could also affect the human mind.

She felt a kind of ticklish heat on both breasts through her shirtwaist and camisole, as of fingertips trailing over them very, very softly. Her heart raced; her lungs pumped. Then came a breathless warmth as the hands caressed her more firmly, but still with a mesmerizing gentleness.

It isn't real, she told herself, even as she luxuriated in the soft friction, her breasts seeming almost to swell, her nipples tightening into stiff little nubs. None of this was real. It was her mind playing tricks on her, giving her that which she most desired—the pleasure she must deny herself in reality, but about which she was wildly curious.

The hands moved downward to her skirt, gathering up the heavy brown wool and the linen petticoat beneath. She felt them on her stockinged legs, and then her bare thighs, which they parted. Feeling starved for breath, Catherine folded both arms over her face, her eyes tightly shut, whispering, "This isn't real. It isn't happening."

There came a little creak of bedropes as the mattress dipped between her outspread legs, almost as if someone had lowered himself there. She felt the brushing of fingers through her linen underdrawers and a little plucking sensation as one of the buttons securing the slit in the drawers popped from its buttonhole. Or seemed to.

A second button slid free, and a third, and a forth, with maddening slowness, the fingertips grazing her very lightly along her most sensitive flesh. When at last the slit was unbuttoned, she felt the fabric being spread open, exposing that part of her that even she had never really seen, never touched except to bathe. The cool air was a shock on her hotly aroused sex, magnifying her sense of exposure.

She should have been appalled. She should have bolted off this bed and fled from this strange place, this dark and delicious phantasm. Instead, she lay still and trembling as the unseen hands parted, caressed... A soft moan escaped her as the touch turned rhythmic, but still teasingly light, compelling her to lift her hips to meet it.

Her lungs stilled when she felt hot gusts of breath on her inflamed sex, and the tickle of what could only be hair brushing her legs. *No, surely not,* she thought as something soft and wet glided between her labia, sending shivers of arousal throughout her body. She clutched the quilt in her fists, thinking, *He can't be... He wouldn't...*

The tongue—for that was what it was, or what she imagined it to be—lapped and flicked and explored until she was writhing and moaning as if maddened by fever. She felt a prickly scraping on her inner thighs, as of several days' growth of beard. The contrast of the sharp bristles with the hot, wet, wonderfully curious tongue only served to stoke her escalating arousal.

She caught her breath as a finger slid into her, moving slowly, thoughtfully, as if investigating the snug, ultrasensitive passage. It could enter only to the first knuckle and no farther. Still, the sensation of being caressed from within was so gratifying that she strained her hips upward, wanting more, wanting *him.*

The finger withdrew. He shifted position, settling his naked hips between her thighs. His hand moved between them, and then came a different kind of pressure as something much more broad and rigid pressed into her. She realized what it was and whispered, "Yes. Yes..."

But then the pressure became a burning ache as he pushed against her hymen. Alarmed, for it hurt, hallucination or no, she opened her eyes and tried to sit up.

A hand took hers; she felt warm lips against her palm. "Shh, it's all right," whispered her imaginary lover in a deep, vaguely accented voice. He eased her back down and lowered himself onto her, scooping both hands beneath her hips to lift her. When she closed her eyes again, he seemed as real as if he were actually there, warm and weighty and masculine. She wrapped her arms around him, feeling the hard-packed, straining muscles of his back and shoulders.

"It's all right," he repeated as he pushed, just slightly, and again, and again. She felt impossibly stretched, but that sensation was overwhelmed by the primal thrill of being penetrated, possessed. He inched into her gradually, breaching her maidenhead by increments until he was completely inside her, a thick, solid presence that seemed to fill her up so completely, she could scarcely breathe.

He took her face in his hands and kissed her, and then he began moving again, slowly and shallowly at first, then more deeply and with mounting urgency. His breathing grew harsh; every muscle in his body was as taut as a bowstring.

The lingering pain of defloration dissipated, replaced by the same pleasure she'd felt when he'd been stroking and licking her, only more intense because he was inside her. She met his thrusts with increasing fervor, driven by a wild and primitive hunger she'd never felt before. The pleasure seemed to expand inside her until it felt, suddenly, as if she were teetering on the edge of some heart-pounding abyss over which she had no control. Bewildered and apprehensive, she tried to hold still in the hope of staving off whatever was about to happen.

"Don't be afraid," he whispered. "Let it happen. Give yourself over to it."

"I can't. I just—"

"You can." He reached between them to touch her where they were joined.

It was like firing a bullet into a stick of dynamite. Her body erupted in convulsive ecstasy, tearing a raw cry from her throat as she tumbled over the edge.

Three

BY THE time Catherine returned to the chateau that night, having made her way back down the mountain in the dark, she found the dining room empty but for a few maidservants clearing away the remains of an elaborate dinner. They directed her to a nearby sitting room, in the doorway of which she paused, hesitating to enter dressed in her grimy day clothes, her hair springing from her chignon in sweat-dampened tendrils.

Six people—her father, Thomas, Archer, Inigo, Lili, and Elic—were relaxing over coffee and brandy in the sumptuously appointed room, the men in dinner suits, Lili in an off-the-shoulder gown of shimmering aubergine silk. Her lush mane of black hair was piled atop her head in a luxuriant mass; diamonds dangled from her ears and encircled her throat. She was perched on the arm of the velvet-upholstered club chair in which Thomas sat with a book open on his lap—of course—her arm brushing his as she leaned over to turn the page.

It looked like a painting by Sargent—the rich interior gilded by candlelight, the careless grace of the subjects. Lili and Thomas looked as if they belonged together, with their dark, gleaming hair and elegant attire. White tie was flattering on most men, and Thomas was no exception. It made him look older, more sophisticated, especially since he seemed so comfortable in it. Catherine had seen him in dinner attire many times but the sight had never struck her quite the same way before. Perhaps, she thought, it was because she was seeing Thomas through Lili's eyes, without so many of her own preconceptions.

Lili pointed to the page and said something too softly for Catherine to hear.

It must have been some witty comment, because Thomas chuckled as he turned toward her, his gaze lighting for a fleeting moment on her bosom before he looked up and met her eyes. He looked at her the way a man looked at a sexually desirable woman, not leeringly, of course, but with an unmistakable glint of admiration. That look shouldn't have surprised Catherine—Lili was magnificent, after all—but for some reason she'd never thought of Thomas as susceptible to feminine allure in the same way that other men were. Absurd, of course. An ivory-tower academician he might be, but he was still a man.

Catherine's father was the first one to notice her standing there in the doorway. "There you are, my dear. Back from your adventures at last." Elijah set aside his own book and rose to his feet, as did the other gentlemen. "We went ahead and ate without you."

"Are you all right, Catherine?" asked Thomas as he took off his reading spectacles.

"I'm fine. I hope I didn't worry you."

Flipping up his coattails as he lowered himself back onto a couch strewn with books, her father said, "Kit and Thomas wanted to send out a search party, thinking you'd wandered too deeply into the cave and gotten yourself in a pickle. I assured them you were an old hand at such adventures, you and your trusty compass, and that you wouldn't dream of venturing beyond *Cella*."

"I lost track of time," Catherine said.

"That's easy to do, in certain areas of the cave." Mr. Archer, seated across a backgammon board from Elic, was studying Catherine a bit too fixedly for her comfort. "People have reported all sorts of strange incidents."

He knows, Catherine thought—or he suspected. Had other people really experienced the same types of phenomena that she had? If so, that would make the vortex theory likelier than the thirst-fatigue-stress theory. The notion, however, that terrestrial magnetism could produce not just compass anomalies but full-blown delusions would no doubt be greeted with hilarity by the scientific community.

Steadfastly avoiding Archer's gaze, Catherine said, "Actually, I fell asleep," which was true, if a bit disingenuous. She *had* dozed off after that remarkable fantasy of lovemaking, but not for long, she was fairly sure. When she awoke, it took her a moment to recall where she was and what had happened—or what she'd imagined had happened. The delusion had extended to a feeling of actual soreness between her legs, which had diminished only slightly in the interim. What she wanted to believe, what she *had* to believe for the sake of her sanity, was that it was just a residual imprint of an exceptionally powerful hallucination.

"Are you sure you're all right?" asked Thomas, eyeing her with concern. "You look a bit worse for wear."

"I've no doubt of that," she said. "All I really need is a nice warm bath and a good night's sleep."

"And some food, I'll wager," Thomas said. "You missed a splendid dinner. A leg of lamb with onions and potatoes in white wine."

"Gigot Brayaude," Elic said. "One of our cook's specialties."

"I'll have someone in the kitchen bring you a plate," said Archer as he heaved himself out of his chair and reached for the bellpull.

"No, please don't," Catherine said. "I can't stay. I'm not . . ." She gestured toward her grubby clothing.

"Nonsense." Lili came over and put an arm around

Catherine, drawing her into the room. "We don't stand on ceremony here. Please join us. Have a brandy while you're waiting for your supper. You look as if you could use it."

"Or something a little stronger, perhaps?" Inigo lifted the stemmed glass in his hand, which held a milky, pale green liquid with an almost phosphorescent quality. On a cut-crystal tray next to him were a pitcher of water, a slotted spoon, a bowl of sugar cubes, and a bottle of Pernod.

"Inigo, if you turn my daughter into an absinthe fiend," drawled Elijah without raising his gaze from his book, "I shall be forced to reconsider my high opinion of you."

"A brandy would be lovely," said Catherine as she took a seat on the couch next to her father, shoving some of his books aside and piling others onto the floor. "Thank you."

A maid entered in response to Archer's summons. "A supper plate for Miss Wheeler," he said, "and have one of the chambermaids draw her a bath."

The lamb *was* splendid, and Catherine was famished. She had to struggle to keep from wolfing it down as Elijah delivered a lecture on the history of Auvergne, working backward in time from Frankish rule to Visigothic to Roman.

"The Romans occupied this area for just over five hundred years," her father said, "beginning in 52 B.C., when the armies of Julius Caesar defeated the legendary Gallic warlord Vercingetorix at the Battle of Alésia. The battle and the fighting that led up to it are described in excellent detail within these pages." Lifting a very old-looking book from the stack on the floor, he opened it to its title page.

C. JULII
CÆSARIS
COMMENTARII
DE BELLO GALLICO
ET CIVILI
TOMUS VII.

Lili came to look over Elijah's shoulder, leaning down so that her hair brushed his. A warm, floral scent wafted about her, as if she were a rare and exotic flower. "Julius Caesar himself wrote this?" she asked.

"He, er, he did," said Elijah, seeming a little rattled by the feminine attention. "And it's the most authoritative account available, not only of the Gallic Wars, but of the Gauls themselves—or, what he called the Galli. They called themselves the Celtæ. The Romans had been colonizing Gaul for some time before they invaded, so there'd been a great deal of trade and communication between the two civilizations."

Mr. Archer said, "I actually have a little collection of Roman coins that have turned up here over the years, along with various other Roman and Gaulish *objets.*"

"Thomas sniffed out a Gaulish glossary in the appendix of a book in the library this afternoon," Elijah said. "It's not much of a glossary, because the Gauls weren't much for writing, but he looked up *væsus,* and there was a definition. It means great, or worthy, so it would stand to reason that 'Dusivæsus' translates as 'Great and worthy dusios.'"

"What of the second inscription?" Lili turned toward Elijah, their faces so close one would have thought they were about to kiss. "The one that's sort of hacked out roughly over the first? Did you manage to translate that?" She met Elic's gaze across the room in a very brief, unspoken communion of some sort. He paused in the act of moving some backgammon checkers to give her the kind of smile you gave someone for whom words are never necessary.

They had a bond, Elic and Lili; it was clear from the way they looked at each other, the way they acted, the little touches and smiles. Unless Catherine was very much mistaken, they were lovers. Yet, both last night and tonight, she'd flirted shamelessly with both Elijah and Thomas, and Elic hadn't so much as raised an eyebrow.

Perhaps, Catherine thought, they were free lovers. Given the sexual liberality that appeared to be the norm at Grotte Cachée, it seemed possible, perhaps even probable. The only real question in Catherine's mind was what a woman like Lili saw in scholarly types like Elijah and Thomas, especially since she'd evidently already captured the heart of Elic, who was almost preternaturally handsome, seemingly intelligent, and with a most amiable disposition. Her father, though fit and good-looking for his age, had to be a good twenty years older than Lili. As for Thomas…

She stole a glance at him. He was looking at her with an expression that was contemplative and vaguely sad, his snifter of brandy cupped loosely in his hand, seemingly forgotten. She looked away, confounded by his melancholic beauty, then back again. Clearly sensing her discomfiture, he gave her a reassuring little smile that, in light of all that had transpired between them of late, wasn't hard to interpret.

It's all right, that smile seemed to say. *You don't want me, so I shall trouble you no more with my attentions. We can carry on as friends.*

"We, er, we did translate that second inscription," said Elijah as Lili leaned in even closer, one hand resting nonchalantly on his shoulder. "It was written in the oldest runic alphabet we know of, which is called Elder Futhark, and it's actually two linked words in Old Norse—*kjønn,* meaning… well, 'sex,' and *præll,* meaning 'thrall,' or 'slave.'"

"So it means sex slave," said Inigo. "Funny, I can't recall having posed for it. Must have been in my cups at the time."

He shot a grin, for some reason, at Elic, who rolled his eyes in response.

Elijah said, "Kit was kind enough to point me to a handwritten *Histoire de Grotte Cachée* as recounted by Seigneur des Ombres's… grandfather, was it?"

"Great-grandfather," said Kit.

"Of course," Elijah said, "it's a bit cursory regarding the pre-Roman history of this valley, which is understandable, given the Gauls' disdain for the written word. There were exactly one and a half pages in the *Histoire* devoted to the Gallic settlement in this valley, which was called Vernem. The Vernae, or most of them, fled the village for parts unknown, one step ahead of Caesar's army. The Romans, you see, had a habit of enslaving conquered tribespeople, and to a Gaul, there was no worse fate than enslavement."

"If that's so," Catherine asked, "why didn't they all leave? You said *most* of them fled. What of the rest?"

"They stayed behind and were turned into slaves. They did have a sort of leader, apparently, someone referred to in the *Histoire* as Anextlomarus, which translates as Protector. He's credited with having ensured that the Vernan slaves were treated well and permitted to remain in the valley. Kit, you probably know more about the Vernae than any man alive. Any idea why that group stayed here?"

Mr. Archer frowned into his brandy as if considering the question. "Couldn't really say, old man." His gaze shifted briefly, but never met Elijah's.

He's lying, Catherine thought. *But why?*

"I'd love to know the answer to that," Elijah said. "And, of course, I'm desperate to sort out the mystery behind those damned—" He glanced at Catherine. "Excuse me, ladies. The mystery behind those satyrs at the bathhouse. They're just so un-Roman. It simply makes no sense. It's maddening, utterly maddening." With a self-deprecatory little chuckle, he said, "Julia—my late wife..."

"Yes, you've mentioned her," said Lili as she crossed the room to sit next to Inigo. In fact, he'd mentioned her at least a dozen times since they'd been there.

Elijah said, "Once, when I was obsessed with unraveling a particularly thorny historical enigma, Julia told me I would never be satisfied unless I could travel back in time and witness the event for myself. She was right about that," he said soberly, "as she was about so many things."

Lili smiled as Inigo whispered something into her ear. "What a splendid idea. Dr. Wheeler, why don't you join us tomorrow, Inigo and me, for a little picnic in the woods. You shouldn't waste this beautiful weather cooped up in that dusty old library. There's a little clearing in a thicket of oaks that you might find—"

"The nemeton?" Archer sat up, scowling. "Do you really think—?"

"He's a mythologist," Lili said. "If anyone could appreciate the nemeton, it would be Dr. Wheeler."

"A nemeton?" Elijah said excitedly. "A druidic sacred grove?"

"Well," Archer said, "it hasn't been used for ceremonial purposes in some nineteen hundred—"

"Of course I'd like to see it," said Elijah. "I'd *love* to see it. Thank you for asking."

As her father launched into yet another lesson, this one on the subject of druidic rituals, Catherine excused herself and went upstairs to the bathroom. The wood-paneled tub was filled and steaming, her blue-checked wrapper draped over the back of a chair. She undressed, nonplussed to find the inner skin of her thighs pink and raw from having been rubbed by a beard-roughened jaw.

Except that it didn't really happen, it couldn't have—just as she couldn't have really lost her virginity this afternoon, despite how tender she still was between her legs. She'd imagined it—hadn't she? Would she ever know the truth of what had transpired in that strange little bedchamber in the cave?

Possibly not. Probably not.

Just because you don't know the answer doesn't mean it's not there. Something happened. A hallucination or . . . something else. Oddly enough, given Catherine's analytical nature, she felt no need to solve this particular mystery through rigorous application of the scientific method. Perhaps, as her father and Thomas maintained, not all answers could be found within the realm of bloodless science.

And perhaps some mysteries were never meant to be solved.

Catherine unpinned her hair and lowered herself into the rose-scented water, sighing as it enveloped her. Laying her head back against the lip of the tub, she closed her eyes and let the warmth of the water permeate her bone-weary, dirt-caked body.

She stroked the flesh of her inner thighs, which felt just as chafed as it looked. Tentatively, for this was new territory for her, she felt between her legs until she located her vaginal opening, which stung when she touched it. She probed it gingerly, finding it smaller and tighter than she would have thought, given what it had accommodated this afternoon, and slick with secretions.

Emboldened, she explored the delicate little folds and furrows of her sex, her inquisitive fingers exciting a buzz of pleasure that, paradoxically, seemed to transport her out of her body. Closing her eyes, she let her mind drift where it would.

She saw Thomas smiling that sad, resigned smile . . . *It's all right* . . . She saw the books straightening themselves on the shelf in that little bedchamber in the cave, saw the candles puffing out of their own accord . . . She saw her walking stick quivering on end, felt the thrill of penetration, the wholeness of it, the rightness of it . . .

She heard her ragged breaths and the lapping of the bathwater, felt the pleasure mounting toward its inevitable climax, panic squeezing her heart . . .

"You're afraid," he whispered. "Don't be. Let it happen. Give us a chance. I love you, Catherine. I want to marry you."

The pleasure exploded and ran its course, leaving her breathless and reeling, her face wet with tears.

Four

"THIS IS the nemeton?" asked Elijah Wheeler in reverential tones around noon the next day as Lili and Inigo led him into a sun-speckled clearing in a grove of ancient, strangely twisted oaks. In the center stood a stone altar, and next to it a patch of ashy earth enclosed by a circle of soot-blackened stones.

"This is it, brother." Setting down the wicker hamper their cook had packed, Inigo took the blanket from Lili, shook it out, and laid it on the grass.

Elijah was filled with awe as he approached the ancient altar, essentially a table supported by four lava boulders. The top was a rectangular slab of the same dark stone about the shape and size of a door, its edges scoured by time—for it was at least two thousand years old, possibly a good deal older.

Elijah circled the altar slowly, tracing with his fingers the timeworn, convoluted pattern inscribed on its surface. The center bore the inscription DIBU E DEBU surrounded by a design of oak branches knotted together. In each of the four corners was carved a circle about eight inches across, enclosing a different stylized image.

"These corner symbols would appear to represent four of the most important Celtic deities," he said. "This female figure on the horse has to be Epona, a goddess of fertility. She was especially revered among the Gauls. The old man with the bow and club is Ogimos, god of warcraft and poetry. The figure cutting branches with an axe is Esus, the god of agriculture and commerce. And this three-headed fellow with the raven on his fist is Lugus, whom Caesar equated with Mercury. He was a very important deity to the Gauls, the protector of travelers and source of all the arts. I can't believe a relic this extraordinary has stood here undiscovered for all these years."

"Seigneur des Ombres takes great care, as did his ancestors before him, to keep Grotte Cachée's historical artifacts away from prying eyes," said Lili as she knelt to empty blue china plates, cut crystal glasses, and covered dishes from the hamper out onto the blanket. She was clad, as she'd been yesterday until supper, in a saronglike swath of colorful silk—gold-trimmed plum today—which she called a *lubushu*. Her hair hung in a single braid down her back; her only jewelry was an exotically archaic-looking gold and lapis anklet. Not once, in his entire life and all his travels, had Elijah met a female as unself-consciously sensual as Lili. When he'd asked where she was from, she'd said she'd been born on the bank of the Euphrates, and changed the subject.

"Is anyone hungry?" she asked, unwrapping a linen napkin from what looked like a large, golden brown onion tart.

"First things first," said Inigo as he uncorked a bottle of wine—one of four local vintages tucked into the hamper.

"No more—please," Elijah said in a drowsy slur a couple of hours later, as Inigo, reclining next to him on the blanket, tilted a bottle over his half-empty glass. "I haven't drunk this much since I was in college. I won't be able to keep my eyes open."

"You needn't keep them open on our account." Lili, sitting behind him, lifted the glass from his hand and pressed down gently on his shoulder until he was lying with his head in her lap.

He should have refused—the only woman he'd ever had that kind of physical contact with was Julia—but dreamily contented as he was, with his belly full of wine and wonderful food, and in the company of such agreeable companions, he couldn't bring himself to protest.

"Go ahead," she murmured as she stroked his face very lightly, her fingertips soft, cool, hypnotic. "Close your eyes." She whispered a singsongy phrase over and over again in a language he'd never heard before—like Aramaic, but not quite—as she continued to caress his brow and cheeks and chin. The intoxicating scent of jasmine enveloped him. Warm breezes ruffled his hair, or perhaps it was her breath.

Inigo, sounding oddly distant, started saying something in an entirely different, but equally unfamiliar language. Except that it didn't really sound like Inigo. It was another voice, that of a much older man.

Elijah opened his eyes, thinking how unseemly it would be for strangers to happen upon him lying there with his head in Lili's lap. He expected to see her face smiling down on him. Instead, all he saw was the sun glittering through the canopy of oak leaves overhead.

He turned his head toward the old man's voice and discovered, to his bewilderment, that there was no soft leg beneath him, no blanket either, just the cool, prickly grass. Lili and Inigo were nowhere to be seen, but under one of the old oaks at the edge of the clearing there sat two men, one young and one quite elderly. The old fellow, bearded and wizened, sat on a squarish boulder against the tree, the clean-shaven, blond-haired young man a few feet away on a tree stump, leaning over a plank of wood balanced across his lap. A large, powerfully built dog—a mastiff, or something like it—slept between them with its broad-skulled head resting on the old man's feet.

The younger man was writing, Elijah realized, with a reed pen on a length of paper—or was it parchment?—as the old man droned on. He paused and asked the speaker something, addressing him as Brantigern; upon receiving an answer, he nodded and continued writing, as if he were taking dictation. There was an Italic quality to many of the words and phrases that Brantigern spoke, but Elijah was at a loss to translate them.

Their clothing was exceedingly odd. They both wore woolen tunics—the older man's saffron, the younger, a rusty brown—and trousers that had stripes woven into the fabric. More curious still was their hair, which was as long as Elic's; but instead of tying it back in a queue, as Elic did, they'd plaited it into multiple braids that hung down past their shoulders.

There were isolated pockets of peasant folks all over Europe who still wore their ancestral garb and spoke nearly extinct dialects. Elijah hadn't been aware of such indigenous folks in Auvergne, but that didn't mean they didn't exist. Clearly, they did.

Elijah stood up, feeling surprisingly sober, and walked toward them. "Good afternoon, gentlemen."

They ignored him entirely, perhaps because he'd unthinkingly greeted them in English. "*Bonjour, messieurs,*" he said.

Were they deaf?

Although only a few yards away from them now, he raised his voice and waved an arm. "*Bonjour!*"

There was no response from the two men beneath the oak, but from the woods to the south, toward the chateau, a boy's voice yelled, "Brantigern! Sedanias!"

The two men and the dog all looked up sharply as the boy, also in traditional clothing, but with his red hair flying loose, burst into the clearing from the path in the woods, yelling something breathlessly as he pointed in the direction from which he'd come.

The young man, Sedanias, bolted to his feet, hurriedly rolling the scroll around a stick. He wrapped it in a length of leather as he sprinted toward the altar, which looked different than it had earlier, during the picnic—newer, less timeworn. One of the circular corner designs, that depicting Lugus and the raven, was missing, leaving a hole where it should have been. Sedanias shoved the leather-wrapped scroll vertically into the hole, then lifted a stone disc from the grass and fitted it into place, positioning it just so.

Brantigern, meanwhile, tucked the wooden plank between the tree and the boulder on which he sat, then gathered up the younger man's reed pen, ink pot, and pen knife, and stowed them in a knothole.

The boy darted back into a different section of the woods as hoofbeats approached along the path.

A man around thirty years of age with dark, neatly shorn hair rode into the clearing, reins in one hand, a club in the other. Elijah gaped in astonishment at the horseman's appearance, for he was clad in a belted, Roman-style *tunica*—white with a wide purple stripe from right shoulder to hem—and red boots secured by leather thongs. The iron ring he wore, in conjunction with the *tunica laticlavia* and the red boots, identified him as a patrician male of ancient Rome. The horse was draped with a long scarlet saddlecloth trimmed in gold braid, on which the rider sat directly, without benefit of saddle. Like the two peasants and the boy, he seemed entirely, perplexingly, unaware of Elijah's presence.

Reining in his mount, he pointed his club at Sedanias and barked out, "You, there!" in Latin—not quite the classical form with which Elijah was most familiar, but still reasonably understandable. "What do you think you're doing here, Sedanias? You're supposed to be cutting marble down by the cave. Are you that eager for a beating?"

"It's my fault," said the old man as he struggled to his feet with the help of a tall, age-burnished oak staff that was peculiarly twisty and knotted toward the top. Elijah hadn't noticed before that he had only one hand, the left. His right arm ended in a stump above the wrist.

"Brantigern Avitus." The horseman bent his head in respectful greeting, which struck Elijah as odd, as did his use of the cognomen Avitus, which suggested something akin to a grandfatherly relationship. "I didn't see you there."

"I heard of the death of the great Augustus," Brantigern said, "so I asked my grandson to bring me here, to our sacred place, to beseech the gods to welcome the Emperor as one of their own. Forgive me, Quintus Vetus—and forgive Sedanias, too, I beg you. He was only indulging a trying old man."

"Yes. Well," said Quintus, clearly at something of a loss. "Praying for the late Emperor... It's a most commendable gesture, but I hope you understand that I can't have slaves just walking away from their assigned tasks without asking my leave." To Sedanias, he said, "Return to your work. But first, see your grandfather back safely to his hut. If anything happens to him, it's I who'll take a beating, at the hands of my father. You know how he depends on the old man's soothsaying." He turned his horse around and left.

Sedanius and Brantigern shared a conspiratorial little smile. "Come, Yannig," said Brantigern, and then the two men and the dog disappeared down the path, the dog staying close by the old man's side as he shuffled along with halting steps, leaning on his staff.

Was he going mad? Elijah wondered. This didn't feel like a delusion, and he'd never once, in the past, experienced any form of mental derangement. Why, then, had he just seen what he'd seen?

He saw a hint of movement and looked up to see a gray cat walking along a branch of the oak tree beneath which the pair had been sitting. It jumped down, looked directly at Elijah, and mewed.

"Well, at least I'm not invisible to *you,*" Elijah said.

The cat strolled through the clearing to the edge of the path and sat, staring at Elijah, who walked over to it. When he was about a yard away, it got up and padded down the path.

Elijah took one last look around the clearing, wondering what the devil had become of Lili and Inigo—never mind his sanity—and then he followed the cat along the path toward the chateau.

Only, when he emerged from the woods, the chateau, which should have been tucked into the lowest part of the valley about two hundred yards away, wasn't there. In its place, he saw a sprawling white house with red-tiled roofs surrounded by formal, colonnaded gardens.

"A villa," he whispered, for it looked precisely like the country homes built by wealthy Roman citizens, both in Rome and in their provinces. With every blink, he expected it to disappear, but there it stood, like a drawing in a history book.

He recalled what he'd said last night, about Julia telling him he'd never be satisfied unless he could travel back in time and witness historical events for himself. Was it possible this was all a dream in which his desire to know more about Grotte Cachée's enigmatic past was being subconsciously fulfilled? A tempting theory, except that this didn't feel remotely like a dream; it was far, far too real.

So if he wasn't dreaming, and he wasn't mad, what on earth was happening here?

There had been times, many times, in his studies of occult phenomena and his sojourns among peoples who believed in such things, that he'd found himself weighing the possibility that certain forms of "magic" might fall within the realm of reality. There were, after all, many unanswered questions in the universe, and physical scientists had barely scratched the surface in terms of what they knew about space, time, and matter. That given, was it entirely impossible that the things he was seeing had actually existed some two millennia before? The best course of action, Elijah decided, would be to relax, observe, and remember.

Oh, and figure out how to exit this new reality and return to that in which he'd been living his life for the past forty-six years.

Elijah heard a repetitive *thunk, thunk, thunk* from the direction of the bathhouse—or where the bathhouse should be, at the entrance of the cave in the extinct volcano on the eastern edge of the valley. He made his way through a small woods that didn't exist in his own time, at the edge of which a team of axe-wielding men dressed like Sedanias and Brantigern—slaves, he presumed—were felling trees in order to enlarge an already sizeable clearing. Not one of them turned to look as he walked past.

In the clearing, other slaves, shirtless and sweating in the harsh afternoon sun, were cutting slabs of white marble into smaller blocks with hammers and chisels. An enormous white linen tent stood against the base of the mountain, concealing the mouth of the cave. From within it, Elijah heard a man saying, in Latin, "Not much longer now, my darling Inigo. Just mind you stay good and hard till I'm done with you."

Inigo?

"Tita, keep those legs spread. What do you think you're getting paid for?"

Elijah found an opening in the tent and slipped through. Inside, bathed in a haze of filtered sunlight and marble dust, he found the bathhouse, or a partial version thereof. There were no walls and no roof, just the marble floor, the pool itself—devoid of water and with the mosaic half-finished—and the four columns, each with a massive chunk of white marble appended to it.

A muscular fellow in a dusty blue *tunica* stood chiseling away at one of the blocks, which was well on its way to being a finished sculpture, while his models—Inigo and a voluptuous raven-haired beauty, both naked—posed for him. The young woman, Tita presumably, was bent over with her legs widespread, hugging a thick tree trunk stripped of its bark—a stand-in, obviously, for the column—while Inigo stood behind her with his hands around her waist, his back slightly bowed and his hips tucked.

The first remarkable thing Elijah noticed about Inigo was his erect penis. About as thick around as a woman's forearm, it was actually penetrating Tita, with about five or six inches showing. Never in his life, even among primitive tribespeople who weren't terribly shy about such matters, had Elijah witnessed an act of coition taking place right in front of him. Not that this was sex in the usual sense. Inigo and this woman, although physically joined, weren't even moving; they were posing. It made sense, now that Elijah thought about it, that such accomplished sculptures would have required live models. Silently chiding himself for his priggish reaction, he strove to take an intellectually detached view of the situation. He was a scholar of human beliefs and practices, not some judgmental Philistine. And what was happening here was, after all, an artistic endeavor.

"Stop thrusting, Inigo," the sculptor ordered. "I'm doing the crack of your ass."

"You *wish* you were doing the crack of my ass," Inigo retorted with a snort.

Tita chuckled. The sculptor cast his gaze wearily to the heavens, but Elijah could see that he was fighting back a smile. "Don't get a big head over it, darling. It's not *you* that gets my heart beating like a bird's. You're an overgrown child, and I loathe children. It's that truncheon of yours. I swear, it's the most lickable thing I've ever seen, and I've licked a few in my day."

With a snicker, Inigo said, "Curious thing, Marcus, how you always manage to bring the conversation around to that particular subject."

"People enjoy talking about their areas of expertise," Marcus said as he blew a puff of dust off the statue's marble buttocks.

"That good, are you?"

"I've been assured there are none better."

"All right, then." Withdrawing from Tita—by God, that thing was huge—Inigo turned and strode toward Marcus, his fist wrapped around the proffered organ. "Prove it."

That was when Elijah noticed the second remarkable thing about Inigo, which was that he had a tail that swung back and forth as he walked. Beyond shock at this point, Elijah just stared, wondering what was next.

Marcus recoiled from Inigo's outthrust, glistening erection. "Not after it's been in *that,*" he said, pointing to Tita's exposed sex with his hammer. "Tonight, after we're done here, I'll meet you—"

"You had your chance," taunted Inigo as he returned to Tita, grabbed her hips, and pushed himself back in, causing her to purr delightedly.

"Bitch," Marcus said as he returned to his work.

The third remarkable thing Elijah noticed about Inigo—and at this point, it was a mere footnote to the rest, a mild curiosity—was that his ears were pointed and he had a pair of small, bony horns poking through the cap of black curlicues on his head.

"*Will* you stop that damned thrusting?" Marcus demanded.

"You want me to stay hard, don't you?"

"Think arousing thoughts."

"I've been thinking about you licking me. It isn't doing the job."

"I like it when he thrusts," said Tita, squirming with pleasure.

Reaching around to touch her between her legs, Inigo said, "So you do." Tita moaned as Inigo caressed her. He thrust harder, more purposefully.

"Stop that!" Marcus snapped, but the command fell on deaf ears. "Oh, hell," he muttered. "Will you at least be quick about it this time?"

"Oh..." Tita sighed, clutching at the tree trunk, her breasts and hair swaying with every thrust. "Oh, yes...yes...yes..."

Without pausing in what he was doing, Inigo turned and looked directly at Elijah. "Wake up, sleepyhead," he said in Julia's voice.

Elijah opened his eyes to find himself back in the clearing, lying on the blanket. A woman was crouching over him to unbutton his trousers, her face obscured by a swath of rippling, golden-brown hair. The gauzy morning dress she wore, apple green with tiny white dots, had always been his favorite.

"Julia?" he said incredulously.

She turned and smiled at him, the breeze lifting her hair. He breathed in the Roger & Gallet eau de cologne he gave her for Christmas every year, tears stinging his eyes.

"Oh, my God." Elijah reached out with a trembling hand to touch her hair, her face, his arm oddly heavy, as if he were underwater. "Oh, my God. Oh, my God. Julia. How can this . . . ? How can you . . . ?"

"I can't stay long," she said as she caressed him. "I just want to feel you inside me again. Just let me . . ."

"Yes," he whispered. "Oh, God, yes." How long had it been since he'd made love to her? Since well before he'd lost her, because she'd been so ill for so long. He moaned her name as she stroked him, reveling in her cool, soft fingertips, her familiar touch.

Tucking her skirts up, she knelt astride him, easing him into her, and it was so sweet and warm and perfect, just like it used to be. She kissed him as she moved, rocking slowly and gently at first, then deeper, faster . . .

They climaxed together, as they often used to, she coloring hotly as she always did, breathy little moans issuing from her. They lay together quietly as he softened inside her, their hearts beating next to each other, their lungs slowing in unison.

"I've missed this," he said, his breath ruffling her hair as she lay atop him with her head nestled heavily in the crook of his neck. The feel of her body conforming itself to his, the warmth of her skin, the knowledge that there was one person in the world who lived for him as he lived for her... God, he'd missed it so much.

"You can have it again," she said.

"But... you said you couldn't stay."

Rising up a bit so that she could meet his gaze, she said, "After I leave here, you'll never see me again. But there are other women..."

"No." He tried to shake his head, but it was too difficult. "No. I couldn't."

She chuckled softly, as she did whenever he was being unaccountably stubborn about something. "Of course you can. You must. You were never meant to be alone, Elijah. No human is."

"But—"

"I can't rest easy if I know you're alone, wanting this," she said, indicating the two of them lying together as one, "*craving* this, but thinking you mustn't. What we had was beautiful, but I'm gone now, and you're still here, stuck in this human form that needs so much. Grief has its natural limits, Elijah. It's time for you to tuck me away in your memory and open that generous heart of yours to someone else."

"Julia..."

"You know I'm right, Elijah. You know it here." She kissed his forehead. "But you need to feel it here." She rested a hand on his chest, over his heart. "Will you try?"

He searched her eyes, accepting the wisdom of what she was saying, but loath to tell this woman who'd been the other half of him that she was replaceable.

As if he'd spoken that thought aloud, Julia said, "She won't be me. She'll be the woman you need now, not the one you needed when we fell in love. It won't be a betrayal. It will be what you need, what I want for you. Will you try, my love? For me, if not for yourself?"

He managed to say, "I'll try. I will."

She smiled, and touched her lips to his. "Sleep now."

"No," he said, knowing that when he awoke, she would be gone. "No. Stay, Julia, please. I need you."

"You have me. You'll always have me."

"But—"

"Close your eyes, love," she murmured, stroking his forehead with a feathery touch. "Just for a few moments."

She whispered something else, then, strange, foreign words that he couldn't make out. Elijah's eyes drifted shut, and he found himself floating on the edge of sleep, thinking, *Don't leave. Please don't leave.*

He strained against the darkness, the swirling nothingness, forced his eyes to open, his limbs to move. His heart leapt when he saw her on the blanket next to him, lowering her skirt as she rose to her feet. But then he saw that her hair was black, hanging in a braid down her back, and that the skirt she was smoothing down wasn't green gauze, but plum-colored silk.

"Lili?" he said groggily as he sat up.

"You're awake," she said, with a little note of surprise.

"Wh-where is . . . ?" He looked around the clearing as he heaved himself unsteadily to his feet.

"Inigo went back to the chateau a little while ago. Don't you remember?" She crouched down to take hold of the blanket. "Would you help me with this?"

"Oh. Of course." Elijah stole glances at her as they folded the blanket—at her wrinkled *lubushu*, her slightly disheveled hair, the high color on those exotic cheekbones.

Had she . . . ? Had they . . . ?

Lili raised her gaze to him, her smile sweetly intimate, then lowered it again.

Good God. His stomach twisted with guilt, until he recalled Julia's words—or her words as he'd dreamt them. *It won't be a betrayal. It will be what you need, what I want for you.*

"It's gotten warm," she said, taking his arm. "We can go to the bathhouse and cool off in the pool."

A few yards down the path, Elijah paused and said, "If you don't mind, I'm going to linger a bit and have another look at that altar."

"Of course. Take your time." She kissed his cheek and walked away.

The altar looked just as it had when they'd first entered the clearing, the stone weathered and discolored by more than two thousand years of exposure to the elements. Elijah ran a hand over the corner design depicting Lugus, tracing its circular border for any gap or sign of looseness; there was none.

It was just a dream, he told himself, feeling a little foolish. But then he noticed the wing of the raven, which had been carved, unlike the rest of the image, in high bas-relief, as if the bird were about to rise up off the god's fist. Elijah closed his hand around the wing, feeling indentations beneath it that conformed perfectly to his thumb and fingertips.

He pulled; the disc shifted. He smiled in amazement, and pulled harder. It stuck, so he jimmied it a bit, twisted it this way and that. Presently, it lifted free. It was about three inches thick, rimmed with wax-coated bronze and curved inward so as to remain securely seated in the opening. Where it had been, there was a vertical tunnel, also lined with bronze, within the boulder that served as a leg for that corner of the altar. Looking down into it, he saw a cylindrical parcel wrapped in leather.

"My God," he whispered as he reached down into the hole to lift the parcel out. "My God Almighty."

He laid the parcel on the altar and pulled away the leather, which was stiff with age, as carefully as if he were unwrapping a priceless Egyptian mummy. The scroll within was parchment, which was excellent, parchment being a good deal more durable than paper. He unrolled it slowly, shaking his head in disbelief. It was heavily inked, from beginning to end, in neat rows of writing. The alphabet was Roman, which the Gauls—for this was surely a Gaulish manuscript—had adopted long before their homeland came under Roman rule about fifty years before the birth of Christ.

What was so astonishing about this document was that there was nothing else like it in existence, given the reluctance of Gaulish druids to allow important matters to be committed to writing. Of course, there was always the chance that the information on this scroll was of little historical import, but if so, why had it been secreted here with such care?

Elijah shivered with excitement as he recalled Sedanias recording every word spoken by the old man, Brantigern, who, slave or not, was clearly a revered elder—a soothsayer, no less, as respected by his Roman masters as by his Gaulish kin. Was it possible that this Brantigern, knowing that Roman occupation spelled the death knell for his people, was endeavoring to capture for posterity centuries of Gallic history and knowledge?

Elijah considered what to do with the scroll as he rolled it back up. By rights, he should return it to its resting place. Kit was exceedingly protective of Grotte Cachée's artifacts. He'd issued several stern reminders since their arrival that nothing of historical value was to be disturbed. But whereas Elijah respected his friend's curatorial diligence, how could he possibly ignore a document as potentially significant as this?

He couldn't. But neither could he let Kit know that he'd found it, much as he loathed the notion of keeping such a volatile secret from his oldest friend. There was a compromise, though, that he could live with. He would return the scroll to its hiding place tomorrow morning, before he left here with Catherine and Thomas. But first, he would copy it down, word for word, so that he could translate it later.

Elijah replaced the stone disc, rolled the scroll back up in its leather wrapper, tucked it inside his shirt, and returned to the chateau.

Five

IT'S JUST I," said Catherine as she knocked at the library door that evening.

She heard her father's chair scrape away from the table at which he'd been copying that scroll all afternoon, a task he expected would take him many more hours. "Are you alone?" he asked.

Catherine sighed. "Of course."

The key turned in the lock. He let her in, then returned to the table and picked up his pen. "This part I just copied down looks like a five-year calendar," he said excitedly. "It's known that the Romans forced the populations they conquered to use the Julian calendar and none other, but no one has ever known how the Gauls kept track of time and the seasons. Until now," he added proudly.

"Are you—"

"Oh, and the very beginning of the scroll looks most promising," he said, turning to the first page in the notebook he was filling with transcription. "Look," he said as he pointed to words on the page. "Alisiia, Vercingetorix, Titus Labienus, Mark Anthony, Julius Caesar... It must be a recounting of the Gallic Wars from the perspective of the Gauls. Until now, all we've had was the Roman side of the story. If I have time tonight after it's all copied out, I'll go back and start translating it right from the beginning. Perhaps there will be an explanation as to why some of the Vernae fled the Romans and some stayed."

"Splendid, but are you sure you should be doing this?"

"You sound like Thomas and Inigo," he grumbled.

"*Inigo* knows about this?" Thomas had been assisting in the copying all afternoon, albeit grudgingly, given the subterfuge involved. But why would Elijah have confided in Inigo, of all people?

"He came in before I had the foresight, in my zeal, to lock the door. He asked me if I thought it was 'quite kosher to slink around behind Archer's back this way.' "

"What's 'kosher'?" she asked.

"It's a Jewish thing," he said with that little wave of the hand that meant he was too preoccupied for long explanations.

"Is Inigo Jewish?"

"I suspect he's of Greek origin," Elijah said as he bent over his work, "but he came here with the Romans."

"With the *Romans*?"

"Oh..." Another dismissive wave, this one a bit flustered. "With... *some* Romans. You know what I mean."

"No."

"He said people had all kinds of reasons for writing things down, and that there was no reason to think the scroll was ever intended to be widely distributed. I told him it might contain vast stores of new information about the history and beliefs of the Gauls. He said that was all the more reason to think long and hard about releasing it, given how secretive the Gauls were about those things."

"Those sound like good points," Catherine said, surprised to find herself caring about the wishes and superstitions of an ancient people.

"Not from a historian's perspective." Glancing up at her, he said, "Are you just here to add your voice to the chorus of outrage, or is there another purpose to your visit?"

"I've been dispatched to shepherd you and Thomas and Inigo to the dining room," she said. "Supper's about to be served."

"I don't have time for supper if I'm to get this all copied by tomorrow morning. Neither does Thomas."

"I'll let him be the judge of that. Where is he?"

"Out there." He gestured across the cavernous library to the French doors that let out on the balcony, through which Catherine saw two male forms silhouetted against the twilit sky. "He's taking a cigar break with Inigo."

"You let him have breaks?" Catherine inquired wryly as she crossed the room, fluffing up the bustle of her dinner gown and smoothing her chignon.

"Ten minutes every two hours," replied her father, who if he'd recognized her tone, had chosen not to acknowledge it.

As she approached the French doors, one of which was ajar, Catherine heard her name spoken by Inigo.

"It is my fondest desire," Thomas said through a flutter of smoke, "but she won't have me."

"You've asked her?"

"I have." Thomas turned with a sigh to lean back against the balustrade.

Catherine ducked behind the velvet draperies.

"Are you sleeping with her?" Inigo asked.

"My God, man, what kind of a question is that?"

"I take it the answer is negative," said Inigo with a hint of humor in his voice.

"I don't know how you can even ask that." Thomas sounded genuinely taken aback. "She's Dr. Wheeler's daughter, and a . . . well, she's obviously completely innocent in such matters."

"Obviously?"

After a brief pause, Thomas said, in a deadly serious tone, "Do I need to punch you in the head, Inigo? Because if you ever suggest such a thing in anyone else's presence, I will."

"Please don't. I hate being hit, and I've never learned the art of hitting back, so it's always pretty much an exercise in humiliation."

Thomas said, "You're an ass, Inigo, you know that?"

"Of course."

"What you've got to understand," Thomas said, "is that other parts of the world—even other parts of France—are nothing at all like Grotte Cachée. Your way of life, the self-indulgence, the... intemperance..."

"Intemperance? You mean sex?"

"You live in this remote little valley where no one ever comes unless they're invited, and even then they have trouble finding it. You and your friends are like some primitive tribe that's been cut off geographically from the rest of civilization for so long that you've become a world unto yourself, with your own distinct customs, mores, and taboos... or lack thereof."

"But you've at least kissed her, right?"

"I'm not going to discuss my love life with you, Inigo."

"Or lack thereof," Inigo echoed with a little snort of derision.

"Insolent fucker," Thomas muttered, chuckling. Catherine's mouth flew open, not so much because she was shocked, although she was, a little, but because she'd never thought to hear an epithet of such extreme vulgarity from the lips of quiet, scholarly Thomas Lee.

Thomas said, "I'm trying to... I *was* trying to conduct an appropriate courtship."

"An appropriate courtship." She could hear the mocking shudder in Inigo's voice. "Sounds more like a business arrangement than a romance."

"As I said, Inigo, you have no notion of what's acceptable and what's not in the civilized world."

"Please tell me you're not a virgin."

This time it was Thomas who snorted with laughter. "I'm twenty-four years old."

"That's a no, I hope."

"It's different for men than for women."

Catherine stood paralyzed with shock. It had never occurred to her, ever, that Thomas might have had sexual relations with women. She'd never even thought about, never considered the possibility.

"Whores?" Inigo asked.

"We had a laundress when I was sixteen." Thomas's voice took on an entirely different tenor than when he'd been discussing her—lower, vaguely roguish. It was the kind of voice she'd heard before among men sharing masculine exploits in the company of other men when they didn't realize she was listening.

Sixteen. Good Lord, sixteen?

"She was older," Thomas said, adding, with an amused edge to his voice, "and *most* instructive."

"Thank God for laundresses," said Inigo.

"And there were others while I was at Yale," Thomas continued. "Not whores per se, but they liked their little baubles and trinkets."

"Of course."

"My only long-term relationship of that sort was a mistress I took in India when I was doing fieldwork there after my senior year."

Catherine could literally not believe her ears. Thomas had spent many long hours describing his year in India studying ancient Hindu mythology. Never once had he mentioned a mistress. But why would he have? A gentleman would never discuss such a thing with a young woman—or rather, a young *lady*, a status that had evidently condemned Catherine to appalling ignorance about that which transpired between men and women.

Or at least the interesting things.

"Lili fancies you," Inigo said.

Catherine edged closer to the window.

"I think Lili fancies every man she meets," Thomas said.

"That's what makes her so perfect for your needs."

"My needs?"

"Don't pretend you don't have them, after telling me about the laundress and the trinket-and-bauble girls and the Indian mistress. And what with Catherine having given you the heave-ho, I shouldn't think there'd be anything to stop you from paying a little call on Lili tonight in her apartment. I'll tell her to expect you."

"Don't do that."

"But she'll be delighted."

"But Catherine—"

"Catherine's not interested. Lili is. Why are you making a simple tryst so bloody complicated?"

"Because the woman I've just recently asked to marry me would be sleeping under the very same roof. Have you no standards at all?"

"We've already established that I don't. And I can't believe you're letting Catherine get in the way. She rejected you, for God's sake. *She* rejected *you.*"

"I still love her," Thomas said soberly. "That will never change."

"Yes, but it would appear that she doesn't return the sentiment, and this is, after all, your last night here in our remote little valley of low standards and raging intemperance."

"I've got that manuscript to copy."

"You do know which Lili I'm talking about, don't you? Beautiful, seductive, loves fucking more than life itself?"

"Have *you* slept with her?" Thomas asked.

"Nah, we don't do that."

"We?"

Inigo hesitated as if choosing his words. "We're like brother and sister. See? I do so know about taboos."

"What about Elic? Aren't they—"

"He won't care. There's not a thing in the world to stop you from enjoying a friendly good-bye romp with the indefatigable Lili."

Thomas sighed. "I don't know."

He didn't know? That meant he might. Catherine felt as if her stomach were turning inside out.

"You won't have another chance with Lili after tonight," Inigo said. "And as for Catherine... it's a big roof, brother."

Six

CATHERINE STOOD outside the library door around midnight in her bedroom slippers and blue-checked wrapper, two towels draped over her arm, taking deep, calming breaths. Through the door, she heard Thomas say, "Have you finished that section, Dr. Wheeler?"

"Hm? Oh, er, yes."

Do it. She knocked on the door. "It's Catherine."

Thomas opened the door and ushered her inside, taking off his eyeglasses as he greeted her. Like Elijah, he was in rolled-up shirtsleeves and no collar, his hair uncombed. His beard-darkened jaw reminded Catherine of her hallucination in the cave, when her invisible lover pleasured her with his mouth, his prickly jaw scraping her inner thighs.

Thomas has probably done that to women, she thought. He'd kissed them and touched them in their most intimate places, unlaced their corsets and rolled down their stockings, knelt between their legs and shoved himself inside them. She pictured him lying atop a woman, thrusting and groaning, and felt a flood of heat rush up her throat into her face.

"Catherine? *Are* you . . . ?" asked her father.

"Am I . . . ?"

"Headed off to bed," he said with a little nod toward her attire.

"Oh. No, I, um . . . I thought I might like to take a little midnight dip in the pool. It's such a lovely bathhouse, and I won't have another chance after tonight."

Thomas said, "You took Lili up on her offer of a bathing dress?"

"Yes, I borrowed it from her this evening, after supper. I, um, I thought perhaps . . . you'd like to join me."

Thomas stared at her for a moment. "Oh," he said, looking pleasantly surprised. "Well, yes, of course. Except . . ." He looked at the table at which he'd been sitting side by side with Elijah, transcribing the scroll. "I'm actually in the middle of translating the calendar, and—"

"Translating?" she asked. "Not copying?"

"We've finished the copying. Your father wanted to get started on the translation, no easy task with such an inadequate glossary. He had me do the calendar, and he's been doing the very beginning of the scroll, which I take it had to do with the Gallic Wars and the initial years of Roman occupation."

"Did you find out why some of the Vernae stayed here and let themselves be enslaved by the Romans?" Catherine asked her father.

He just sat there, gazing at his open notebook, and the half-inked page on top.

"Elijah?" she said.

He looked up, blinking.

"You told me you thought this beginning section might tell you why some of the Vernae stayed behind," she said. "Did it?"

"Um, yes. Yes, it did."

"It *did*?" Thomas exclaimed. "Why didn't you tell me?"

"Why did they stay?" asked Catherine, surprised that she cared.

"It had to do with one of their gods," Elijah said. "It's . . ." He shook his head. "It's difficult to summarize."

Thomas picked up Elijah's notebook and read the page to which it was opened. He frowned. "Hm."

"That's something else," Elijah said, "something that came at the end of that section."

Catherine took the notebook out of his hand.

"Not all of the words are translatable," Thomas told her as he looked over her shoulder. "Where there's doubt as to the meaning, we insert a question mark."

Elijah's neatly printed translation read:

And thus came we few ? Vernae to live in thrall to our Roman (masters?), a ? race (doomed? condemned?) to servitude under those who would ~~name~~ call our gods by their ? names and turn our sacred (spring? cave stream?) into a place of (? something negative about the bathhouse).

And so do I, Brantigern Anextlomarus (Brantigern the Protector) (record? write down?) the ? of our people, not for Roman eyes, nor for the eyes of any man, but for the gods and goddesses alone. Always ~~has~~ have our ? and secrets been (safeguarded?) from those who would (destroy? burn?) our gods and make mockery of our truths. Always shall it remain so.

Catherine looked at her father, who sat staring at the spot on the table where the notebook had been.

"Dr. Wheeler," Thomas said. "Do you think we really ought to be—"

"Go ahead to the bathhouse, Thomas," said Elijah without looking at them.

"But the calendar."

"You've done enough for one night."

Thomas hesitated.

Catherine caught his eye and nodded, beckoning him toward the door.

"I'll need to change into my bathing suit," he said.

She said, "You're wearing drawers and an undershirt, aren't you? They'll do."

"You can't be serious."

"Thomas, your bathing suit looks *exactly* like underwear. What's the difference?"

"She's right," Elijah said. "Don't be such a square-toes, Thomas."

Thank God there's just a sliver of moon out, thought Catherine as she and Thomas entered the bathhouse. The less moonlight, the better. What little there was reflected off the white marble edifice, casting the pool into a dreamy, indigo twilight.

Sitting on one of the iron chairs against the wall, Thomas removed his shoes and socks, shrugged off his suspenders, and set about unbuttoning his shirt. "What prompted you to ask me to join you?"

"Why wouldn't I?" she asked, standing near a corner of the pool with her back to him. "We've been friends for years."

"You know what I mean."

Catherine didn't respond to that. Instead, she laid the towels on a little marble bench, her hand trembling ever so slightly. She unbuttoned her wrapper and let it fall to the floor, leaving her entirely naked.

The soft sounds that had accompanied his undressing ceased.

She stepped down into the pool, submerged herself completely in the warm water, and stood, still with her back to him, to skim her hair off her face.

A thrumming silence filled the bathhouse.

She turned to look over her shoulder. Thomas was on his

feet, staring at her, his trousers and shirt unbuttoned, suspenders dangling, eyes huge in the bluish half-light.

His throat moved as he swallowed. "I thought you said you borrowed a bathing dress from Lili."

"I didn't say I was wearing it. I tried it on, and decided it was too long and heavy—too much soggy wool."

She glanced at him again. He was still looking at her with those big, dark eyes, as if sorting through this unexpected new development in his mind.

"You needn't wear your undershirt and drawers on my account," she said. "It's lovely having nothing between oneself and the water. I won't look, if you don't want me to."

"Accusations of deformed toes aside, I'm not as shy as all that."

It took him a minute to undress, and then he walked along the edge of the pool to the opposite corner, as if trying to put a respectable distance between them. It amused her to think that he was making up a code of propriety on the spot in order to deal with the novel situation of sharing a pool with her, stark naked.

Unclothed, Thomas Lee was a revelation. Leanly muscled and perfectly proportioned, he put her in mind of a classical statue—which, in turn, put her in mind of the four lewd statues erected at the corners of the pool. She couldn't help wondering if Thomas had done the things that the satyr was shown doing with the nymph. Had he ever bent the laundress over her washtub and taken her from behind? Had he held any of the bauble-and-trinket girls up against some lamppost or alley wall, and taken her that way, or lifted her on his shoulders so he could bury his face between her legs? Had he ever made his Indian mistress kneel before him and lick his erect penis? Had he ejaculated that way? *Could* a man ejaculate that way? Now that Catherine knew that women, as well as men, could reach a sexual climax, she thought perhaps it was possible.

She tried not to stare at Thomas's male member as he

lowered himself into the pool, but neither could she seem to tear her gaze away. It was, of course, not quite as generously proportioned as that of the satyr; it more resembled the penises of the men in the book of lascivious etching she'd seen in the cave. The major difference was that it wasn't erect—or rather, fully erect, for it was indeed, more distended than she would have expected.

He was at least somewhat aroused, she realized. The knowledge that she'd done that to him, simply by taking her clothes off and asking him to remove his, gave her a sense of gratification unlike any she'd ever known.

He settled into his corner a bit stiffly and gave her an awkward little smile. "So."

She stood up and waded toward him in the waist-high water, watching his darkly intent gaze shift from her face to her breasts, and farther down.

Quietly, seriously, he said, "Catherine, please tell me you're not doing this to tease me."

"You know me better than that, Thomas."

"I do. But then . . . why?"

She came up to him, took his face in her hands, and kissed him. He kissed her back, hard, his hands tangled in her hair, then grasped her arms and pushed her away. He stood, saying, "I've got to leave."

"Why? Because you want me?"

The look he gave her sent shivers of heat down her spine. "Yes," he said.

"I'm glad," she said. "Because that's what I want, too."

"Does this mean you've changed your mind about marrying me?"

"Ask me afterward," she said as she wrapped her arms around his neck.

He gripped her by the waist to keep her from pressing herself against him. "Catherine . . . darling. We can't. I couldn't . . . do this without offering you a commitment of marriage."

"You *have* offered that."

"And having you accept it. For *your* sake."

"Thomas, I know the unspoken rules. If a lady is engaged, and is discovered in a . . . compromising situation with her intended, she is generally forgiven—so long as they're wed within a decent interval. But I don't want this to be about rules and customs and what's appropriate and what's not. I want it to be about us. About you wanting me and me wanting you."

His hands tightening around her waist, he said, "What I want most of all is to marry you. If you're saying you won't—"

"What I'm saying," she whispered as she stroked his face, "is that you'll need to ask me afterward."

"But—"

"Thomas, I love you. I just want to—"

"You love me?" He looked astounded, thrilled.

"Deeply, madly, and completely. So, if you would just please stop fretting over what's proper and what's—"

He hauled her to him and banded his arms around her, kissing her so passionately that she felt as if her heart might explode from sheer elation. She felt his restless hands everywhere, on her throat, her back, her breasts, her bottom—and, more gently, on her sex, which he caressed with a slow, deft touch as his erection rose between them.

Curious, she reached down and glided her fingertips very lightly along the rigid shaft, which was much smoother than she would have thought, with a network of ropy veins beneath the tightly stretched skin. "Oh, God," he breathed as she conducted a lingering perusal of his male anatomy—the satiny glans with its tiny aperture, the weighty scrotal sac. His breath quickened as she stroked and explored; his hips flexed. "You'd better stop that," he said, "or this will end far too soon."

Thomas lowered himself onto the submerged bench, lifting her by the waist to seat her astride him. He clasped her to him and kissed her deeply, his tongue flirting with hers in a way she found incredibly arousing. Drunk with desire, she rocked her hips unself-consciously, her sex growing slick as it rubbed against his, the outer lips swelling open in anticipation.

He thrust hard against her, groaning into her mouth, and then abruptly stilled. "Stop. *Stop,*" he pleaded, holding her away from him, his lungs heaving. "I'm too close. I'm... We need to—"

"Here." Rising up on her knees, she began to position him to enter her.

"No. Not... not like this. Let me take you inside, to a proper bed."

"If I'd wanted you in a bed," she said, "I would have tricked you into coming to my room instead of here."

He chuckled, shaking his head. "The thing is, it's your first time, and water washes away... It... tends to make things a bit trying, especially for the lady. I don't want that for you."

"All right, then." She climbed up onto the marble floor of the bathhouse, sitting on the edge with her feet in the water. "How is this?"

He swam to the opposite corner in two strokes to retrieve the towels. Laying one out behind her, with the other rolled up for a pillow, he lowered her down so that she was lying on her back with him kneeling on the bench between her legs.

"You must tell me if this hurts," he said as he positioned himself, his other hand holding her hip to steady her.

There was some discomfort as he nudged into her, partly because she was still raw from the experience in the cave, but for the most part, what she felt was inexpressible joy at being united with this man she'd known for so long, but had never really known until now. He felt so hot and hard and *right* inside her, so utterly perfect.

Bracing his hands on the floor to either side of her, he leaned down for a tender kiss. Unshaven and naked, his disheveled hair hanging across his forehead, he looked so devastatingly virile that she could scarcely believe she'd spurned him as she had.

"Are you all right?" he asked.

"I'm wonderful," she sighed. "*This* is wonderful."

"This is incredible," he said as he began moving inside her, his thrusts hypnotically slow, deliciously deep. "You're so beautiful, Catherine. I've wanted this for so long. I can't tell you how many nights I've dreamt of this."

Thomas took her in his arms and sat her up, then cupped one of her breasts and drew the nipple into the heat of his mouth, making her gasp in startled delight. He pleasured her this way, using his clever lips and tongue—and even, from time to time, the edges of his teeth—until she was moaning in ecstasy. They embraced so tightly as they writhed in unison, her legs banded around his hips, that it was as if they were a single being gripped in a delirium of pleasure.

She clawed at his hair, her breath coming faster and faster as her climax approached. Pressing on the small of her back, he ground against her in a way that caused it to detonate like a thunderclap. He held her through the last, shuddery tremor, whispering endearments into her ear, and then he pulled himself out of her and crushed her to him, groaning hoarsely as warm fluid pulsed between them.

"I'm sorry," he panted, stroking her hair and back with a quivering hand. "I just . . . I don't want you to get in trouble, and I don't have any . . ."

"I understand. Thank you."

He dampened the rolled-up towel and used it to clean them off, and then they sank deeper into the water and held each other, kissing and whispering and laughing, and kissing some more.

"Wait here." She climbed out of the pool and crossed to his little mound of clothing on the iron chair.

"Where are you going?"

"I need to put something on," she said, rummaging around.

"A bit late in the day for modesty, I'd say, but if you want my shirt, it's yours."

"I don't want your shirt," she said as she rejoined him in the pool. Showing him the ring finger of her left hand, on which she wore the diamond and emerald engagement ring he'd told her he would keep in his pocket for a year, she said, "I want this. If... if you still want me to—"

Thomas silenced her with a kiss that went on for a very, very long time.

Early the next morning

INIGO WATCHED from behind an oak at the edge of the woods surrounding the nemeton as Elijah Wheeler, whom he'd followed from the chateau, entered the clearing from the path, carrying a leather satchel.

Laying the satchel on the altar, he unbuckled it and withdrew the Sacred Scroll in its leather wrapping. He studied it for a moment, smoothing his hand wistfully along the leather, and then he pulled out the Lugus disc, returned the scroll to its rightful place, and shoved the disc back in.

He looked at the satchel for several long minutes, and then he took out two notebooks, the ones in which he and Thomas had copied the contents of the scroll last night. He took out something else, too: a match safe.

Crouching over the long-disused fire pit, he tore all the pages out of the notebooks, crumpled them and their covers into a pile, and touched a match to it. He tended the fire—relighting it a couple of times, stirring it with a stick—until all that remained was a heap of gray ashes.

For quite some time, he stood over the remnants of his precious transcription in grave contemplation. And then, as solemnly as if he were reciting a prayer, he said, "And so did Brantigern Anextlomarus record the lore of his people, not for Roman eyes, nor for the eyes of any man, but *dibu e debu*—for the gods and goddesses alone. Always have the secrets of the Vernae been safeguarded from those who would destroy their gods and make mockery of their truths. Always shall it remain so."

Looking up, Wheeler noticed Darius, in his feline incarnation, watching him from a patch of sun across the clearing.

"Good morning, Darius, and good-bye," said Wheeler with a respectful bow. "May you live in peace and solitude."

Darius nodded to acknowledge the bow, and gave Wheeler a mew of thanks.

Wheeler picked up his satchel and walked back down the path, smiling.

[illegible]

[illegible]

[illegible]

[illegible]

[illegible]

[illegible]

A Demon of Flesh and Stone

One

October 52 B.C.

BRAN AWOKE with a moan of terror on his lips, shaking and sweating, the images from his dream seared into his mind's eye: an eagle crushed to death beneath the wheels of a Roman chariot, his two fledglings hobbling about with their wings ripped off, pouring blood. Nearby, a majestic old oak tree surrounded by a double row of wooden ramparts burst into flame.

Throwing off the bearskin beneath which he'd slept, he rose from bed, grabbed his tunic and trousers off their hooks, and dressed quickly—or as quickly as he could, having been born with but a single hand. The house felt quiet and empty this morning, or rather the houses, for Bran's family home had grown over time into a cluster of round stone huts with conical thatched roofs connected by passageways. It was the grandest domicile in the village, Bran's father, Tintigern Dovatigerni, being high chieftain of the Vernae, and his maternal grandfather, Artaros Biraci, their revered druid.

When Bran was growing up, the house and outbuildings—

some nearby and others, like the stable, storehouse, grain pit, and beehive, at the outskirts of the village—were filled day and night with the comings and goings of Bran's family and the various *vassi* who saw to their needs. But his sisters were married now, with homes of their own, and his father and two older brothers had left some weeks ago to fight alongside the great Vercingetorix at the besieged city of Alisiia to the north, the last real hope of the Celtæ to resist the invading Romans. Bran had begged to join them, but his druidic vocation—he'd been apprenticed since birth to Grandfather Artaros—and that missing hand had conspired to keep him home.

It didn't help that, in a race of red- and yellow-haired giants, he'd been born not just deformed, but strangely dark, and of comparatively modest stature. There'd been whispers, after his birth, that he'd been sired not by Tintigern, but by some foreigner during a trading excursion by his parents to Narbonensis, the Roman colony on the southern border of Celtica. Bran's mother, Vlatucia, had silenced that rumor by slicing out the tongue of the woman who'd had the poor judgment to start it. There'd been not a peep since.

It was just Bran, Artaros, and Vlatucia in the house now, so it was fairly tranquil all the time, but not usually so deathly quiet first thing in the morning. After checking the main hut and those of his mother and grandfather, and finding no one about, he stepped outside and ducked into the cooking hut.

"Bran." The *vassa* Adiega looked up from the butter she was churning to give him one of those big, sweet smiles that were like rays of sunshine warming his soul. Her eyes were the clean, bright blue of a cloudless sky, her hair alight with streaks of gold. Even with her braids tied back with a strip of rag, and wearing the patched old dress in which she cooked and cleaned, she was the most radiant creature Bran had ever seen.

"Morning, Bran," greeted Adiega's widowed sister, Paullia, as she stirred a pot of porridge over the central hearth. "Hungry?" Leaning over the pot so as to display her ample bosom above the neckline of her red dress, for she was as voluptuous as Adiega was slender, she tossed him a saucy grin. "See anything you like?"

"Yes." Taking Adiega by the hand, he pulled her away from the open door—and the view of passing villagers—and drew her into his arms. Without being asked, Paullia moved to the opposite side of the hearth so that she could see through the doorway, the better to watch out for prying eyes. If Vlatucia were to find out about Bran and Adiega, who knew what retribution she would exact.

"You're trembling, my love," whispered Adiega as they embraced.

He told her about his dream.

"What could it mean?" she asked.

"Only bad things," he said gravely. "The oak tree is Vernem, or possibly even Celtica as a whole, and the ramparts are the type the Romans have built around Alisiia to keep Celticum relief forces at bay."

"And the eagle?" she asked. "The two fledglings?"

"I'm not sure," he lied, loath to even think about the implications, much less voice them.

"Did you have the other dream, as well?" she asked. "The one about the demon from the north?"

"I have it every night. He's getting closer."

"You think he's really out there somewhere, in the woods?"

"I know he is," Bran said, although right now, a wandering demon who seemed content to keep his distance from their village was the least of his concerns. "Adiega, have you seen my mother and grandfather this morning?"

Nodding, she said, "A messenger came, and they went running out to a cart coming into the valley along the road from the north."

"*Running?*" Vlatucia never ran; it lacked dignity. And Artaros was aged and nearly blind. Bran went to the doorway to peer at the road, some distance away. He saw the cart sitting still, the driver hunched over in his seat. Two tall figures stood nearby, with a smaller form, that of Artaros's gray wolf, Frontu, pacing back and forth. A pair of horses was harnessed to the cart, with three others tied to it in back.

Bran concentrated his hearing, sorting through the morning cacophony of the village—goats bleating, geese honking, children shrieking with laughter, Vectito Donati's fat little dog yipping and barking, the *clack-clack-clack* of a loom, the ringing strikes of Brude Ironsmith's hammer . . . All of these sounds he filtered out of his ears as he focused in on the conversation taking place next to the cart.

"I know he's only nineteen," Artaros was saying, "but he was always a clever boy, and he's wise for his age, with a quiet strength."

"What are they saying?" asked Adiega as she peeked out from the edge of the doorway.

"I think they're talking about me."

"Let me hear," she said.

Bran waved a hand in the direction of the cart, murmuring, "*Uediju rowero gutu,*" and suddenly Vlatucia's voice was as audible as if she were standing right in front of them.

"Strong? He's the runt of the litter, and a cripple, at that. I should have drowned him at birth."

"Shit," muttered Paullia, sounding both awed and appalled by Vlatucia's cold-bloodedness.

Bran suddenly regretted having made the sisters privy to this particular conversation, especially his beloved Adiega.

"Bran is your son," Artaros said sternly.

"He's an embarrassment."

Adiega reached over to squeeze Bran's hand.

"He has powerful gifts," said Artaros, "the like of which I've never seen."

"But not the kind of gifts that make for an effective leader. Branogenas is weak, Father, and well you know it, weak not just in body, but in spirit. He's not equipped to lead the Vernae, especially in a time of war. It was his brothers who were trained for that role, not he. His role is to serve the gods, counsel the elders, and prophesy the future. He was to be our druid someday, not our chieftain."

"But the fates have changed all that," the old man pointed out. "Your husband and your two elder sons are gone, Vlatucia, and now it is Bran who must wear the golden *torka*."

Bran leaned against the doorsill and closed his eyes. He'd known, from the moment he'd awakened, what that dream had meant; he just hadn't wanted to acknowledge it.

"Bran, I'm sorry," said Adiega as she embraced him from behind. "I'm so sorry."

"I must go speak to them."

Bran's mother glanced at him as he approached the cart, then carried on with her litany of his shortcomings. Vlatucia matir Saveras was tall even for a Celticum female, with sharp, alert bird eyes. By all accounts, she'd once been the most beautiful woman in their clan, but in recent years her face had begun to collapse from within, like a bad apple shriveling around a puckered little wormhole of a mouth. She was clad, as usual, in a dress hemmed short to reveal a pair of men's plaid trousers, a dagger and a ring of big iron keys hanging from her belt. Her long mane of wiry hair—iron gray with some strands of copper still remaining—hung loose but for two side braids strung with golden beads.

Bearded old Artaros, leaning on his gnarled oak staff, his eyes as eerily pale as Frontu's from the film that clouded them, patted Bran's shoulder.

There were three corpses on the back of the cart, each hidden beneath a blood-soaked blanket save for their mud-crusted boots. On the chest of each body sat an iron helmet.

Bran recognized the one in the middle as Tintigern's because of the boar tusks.

"I want to see my father," Bran said.

"You haven't the stomach for it," Vlatucia replied.

Artaros pulled the blanket away.

The air left Bran's lungs. Tintigern's face was blackened and swollen, with a yawning wound where his right eye had been; his mouth was agape, his other eye half-open. Blood caked his trailing moustache and his magnificent head of silvery, limewater-stiffened hair, scraped back from his head to reveal the small gold hoops piercing his ears. Around his neck, half-hidden beneath his cloak of shaggy, crimson-dyed fleece, he wore the golden *torka* that identified him as chieftain of their clan.

"Look, he's gone white as milk," Vlatucia told Artaros with a little sneer.

Gathering all his strength of will, Bran whipped the blankets off the other two bodies only to find that they weren't his brothers at all, but two other men of the village who had accompanied Tintigern and his sons to Alisiia.

"What of my brothers?" he asked.

"You have no brothers," his mother replied.

Artaros said, "Dovatucas and Narlos surrendered and were taken as personal slaves of Roman soldiers."

"My own sons," said Vlatucia, her face twisted in disgust. "They should have cut their own throats rather than allow themselves to be taken captive. Their subjugation only makes our defeat more shameful."

Our defeat. So—the Romans had vanquished the forces of Vercingetorix and taken Alisiia. Bran pictured the burning oak tree from his dream, wondering how much time they had—weeks? months?—before there were Roman soldiers marching into their little valley.

Vlatucia leaned over the side of the cart to wrest the blood-stained *torka* from her dead husband's neck and close it around her own.

"That *torka* belongs on Bran," Artaros said.

"He hasn't the right to wear it," she said, as if he weren't standing right there. "Not yet, anyway—probably not ever."

"That's for the elders to decide," Artaros said.

"The elders will follow my lead," she said. Of that, Bran had little doubt; they were all utterly cowed by her. "When Branogenas grows a set of balls—and a sense of duty—he can wear this *torka.*"

"He's not Branogenas any longer," said Artaros. "He's Brantigern, chieftain of the Vernae."

Vlatucia chuckled disdainfully.

"Have I not proven myself a dutiful son?" asked Bran, in a rare display of boldness. He'd learned long ago that it didn't pay to go head-to-head with his mother.

"If you truly knew your duty, *Branogenas,*" she said, "and were willing to accept it, you'd have married Briaga long before this."

The cart's driver, Adiega's brother, Sedna, glanced from Vlatucia to Bran, then looked away.

"If you were a *man,*" Vlatucia continued, "and not a selfish little boy, she would already be big with child, and I wouldn't have to fret so over the fate of our druidic line. It's dying out, or haven't you noticed?"

There remained but thirteen other members of the clan who shared Bran's increasingly rare gift of spellcasting and second sight, though their powers were, like those of Bran's parents, far weaker than his, and undeveloped through druidic training. In order to produce children with druidic gifts, it was necessary for both parents, not just one, to be gifted, but an appalling number of gifted men had died these past few years fighting the Romans. Two of the precious thirteen, a boy and a girl, were small children with widowed mothers. The rest, Bran's two pregnant sisters and eight others, were adult females wedded to ungifted men. That left Briaga matir Primius, who was not only gifted, but a highborn *uxella,* as the natural choice of a wife for Bran—

the *only* choice if, as his mother was forever reminding him, he was to be ensured of druidic offspring.

Much as Bran hated to admit it, she had a good point. For the sake of their clan's druidic lineage, he really should marry Briaga. Were he not so passionately in love with the lowborn, ungifted Adiega, he might have already succumbed to his mother's unceasing pressure and asked Briaga to be his wife, though she left him entirely cold. But Adiega, who'd grown from a childhood playmate into the woman he loved with his entire heart, was the other half of his soul. The notion of forsaking her for the vain, shallow Briaga was unthinkable.

"If your children aren't druids and druidesses," Vlatucia said, "if they aren't born with your gifts, then you will be the last in a line of Vernan druids stretching back centuries. Is that really what you want?"

"What I really want," Bran said wearily, "is to mourn my father in peace, without having to argue with you about whom I'm going to marry."

"You go ahead and wallow in your grief," Vlatucia said. "I've no time for it. The Romans are advancing on us even as we speak. I must make plans for the future of our clan. Your father would have been the first to understand that."

"*We* must make plans," Artaros said. "Tintigern never acted without my advice and that of the elders, nor shall you. Tomorrow, we shall bury our chieftain and his fallen comrades. Afterward, you and I and the elders will gather for a council in the nemeton and sort out what needs to be done to protect us against the Romans."

Vlatucia conceded to that with a sour little nod of her head. To Bran, she said, "See to the funeral preparations. Tintigern is to be buried with his best possessions. His sword and helmet, obviously. His comb bag, razor, daggers . . . his favorite drinking horn, the one with the silver on it. Have Adiega and Paullia wash him and dress him in his finest clothes, with his gold wrist *torkas* and enameled cloak pin. Make sure they arrange his hair the way he wore it in battle, like a horse's mane. And tell them to gather as many flowers as they can from the fields and the woods. Oh, and keep an eye on them. Don't let them steal the *torkas* and cloak pin."

She turned and left without so much as a backward glance at her husband.

Artaros told Sedna to take the bodies to the nemeton and the horses and cart to the family stable, and then he and Bran started back toward the village, Frontu loping along by the old druid's side.

"Did you have the dream again?" Artaros asked. "The one about the demon from the—"

"Every night," Bran said.

"Are you still unsure of the sex?"

"He's male, I think. But he still occasionally appears to me as a female."

Artaros nodded thoughtfully. "How far away is he now?"

"Eight or ten *luegae,* not much more than that."

Artaros stopped in his tracks. "That close?"

"I wouldn't worry," Bran said. "He doesn't seem interested in coming here. Quite the opposite, actually."

The old man nodded again, then continued walking. "We'll have to trap him, then."

"*What?*"

"I'll explain when we meet with the elders tomorrow night."

" 'We'? Can you imagine my mother's rage if I show up at a council of elders?"

"She may be too old for me to spank, though I'm frequently tempted, but she *can* be overruled. I still wield a certain amount of authority with the elders."

"Forgive me, Grandfather, but I think it's safe to say Vlatucia wields more, if only through fear. Gamicu Ivageni is still fresh in their memories." Shortly after Bran's father left for Alisiia early last month, Gamicu, one of the elders, had had the temerity to question Vlatucia's insistence on serving as chieftain in her husband's absence. One night, Gamicu was snatched from his home by three Germani thugs Vlatucia had retained to do her bidding, though they lived in the woods somewhere nearby, not in the village proper. The next morning, one of the villagers on his way to do some trading with a neighboring village happened upon Gamicu's charred remains in a field. He'd been enclosed in a man-shaped wicker effigy and burned to death.

"I'll never be allowed at that council," Bran said. "She'll order me away, and there's no one in this village, including you, who would dare take her to task over it."

Artaros smiled. "There's one I can think of."

Two

"WHAT IS *he* doing here?" demanded Vlatucia the following evening as the Vernan elders, all aged members of the *uxelli* class, gathered around the fire in the nemeton. She still wore Tintigern's golden *torka*; Bran wouldn't have been surprised if she'd slept in it.

Artaros, standing behind the altar with Bran to one side and Frontu to the other, said, "Branogenas is a *uelis,* a gifted seer. Someday, he will take his place as druid of our clan. It's time he learned how important decisions are made among our people."

Vlatucia fixed Bran with her most venomous look. "Leave," she said.

A gray cat jumped up onto the altar, prompting a flurry of mutters and bows from the elders. Frontu stood with his front legs on the edge of the altar to growl at the interloper, who hissed at him.

"Down, Frontu," commanded Artaros, whereupon the wolf seated himself, his silvery eyes fixed on the cat. Ignoring him with feline nonchalance, Darius settled down right in front of

Bran and stared at Vlatucia, as if daring her to defy him; he'd always been fond of Bran.

She looked away, coloring hotly in the way that only red-haired women can. Lifting her chin, she addressed the assembled elders. "Alisiia was a tragic defeat for the Vernae, for our mother tribe, the Arverni, indeed, for all of Celtica. Our days of self-rule are numbered. The Romans have been invading our villages, executing the chieftains, and selling the people into slavery—an unspeakable fate. Our only hope is to do what our sisters and brothers elsewhere are doing, and that is to leave here before the Romans arrive."

"And go where?" asked Guthor Totavali.

"Any place where we can be our own masters and worship our own gods and goddesses."

"What about Darius?" Bran asked. Darius, their god of fire from a far distant land, had made his home in their enchanted cave for centuries. It was the sacred responsibility of the Vernae to keep him hidden and protected, for the world was full of fools who understood nothing about his kind, except how to destroy them.

Vlatucia glared at Bran for having spoken. He avoided her gaze, but Darius glared right back at her.

"Bran is right," Artaros said. "We must think of Darius first. It is he we live to serve, not ourselves. He couldn't travel with us. It's much too risky. He'd be bumping into people constantly, and sooner or later, he'll be recognized for what he is. On the other hand, I hate to imagine what would happen if we were to leave Vernem and abandon him to whoever settles here after we're gone. Even most Celtæ have lost touch with the old ways, the old beliefs and practices, from contact with the worldly Romans and Greeks. People are losing their respect for magic and for the deities who live among us. They think there's only one world, the one they can see, and they're becoming more and more intent upon being the masters of that world. *Some* of them," he added with a sidelong glance at Vlatucia, who gave him a contemptuous look. "They don't want gods and demons getting in the way of their power, so they pretend they're not real. If we all flee the Romans, where would that leave a god like Darius, who relies for his very existence not just on the solitude of our cave, but on certain druidic spells of safekeeping?"

"I'll stay here when the Romans come," Bran said.

Darius turned to look at him, as did Artaros and Vlatucia. The elders all started talking at once.

Holding up a hand to silence them, Artaros said, "I shall stay. It is my place."

Bran shook his head. "You must leave with the rest of the villagers, Grandfather. I know I'm just a *uelis,* but you can teach me what I need to know before the Romans come. I would hate for you, in your advanced years, to have to endure the rigors of slavery under the Romans, and the Vernae need your druidic skills."

"More to the point," Vlatucia told her father, "Darius needs a young druid, one who won't be dropping dead in a year or two."

"Thank you for pointing that out, Daughter," said Artaros dryly.

"And Bran can father druidic offspring to ensure Darius's continued safekeeping," Vlatucia said, adding pointedly, "so long as he consents to marry Briaga matir Primius before we leave, so that she can stay behind with him."

"*Briaga* has to stay and be enslaved?" exclaimed her father.

"No, surely not," said Bran, picturing Briaga as she'd appeared earlier that day at his father's funeral, dressed in a multicolored silken dress with her face brightly painted and her fingernails stained berry-red, a beaded comb bag dangling from her wrist. She'd giggled and whispered with her friends throughout the solemn rite.

"Of course Briaga must stay," said Vlatucia. "We must all make sacrifices for the good of the clan, Brennus."

"Y-yes, but—"

"I'm willing to leave Bran behind, aren't I?" she asked, to which her father responded with a dismissive little snort, knowing full well how much of a sacrifice that was for her.

"But if you end up a slave," Tolagnas Rodani asked Bran, "will you even be able to protect Darius? Will you have the freedom to do so? What if the Romans sell you to some soldier on his way back to their homeland?"

"I'll teach him some spells to prevent that from happening," Artaros said, adding, to Bran, "But I don't like the idea of you and Briaga being here all alone. Your children will need other Vernae, unrelated to you, children with druidic gifts whom they can marry in order to perpetuate the druidic line."

Vlatucia said, "We have but two gifted children in the clan, Sergonas Rodani and Lasrina matir Temari. We shall leave them behind."

The grandfathers of the two children grudgingly consented.

"Their mothers should be encouraged to remain behind with them," Artaros said. "And there may be others who are willing to stay, but they must do so of their own free will. No *vassi* are to be pressured. Bran will act as both druid and chieftain, but in secret, otherwise the Romans will kill him."

"It is decided, then," said Vlatucia. "Father, you must perform the rite of marriage between Bran and Briaga first thing in the morning."

"So soon?" asked Bran, panic speeding his heart as he thought about Adiega. Surely, if he sorted through the problem carefully, he could think of some way to make her his wife and keep her with him.

"We needn't rush the wedding, if Bran would prefer to wait," Artaros said. "Do we have any way of knowing when the Romans will be arriving?"

"I have scouts to warn us when they start advancing on Vernem," said Vlatucia, "but I should think they'll be here by the Cold Time. That will give us time to pack up our households and prepare for our travels. Meanwhile, we've discussed all there is to discuss tonight, so I declare this council—"

"There is actually another matter that hasn't been addressed," said Artaros. "We've resolved the issue of who will stay behind, and how to ensure the druidic line here at Vernem, but what of the Vernae who leave to settle elsewhere? Without little Sergonas and Lasrina, and with no married couples who are both gifted, there will be no one to serve as druid to us after I'm gone."

That observation was greeted with confounded silence.

"There is a way," Artaros said.

All eyes turned to him.

"Branogenas has detected the presence not far from here of a . . . nonhuman traveling south, through the deep woods."

"A god?" Vlatucia asked.

"Not precisely," Artaros hedged. "He's . . . well, from what I can surmise based on Bran's dreams, he's more of an elf, from somewhere far north of here."

"Benign or demonic?" inquired Tolagnas.

"It's hard to say."

"Why was I not told of this?" Vlatucia demanded.

"I was waiting until we had enough information to act upon," her father replied.

Vlatucia said, "The presence of a possible demon so close to Vernem, especially at such a vulnerable time for us, is a matter about which I should have been consulted long before this. We need to do whatever is necessary to keep him as far away from Vernem as possible."

"Actually," said Artaros, "we need to lure him closer." He waited for the uproar to die down, then said, "Unless I'm very much mistaken, and I don't think I am, this particular elf is the type that can shift from male to female, and back again."

"He's a *dusios*?" Vlatucia cried. "The dusii are demons, ravishers of women. Everyone knows that."

Speaking over the elders' outraged mutterings of agreement, Artaros said, "But not everyone knows that after a dusios, in his female form, mates with a man, that man's vital seed is transformed. When he becomes a male again, and mates with a woman, any child that might result from that union is blessed with druidic gifts."

The elders grew silent as they pondered the implications.

"If we can capture him . . . " Artaros began.

"And control him," Vlatucia interjected.

"And control him," her father continued, "then we can use him to sire gifted offspring before we're forced to leave here, thus replenishing our druidic line."

"And how do you propose to effect this . . . siring?" asked Vlatucia.

"By mating him with as many of our married couples as would be willing," he said, "first the males, then the females. If all goes well, by the time we leave, some of the wives will have babes in their wombs—their husbands' babes, but gifted."

"I'm not sure I like the idea of it," said Guthor, "mating our fellow Vernae like cattle."

"Do you like the idea of being left with no druids?" asked Vlatucia. "We shall do it, but—"

"If the elders agree," said Artaros.

The elders were consulted, one by one. Of course they all consented to the plan, even Guthor, who was probably imagining how it felt to be burned alive in a wicker effigy.

"My one requirement," said Vlatucia, "is that this dusios must transfer seed only between *uxelli* husbands and wives. The wife must be gifted, and of course not with child. If gifted children do indeed result from these couplings, they must be reared in a manner befitting druids and druidesses."

"Of course," said Artaros. "The dusios is traveling on foot, through dense forests and difficult terrain, and he appears to be keeping a deliberate distance between himself and us.

We must summon him closer if we've any hope of capturing him."

"Do you have a spell to accomplish that?" asked Vlatucia.

"My spells alone aren't enough," he said. "I'll need a shrine to focus them, a stone figure representing the dusios himself. It must be erected in the *Cella,* and quickly, within a half-month or less, before he moves out of the range of my powers."

"Make it happen," Vlatucia told Bran. "Any man who can move stone and wield a hammer and chisel must help."

"What happens once we lure him close?" asked Bemmos Modagni. "Will he just walk into the village of his own accord?"

"Not this dusios," said Bran. "I can feel his resistance to humans, his fear of them. We'll have to capture him somehow."

"We'll set a trap," said Vlatucia. "We trap boar. We can trap an elf. Meanwhile, don't mention this to anyone, even your wives. We don't need to be alarming people by telling them we're setting out to capture a demon."

"May I speak to you, Grandfather?" Bran asked at the conclusion of the council as Vlatucia and the elders filed down the path to the village and Darius strolled off to his cave.

"Of course."

"In confidence."

"When have you ever had to ask that?"

Taking a deep breath, Bran said, "I want you to marry me to Adiega."

Artaros stared at him. "The *vassa*?"

"I love her, Grandfather. She's—"

"Oh, dear," said Artaros.

"Please, Grandfather. I can't marry Briaga. She's—"

"She's gifted. Adiega isn't."

"But—"

"I know, son," said Artaros, resting a hand on Bran's

shoulder. "I was young once, too. Love is a powerful force. But so is duty."

"You sound like Vlatucia."

With a sigh, the old man said, "In this, unfortunately, she is entirely correct. A god such as Darius can only be properly cared for by druids. He'll live long after you and Briaga are dust, but he'll be safe because your children and your children's children will have the gifts necessary to ensure that safety."

Bran looked off into the black forest of sacred, primordial oaks, fighting the unmanly urge to weep.

"It would be a slap in the face of the gods and goddesses," Artaros said, "for you to allow your gifts to die out with you. I told your mother they were the most powerful I'd ever seen, and I meant it. Mine are much weaker. I get by with powders and potions and shrines. You, my son, are that rarest of druids, a true seer. You whisper a few words, and your magic happens. You must perpetuate that power. You must wed Briaga and beget druidic offspring with her, and that offspring must in turn wed only those who are gifted. In that way, there will always be druids at Vernem, and Darius will live forever in peace and solitude."

Bran didn't trust himself to reply, lest he burst into tears.

"Debu e dibu," said Artaros, pointing to the words inscribed on the altar. "To the gods and goddesses are our lives dedicated. So it has always been, and so it must remain."

Three

ADIEGA AWOKE to a booted foot jabbing her in her ribs. "Wake up, you lazy *slugo.* You, too, Paullia."

Vlatucia!

The sisters scrambled off their pallets in the cooking hut, squinting up at their mistress in the semidarkness, for it wasn't even dawn yet.

"Fetch something to eat—some bread and mead will do. And some soap and washrags, a razor, a comb, some shears, and two blankets. And a bucket. Bring them to the *Cella. Move.*" She clapped her hands twice and left the hut.

"The *Cella*?" said Paullia in a tone of disbelief. The cave was the most sacred place in the valley, even more so than the nemeton. The only *vassi* Adiega knew of who'd ever been permitted to enter it were those, including her brother Sedna, who'd spent the past half-month building Artaros's strange new shrine. She knew its purpose, Bran having told her even though he and the elders had been ordered by Vlatucia to keep their counsel. They had no secrets between them, she and Bran. He shared everything with her, even his mother's insistence that he marry that strutting, primping little goose, Briaga.

It will never happen, Bran had assured her time and again. *I'll find a way to make you my wife. I'd die rather than spend my life without you.*

His sincerity was unquestionable, but of course his mother had her ways. One thing Adiega had learned from her years under that woman's roof was that Vlatucia got what Vlatucia wanted.

Always.

"I am Lothar," said a bearish fellow with a truncheon standing guard outside the entrance of the *Cella.* Two others squatted on the cave floor, lashing tall, heavy stakes into a flat panel. All three spoke the Celtice tongue with heavy Germani accents, from which she deduced that they were the same men who had abducted and burned poor Gamicu Ivageni last month on Vlatucia's orders. "You will leave the food with me. I will let him eat when you are done with him."

"Done with who?" asked Paullia, her arms laden with blankets and washrags.

Lothar chuckled in a way that put Adiega instantly on alert. Turning, he ushered them over a little natural bridge that spanned the cave stream running along the front wall of the *Cella.* The newly carved shrine, a stone statue wearing iron *torkas* and inscribed DVSIVÆSVS, stood against the back wall. "Vlatucia, she say she want you to wash him good, shave the face, and cut the hair all off, for the bugs. Put it there, with his clothings, and I will burn it." He pointed to a heap of tattered rags and animal skins in a bronze-lined fire pit.

"Who are you talking about?" asked Adiega.

He pointed behind them. She turned and started, her bucket of grooming implements clattering to the floor.

Standing calf-deep in the stream, his arms stretched high

overhead with his hands tied to a hook of rock, was a very tall, very dirty, very, very naked man. He was thin, but with long, ropy muscles, as if he ate just enough to keep himself constantly on the move. His dark blond hair hung past his shoulders in a snarled mass studded with bits of leaves and twigs; his beard was nearly as long and just as filthy. There were bruises all over him, a gash on his forehead that was just starting to scab over, a large and ugly abrasion on one shoulder, and smaller ones on his knees and elbows.

He was staring intently at Adiega and Paullia, his blue eyes pale and luminous against his grimy face. He said something in a low, hoarse voice, using words in a guttural language Adiega had never heard spoken before.

"He speak the . . . I don't know how you say," said Lothar. "The *sprâcha von Norvegen.* You know. From the *nord.*"

"From the north," Adiega whispered as she crouched to pick up the items she'd dropped and put them back in the bucket. "By the gods, Paullia, this . . . this man is . . . Well, he isn't a man at all. He's a dusios. They captured him to put gifted babies in the bellies of the *uxelli* matrons before everybody leaves."

"A *dusios*? You mean one of those sex demons?" Paullia was eyeing the demon in question up and down with an expression of carnal fascination that was all too familiar to Adiega. Following the death of her husband in battle two years ago, which had put an end to eight years of misery and regular beatings, Paullia had resolved never to marry again. Instead, she cheerfully assuaged her lust with any man who took her fancy, an arrangement that suited both Paullia and the unattached males of Vernem.

"You be good for these womens, *ja*?" Lothar went over to the dusios and yanked his head back by the hair. "So I don't hurt you no more."

The dusios bared his teeth and snarled as he kicked out savagely, water spewing all over the *Cella.* The Germani landed on his back with a howl of pain. Sputtering invective in his own tongue, he leapt to his feet and slammed his truncheon into the stomach of the dusios, who kicked again, roaring, "*Hrøkkva!*" This time his captor managed to scramble away in time.

Dusting himself off, Lothar told the sisters, "Vlatucia don't want me to hurt him too bad. You tell me when you cut off hair so I can burn it." He returned to his post in the corridor outside.

The dusios, still a little breathless from his tussle with Lothar, was staring at them again, in a way that made Adiega shiver. He growled in frustration as he yanked at the ropes binding his wrists, but they held tight. That part of him that hung between his legs seemed to be somewhat larger than when they'd first entered the *Cella,* she noticed.

"What are we going to do?" she whispered to Paullia.

"You shave him and cut his hair," she said, setting her blankets on the floor but keeping the washrags. "I'll wash him."

"But..."

Paullia took the dish of soft yellow soap from Adiega and approached the dusios slowly, giving him her best man-tamer smile. "I wash?" she asked, miming the rubbing of a washrag on the soap, and then on him.

He stared in apparent bewilderment and suspicion at the soap as she stepped down into the stream, the bottom of her skirt floating on the surface of the water. "*Hverr... ?*"

"Soap," she said, dampening the rag in the river and rubbing it on the soap. "Don't you have this where you come from?"

He recoiled when she reached up to wash his face. "*Ekki!*"

"It won't hurt you." Paullia rubbed the soapy cloth on her forearm, then dipped her arm in the water to rinse it off. "See? Clean." She sniffed her arm, smiling as if in pleasure as she inhaled. "Wouldn't you like to be nice and clean?"

This time, when she went to wash his face, he stood still for it, though he still looked apprehensive. He seemed to relax somewhat as she carefully dabbed the wound on his forehead; her gentleness must have put him at ease.

"Could I have that bucket, Adiega?" Paullia filled it with water, telling him to close his eyes as she held it over his head, but of course he didn't understand. "I don't want your eyes to sting. Your eyes." She pointed to his eyes, and then her own, which she closed tightly as she mimed pouring water over her head.

He closed his eyes. She rinsed his face. "Adiega's going to cut your hair and your beard now," she said, making a scissor shape with her fingers and pretending to chop off her braids. "Go ahead, Adiega. I don't think he'll give you any trouble."

"Adiega," he said, as if testing the feel of the word in his mouth.

"Yes, that's right." Paullia pointed to Adiega and said her name again, and then she pointed to herself. "Paullia. Paullia."

"Paullia."

"You?" She pointed to him, waiting with an expectant expression.

He hesitated, as if unsure just how friendly he wanted to be with members of a clan that had just captured him and tied him up in a cave. Finally, he said, "Elic."

"Elic," Paullia repeated as she lathered up the washrag again. "What a lovely name." Gesturing to herself, she said, "Woman." She pointed to Adiega, and then to herself again. "Woman, woman. You?"

He didn't answer.

"Dusios?" she asked.

He looked dismayed that she knew this. "*Álfr ok dusios,*" he said.

"I think he's saying he's both an elf and a dusios," said Adiega. Elic watched her closely as she stood at the edge of the stream, cutting off tangled chunks of hair and setting them aside to be burned. She'd planned to trim it close to the scalp, but since he appeared to be free of lice and fleas—perhaps his kind were immune to them—she decided to leave it brushing his shoulders.

"Let's get those ears clean. *Ear,*" she said as she ran the washcloth around it.

"Ear."

"That's right."

"*Eyra,*" he said.

"That's your word for ear?"

"*Eyra.*"

Paullia scrubbed and rinsed and scrubbed and rinsed, trading the names of body parts with Elic as Adiega snipped his hair. Feeling more at ease now that Elic hadn't managed to rape and kill them both, she washed it, then trimmed and shaved his beard.

"Ooh, Adiega, look how handsome he is without all that nasty hair," Paullia said, standing back to take him in. "Makes you wish you were one of those *uxelli* matrons he's going to be siring babes on, doesn't it?"

"Not me," said Adiega, noting with amusement how Elic was looking back and forth between them as they spoke, although he couldn't understand a word they were saying. "The only man I want to . . . you know . . . do that with is Bran."

"Then do it!"

"I'm not like you, Paullia. I can't feel right about it unless I'm married."

Paullia was kind enough not to mention the fact that a marriage between Adiega and Bran was looking unlikelier by the day.

"Chest," Paullia said as she ran the soapy cloth over Elic's upper torso.

His gaze lowered to that part of Paullia's body. What with her standing knee-deep in the stream and pouring bucket after bucket of water, her dress had gotten soaked through, conforming all too well to her feminine contours.

"*Brjóst,*" he said, his voice pitched a bit lower than it had been, that hungry look returning to his gaze.

"*Brjóst,*" she repeated, trailing a hand lightly over her right breast.

Elic met her gaze. She smiled into his eyes.

Paullia trailed the washcloth down his belly to his masculine organ, which she proceeded to wash with exceptional thoroughness, Elic straining toward her as he grew fully erect. She closed her soapy fist around him and stroked.

"*Betr,*" he murmured, thrusting into her hand.

"What are you *doing*?" whispered Adiega. "Are you *crazy*?"

"I've never seen a man get so hard so fast," Paullia said. "What I wouldn't give to feel *this* inside me."

"That Lothar fellow will come in and see you," said Adiega as she darted a wary glance at the corridor.

"Just warn me if he starts heading this way."

"Paullia, *please,*" Adiega begged.

"You've never seen a man expel his seed, have you?" Paullia asked. "You should watch this. It'll be an education for you."

"*Ekki,*" Elic groaned. He was twisting his body as if trying to make Paullia let him go.

"Um, Paullia," Adiega said. "I think he wants you to stop."

"Of course he doesn't want me to stop," said Paullia as she stroked him harder, faster.

"No, I think that's what *ekki* means—'stop,' or 'no.' He's grimacing."

"They do that."

"*Ekki, ekki!*" Elic was quivering, his expression pained. "*Ekki!*"

Startled, Paullia released him, saying, "I . . . I'm sorry. I'm sorry, Elic, I . . ."

He shook his head, his breath coming fast, his face flushed. "I'm sorry. I'm sorry."

Late that night, Adiega was awakened by straw crackling in her sister's pallet on the floor beside hers in the cooking hut. At first she thought Paullia was just restless, but then she heard a low, masculine moan, and she realized her sister wasn't alone. It wasn't the first time Paullia had brought a man to her bed while Adiega was sleeping—or trying to sleep; it wouldn't be the last.

Looking over, Adiega saw the moonlit form of a man rearing over her sister, blankets covering him to the waist, the muscles in his back and arms straining with every thrust. He was very tall and clean shaven, with unbraided blond hair.

Elic? By the gods, it *was* him. How could this be happening? How could he have gotten free? As Adiega and Paullia had taken their leave of him this morning, the three Germani were securing their barrier of wooden stakes over the entrance to the *Cella* by means of iron bands encircling the natural columns to either side of it. In addition, one of them, Lothar said, would be standing guard at all times.

Elic's thrusts grew swift and hectic as Paullia clutched at him, her breath coming in high-pitched little pants. He stilled, a strangled groan issuing from his throat as Paullia bucked beneath him.

He settled on top of her, rubbing his face on her hair.

She let out a deep, satisfied sigh. "That was lovely."

"*Líkaði*," he murmured.

Sitting up in bed with her blanket clutched to her chest, Adiega said, "Paullia, Elic can't be here. He must have escaped from the *Cella*. We'll get in terrible trouble if he's found here."

"Oh, we woke you up," her sister said. "I'm sorry."

"I'm sorry, Adiega." Elic gave her a disarming smile as he left her sister's pallet and came to hers.

"Stop it," said Adiega as Elic tried to get under her blanket. "Paullia, tell him to stop it."

"Why?" she asked as she snuggled under her blanket. "He's wonderful, and I won't tell Bran. It'll be our little—"

"*What?*" cried Adiega.

"Shh! Someone will hear you." Giggling excitedly, Paullia said, "Can you believe he wants to do it again so soon?"

"Get him off me!" Adiega exclaimed.

"Oh, just let him," Paullia said. "You'll thank me tomorrow."

"*Ja,* let him," Elic echoed as he yanked at her covers. "Let him."

"*No!*" She yelled, pushing him away as hard as she could, but he was surprisingly strong for such a thin man. "Get away from me!"

Footsteps came running. The door banged open.

Vlatucia's three Germani hauled Elic off of Adiega, knocked him unconscious, and dragged him away.

Four

ELIC SPENT the next day chained to the Dusivæsus statue by a neck manacle, a blanket wrapped around his nakedness, watching his three hulking guards build a most curious structure right there in the cave chamber they called the *Cella*. They constructed it from the ground up, cutting and weaving willow branches for hours—no easy task for them, given their thick, clumsy Germani fingers. At first, Elic thought it was just a simple human figure, but then he saw that telltale bulge take form between the legs, and he realized it was destined to be an exact replica, a little larger than himself, of Dusivæsus.

Late in the afternoon, when the wicker dusios was nearing completion, there appeared in the entrance of the *Cella* a tall, sour-looking woman of middle years accompanied by a young man carrying a bucket, with a green, folded garment that looked like a cloak tucked under his arm. He was somewhat shorter than she, and with hair so dark that Elic would never have taken him for a Galli had he encountered him anyplace else. No hand emerged from his right sleeve; Elic wondered if he'd lost it in some farming accident or battle, or if he'd been born that way. The woman wore mannish clothes, with a gold *torka* around her neck of the type Gallico chieftains often wore.

The guards sprang to their feet when the woman—whom they greeted as Vlatucia—entered the *Cella,* stepping carefully over the shattered remains of the wall of wooden stakes that Elic had kicked down last night so that he could get to the woman called Paullia. The guard he'd punched unconscious had awakened sooner than Elic had expected and fetched his comrades. He had hoped to bed Paullia and be many *luegae* from here by the time the man woke up, but it was not to be.

All day, as he'd sat on the statue's platform watching those three brutes build their wicker effigy, all he could think was, *I should have killed the bastard.* Not that he had the stomach for killing. He hadn't taken a single life in all his many years of existence, and he hoped he would never have to. But it felt good to think it.

Vlatucia barked something to the guards, who swiftly retreated—so swiftly, in fact, that one of them left the knife he'd been using on the floor not too far from Elic's right foot, amid a scattering of willow branches. The branches helped to disguise it, but they did not conceal it altogether. *Please, Frøya, don't let them start casting their eyes around the floor.*

"Bran!" The woman nodded toward the bucket the young man was carrying and said something.

Bran approached Elic warily, setting the cloak on the platform next to him, and also the bucket, the contents of which he emptied out: a washrag, a comb, and a dish of soap.

Elic picked up the soap dish and hurled it against the cave wall, where it shattered.

Vlatucia pointed to the mess and said something to Bran, who started toward it, then hesitated, as if unsure that he wanted to obey that particular order. Vlatucia snapped at him. He glanced very briefly at Elic, clearly embarrassed to be seen by him in such a position of servility, and then he turned toward the entryway and called out, "Lothar!" One of the guards came in, cleaned up the broken soap dish at Bran's behest, and left.

Vlatucia, clearly vexed by Bran's defiance, snarled something at him, then pointed to the low flames crackling in the fire pit and issued yet another order. The young man took out a tiny purple leather pouch from inside his tunic and sprinkled a few grains of glittery black powder upon the fire while murmuring an incantation. The flames immediately turned a bright, searing green with purplish tips.

Bran made a go-ahead gesture to Vlatucia, who turned to Elic and said, "It is called Powder of Tongues. It comes from somewhere far to the east."

Elic sat up straight on the platform, surprised by the fact that he'd understood her, even though she'd spoken in the Gallitunga. He knew enough about spellcasting to know that a powder alone, although it might focus or enhance an enchantment, couldn't effect such potent magic without the intervention of an extremely gifted magus.

"The powder is extremely hard to come by even in its native land," she said, "and quite expensive, so we have only a very small supply, most of which my son has just poured onto that fire so that I can explain some things to you. When those flames return to their normal color, which won't be long from now, you won't be able to understand me anymore. If you waste that precious time by throwing things, like a temperamental little child, I will have you beaten, which is a pastime my Germani approach with great artistry and relish."

"Can you understand me, too?" he asked.

"I can."

"Why was I brought here?" One moment he'd been tracking the scent of deer through the woods. The next, he was in a hole in the ground, looking up at the faces of the three Germani guards.

"We need to perpetuate our druidic line, and you're our only hope for doing that." She went on to explain about her clan's need for gifted offspring and the role they had in mind for him. "I can't imagine you would find much to object to in the arrangement," she said. "As I understand it, dusii exist to mate."

"Yes, but on our own terms," he said. "*I* choose the women I lie with."

"Actually, *I* do," she said, "at least until the Vernae leave this place. If you've planted enough babes in enough wombs by that point, I may let you stay here."

"What if I refuse to fuck who you tell me to fuck?" he asked, enjoying the scalding blush that crawled up her throat. The young man, her son, looked to be fighting back a smile—understandable, given the way the she-bitch treated him.

"You can't help but have noticed our new friend." She looked toward the wicker effigy, as did Bran.

Elic took advantage of their having turned away to extend his right leg, cover the knife with his foot, and slide it back.

"If you refuse to"—she lifted her chin and leveled her gaze at him—"fuck whom I tell you to fuck, then you will be enclosed in that effigy and I will have it lit on fire. Don't do yourself the disservice of doubting that. Bran, tell him."

"She'll do it," he said, with an expression that seemed to meld shame and disgust. "She's done it before."

"It is the punishment I favor for those who defy my authority, inasmuch as it tends to have a quelling effect on the defiance of others." With a glance at Bran, she said, "*Most* others. And of course it is a particularly apt punishment for one such as yourself. By the way, you will also be burned if you continue spreading your seed around to every *vassa* who captures your fancy. You broke out of here last night to lie with my serving women."

"Not both," he said. "Just the one." Though he would have gladly taken the other, too, had she been willing.

"There will be no more such nocturnal escapades," she said. "You are to service my hand-chosen couples only."

"When is this coming off?" Elic asked, tugging on the neck manacle.

"It isn't."

Bran said, "Is it really necessary, Mother? He knows he'll burn unless he does exactly as you—"

"If you weren't such a child," she replied, "you wouldn't ask that. Acknowledging a threat and taking it seriously are two different things. I can't take the chance that he'll decide to make a run for it the moment we let down our guard."

Elic knew better than to argue with the likes of her. "How many couples am I to . . . 'service,' as you put it?"

"We have ten highborn couples with gifted wives, but my two daughters are with child, so that leaves eight. You are to transfer seed between four couples per night until the wives conceive."

"That would be eight changes of gender in one night," he said. "I can't handle it, especially undernourished and weak as I am now. It's too much of a strain on my body. I'll do the men first, then the women. That way, I only have to endure The Change twice."

"Impossible," she said. "The offspring must be those of the husband. If you collect all the seed at once, different men's seed will get mixed up together."

"In such a case," he explained, "the seed tends to seek the womb in which it's meant to take root."

"Do you have a different name in your female form?" Bran asked.

His mother looked at him as if it were an absurd question, but of course it wasn't.

"She's had several names," Elic said. "You may call her Elina."

Pointing to the flames in the fire pit, Bran said, "The colors are fading, Mother. You've very little time left."

She said, "These couplings will take place in the nemeton—our sacred oak grove—every night until we leave. You are to bathe beforehand. I shall have some more soap sent to you."

Elic had never encountered a people so obsessed with cleaning themselves. It couldn't be healthy. "I'll need a razor to shave with," he said.

"Do you think I'd really allow you to get your hands on a blade?" she asked.

You allowed me to get my foot on one, he thought with a smile.

After Bran and Vlatucia left, Elic sat on the floor in front of the platform and considered the name so precisely carved into it: DVSIVÆSVS. *Great and Worthy Dusios.* Funny, he didn't feel so great and worthy when the lady chieftain of the Vernae was telling him who to fuck, where to fuck, and when to fuck if he wanted to avoid a fiery death.

Taking the knife he'd just filched, he started scratching out a better, more appropriate name on top of the first, using the runic alphabet of his homeland.

The slow, measured thudding grew steadily louder as Bran guided the procession of four *uxelli* husbands, naked beneath their hooded cloaks, into the nemeton.

Artaros sat on the square boulder at the edge of the clearing, beating on his goatskin hand drum, a bronze ewer and cup on the stump next to him. Between the old druid and the altar, flames leapt from the herbs burning in the fire pit, to which Frontu was lying so close, as usual, that it was a wonder his fur didn't singe.

A tall, astonishingly beautiful woman—Elic's female incarnation, Elina—stood next to the altar. She wore the green cloak, its hood lowered to reveal her honey-blond, roughly chopped hair. Around her neck was locked the iron manacle Vlatucia had insisted upon, its chain wrapped around one of the boulders supporting the altar.

Setting down his drum and beater, Artaros filled the cup from the ewer and offered it to each husband in turn, instructing them to drain it completely. It was a brew Artaros called Lightning and Clouds, which he'd formulated both to excite one's sexual appetite and to blur one's memory. As Artaros had explained it, husbands and wives who weren't in the habit of straying might need a little help in overcoming their natural reluctance to couple with someone other than their spouses—but there was no need for them to remember, the next day, the things they'd done the night before in the nemeton.

Artaros gestured for Bran to depart, for his role in these ceremonies was solely that of escort for the husbands and wives. He was to wait at the head of the path and listen for a series of rapid drumbeats. This would be his signal that the husbands had all taken their turns with Elina, at which point he was to gather them up and walk them back to the village, returning with the four matrons. In the interim, Elic would have transformed back into a male so as to transfer the husbands' seed to their wives.

Halfway down the path, curiosity overcame him. He veered off into the dark forest and circled back to within a few yards of the firelit nemeton, where he heard Artaros chanting incantations of fertility while beating on his drum. Peering between the trees, Bran saw Epillus Brocagni open his cloak and lift Elina, now naked, onto the altar as the other three husbands watched from the perimeter of the clearing.

Standing between Elina's legs, Epillus kissed her neck and breasts while caressing her, first gently, then more and more heatedly as his passions rose, along with hers. He reached between them for a few moments, his arm working, and then he closed his hands around her hips and began pushing in rhythm with the drumbeats—which was when Bran, who had no personal experience of such matters, realized he'd actually entered her and was performing the sexual act.

Oncus Queniloci, driven, no doubt, by the lightning aspect of Artaros's Lightning and Clouds, came up to the altar and laid Elina on her back to suckle her breasts as Epillus took her, his thrusts growing quicker, more abrupt. The other two men drew closer, both pleasuring themselves as they watched, their eyes glittering in the firelight. Elina's breath came in rapid little hitches, and then she cried out, her body convulsing in a way that made Bran's own sex stiffen and rise beneath his trousers. Epillus hunched over her, shouting. He shouted over and over again, ramming himself into her as he shot his seed.

Oncus went next. He placed her on all fours on the ground and took her that way, gripping the chain attached to her neck manacle, as she licked the sex of Solas Battigni, kneeling in front of her. When it was Solas's turn, he laid her faceup on the altar and lifted her legs over his shoulders while Caliacas Corbbri straddled her breasts, squeezing them together so that he could thrust between them. When Solas was done with her, Caliacas curled her onto her side at the edge of the altar and penetrated her from a standing position.

Surrendering to his aching need, Bran had reached into his trousers to ease his lust, but he'd barely begun to stroke himself when Artaros commenced the rapid drumming that indicated it was time to usher the husbands back to the village and return with the wives. This he did, grateful that his tunic was loose enough so that his erection wasn't obvious to one and all.

The wives took their turns with Elic in a more orderly, one-at-a-time manner than had their husbands—not that there was anything particularly civilized about the couplings. Elic was like a rutting beast, shoving the women into positions Bran had never imagined and taking them with wild, carnal ferocity.

In an agony of arousal now, Bran braced his back against one of the old oaks and relieved his terrible lust with his fist, gritting his teeth to keep from groaning as his seed spurted in long arcs onto the forest floor.

As he tucked himself back into his trousers, panting and shaking, he heard the battery of drumbeats that marked an end to the fertility rite—the first of many, he reminded himself, wondering how he was going to get through them.

Five

The Cold Time

WHERE'S ADIEGA?" Bran asked Paullia as she dumped a sack of apples and another of onions into the back of the cart sitting outside the cooking hut, alongside a cageful of chickens. "I've been looking for her all morning."

Paullia blew on her hands and rubbed them together as she strode back into the hut. "I don't know, but if you see her, would you tell her to come give me a hand?" Lifting the big iron cauldron off its hook, she started dragging it outside, her breath smoking in the icy air.

Bran grabbed the handle and helped her to heft it into the cart alongside various other possessions of Vlatucia's that she had earmarked as being critical for a long journey. All over the village, families were packing up their household belongings for their lives away from Vernem, for they'd received word that morning from one of Vlatucia's scouts that a Roman cohort was marching in their direction and would be there by nightfall. The only villagers not scurrying about in frantic preparation were those few individuals, including the two gifted children and their mothers, who would be staying behind with Bran.

One who anticipated staying was Briaga, who was spending the day getting dressed and groomed for the wedding rites she expected to participate in this afternoon. This despite the fact that Bran had never actually asked her to marry him; in fact, he'd barely ever spoken to her. The arrangements had been made by Vlatucia in concert with Briaga's mother. From what Bran had been told, Briaga was torn about her impending nuptials and future life in Roman-occupied Vernem. On the one hand, she would be a slave married to a cripple who had to keep his leadership status a secret. On the other, she'd be living in close proximity to Romans, whom she viewed as paragons of sophistication. Surely they would recognize her as a kindred being and treat her like a free woman.

"I've been asking all over the village for Adiega," Bran said, "but no one's seen her."

"She's in the storehouse."

Bran turned to find his mother standing behind him. Despite the weather, she wore no cloak or wrap, but she looked as unperturbed as if it were a balmy summer's day.

"What is she doing in the storehouse?" Bran asked, suddenly much more worried than he'd been before. Vlatucia's storehouse at the edge of the woods, her stronghold for valuable crops, among other things, was thick-walled and windowless, with a heavy oaken door fitted with an iron lock. By far the most secure building in Vernem, it had been pressed into service on more than one occasion to detain miscreants pending judgment by the elders.

From the corner of his eye he saw Paullia move around to the other side of the cart, where she could eavesdrop unobtrusively.

"After I learned this morning that the Romans are on their way," Vlatucia said, "I went to Artaros to tell him he needed to get ready to marry you to Briaga this afternoon. He told me he would make the necessary preparations, but that he didn't know if you'd go along with it. He said your reluctance to wed Briaga wasn't so much a matter of immaturity as the fact that you were in love with someone else."

"He . . . he *told* you?"

Vlatucia shook her head. "He told me you'd given him the girl's name in confidence, and that there was nothing I could do to force him to reveal it. So I just sat down and thought about it. I was bewildered at first, because you've never courted any woman, nor shown any interest in doing so. But then I realized that there was one woman in whose company you've spent a great deal of time for years, because she's lived under our very roof since she was orphaned. I would have thought of Adiega right off—in fact, I would have realized it long ago—but it had never occurred to me that you would shame our family by seducing a *vassa.*"

"I didn't seduce her," Bran said hotly. "We've never even—"

"Good, then I don't need to worry that you might have gotten her with child. She's a virgin?"

"Of course."

"All the better. The gods smile on virgin sacrifices."

Bran had been cold all morning, but now he felt as if every nerve in his body were crackling with frost. Shaking in dread and disbelief, he said, "You can't be serious."

Circling around the cart to stand face-to-face with Vlatucia, Paullia said, "You evil, shriveled-up sack of puke. By the gods, if you hurt my sister, I'll take my meat knife and tie you up and start cutting bits off. First your nose, then your tongue, then your fingers, one by one, then—"

"Yes, yes," Vlatucia drawled, rolling her eyes. "A most terrifying threat. I do hope you realize you're never welcome under my roof again."

"You won't have a roof after today," reminded Paullia. "And

anyway, I've decided I'm better off staying here and taking my chances with the Romans than fetching and cooking for the likes of you."

"Mother, have you lost your wits entirely?" Bran asked. "We don't do human sacrifices anymore, we haven't in decades."

"Because of your father's softheartedness," she said. "And see where it got us? We've lost our homes, our lives, everything. We need to burn a virgin to ensure our safe travels through—"

"*Burn?*"

"My Germani are constructing a wicker effigy in the wheat field. She's to be burned at noon."

Nodding in understanding, Bran said, "And I'm to be wed to Briaga shortly thereafter, your reasoning being that, with Adiega gone, there will be nothing to stop me from doing my duty by the clan. Well, it won't work, Mother. I will marry Adiega or no one."

It was only when Bran saw Paullia giving him a look of pride and respect—underscored with shock—that he grasped how fearlessly he'd spoken to this woman who'd kept him so firmly under her thumb for nineteen years.

"Then you will marry no one," said Vlatucia with studied calm, "for Adiega *will* burn, and there is not a thing you can do about it."

Paullia opened her mouth for another dressing-down, but Bran caught her eye and gave her a surreptitious little *not now* look.

Adopting his most solemn demeanor, Bran said, "I won't attempt to argue you out of it. After nineteen years as your son, I know full well the futility of that. But I beg you, if you've a whit of human compassion, let me say good-bye to her. At least then, I'll be able to live with . . . whatever happens."

"Only if you promise me you'll consider marrying Briaga."

"I promise," he said gravely. He could *consider* flying to the moon, but that didn't mean it would ever happen.

After a moment's pinch-faced thought, Vlatucia said, "I can't let you visit her unaccompanied. Someone will have to go with you, either me or someone I can trust to keep you from getting any clever ideas."

"Artaros can come with me. He feels exactly as you do about Briaga. He's forever pressuring me to marry her."

"Send him to me. I'll give him the keys to the storehouse."

"*Marry* you?" exclaimed Artaros as he stood outside the storehouse, sorting with some difficulty through the keys on Vlatucia's big iron ring. "To *Adiega*?" He stroked his long beard as he contemplated the request. "Well, I suppose, if she's condemned to die anyway . . . I mean, what harm could it really do? And if it will give you some comfort . . . You'd be a widower after she's gone, so you could still wed Briaga this afternoon if you decide to accept your duty and do the right thing. Yes, all right. I'll do it."

"One other thing, Grandfather," said Bran as the old man chose a key and struggled with the task of fitting it into the lock. "Another favor, a big one. After you marry me to Adiega, I'd like you to take those keys to the *Cella,* free Elic from his neck chain, and bring him here. Then leave, and don't tell anyone what you've done."

Artaros stilled, his frown softening into a smile as he thought it through. "I always knew you were a clever boy."

"Powder of Tongues," Elic said in the Gallitunga when Bran produced the little purple leather pouch after locking the door from inside. It looked to be a storehouse he'd found himself in, along with Bran and the young Adiega, who sat on a blanket on the floor with her arms banded around her, refusing to meet his gaze.

It was warm in the round stone building, and dark save for

the light from a small brazier in the middle of the room and the smoke hole in the roof, the perimeter of which was piled high with sacks, crates, and barrels. Bran upended the pouch over the brazier and shook it, emptying its few remaining grains of black powder upon the coals as he recited the words that generated the magic. Green flames with purple tips leapt up from the spots the grains had struck.

"We don't have long," Bran said as he put away the pouch. "My mother intends to have Adiega burned at noon as a sacrifice—but really as a way of pressuring me to marry someone I don't want to marry before they all leave."

"*Bikkja,*" Elic muttered under his breath.

Crouching next to Adiega to put an arm around her shoulder, Bran said, "Artaros married us to each other a little while ago, in secret."

Elic smiled and bowed to Adiega. "It is a wonderful thing to find the mate of your heart. I am truly happy for you."

She looked up a little shyly to return his smile. Strange... Though she'd struck him as more reserved than her sister Paullia that time in the *Cella,* she wasn't what he'd call shy.

The reason for her bashfulness became apparent when Bran said, "We want you to... do for us what you do for the others, the *uxelli* husbands and wives."

Elic looked from Bran to the blushing Adiega and back.

"Adiega doesn't share my gifts," Bran said, "so the only way for us to have druidic children is if you help us. And it will protect Adiega from my mother, too, if she can be with child after we... well, afterward."

"You're absolutely sure you want this?" Elic asked Adiega.

"Yes." Looking at Elic for the first time, she said, "But I know that Vlatucia has threatened to have *you* burned to death if you... have relations with people other than those she's chosen for you."

"I'm sick of Vlatucia," Elic said, "sick of fearing her, of being her obedient sex slave. Of course I'll help you."

Adiega said, "We . . . we'd want to be together when you . . . when we . . ."

"Certainly," Elic said.

"And no potions or herbs," said Bran. "Just us. Just . . . the three of us." He said something else, then, but although Elic could hear the Gallitunga words, he could not understand them.

He looked at the brazier to find it filled with ordinary, glowing coals. The Powder of Tongues had worn off.

Elina knelt with her back to Bran and Adiega until The Change was complete, her green cloak wrapped tightly around her so as not to make them witness the transformation from male to female, which humans tended to find nauseating.

She rose and stretched, shaking out her legs, craning her neck this way and that. Turning and peering across the dark storeroom, she saw the young couple lying together on the blanket, their arms wrapped tightly around each other. They were both barefooted, but otherwise still fully dressed. Bran was whispering something earnestly into Adiega's ear. He kissed her forehead, searched her eyes, and asked her something. She nodded, and then her gaze shifted to Elina coming toward them.

Bran glanced at Elina as she lowered herself to the blanket next to him, then he took Adiega's face in his hands and kissed her again, on the mouth this time, lingeringly and with deep passion. He stroked her breasts through her dress, drew her toward him and rubbed against her.

Elina untied Bran's trousers, took Adiega's hand, and closed it around his erection. He thrust into her hand, moaning something that made Adiega smile. She stroked him with an expression of wonderment at her ability to bring him such pleasure, until finally he removed her hand and kissed it, saying something in a hoarse, breathless voice; he was close.

Elina rolled him onto his back and straddled him. Wanting to spare Adiega's feelings, she arranged her cloak so as to conceal the juncture of their bodies as she positioned Bran to enter her. He sucked in a breath, squeezing Adiega's hand.

To Elina's surprise, Adiega pulled the cloak aside to watch as Elina lowered herself onto Bran's straining erection. Elina unpinned the cloak and tossed it aside, whereupon Bran said something to Adiega, tugging impatiently at her dress. The young woman hesitated, then pulled the garment off over her head, leaving herself as naked as Elina. She was pale and lissome, with sweet, high little breasts. Bran looked at her the way every female dreamed of being looked at, with both awe and desire.

Bran embraced Adiega, kissing and caressing her as Elina rocked atop him in a steady, languid rhythm. Adiega pulled his tunic up to kiss his chest. He shucked the garment off and gathered her in his arms, his breath coming in harsh gasps, his body bucking to meet Elina's quickening thrusts. She contracted her internal muscles, released and contracted again, and again, like a fist pumping, squeezing…

Bran groaned helplessly, his back arched, arms tightening around Adiega. Elina felt the hot bursts of his seed as her own pleasure erupted, wave after wave of it, the spasms drawing Bran's seed deep, deep into her body.

Elic, wrapped once more in the green cloak, felt the same relief he always felt upon returning to his masculine form. He felt the presence, low in his belly, of Bran's seed, the pressure of it making him hard and ready. Rising, he saw Bran and Adiega, both now completely unclothed, lying on the blanket with their arms and legs entwined as they whispered and kissed.

Settling himself behind Adiega, Elic removed his cloak and pressed his body gently to hers. She started when she felt his erection against her bottom. Bran stroked her face and murmured something. She nodded. He kissed her, caressing her breasts; she sighed in pleasure.

Reaching between Adiega's legs from behind, Elic eased a finger inside her until he encountered her virginal barrier, which was pliant but almost completely intact; not surprising, given how young she was. Luckily, she was slippery with arousal; that should help.

Lifting her outside leg so as to give him better access, Elic pressed the head of his penis against her sex. She tensed. Bran whispered something in a reassuring tone of voice, and she seemed to relax.

Slowly, Elic told himself as he flexed his hips, entering her just slightly, and then a bit more, until he could penetrate no farther. He pushed against the delicate membrane; it stretched, but didn't give. He pushed again, and again, with no success. Trembling, Adiega said something to Bran, who gave Elic a worriedly inquiring look.

"It's all right," Elic said, although he knew Bran couldn't understand him. "Here. Touch her like this." He lowered Bran's hand to Adiega's sex, showing him how to lightly stroke the little knot at its apex. She writhed to his touch, moaning softly, as Elic resisted the maddening urge to thrust.

Not yet, he thought as her breath came faster, her hips quivering. *Not yet*...

She cried out, her body shuddering wildly as her pleasure peaked.

Now. Elic gripped her hips and shoved, driving through the thin membrane to bury himself inside her as she groaned—more in pleasure, he hoped, than in pain. He lay still as the tremors waned, and then he began to thrust.

Bran kissed and suckled her breasts while continuing to caress her intimately, coaxing her toward a second climax just as Elic reached his own crisis of pleasure. He let out a low, grinding moan as he pumped a torrent of seed into her, and then he slumped down, breathless and damp with sweat.

Elic withdrew his bloodied organ slowly and carefully from Adiega's body. Sitting up, he reached for his cloak.

"Elic."

Bran was smiling at him as he held Adiega in his arms. He said something that didn't require Powder of Tongues to translate.

"You're welcome," Elic said.

"There she is," said Bran shortly before noon as he and Adiega walked hand in hand through the village, with Elic, Artaros, and Frontu following behind. All around them, people paused in their packing and preparations to stare. He heard whispers about himself and Adiega, whispers about Elic...

Vlatucia stood in front of her house with her hands on her hips, her expression furious, the golden *torka* around her neck gleaming in the frigid morning sun. Behind her stood her three Germani thugs.

She turned to them and said, "The woman, Adiega—take her and burn her."

Bran thrust the trembling Adiega behind his back as Artaros stepped forward. "You can't burn her, Vlatucia. It would be anathema. She's your daughter by marriage."

"*What?*"

There came a chorus of excited murmurs from the crowd that was gathering around them.

"I married them myself just this morning," Artaros said.

She raised her hand; like well-trained dogs, the three Germani stopped advancing.

"You're lying," she told her father. "You wouldn't have done that. Bran must wed Briaga. You know that. You've told me so yourself. His children must be gifted."

"His first child *is* gifted," the old man said. "He's curled up in Adiega's womb even as we speak."

"Impossible."

"See for yourself, Vlatucia. You have druidic gifts of your own, though you dismiss them. When you were a child, you saw the brightest, most colorful auras. Concentrate on Adiega. Tell me if you don't see silvery ripples, little sparks..."

Bran stepped aside so that his mother could study Adiega.

Vlatucia shook her head in disbelief as she stared at her son's new wife. "It... it's not possible... How could she... ?" Her expression turned venomous as her gaze lit on Elic. "*You.*"

Elic smiled and bowed.

"You were forbidden to do anything of the sort. I *expressly* forbade it! How *dare* you?"

Elic, who couldn't understand a word of what she was saying, stood calmly by while she ranted at him.

"Perhaps I can't burn that worthless little *vassa* who married my son, but I can burn *you,*" she said, pointing a quivering finger at Elic.

"Only the chieftain can order such a punishment," Bran said.

"We have no official chieftain," she said. "There's no one who's qualified, so I'm serving until—"

"Give me the *torka.*" Releasing Adiega's hand, Bran walked toward his mother, his arm outstretched.

"It's rightfully Bran's," said Artaros. "You know it." Gesturing to the onlookers, he said, "*They* know it, even if they're too afraid of you to say it out loud."

"It's *mine*!" she cried, clutching at the *torka* with both hands, her face flushing crimson. "The *gall* of you," she told Bran, "thinking you deserve to wear this. You're a *child,* a *cripple.* You can't even put this on with one hand. You need two to pull it apart."

"If you don't give it to me, I will take it from you," Bran said.

She let out a burst of hectic laughter. "I'd love to see you try, *cripple.*"

Bran pointed at the *torka* while saying an ancient, simple, but very effective spell.

Vlatucia's eyes widened in alarm as she felt the *torka* grow warm, then hot. "Get it off," she told her three Germani, clawing at it. *"Get it off! Get it off!"*

They yanked it off her and threw it on the ground, then clustered around their mistress as she rubbed at the livid ring around her neck, whimpering.

"Frontu." Artaros, knowing the *torka* would be cool to the touch now, pointed to it. The wolf obediently loped over, picked it up in his mouth, and brought it back to his master.

Artaros strained to widen the opening in the *torka* with his feeble old hands, but finally he gave up and handed it to Elic, who bent the soft gold easily and closed it around Bran's neck.

It felt so cool and heavy and *right* that it took Bran a moment to notice that his fellow Vernae were cheering him.

The villagers spent the next few hours loading up their belongings, and then they all left together, in a long string of carts and wagons—except for those few who had chosen to stay behind with Bran and Adiega.

"Do you hear that?" Bran asked as they stood at the edge of the village, watching the last of the carts disappear far beyond the valley.

It was the ground beneath them, beginning to rumble with the thunder of distant marching feet.

Dawn,
July 31 of this year

"CAN YOU hear what they're saying?" Emmett Archer asked Adrien Morel, Seigneur des Ombres, as they stood at an open window in *le seigneur*'s gate-tower study. Forty feet below and some distance away, barely visible in the morning mist enveloping the castle courtyard, Viktor Larsson and Heather Armstrong stood beside the large central fountain with their luggage at their feet. They weren't the first guests of the chateau to slip away before sunrise without saying good-bye; they wouldn't be the last.

"He's apologizing for being such an ass." Extraordinary hearing was one of several gifts, both sensory and extrasensory, with which Morel had been graced at birth, and which he referred to in toto as The Gift. He retrieved a pack of Sobranie Black Russians from the pocket of his dressing gown and flipped it open.

Igniting Morel's gold-tipped black cigarette with his monogrammed lighter, Archer said, "You should quit those things, *mon seigneur*—now, while there's still time for it to do you some good."

"As should you, my friend," said Morel as he offered the open pack to Archer.

Accepting the cigarette with a wry nod of thanks, Archer said, "At my age, it's not so easy." What he was thinking, but didn't say, because theirs was not that sort of relationship, was *Thank you for calling me your friend.* Acquaintances of Archer's—especially the Americans, who rarely understood such things—sometimes asked him if he didn't find it demeaning to address a man twenty-seven years his junior as "*mon seigneur.*" He would explain that it was similar to his experience as a flight lieutenant in the RAF, in that one is expected to show deference to a man of superior rank, regardless of age or personal feelings. Of course, it was actually a bit more complex than that. A glance at the golden torque and gnarled oaken staff encased in glass on the wall opposite *le seigneur*'s desk was enough to remind Archer that Adrien Morel was not so much of superior rank as of superior . . . everything. Young he might be, and a mortal human just like Archer, but there was ancient magic flowing in his veins, and if that wasn't worthy of homage, what was?

"Do you *sleep* in a suit and tie?" Morel asked Archer as his *administrateur* tucked his lighter back into his inside coat pocket. "I ring you before the sun has even risen, no one up at this hour but myself and our departing guests, and you arrive ten minutes later looking as if you've just stepped out the front door of . . . What is that Savile Row shop you like so much?"

"Huntsman's. And for your information, sir, this is not a suit, but a blazer and trousers—summer-weight worsted, quite informal, really." Morel was probably wrong about no one else being awake yet, Archer thought. Darius preferred to do his roaming at ungodly hours, the better to avoid contact with visitors. Elic and Lili were sometimes up early, as well, but Inigo would sleep until noon today in his air-conditioned suite in the southwest tower, as was his custom, with Kat and Chloe curled up on either side in his king-size Tempur-Pedic.

Nodding toward the couple below, Archer asked, "Are they still talking?"

Morel waved a hand across the open window. "*Uediju rowero gutu.*"

". . . not blameless myself," Heather was saying softly. "The way I flirted with Elic yesterday, in the bathhouse—"

"I'd been begging for that," Larsson said. "I don't know what came over me, letting that woman get to me that way. It's this place, no? Not to say I'm without fault, but this place . . . It's like there's something in the air here that makes you . . . You don't know what's real and what's . . ." Archer could hear Larsson swallow. "Last night, b-before you came to bed, I . . . I awoke and—" He shook his head, groping for words.

"You, too?" she asked. "I dozed off in the bathhouse, and when I woke up, I'd had this . . . I guess it was a dream, but at first I thought it had actually happened, 'cause it felt so . . ."

"But it didn't, right? It was just a dream?"

"Well, yeah, I guess so. Sure. Of course. I mean, I did things in that dream that I would never . . ." She looked away. "Things I couldn't imagine doing if I were . . ."

"*Ja.* Me, too," he said, but there was an edge of uncertainty to his voice.

"Listen," she said, "as long as we're clearing the air, I'm sorry I brought that up about Lars in front of everybody yesterday. I know how you feel about—"

"*Nä,* you were right to do so. He's my brother, and the problem—if there *is* a problem—is mine, not his. I need reminding sometimes not to be such an *åsna.* You're good that way. You make me a better person." Burrowing into the front pocket of his khakis, he produced a glittering little object—Miss Armstrong's engagement ring, Archer realized when he lifted her left hand. He hesitated, as if waiting for permission; almost made Archer feel sorry for the poor wanker.

She smiled and nodded. Sighing in relief, Larsson slid the big diamond onto her finger, then gathered her in his arms for a lingering kiss.

Clearing his throat, Archer drawled, "How very stirring," through a plume of smoke.

Morel waved his hand again, turning off the "surround sound," as Inigo called it.

"Did it take?" Archer asked as he watched the couple stroll through the tree-lined courtyard toward the gatehouse, Larsson hauling their matching leather duffels.

Le seigneur nodded as he drew on his cigarette. "Her aura is filled with little silvery sparks. She's carrying Elic's child—a druid." He always called them druids and druidesses, the gifted ones.

"A boy," Archer said. "Excellent." There'd been an unusually long run of girls lately. Which was fine, but one did like to maintain a certain balance in these matters.

"A boy with extraordinary powers, judging by the energy."

"It's not just Elic's child Miss Armstrong is carrying," Archer pointed out. "It's Larsson's, too. It's entirely his DNA, after all. Elic just supplied his—"

"*Just?*"

"Point taken, *mon seigneur.*" Archer executed a conciliatory little bow, which set off a mild wave of dizziness. Steadying himself with a hand on the windowsill, he straightened up to find Morel studying him in that unnervingly intent way of his.

"Are you all right, Archer? Your aura, it's been looking a bit... dark in parts."

"Encroaching old age," Archer said with a mild shrug. "Damned galling, really, but what can one do but stiffen one's back and carry on, eh?" No point worrying *le seigneur* about a problem even he was helpless to do anything about.

Leaving his fiancée to wait with their luggage by the gatehouse, Larsson sprinted across the drawbridge and up the driveway to the stable-cum-garage.

"Do you think they'll ever return to Grotte Cachée?" Archer asked.

"I shouldn't think so," said Morel as he drew on his cigarette. "But as you know, one can never predict these things."

Miss Armstrong chatted for a moment with the gatehouse guard, Mike, an American like herself. She crouched down and made a beckoning gesture, which was when Archer first noticed the cat lounging nearby, its dusky fur blending so perfectly with the volcanic paving stones that it was all but invisible. When it made no move to rise, she walked toward it, only to have it dart away.

"So Darius *is* awake," Archer said. "I thought he might be."

"So are Elic and Lili," Morel said, pointing through the mist to the northeast tower, where two shadowy figures, one quite tall, stood in the top-floor window of Elic's suite.

Morel watched, seemingly riveted, as the figures merged in a lengthy embrace, Elic's chin resting companionably on Lili's head. *Le seigneur* took a puff of his Black Russian, expelling the smoke in a lingering plume, then crushed the cigarette out with a melancholic frown.

Archer reflected for a moment, weighing the wisdom of bringing it up; they rarely discussed *le seigneur*'s personal situation. Reasoning that he might not have that much more time to address the matter, he said, very quietly, "There is a way, you know."

Morel looked up quizzically.

"You needn't be alone, *mon seigneur,*" Archer said carefully. "You needn't die childless."

A testy edge crept into Morel's voice as he said, "I *can't* die childless, as you very well know. I need an heir. Grotte Cachée needs it. The follets need it. You must redouble your efforts, Archer. Find someone."

"With respect, *mon seigneur,* if it were a simple matter to locate a woman with The Gift, I would have long since—"

"There are druidesses all over the world—hundreds, perhaps thousands of them."

"But how many of them realize what they are?" Archer asked. "And of those who do, how many are willing to make their true nature known? Even you can't always spot them, if they're in deep enough denial. But the thing of it is . . . there might be another way."

"If you're suggesting I wed some ordinary woman and risk siring a civilian . . ." That was *le seigneur*'s term for those without The Gift: civilians. Shaking his head, Morel said, "The follets need a *gardien* who can see beyond the surface of things, probe the hearts of strangers and listen to their distant whispers—a *gardien* who can sense danger in time to avert it. No civilian can be entrusted with the welfare of living gods, only someone with The Gift—a druid or druidess."

The problem was that The Gift was a recessive gene. There were mutations from time to time, druidic children born of civilians, or of a civilian and a druid or druidess, but such instances were rare. For countless generations, Morel's ancestors had been careful to wed their children to others with The Gift, thus ensuring the best possible guardianship of the follets who'd been in their care for over two thousand years.

"There might be a way you *could* marry an ordinary woman," Archer said, "just someone you met and fell in love with, not a druidess, and still sire offspring with The Gift." Morel was a handsome fellow, with his soulful eyes and unruly thatch of brown hair. Archer had seen the way women looked at him on those rare occasions when he mingled with the visitors. If he would just open himself up to the possibility, he could have his choice of desirable women.

"Barring an unlikely stroke of luck," Morel said, "any union of a druid and a civilian is destined to produce civilian offspring. After twenty years in my service, I hardly think you can have forgotten that much."

"Nineteen," Archer corrected as he stubbed out his cigarette. He had assumed his present post after the previous *administrateur,* his father, perished along with Morel's parents in the crash of their private jet. The eighth generation of his family to serve as second-in-command to the high druid or druidess of the ancient Vernae Clan, Archer regarded the position as more of a sacred calling than a job. When it came time for him to join his predecessors in the little cemetery in the woods to the north—which could be months or years from now, depending on which doctor he listened to—Morel might actually be forced to look outside the Archer family for a replacement. It was a prospect that Archer found excruciating.

Had he no offspring to carry on the ancestral vocation, it would pain him less, but in fact, he had a thirty-four-year-old daughter. Isabel was the only good thing to come out of a marriage that had ended nineteen years ago when his socialite wife decreed that he could either remain in London as her husband or step in as *administrateur* to the newly orphaned Adrien Morel. There was no way she was following him to some "dreary old pile of lava" in the most isolated and rural region of France. He would have fought for custody of Isabel, but the child's few visits to Grotte Cachée during the separation had "creeped her out royally," and she'd sworn never again to set foot in "Château des Freaks."

Archer's ex had remarried with unseemly speed and moved with their daughter to New York City, where Isabel now worked as a freelance graphic designer. Archer visited her often in New York, but whenever he brought up the possibility of her succeeding him in his post, she rolled her eyes and changed the subject.

"Here's the thing," Archer said. "It's ultimately your child who needs to have The Gift, not your wife."

"Yes, but if she doesn't have it, how can the child—"

"You know the tale of how your ancestor, Brantigern the Protector, begat a druidic son with Adiega even though she was a normal woman without The Gift—how Elic transformed himself into Elle to extract Brantigern's seed, which he then imbued with his essence and transferred to—"

"You can't be serious."

"Elic is a dusios, *mon seigneur.* It's what he's meant to do. He'd be a female when he . . . when you . . ."

"When we fuck?"

Archer was struck dumb. He'd never known Morel to utter a vulgar word.

"Elic was a virtual stranger to Brantigern and Adiega," Morel said. "They hardly knew each other. But I've known him all my life. I grew up with him. He used to carry me about on his shoulders when I was little. I could no more share my bed with him than I could share it with, well, any old friend, regardless of how female he looks. I'd know it's really him."

"You won't remember," Archer said. "He can make you forget. He can even keep you asleep while—"

"Not me. The Gift prevents their powers from working with me."

Archer hadn't known this. "Are you quite sure?"

Unexpectedly, Morel smiled. "Did I ever tell you about the time I woke up with Lili on top of me?"

"Good Lord," Archer exclaimed through an incredulous chuckle. "You're joking, surely."

"I was seventeen—it was right before you came here. She was naked, of course, and whispering one of her *mashmashus,* the one that was supposed to keep me from being able to move while she . . . did what she was born to do. It didn't take, though. I felt a little weak, but I could still move. I said, 'Lili, what the hell are you doing?' She said she wanted to give me something to 'raise the veil of sorrow from those beautiful eyes,' because, of course, I'd just lost my parents and your father, who'd been like an uncle to me. For that matter, Lili had been like an aunt. It just felt . . . I don't know. Vaguely incestuous."

Archer glanced across the courtyard to the northeast tower window, but Elic and Lili were no longer there. Picturing the

Babylonian enchantress in his mind, Archer said dryly, "I think I might have managed to overcome those misgivings had I been in your place."

Morel smiled to acknowledge the point. "She's magnificent, to be sure, but when you've known someone since infancy…" He shook his head. "In any event, their magic is apparently ineffective with druidic types. Were Elic—or rather, Elle—to attempt to, er, extract my DNA, I would be fully aware, and fully appalled, the entire time. And then, of course, I'd have to deal with the knowledge that Elic was going to be seeking out my wife right after leaving me. Can't you see how I might find the situation a bit sordid?"

The purr of an automobile engine drew their attention to the window across the room that looked down onto the front of the chateau. Larsson pulled up to the drawbridge in his steely Lamborghini Roadster, jumped out, and loaded their bags into the boot. Raising the passenger-side gullwing door for Miss Armstrong, he gave her another quick kiss as he helped her into the sleek little car.

"*Mon seigneur,*" Archer said as the couple drove away, "if you would just consider what I've proposed, keep it in your mind as an option…"

"*Non.* It's unthinkable. *Répugnant.* Find me a druidess." Morel turned back to the window, his arms folded, his expression grim. "Make it a priority."

Archer knew when he was being dismissed. He crossed to the doorway, paused, and looked back.

Morel stood at the window, lost in his thoughts as he watched the Lamborghini grow smaller and smaller on the gravel road leading away from their dark and enchanted little valley.

About the Author

LOUISA BURTON, a painter and former freelance illustrator, lives in New York with her husband and two cats, one a Russian Blue who bears a striking resemblance to Darius in his feline incarnation. The Hidden Grotto series, beginning with *House of Dark Delights,* is inspired by a lifelong passion for mythology, history, and Victorian erotica.

Explore the mysteries of Grotte Cachée at www.louisaburton.com

Read on for a sneak peek at

BOUND IN MOONLIGHT

The next scintillating and erotic novel

by

Louisa Burton

Coming from Bantam in Fall '07

Bound in Moonlight
Coming Fall '07

One
London
June 19, 1817

"HAVE YOU any objection to being raped?" inquired the silver-haired, nattily attired Sir Charles Upcott as he dipped his quill in a cut-glass inkwell.

Caroline Keating stared at Sir Charles, barrister and baronet, across the marble and ormolu desk that was the focal point of his imposing Regent Street office. Taken aback by the query—indeed, deeply dismayed by it—she said, "Is it not in the nature of... such an act for the lady to object?"

Sir Charles glanced at her over the top of his spectacles and wrote something on a sheet of foolscap. "Should you be chosen to go on the block, the gentleman who purchases you—your master—may subject you to any number of secret proclivities that he would be loath to reveal to his wife or mistress. He may have wondered, for example, how it would feel to force himself on an unwilling female—something no civilized man would do in the normal course of events, even to a lady of limited virtue. But even civilized men have their dark fancies. As I explained at the outset, Miss Keating, your master may enjoy you in any manner he sees fit during the seven days in which you are his property, short of causing injury so severe as to require the attention of a physician—although there will, of course, be a physician on hand at all times."

"But if I am, indeed, forbidden to resist my . . . the man who . . . buys me, how *could* he force himself on me? He would have no cause to do so—indeed, no opportunity—were I to submit willingly every time he . . . requires it."

Without looking up from his notetaking, Sir Charles said, "He may order you to resist. Or he may employ such brutishness in the act, or encourage it on the part of others, that you will naturally resist."

"Others?" Caroline asked in a thin voice.

"He will be at liberty to lend you out, as it were, to another gentleman at the chateau, or to several at once if the fancy strikes him. A slave must be prepared for any contingency."

"But did you not say that I would be forbidden to . . . give myself to any man but my master during the week of my servitude?"

Looking up with a sigh, Sir Charles said, "Unless it is at the *behest* of your master. Should he command it, you must do it, unquestioningly and without reluctance. It is really a very elegantly simple arrangement."

"But why would he encourage someone else to . . . ?"

"Usually it is so that he can watch."

Watch? Caroline blinked at the barrister. Violent ravishment . . . by more than one man! Good Lord, what else did she not know about the "secret proclivities" of ostensibly civilized gentlemen?

Sir Charles removed his spectacles and sat back in his chair with a squeak of leather, studying her with quiet speculation. No doubt he was pondering the wisdom of selecting such a naive creature as she to go under the hammer two weeks hence at some mysterious, isolated chateau in France.

"Miss Keating," he said, "I am required by the party I represent in this matter to ask you these questions in order to ensure your aptitude for sexual enslavement. I must warn you, however, that if you offer even one negative response, you will not be chosen—and as I'm sure Lord Rexton explained when he recruited you last night, there is a great deal of money at stake, thousands of pounds."

Caroline turned to gaze through a window curtained in whispery, sun-hazed silk billowing lazily on a warm breeze. This time yesterday morning, she'd been standing in a crush of onlookers on the north bank of the Thames watching the opening ceremony of Waterloo Bridge and reflecting that she didn't even have the halfpence they were charging for a toll.

Sir Charles allowed her a few moments to contemplate the magnitude of her plight, then put his spectacles back on. "As to the question of rape?"

"All right," she said on a sigh, recalling the deal she'd struck yesterday evening with Bram Hugget, the street sweeper who'd been begging for a kiss for weeks.

"Just one," she'd said, "but it will cost you a halfpenny."

He'd scratched his prickly boulder of a jaw. "Only if I get to feel them diddies, too."

She'd clenched her teeth against the urge to weep and scream. A halfpenny to die, quite a bargain, really; but it was a halfpenny she didn't have. "Over my clothes, not under. You've a minute to be done with it."

"Miss Keating?"

She looked toward Sir Charles, regarding her expectantly, his quill poised over the inkwell.

"Fellatio?" he said.

She frowned in bewilderment.

"Oral copulation. Are you willing to perform it?"

"Oral? Do you mean kissing?"

Sir Charles withdrew from a drawer a leather folio, which he untied and opened, revealing a stack of pictures. He sorted through them, chose one, and handed it across the desk to Caroline.

It was a tinted engraving executed in loose, jaunty pen-strokes of a man, fully clothed, and two plump, naked women. The man lay on a bed with his feet on the floor and his breeches wide open, kneading the breasts of a woman who was squatting on his face. The other woman knelt between his outspread legs, sucking on his erect organ as she fondled both him and herself.

Caroline stared in unblinking shock.

"Lord Rexton gave me to believe that you were a lady of some experience in these matters," said Sir Charles. "When he recruited you yesterday, did you not tell him that you'd been ruined through a liaison with a soldier?"

Finding her voice, she said, "It was a very brief liaison."

"How brief?"

"One night."

"How long ago?"

"Somewhat over two years."

Frowning, he dipped his quill and noted this information.

Thousands of pounds.

"My . . . my experience is limited," she said, sitting forward, "but I assure you, Sir Charles, I will not balk at—"

"Yes or no on performing fellatio, Miss Keating?"

She swallowed hard as she returned the picture to the barrister. "Yes."

"Are you willing to have relations in the Greek manner?"

"I'm sorry, sir. I do not know what that is."

With an expression of weary forbearance, Sir Charles chose another engraving from the stack and handed it to her.

A man and a woman, both naked, were coupling on an

elaborately draped bed, she with her bottom raised high, he taking her from behind. Caroline had to study the picture for a moment before she realized that he was penetrating her in an aperture other than that intended by nature.

"Oh," she said quietly.

Sir Charles regarded her expectantly over his spectacles.

"Is it painful?" she asked.

"That depends largely on whether the gentleman wishes it to be so. Yes or no?"

She handed the picture back, nodding listlessly.

"Are you willing to suffer such physical punishments as spanking, birching, and caning?"

She hesitated, wondering with a surge of dread what punishment had to do with copulation.

He produced another engraving, this one depicting a terrified-looking young woman lying facedown astride a narrow bench, her petticoats canted up to reveal a bare posterior ribboned with welts. To the side of her stood a dapper, maliciously grinning gentleman stroking his exposed penis with one hand as he raised a length of bamboo with the other.

Caroline's stomach clenched as she fought the urge to bolt up out of the chair and flee the room.

"Well?" prompted Sir Charles.

She thrust the picture back at him, bombarded by the memory of all those beatings her father had dealt to her and her brothers, hundreds of them over the years, for infractions as trivial as forgetting a line of a psalm. Hanging in the little schoolroom on the third floor of the castlelike rectory in which she'd been reared were a broad leather strap, a birch cane, and a perforated wooden paddle, all well-worn. She couldn't remember a time when she wasn't mottled with bruises from his sudden, impulsive batterings, mostly on her back, sometimes her chest or legs—but never on the face or arms, where they might have been visible to the Reverend Mr. Keating's parishioners. He was cruel and pitiless and probably half-mad from the French disease, her brothers whispered, acquired during his reckless youth—but he was far from stupid. Caroline had promised herself, when Aubrey rescued her from the dismal gaol that was her family home, that no man would ever strike her again.

"Miss Keating? Yes or no?"

The air left her lungs on a whispered, "Yes."

"I beg your—"

"*Yes,*" she said, feeling perilously close to tears. "Yes. Yes. Yes to all of it."

"Still, I am required to elicit clear and unequivocal consent to each act, lest you protest later that you weren't adequately warned as to what might be done to you. You are willing to be bound, gagged, blindfolded . . . ?"

"Yes."

"Are you willing to perform sexual acts before an audience?"

"Yes."

"Are you willing to engage in sexual activity with another female?"

Dear God. "Yes."

"Do you achieve orgasm, Miss Keating?"

Heat swept in a wave from her throat up to her hairline.

"I shall take that for an affirmative," said the barrister as his pen scratched over the foolscap. "Your age?"

"Twenty."

"Height?"

"Five feet, six inches."

"Weight?"

"I couldn't say with certainty anymore."

"Eight stone at the most," he muttered as he wrote. "Complexion pallid but unblemished. Hair golden blond."

"I was wondering, about my hair . . ."

"Mm?"

"I thought I might henna it, if that would be permissible."

"In order to help disguise your appearance? Some of the ladies do change their hair color and employ cosmetics for that purpose. I must say, it would be a shame in your case, but you are within your rights to do so if you wish."

"Thank you."

Setting his pen aside, Sir Charles slid off his spectacles and scrutinized her thoughtfully.

"Will I do?" she asked in as even a voice as she could muster.

"It is a pity you've been deflowered, Miss Keating. An intact maidenhead is highly prized in a slave. Virgins tend to command the highest prices, debauchees nearly so—the innocent on the one hand and the unabashedly wanton on the other. You, unfortunately, are neither. But then, great beauty is also a factor of some consequence, which will serve to your advantage. And you are, if not entirely untarnished, nearly so, with a guileless manner of the type that certain gentlemen find irresistible."

He closed the folio of lewd pictures and returned it to the drawer, then took out what looked like a visiting card and handed it to her. Engraved on heavy, cream stock were the name and address of a Dr. Humphrey Coates.

Sir Charles said, "You will report to Dr. Coates tomorrow afternoon at five o'clock for a physical examination. This is to ensure that you are of an adequate constitution to endure the rigors of Slave Week, to pronounce you free of disease, and assuming you pass inspection, to provide you with a means to prevent you from getting with child. Pending a positive report—"

"That's possible?" An unwed pregnancy had been one of the things Caroline had lain awake all night fretting about. "To... have relations without conceiving?"

"There are two devices that serve this purpose, a sheath of sheep-gut for the gentleman and a vinegar-soaked sponge for the lady. As it wouldn't do to inconvenience your master, you will be given a sponge, which you will be required to wear internally at all times, removing it only to clean and replace. Should you neglect this precaution and find yourself afterward in a delicate condition, it will be on your head entirely. By the terms of your contract, you will be forbidden to communicate with your master or to name him as the father of your child."

"Contract?"

"As I *had* been explaining," he continued wearily, "pending a positive report by Dr. Coates, I am willing to approve you to go on the block. In that eventuality, you will return here to execute a binding legal contract setting forth the rules by which you must abide during your week of enslavement. Primary among them is the requirement of utter and absolute obedience to your master, to whose every command you must submit without hesitation or protest of any kind. Should you fail in this even once, you will be sent home with nothing but your traveling expenses." Sir Charles recited this information in a disinterested drone, as if he'd done so scores of times, which she supposed he had.

"In addition," he continued, "you are obligated to secrecy about the location of the chateau to which you will be taken, as well as the identities of the participants, master and slave alike. Should you, at some future point, find yourself in the company of someone whom you recognize from the chateau, you are to conduct yourself as though you'd never met. The contract that the gentlemen sign stipulates the same requirement. The punishment for violating this crucial confidentiality, for the gentlemen as well as for the slaves, is complete social ruin."

Caroline said, "How can you . . . ?"

"Certain exceptionally grievous sins, should they become public knowledge, will make a pariah of even the most revered member of the *ton*. Such sins will be invented, if necessary."

Sir Charles gave her two other cards, one for a dressmaker who would supply her with the required frocks and underpinnings, and the other for a master swordsmith. "He will measure you for a collar, a pair of wrist cuffs, and a pair of ankle cuffs," the barrister explained. "These he fashions of gilded steel, with rings for the attachment of chains and leashes."

Caroline stared at Sir Charles.

He held her gaze steadily until she looked away, letting out a tremulous breath.

"You will be contacted regarding transportation arrangements to Calais and from there to the chateau." Recharging his quill with ink, he said, "Where do you live, Miss Keating?"

"St. Giles," she said, noting how his eyebrows quirked at the mention of the notorious slum. "I share a bed in a lodging house on Denmark Street and Charing Cross Road. But..."

"Yes?"

"When I left yesterday evening, I told my landlady I wouldn't be returning, and I... I don't know if she'll let me back in, because it's tuppence a night, and I haven't been able to pay it in some time."

With a little grunt of acknowledgment, Sir Charles wrote anote on a sheet of writing paper, folded it up around four gold sovereigns, and sealed it with wax. "Give this to Mr. Peckham at the St. James's Royal Hotel on St. James's Street. The payment covers your bed and board for two weeks. See that you eat your fill, and then some—your thinness detracts from your beauty. Eat beef and mutton washed down with plenty of good, rich burgundy. It will put some much-needed color in your cheeks."

She murmured her thanks as she took the note, heavy with the weight of the coins. It was more money than she'd had in her hands—more than she'd *seen*—in a very long time. With any luck, she would see a great deal more at the conclusion of her one-week "enslavement."

One week of appalling degradation. If she could stomach it, she would be free forever from the ever-worsening squalor and hunger and hopelessness in which she'd been mired these two years past. She could buy a little cottage in some village in the Cotswolds, where no one had ever heard of Caroline Keating and her tattered reputation. Perhaps she could even open the school for girls that had been her dream since childhood.

"If you've no further questions..." Sir Charles scooted his chair back.

"The money," she said, sitting forward. "You said thousands. Lord Rexton did, too. Is that true? Is that how much a slave can expect to... sell for?"

"Two thousand at a minimum," he said, "and possibly quite a bit more. The highest price in the history of Slave Week went to a young lady last year, an astonishing beauty, the virginal younger daughter of a duke. She cost her master twenty-three thousand guineas."

"My God."

"Once the winning bid has been accepted, the gentleman is required to sign a note of indebtedness for that amount payable to the lady whose services he has purchased, which note is held in escrow by Lord Rexton."

"He will be there?"

"As a representative of Childe and Upcott, yes. Our client, I shall call him Seigneur X, retains us to handle the legal and pecuniary aspects of Slave Week. The auction itself is overseen by Riddell's, which has distinguished itself in that business for the better part of a century. Needless to say, we will have ensured in advance the financial solvency of the invited gentlemen, although it goes without saying that some are in a position to bid a good deal more than others. At the end of the week, if all has gone well and the lady has upheld her end of the contract, the note and the funds it represents will be handed over to her."

"All of it? None is held aside as a commission for you or the auction house?"

"We are remunerated separately by Seigneur X. You see?" He pressed his lips together in what she took to be his idea of a smile. "Elegantly simple, the entire affair."

